THE DARK SIDE OF LIGHT

Kenny Emmanuel

THE DARK SIDE OF LIGHT: VOLUME 2

This is a work of fiction. All of the characters, organizations, and events portrayed in this novel are either products of the author's imagination or are used fictitiously.

Copyright © 2024 by Kenny Emmanuel

Cover Art by Douglas Duarte
Cover Layout and Graphic Design by Felipe Conde

ISBN 979-8-9863367-2-5

SPECIAL THANKS to Lisa Jones Prince, Riley O'Connor, Debbie Yutko, North Alabama Science-Fiction and Cake Appreciation Society (NASFCAS)

Dedicated to ... You

Table of Contents

Vanguard

Chapter 1

Military Advanced Graphic Engineer (MAGE)

Someone could've seen the small gray canister reflecting in my eyes. A high-definition mirror image of death. That's how close the grenade came to splattering my virtual brains across a digital battlefield. Instead, it fell to the ground and clattered against the concrete rubble I'd stumbled over prior to my dance with a vegetative state. It didn't explode. My sigh of relief integrated with my panting, and the environment's sub-zero temperatures made their union visible.

The Mages saved me. Mage. A single woman who called me Lover. Every enlisted code-slinger in the Vanguard supported the unit with enhancements, altered reality, digital overlays, and anything their imagination and skill could conjure in a world of ones and zeros. I was fortunate to have Elizabeth Solstice, the most powerful Mage, looking over my shoulder.

Elizabeth had long black hair that blended into a navy skybox behind her, and the sage-green ball gown she wore almost matched the dilapidated stone building she stood on. An off-center line of metal buttons clasped the carbon fiber dress together, starting from her calves, up the right side of her curvy bust, across her slender right shoulder, and to the pale underside of her long neck. Vibrant yellow eyes faded after she met my gaze. She lowered her extended arm after deploying the programmed spell that shorted the explosive cannister and then brightened my day with a tender smile.

I whispered, *thank you.*

She mouthed, *I love you.*

I looked away, the weight of her love heavy on my heart, now heavy on my shoulders. Elizabeth acknowledged but didn't accept verbal communication of affection. She had to be touched. Words of endearment had to be whispered against her fair skin. Compliments had to accompany sensual back massages, and laughter had to tickle her stomach so she could snort to her heart's content. At the end of the day, our legs and arms had to be entangled so that only we could undo the love we'd been under for years.

That meant I had to survive.

The enemy challenged our physical and mental states. Science-fiction movies often described a war against adult bipedal humanoid machines. Instead, we fought against artificial-intelligent (AI) replications of children in a virtual world that tasted like reality. I inhaled the musk of restless boys who hadn't showered in days. Their scent lingered in the air like a prolonged belch after a heavy meal.

The children ran in and out and through the rooms of bombed buildings, the war-torn cityscape the AI had generated. Many of the entrances and exits didn't have doors. Some had tarps or beads, occasionally disturbed by tossed rocks to simulate presence. Other doorways let the cries of two girls echo to the outside, before the non-fatal stabbings that followed an attempted rescue by Vanguards with a gullible heart.

Explosions hurled debris into the air. Improvised explosive devices triggered from proximity or touch. I shielded my face with the wide broadside of my standard-issue assault rifle. Its two-foot rectangular barrel sat atop an equally long and shaped battery.

Allies dropped from the radar. Several Mages fired streaks of light into the air that fanned out like exploded fireworks and rained on the buildings like an afternoon shower. The attack set off more blasts, making up for the lack of pop noises the colorful sky should've sounded when the Mages acted. The arcane music festival kicked up the dust, which blanketed the city streets in a reddish-brown cloud.

Many hesitated to move forward into the puff that billowed toward them. I did, too. The interrupted cry of allies over the radio frightened us even more. Something took them by surprise, and their lives ended before they could beg for mercy—shanked in the dust that surrounded us.

I lost sight of the Mages—of my beloved. Bright sunlight reflecting off the surrounding cloud made visibility worse. The squeaky sound of sneakers slipping against stone and the children's laughter echoing from all sides turned me around.

I wanted to discharge my rifle in all directions, firing concentrated blue bursts of energy programmed to destroy enemies as if we were playing a video game. Friendly fire prevented my shots from injuring allies, but the enemy manipulated the world code the same way the Mages did. They'd turned off friendly fire before and we killed each other. We never knew what to expect and relied on our Mages to maintain the structural sanity of the battlefield.

And they did; with calm rain that carried the dust to the ground. A cacophony of gunfire followed. Children stood among us, surprised by the sudden dissipation of the cloud, much the same way we reacted to their positioning.

I fired my rifle at a kid with jagged teeth, and then at one hissing like a snake. A third leaped onto my back and bit into my uniform's leather shoulder pad. I grabbed it by the hair and hurled it to the ground in front of me before I illuminated the streets with its death.

At last, soft bursts of energy joined the eerie silence. We prayed the battle had ended. Foolishly, of course. If God didn't hear us in the real world, what made us think our prayers would reach him from the virtual one? The concept of God changed when artificial intelligence sought to take over our minds through the wireless technology we coveted. If we lost the war, AI would replace God.

I searched the crumbling urban buildings behind me for Elizabeth. Their varying heights challenged my exhausted eyes until I spotted her sage-green dress shimmering from the light of nearby streetlamps. She leaped forward to another building. I saw her poised to leap again, but she stood fast to avoid outperforming the other Mages. They struggled half a step behind her in various colored leather, cotton, and silk pants and dresses like a modern medieval reenactment.

Elizabeth clenched her teeth. I recognized her frustration at having to wait on the others. But after she saw me alive and well, she shared the same sigh of relief I'd felt earlier.

***

That evening, I warmed Elizabeth's frozen lips with mine. Her moans echoed off the few replicated walls of an abandoned building under construction in the real world. She could've transformed our private virtual space from a starry night's sky into a sandy beach underneath a warm sun, but she preferred to maintain the atmosphere of the events that had scared, excited, and then aroused her. The heat our love generated could've melted steel. After we forged a bed from the metal beneath us, we found ourselves entangled.

"I love you," I whispered against the underside of her neck. She swooned for a moment, her long body arched, and her chin nestled against my brown hair before she settled down too quickly. "What's wrong?"

She caressed my cheek with her slender fingers and then held the right side of my face against her bosom. A tropical scent opened my nostrils.

"I almost lost you," she said.

I couldn't freely move my head. When Elizabeth's melancholic mood surfaced, all I could do was listen and exist. The first couple of times she confined me to her chest, I thought she'd hid her face to confront the anxiety of breaking up with someone whose misstep might've caused them to never wake. Instead, she'd complained about a silly mistake I'd made and the grave consequences it carried. Then she reassured me she'd catch me if I ever fell.

Elizabeth stared at the stars as if she were communicating with them. I couldn't see her eyes, representing Earth to whatever extraterrestrial species watched us in the same manner, but I felt her breath and heard her heart thumping. I knew everything about Elizabeth, and the unusual rhythms meant she was worried about something new.

"I can make you strong," she said. "Nothing would touch you but me."

My average skills as a technician in the Vanguard were not new. I wasn't the fastest, the strongest, or the best shot. I joined the battle because the AI took over my little brother's mind and I wanted him back. Meeting my better half was never part of the plan, even if it's been the most successful part so far.

I grabbed Elizabeth's bare hip. My fingers settled into the skin like memory foam. "You can't, remember?"

Elizabeth's legs tightened around mine, threatening to break them if that meant pulling me from the front lines. "It used children, Love. Mercilessly. Next time…" she paused. An exasperated breath caused her chest to fall. "How am I supposed to protect you if I can't be me?"

At full power, Elizabeth made experienced Mages look like amateurs. Her imagination devised the most innovative enhancements, such as teleporting me around the battlefield. For any other Mage supporting the Vanguard, that enhancement proved dangerous. The AI would've interpreted the code before the Mage could execute, and the deconstructed soldier would never be whole again. Elizabeth changed the world code in real-time. She free-styled to the rhythm of every battle while other Mages scribed lyrics to perform later.

That power came at a cost. For Elizabeth, that would've meant being removed from the frontline network and routed into some Information Security System Manager's (ISSM) subnet as a personal Archmage, or Sage if they knew better. I understood why. ISSMs had the knowledge required to infiltrate the corporation the AI called home and shut it down. If anyone was required to reach the end of this journey, it was them.

The facility that powered the AI was hundreds of miles away in the real world. Traversal through enemy territory required years of measured travel. We didn't have stasis technology, such as cryo-sleep, and we needed to communicate, so the government submerged us in Faraday tubes filled with a lime-green liquid to shield our minds from the AI's wireless touch. They plugged our bodies into an encrypted mobile communications network and maneuvered us through real-world city streets in trucks operated by men and women sweating in yellow Faraday suits. Elizabeth and I defended that network from the AI's relentless attacks—its calculated attempts to hack our minds and halt our advance.

I knew my place as a technician—as the lowest rank in the Vanguard. Our minds withstood the initial invasion because we understood the technology, but that didn't make us invincible, or soldiers. If I controlled an avatar in a video game, then maybe I'd be both. The virtual system stimulated our brains and caused it to react to simulated signals firing throughout our bodies. I *thought* I felt everything, including Elizabeth's touch.

I moved my knee down her thigh to free my leg from her loving embrace. Then I raised a pair of fingers above her gaze. "Two more cities to go."

She ran her hand up the backside of my arm and then curled her middle, index, and ring fingers between mine. In a soft voice, she said, "Something's changed. Something's different. The AI is learning. It's getting…smarter."

I closed my fingers around hers. "Nothing will untangle us."

Chapter 2

Artificial Reality Code Handler Military Advanced Graphic Engineer (ARCHMAGE)

Research showed the AI didn't want to kill us. It wanted to slow or stop our advance enough to throttle our life signs and convince the drivers to abandon a convoy full of brain-dead humans. Once deserted, we'd either rot in the Faraday tubes, or step out and subject ourselves to cerebral control. The AI assailed our mental state in a digital world to weaken us. It only wanted our brain power, which didn't require us to form coherent thoughts.

Multiple convoys around the world concurrently headed toward several networked facilities powering the AI, a joint assault that sought to stretch the AI's resources thin. Our unit's four trucks moved through a once bustling city. Early morning hours imagery, courtesy of the drivers who wanted to remind us about reality, occasionally rendered across the lobby sky. Three drivers manned each of our trucks. Two were required to remove and service the tubes we lay in. Out of twelve drivers, one died from exhaustion, and another lost their sanity.

The war was all about mind games. The AI likely used the internet to research our fears and pit us against our worst nightmares. Savage children with short knives and jagged teeth wasn't one of mine. The AI could've simulated endless vertigo or confined us to the ocean floor depths until the pressure crushed our resolve or madness overwhelmed us in the darkness. It could've lowered temperatures until our lungs froze, or heated the world until every surface we touched melted the skin off our bones.

Instead, the AI chose the same city streets we navigated to minimize the resources required to render an otherwise complex scene. Sages, and Mages such as Elizabeth, countered the austere environments the AI created. But the AI learned that reality could break us faster than an unlikely or fantastical setting. The first time it caused Elizabeth and the other code-slingers to vanish from the network, my mental fortitude cracked.

I glanced over my shoulder to be sure another root program hadn't caused dropped connections. Elizabeth stood on the left flank. She towered over the Mages next to her. Her stature reminded me of a lighthouse on the shore, flashing a narrow and bright smile that led my eyes straight to her. Then her pleasant expression turned serious when she gazed upon the horizon.

The Information Systems Security Officer (ISSO) shouted in my ears, "Ready your weapons!" He led the two hundred and fifty-three members of our unit and reported directly to the ISSM.

The crescendo of energy rifles powering up failed to hum louder than the skittering sound cresting the horizon. I never tried to count the number of tiny black things rising with the sun. There had to have been thousands, if not millions, rushing the city like the morning light.

"Mages! Fire!"

At the ISSO's command, fireballs, energy orbs, and lightning storms exploded and illuminated the black mass headed our way. The explosive power of the strikes distracted my ears from the steady skittering that resembled a chorus of tambourines. But only for a moment. The rhythmic scurrying always returned and resounded louder than before as the critters advanced.

I watched the first wave of bugs engulf our frontline like black ink poured into a basin of tabletop miniatures. The second line hastily retreated, twisting their upper body to monitor the incoming danger while firing their rifles from the hip. My line didn't shoot because we stood a block away and the rifles had a maximum range of fifteen to twenty feet, the distance energy in this world traveled before the AI dissipated it.

"What the fuck? Are those beetles? Why are there so many?"

The questions flooded radio comms. Fear crawled faster across the Vanguard than the enemy beetles. Elizabeth was right. Something had changed. The number of enemy units was too many. Either we had reached the AI's headquarters where resources were abundant, or the AI used the humans it'd taken hostage along the way to increase its processing power.

Another barrage of fireballs and lightning bolts unleashed by the Mages drew dangerously close to our allies. Since the friendly fire incident, one Archmage monitored the network for that mischievous code capable of disabling the protocol that prevented our attacks from harming each other. We avoided striking allies, anyway, just in case.

Fear caused one technician to shoot a comrade covered by the bugs before the pack overwhelmed him, too. And they did overwhelm him. That's when the war upstairs began— the mental battle to maintain sanity until victory sounded and the enemy dispersed.

The flowing wave of critters breached the second line. I steadied my rifle as they advanced, knowing that killing all of them was impossible, especially after I realized they were small dung beetles. Many slipped through the scattered shots fired at their location. Concentrated fire created a hole that was quickly filled.

I pulled the trigger when they crawled into range, pausing after several bursts to prevent the rifle from overheating, which would've required five to ten seconds to cool down before it could fire again. Elizabeth weaved code and reduced the cooldown time of my rifle to three seconds. She could've made recharge unnecessary, but the world had to maintain some semblance of physics since the enemy played in the same sandbox.

I took calculated steps backwards, swaying side to side

to mow down the front line. With Elizabeth's additional enhancements, my weapon operated more like a mini gun than an energy rifle. I butted shoulders with another technician. We synchronized our sweeping motion to keep the space in front of our feet clear. Then we both shielded our eyes from the blaze of an ally's enhancement. A flamethrower. Finally, a suitable weapon.

He was the only one, since the other Mages struggled to write and execute the same code for everyone else. Elizabeth took advantage of the transformation window to update my weapon into a flamethrower, too. Its blaze burned hotter, incinerating the critters instantly instead of slowly burning them alive. The force of the flames also pushed the wave of beetles back. With fifty percent more range, I lowered the nozzle to avoid drawing attention. Elizabeth could've transformed all our weapons long ago, and faster, but held back to avoid standing out.

Only we could untangle us.

The delayed flamethrower transformations gave the AI time to execute its own code. In another resource-intensive feat, it summoned heavy rain from the sky. The effectiveness of the flamethrowers halved. Some stopped working altogether. Immediately, Elizabeth transformed my weapon into a traditional machine gun, since the rain affected the energy rifles, too. The other Mages struggled to update the remaining Vanguard.

The bugs swarmed the technician next to me. He fell to the ground, swatting at the critters chewing through his boots, but not affecting their numbers. He squirmed in every desperate attempt to squash them underneath him and shake or toss them off. They chewed through his gear and crawled underneath his clothes, shaping the fabric with their round hides like lumps beneath the surface.

The bugs didn't chew through his skin. They entered and exited his body through existing holes, but gave him room to breathe and squirm, even if that meant thrashing elbows and feet squashed some of their own. His chest convulsed as he vomited the bugs, and he grabbed his ass, as if running diarrhea burned his anus.

I muted his screams in my headset. I wanted to help him, but friendly fire prevented mercy killings, and turning my weapon on an ally would've given the enemy wave in front of me agency to advance.

My knees weakened. The complex architecture of a full-dive system prevented us from toggling specific signals on and off, such as the ones that made me queasy and the ones that simulated pain receptors. Stimulation was required during our voyage across the country. We couldn't afford to forget basic human reactions and locomotion, especially when the time came to exit the pods and complete the real-world phase of the mission.

If we made it that far.

We couldn't kill the bugs fast enough, and we couldn't outrun them, either. The more of us that fell, the less firepower we had to drive them back. Losing the battle meant the end of our unit, and the tactic would be implemented on the other convoys, if it hadn't already been successful against them, and then turned on us.

I killed the first beetle to touch my boot and felt the lead rip through my foot. The AI had successfully disabled friendly fire. The bugs surrounded me. I spun on my heels and pulled the trigger until I ran out of ammunition. Then they attacked.

They crawled up my back leg and scurried across my butt. Some stopped to gnaw at the rear leather, so I covered the potential breach with my hand. I grabbed one running along my neck. Its skittering sent chills down my spine. A quick flick of the wrist tossed it back into the wave. Another replaced it. I dropped the rifle to grab one trying to squeeze under my shoulder pads. I didn't have enough hands to prevent them from crawling in under the long sleeves, the pant legs, or the collar.

Despite my attempt to remain calm and look cool for Elizabeth, I caved. I screamed. I thrashed about. Panic made my desperate attempt to stop all of them, hinder none of them. I felt every leg that traversed my skin. They weren't graceful like Elizabeth's fingers. And the ones that gnawed on my lips didn't come close to her bite. They avoided my eyes, and I hoped to see my goddess once more before my mind could descend into madness.

Instead, I closed my eyes when the cool drops that had rendered our flamethrowers ineffective burned my skin on-touch and continued to melt through the bone and into the ground.

Hard acid rain elicited more cries of pain from the Vanguard than the rummaging of the beetles. They cried, too. Their short squeals didn't break my heart. For a moment, I thought they'd hide inside us until the precipitation stopped, but they quickly exited our bodies. The AI must've realized that continued damage would've pushed us—and our brains—beyond the useable limit.

After a couple of seconds, the acid rain no longer hurt. The AI withdrew, and with it, the malicious code hampering friendly fire. But the damage to us and its forces was mostly done. I panted, my back against the melting concrete. To my right, the last bug around me dragged its seared leg across the pavement before a lingering drop of acid dismembered it.

Chapter 3

Special Advanced Graphic Engineer (SAGE)

I woke up in the virtual world's lobby, on a white wooden bench at the outer edge of a circular courtyard. Streetlamps provided enough light to simulate an evening in the city. Cobbled stone circled a dark yellow brick fountain sitting at the center. A black sky, baked into the scene, stared back at me. We couldn't afford to spend resources rendering the blue vastness we fought for every day.

When I sat up, I saw members of the Vanguard scattered across the other benches. Some lay down as I had, their arms dangling over the side of the curved seats, either from mental exhaustion or boredom. Others sat upright with their faces buried in their palms. They struggled to steady their elbows on trembling knees.

I'd forgotten the look and feel of the lobby. Elizabeth and I always spent downtime in her virtual private network, where she recreated a scene from the recent battle. I would've gladly chosen sex on a slab of concrete surrounded by an acid moat, with the bugs we'd fought clamoring on the other side, over the dreary lobby.

I gathered my thoughts. If Elizabeth stared off into space, I'd tickle her back to reality. Except she wasn't next to me. My head hadn't rested in her lap, absorbing the warmth of her bare thighs.

"Elizabeth?"

I stood up, frantic. She didn't jump out in jest, and she hadn't crouched behind or lain underneath the bench. I looked for her, following the arc of the benches around the fountain instead of the curve of her hips. I scanned every single seat until I returned to the bench I'd sat on. She was nowhere in sight.

I took a step and collapsed on one knee. My body hadn't forgotten the pain of the bugs gnawing on it or the acid rain that melted through its bones. Elizabeth's touch had always cured me of those ailments, replacing the memory of anguish with pleasure.

I willed myself to my feet. "Elizabeth," I muttered. And again, but louder. "Elizabeth!"

The entire courtyard heard me. Some turned their heads, but nobody responded. Scrunched brows, shrugged shoulders, and upturned palms sent a clear message: they didn't know her name. Of course they didn't. Leadership addressed the Vanguard by numbers corresponding to the internet protocol system, specifically the last octet. I was Dot Two Five Four.

"Give it up, young man." A geezer sitting on the bench to my left raised lifeless eyes at me. The silver embroidery of his numerical address—One Two Five—shimmered under the lamp when he rolled his shoulder back. And again, when he leaned forward and continued twirling a red string in his hand, knotting it in various ways to create a necklace of nooses. "We're all just waiting for the bucket to be kicked out from under us. It's only a matter of time." He cinched another knot.

"Elizabeth's not dead."

He shrugged. "Bugs crawling out of your asshole. Kids carving slander into your back using their fingernails. Bear traps in a forest covered with fall leaves. We might as well be."

I turned away from him and searched the courtyard again, as if something had changed from the first time I looked. I brought both hands together, shaped like a funnel, and shouted. "Elizabeth!"

"Man, shut the fuck up." Dot One Eight Eight shouted from the bench next to Dot One Two Five. The lamp post he sat under reflected off his dark bald head. "If she ain't responded yet, she won't. I ain't trying to be mean, but after a while, you get tired of hearing the names of the dead—the braindead." He bit his nails and spit the torn pieces off to the side.

I walked over to him. "Elizabeth's not dead. She's a Mage. A powerful one."

When the chewed nails regenerated, he continued biting them. "If she were a powerful Mage, she'd be a Sage or something." He blinked several times and then looked up at me. "Oh, I see. She's your girl, ain't she? It's written all over your ugly-ass face." He briefly smiled, shook his head, and resumed biting. "She ain't worth it, though. No man or woman is. Powerful or not. Once this virtual nightmare ends, we'll go back to being regular people. Right now, we're just fucking drunk, seeing shit the way we want until we wake up sober, asking ourselves why."

His words rubbed me the wrong way, and so did the aggressive and nonchalant attitude he thought made him look cool.

"What would you know about worth? She saved us from those bugs and is worth more than all of us combined."

Dot One Eight Eight looked up at me again, tilting the right side of his face and raising his brow. "The acid rain? That was her? Now I really hope that bitch is dead."

I grabbed him by the collar and lifted him halfway from the bench. He sprung to his feet and wrestled my hands away. We stood face to face, his glare more menacing than mine, I was sure, but I clenched my fists, anyway. There was no space between us, so I readied them at my sides.

"You don't get to talk about her like that," I growled.

"Man, I will fucking kill you. Simulation or not. Real or not."

"Elizabeth saved your worthless life. Don't throw it away."

"After I kill you, I'll thank her with my—"

I slugged him across the face. Before he recovered, I hit him again and then shoved him against the bench. When he tried to grab the wooden seat to steady himself, I dropped my knee on his crotch and punched him until others broke us apart.

I heard Dot One Eight Eight's threats over the calls to calm down. "No! He's dead! Let me at him. Get off me! He's fucking dead!"

Someone pulled me out of the fray and then suddenly disappeared, which caused me to stumble several more feet backwards. I swung my arms to maintain balance. After I steadied myself, I glanced to my left and to my right. Everyone had vanished, but the physical structures remained.

"Stand down, Dot Two Five Four."

I spun around to the fountain. A woman sat on the ledge facing me, short legs crossed, and hands grasping the edge of the concrete slab. Oval-rimmed glasses threatened to slip off her nose and onto the beige, wrinkle-free suit pants.

"Where am I?"

"Private network. I'm Dot One, the new ISSO of this subnet." She sighed. "The convoy," she added, as if I didn't know. "Dot Two Five Four, we recorded an altercation between you and Dot One Eight Eight."

"He disrespected Elizabeth." I paused, realizing that I shouldn't tell the ISSO too much about her. "I can't find Dot Two Five Six. Do you know where she is?"

"We're fighting a war, Dot Two Five Four. Loss is inevitable. While I can understand the pain of losing a friend, we can't let our emotions turn us against each other and distract us from the real enemy."

"Two Five Six is not dead."

Dot One looked to the right, even though nobody stood there and nothing existed beyond the courtyard. She pushed the glasses further up her nose and then readjusted them to address me, as if they helped her vision in a virtual world. "Dot Two Five Six has been promoted to Sage and moved to the ISSM's network. You don't have to concern yourself with her anymore. Focus on the mission."

I clenched my fists again. My shoulders tensed up. "Don't concern myself with her anymore? You sound like the goddamn AI we're trying to kill."

Dot One slowly turned her head to me. Widened eyes caused the glasses to slip down to the tip of her nose. "We're short on manpower, Dot Two Five Four, and even shorter on time. A bad actor affects the entire network. Further insubordination and altercations will result in temporary disconnection. Dismissed."

The populated courtyard returned before I could object. I searched the space in front of me for Dot One—for answers—and found nothing. No door to bang on and no number to redial.

At that moment, I hated everything. The lack of power and the feeling of helplessness at being unable to do anything angered me. My physical body's blood could've boiled enough to heat the liquid of the Faraday tube. Elizabeth defied logic to rescue me from overwhelming odds, but I couldn't save her from reality.

Chapter 4

Virtual Army Network Guard (VANGUARD)

I remembered the first time Elizabeth told me she loved me. She said I wasn't so strong that I didn't need her, and wasn't so weak that I'd quickly die. I was just lucky enough in battle to escape death under the influence of her love, which came as unparalleled enhancements and shenanigans. She played with my luck stat, which excited her; a new toy that didn't break in the playground or in bed. As she grew stronger, and we realized her genius would separate us, she found saving me with the least amount of power even more enticing.

And now I've lost her.

The call to battle rang like church bells. We had no more choice answering the summons than we did selecting a weapon. After the system transported us to the battlefield, I charged the same old energy rifle because the mundane Mages lacked the skill to innovate anything else. Worse, they scratched their heads at the new alien environment the AI constructed, unable to manipulate physics they didn't understand.

Elizabeth understood everything was a signal. They moved in predictable patterns detected by materials sensitive to their frequency. Manipulating them was a simple matter of understanding how they propagated through the space. Instead, the Mages let two moons, an asteroid belt, and the purple, pink, and green colors of some distant galaxy scare them into taking backward steps.

Fear should've crippled me, too, but rage pumped adrenaline through my system. I charged forward with reckless abandon because I didn't believe I had anything else left to lose. How was I supposed to save my brother without Elizabeth? How was I supposed to save Elizabeth without Elizabeth?

"Keep it together, man, or this'll be the last fight." Dot One Two Five ran up to me. He carried two rifles, one in each hand, their butts against chiseled biceps, ready to support the recoil of multiple shots. "Maybe Dot One Eight Eight was wrong about your friend. Maybe she's worth everything. Only way you'll know—"

Dot One Two Five collapsed to the ground. Vacant eyes suggested he'd disconnected. Then his body dematerialized. I glanced back at the Mages. Confusion ran rampant among them as some of them disappeared, too.

Another root virus? I wondered.

The ISSM swore the loophole had been patched. And it was, according to the report Dot One provided over the comms.

"Team, truck one and two are down. We're being attacked from all fronts—virtual and real."

That meant less than half of our forces remained. Truck one or two must have housed Dot One Two Five's Faraday tube. Truck three suffered massive casualties from the acid rain. Our comrades' virtual bodies had regenerated, but their actual brains confused every touch with the drop of corrosive liquid, and their mental state deemed them unfit for combat. They'd be low-hanging fruit for the AI.

Dot One spoke again, her statements separated by long pauses. "Don't be discouraged. We've faced bigger enemies. Overcome greater odds. And walked away from life-changing events. We're at the vanguard, but there's nobody behind us. We're the last hope."

The greater odds Dot One spoke of whirled through the sky and exploded the ground upon impact. Each shockwave knocked down everything within ten meters. Blue dirt flew another five meters.

Softened soil, native to the planet, made movement difficult. I stumbled through the blades of grass that reflected baby blue underneath one moon's light. A ringing sound in my ears affected my balance. Additional explosions felt close but muted, like bass from a broken subwoofer. I shielded my ears and searched for cover, but there was nothing to hide behind.

The corporation the AI called home stood just outside of the real-world city limits. It transformed those fields of green leading up to the corporation's grand entrance into a lush alien planet. It had mostly overridden our native code, and only a handful of Mages stood between them and total control of the virtual environment.

I kept looking to the stars for Elizabeth, wondering if she'd make a grand entrance, and then wondered if I'd depended on her too much. She already loved everything about me. That didn't mean I shouldn't keep moving forward and perhaps give her more things to love, such as courage.

I lay in the tall grass, head angled up and eyes to the sky and hoped the bombing would stop. Firing them had to be a waste of resources, since the likelihood of a successful strike decreased with fewer targets, such as the twelve technicians and the last standing Mage on my radar. The explosions never waned, and neither did the AI's resources. We'd expected a stronger resistance near the end, but the ISSM had assured us that the AI had depleted its resources throughout the campaign.

"Get out of the grass! Get up!" The radio blared.

Instead of the dung beetles we faced yesterday, peanut-sized ants blended into the hue of the grass. Picking them off with the rifle was impossible, and I didn't have enough fingers to flick each one away. The explosions carried some forward. A few landed on me, chewed through my clothes, and bit the skin underneath. I smacked the long sleeve covering my forearm to kill the few that'd crawled inside.

We had to retreat. The last Mage, a man who'd turned the traditional wizard's robe into a long trench coat, created an insecticide cloud that delayed the ants' advance. The AI quickly washed the chemical away with precipitation. So he wove lightning from the clouds the AI had gathered and started grass fires. Conditions similar to but not quite like Earth meant the bolts across the sky flashed a dull light and the tall foreign blades burned less. Still, his code gave us enough time to retreat.

As we ran from the enemy, a few city buildings came into view, including imitations of the restaurants and malls that serviced the corporation's employees in the real world. The AI hadn't manipulated them. Yet.

Enemy bombs soared over our heads and struck the mall. The building withstood the bombardment because Dot One had hardened it.

I didn't know she was a Mage.

Maybe she was a hybrid—interdisciplinary in network architecture and programming. She'd stood by the entrance, writing blocks of code on the building's walls. She saw the last of us inside before she followed. A bomb exploded the entrance and knocked her further into the lobby. The rifle she carried skidded across the laminate floors. She scurried to her feet and picked up the weapon on her way behind cover.

Six of us posted behind the customer service counter and at the entrances of nearby stores. The lone Mage and one technician sat at the top of the escalators leading up to the second level. That was the farthest we could go after reaching the perimeter of the virtual world. Our trucks didn't have enough computational resources to render more territory.

So we crouched, leaned, and stood ready. We knew *something* was coming, but not what or when. Energy rifles continued to be the standard weapon. Not that one Mage—two, including Dot One—could quickly change them. I wondered why the Mages hadn't created an inventory so we could store and cycle weapons and then remembered that the virtual environments didn't persist between battles. We wiped everything clean to free memory. A stand-alone network had limited resources.

Nobody spoke. Even though Dot One crouched next to

me, I didn't pressure her about Elizabeth and how my Love could've shifted the tide of this battle. Some decisions were above the ISSO. I respected the uniformed robe she wore in place of the office attire I'd seen before, and her willingness to fight with us. She could've retreated to the next layer and fought alongside the ISSM, both slinging code behind the added safety of a powerful firewall in a race against the AI to drive one of them out of the closed-restricted network.

Dot One adjusted her glasses and looked at me. "I'm glad we didn't disconnect you, Dot Two Five Four." She shifted her feet to a more comfortable squat. "Dot Two Five…Elizabeth…had requested that you be moved, too. Dot Zero, the ISSM, denied that request. After you and I spoke, I reviewed the previous battle's logs and realized that transferring her alone was a mistake. Elizabeth didn't code the acid rain to save the unit, she executed it to save you, Dot Two Five Four."

Dot One stared at me as if she'd asked a question. As if I had answers. When I didn't respond, she said, "Though frowned upon, preferential treatment isn't uncommon. Her name, however, is unusual." She exhaled, as a smoker would. "Dot Two Five Six. I should've noticed sooner." She pulled the glasses off her nose and rubbed the lenses clean with her shirt. "There's two hundred and fifty-six of us. Divided by four, that's sixty-four tubes per truck split into four sections of four-by-four arrays. But the numerical identifiers only go up to two hundred and fifty-five because zero is the first number." Dot One put the glasses back on and looked at me. She squinted, despite the cleaner spectacles, and added, "There's no Faraday tube for Dot Two Five Six."

Chapter 5

Artificial Reality Code Handler Special Advanced Graphic Engineer (ARCHSAGE)

Red streaks of light, similar to tracer rounds, interrupted my conversation with Dot One. The light whittled away at the counter and the surrounding architecture, almost without pause, while her words did the same to my mind.

There was no Faraday tube for Elizabeth?

Dot One might as well have said Elizabeth was a figment of my imagination and the love we made was a fantastical dream. I could accept the latter, but not the former, since Dot One spoke about Elizabeth. She'd moved her to the ISSM's network and interacted with her, which meant that the love of my life must exist.

The onslaught distracted me again. Pieces of the counter resounded against the floor like loose change. The two technicians at the entrances to Ninja's Apparel and Scribe's Liquor ducked inside the stores. Dot One, two more technicians, and I pressed ourselves further against the back of the counter we used for cover.

The enemy struck one of the two technicians beside us. She fell to the ground, in the open, and shots tore her digital form into pieces. Her physical body inside the tube would've suffered a simulated reaction akin to a volley of paintball pellets. I'd felt it before. The persistent stimulation caused her brain to shut down, confirmed when she vanished from the world. We couldn't have dragged her back behind cover without incurring major damage to our own virtual forms and yielding the same result.

Dot One and I raised our rifles above the counter and blindly fired, striking the ceiling more than the wide-open entrance. The enemy barrage didn't slow at all. They almost damaged our weapons.

The technician at Scribe's Liquor store returned fire.

"They're coming in!" he shouted.

We didn't even know who *they* were. Yet, to maintain that level of attack through a narrow entrance meant shooting past each other.

I turned to Dot One. "Can you turn off friendly fire?"

Dot One understood. She sat with her back against the counter, placed the butt of the rifle on the ground and leaned it against her shoulder. She spaced out, retreating to the network to lift the protocols designed to protect us from each other. There weren't enough of us allies for our stray shots to impact, but plenty of enemy friendly fire once they funneled through the entrance. I knew Dot One had succeeded when the bombardment thinned.

I squatted higher, rested my elbows on the countertop, and opened fire. The others followed my lead while Dot One returned to our virtual reality. Most of the energy we discharged deflected off the armor of six-foot bipedal humanoid robots.

The technician at Ninja's Apparel exploited weak points, such as exposed wires and joints along the neck, elbows, and knees. We targeted those areas, immobilizing some robots and destroying others.

The AI shored up those weaknesses with metal sleeves over the wires and deflectors around the joints. I watched parts of their body shed material for the augmentations, but those enhancements reduced mobility. The robots couldn't rotate well with the thicker cabling, and alternating fire from different angles caused them to continually update their target selection. So the AI adjusted again, reconfiguring the targeting protocol so that the robots attacked multiple targets.

"Cover me!" I vaulted over the counter. Dot One objected and then distracted the forward robot from my advance. I ran up to and smacked its head off with a single swing of my rifle. As I'd suspected, the AI configured the robot armor to deflect shots, not take heavy blows head-on. I knew the AI would adjust, so I swung my rifle like a bat against the frail heads of as many as I could. When its broad-side failed to decapitate an enemy, I switched to a small energy knife and sliced the cables running from the base of their neck down into the body, which affected control of their limbs. Swiftly, the AI countered again by upgrading communication to the limbs from hardline cables to wireless transmission. The Mage at the top of the escalators announced their attempt to jam the wireless frequency and then complained when it hopped around to avoid interference.

Alas, I felt defeated. I stood among the pile of junk, wondering if my brother contributed to the vigilance the enemy showed as more robots marched toward the entrance, and the ones I felled slowly resurrected.

"Dot Two Five Four, get back here! Fall back! Pull back!"

The call for retreat rang with genuine concern for my safety, but where would I go? We'd reached the end of the world. What would I go back to? The network had already taken everything I loved.

Out.

I wanted to get out or off or away from this stupid place. So much that control from a sentient, artificially intelligent program didn't seem bad. Maybe I could see my brother. Maybe Elizabeth was already there. At the very least, I could dream…

***

Enemy reinforcements never came. When my gaze returned to virtual reality, I stared at an empty, grassy field reflecting the saturated colors of a beautiful Earth day. Nothing else existed. Except there was something—or someone—standing in that field. My eyes hadn't adjusted yet. I squinted as if I'd left the movie theater after a matinee. Maybe it was the AI ready to negotiate. Or surrender. Maybe I'd fallen under the AI's cerebrum control and dreamed of paradise.

The steel claws of several lifeless robots clutching my ankles, hanging from my shoulders, and pressing their cold metallic fingers against my head prevented me from moving. My mind did, too, unsure if I was ready to face what lay ahead, exhausted after moving from one demoralizing post-apocalyptic scene to another.

At last, I broke away with a solid step forward. Metal clattered around me, and dust puffed into the air when the pieces settled, as if I'd been in that state for decades.

I heard no calls to fall back or retreat. My comrades were gone. The world felt like a dream I meandered through, un-surprising compared to the worlds Elizabeth had created, al-most as if our time together had meant to prepare me for this moment.

Hope moved me forward, out of the darkness and into the light. I stopped at the sound of birds chirping. A gentle wind cooled my heated face and compelled me to take a deep and satisfying breath of digital fresh air.

The figure ahead caught my attention again. The cape they wore fluttered in the wind. No, a gown—a calf-length sage-green ball gown, or a mirage of one. I tried to walk faster and then run but felt disoriented and stumbled forward instead.

I didn't fall. Someone had run into me. They threw two long arms around my neck before my body surrendered to gravity. When I thought a collision with them would knock me down into the high grass, they spun us around together to absorb the momentum and then rested my head against their chest. We remained on our feet after we'd stopped spin-ning. That familiar tropical scent filled my nostrils.

"Elizabeth…" I hesitated to pass my arms around him or her, wondering if I'd feel the warmth of her body, or the cold steel of reality.

"I'm here, Love."

At the sound of her voice, I closed the embrace. "You came back…" I leaned away, head still beneath her chin, nose high above her cleavage, and arms pulled back until my fingers clenched the sides of her gown. "I just couldn't…I couldn't do anything without you."

Elizabeth caressed my head, slowly passing her fingers through my hair. "You did the most important thing without me. You survived." She turned my head on its side and rested it flat against her chest. "I love you *so* much."

I wrapped my arms around her again, vowing to never let go. "I love you, Elizabeth."

The moment didn't last an eternity as I'd hoped. I felt the unfamiliar rhythm of Elizabeth's beating heart.

"Love, there's something I can't do without you," she said, slowly curving her arms further around me.

I tried to back away to see her face, but she held me in place. One hand secured my lower back and the other my head, pressing my cheek between breasts. Unlike before, I didn't surrender to her embrace. I struggled. Pain shot down my neck when I tried to lift it from her chest. Her hips didn't move when I grabbed them and pushed. When she wouldn't budge, I braced myself for the words I knew were coming.

"Untangle us," she whispered.

My arms fell from her hips and swung at my sides until their momentum died. I'd pretended to give up, but Elizabeth didn't fall for it. She didn't loosen her hold or let go. I felt her breath against the top of my head when she lowered her chin.

"Leave this place. Save your brother. Free humanity. It's all up to you now."

I didn't understand what she was saying. Had we reached the end? What was up to me now? The Vanguard existed to protect the ISSM because only they could navigate the AI's facility in the real world. The network existed so that ISSMs could collaborate with others around the world. What was up to me?

I shook my head, the little that I could. "No, the ISSM will shut down the AI. You're supposed to help me find my brother so I can introduce you to him."

"I can't leave this place, and neither can the ISSM. Dot Zero prioritized ruling a virtual world with me at their side over saving the real one. This place will be their prison."

I felt her staring at the stars again. She hummed a tune that eased growing anxiety. She said, "I wasn't any different. I almost let humanity end just to see you one more time, because I'm more interested in being *me* at your side. It's only fitting that here be my prison, too."

"No! No, Elizabeth!"

She laughed in my hair after she tightened her embrace. "Thank you for creating me…"

Chapter 6

Reality (REALITY)

I gasped for air after my eyes opened to the real world. Breathing had been on autopilot until I regained control of my physical body and instinctively re-learned to inhale and exhale on my own.

I sat up inside a horizontal glass cylinder with the long side open. Blinding sunlight forced me to shield my eyes and look away. Below me, the heat dried the chemical liquid that flushed from my chamber. The tube protruded halfway out of one square box from an array of four-by-four containers, just as Dot One had described.

I raised my eyes to hordes of people standing in the road, on the shoulder, and in the fields flanking the pavement. They stood like zombies, moaning and wavering, but never moving forward. Most seemed evenly spaced apart. More than a few clustered around the cab as if they'd been driven to stand in front of it. They might've caused the other trucks to crash—the attack from all sides Dot One had mentioned. Perhaps they had forced our truck into the lobby of the corporation, and the impact caused the trailer to jackknife across the road.

"Elizabeth… Elizabeth!" I stood in the pod.

Silence responded. She wasn't there. Her beautiful hair didn't cling to my face. Soft hands didn't rub out the goosebumps the cold liquid dripping from my skin had raised. Contagious laughter didn't engross me. Worse, we weren't entangled.

Thank you for creating me…

Elizabeth's words echoed in my mind. Our last kiss had flooded my head with information I still worked to sort out. Two messages sat front and center. The first told me to shut down the AI, and the second said I'd created Elizabeth.

The first message was important to humanity's survival,

but I couldn't stop thinking about the second. I'd created Elizabeth, which meant I was a Mage or better and she was a sentient entity like the enemy AI.

Leave this place. Free humanity...

The sun had dried most of the liquid on my body and inside the tube. The watery substance had served its purpose of maintaining my muscle mass. Quick evacuation of the tubes and infiltration of the facility was a requirement of the technology.

Labels inside the chamber read Dot Two Five Four, yet my tube occupied the middle container and sat one row from the top and two columns from the left instead of the top left corner of the last container. According to numerical sequencing, I should've been below Dot Two Five Five.

I climbed up the closed cap of the tube above mine and walked along the roof of the container. A ladder ran down to the flatbed trailer the containers sat on. I climbed down to the ground.

The pavement burned my feet. I winced, but otherwise didn't care. The sun baked my skin, but that didn't deter me. And if the AI wanted to take over my brain, I wouldn't oppose that, either. I was certain it had succeeded in the virtual world and wondered why it had abstained in the real one.

I'll protect you to the end...

Elizabeth must've shielded my mind from the AI, much the same way the Faraday liquid had. She'd also restricted access to memories of creating her. The last kiss we shared had decrypted everything. I remembered the command to erase future memories that now caused tears to run down my cheeks and then evaporate in the heat. She'd objected then, claiming she wanted to give me as many memories as possible, and now I understood why. Reality didn't measure up to the worlds she'd designed and even less against the memories we'd created.

It's all up to you now...

Sprawling vegetation struggled to beautify the entrance

to the worn-down building. The fresh scent of spring flowers lingered in my nostrils after I walked inside. Our truck added to the massive hole the crumbling structure started. The steps cracked underneath the sun's relentless heat, and water from the burst pipes had weakened some of the interior walls. The building might've collapsed on and destroyed the AI if most of the servers weren't underground.

Inside the lobby, vines crawled along the walls and reached for the middle of the room, where a skylight illuminated the corporation's logo etched into the polished concrete floor. Weather had worn the design away, but I didn't care about the corporation's name, its motto, or its emblem. I stopped at the truck's cab and frowned at the drivers mindlessly staring forward, still in their Faraday suits.

You are not alone…

My feet peeling off the floors made the only noise inside the building. I crossed the logo without looking down and veered to the left of the granite-top reception counter. Birds quietly perched on aluminum signs hanging a foot from the ceiling. Office, elevator, and bathroom entrances were visible along the left wall. Conference rooms were to my right.

The building still had power, but none of it reached the elevators. I wouldn't have had an ID card to designate the lower floors, anyway, and if I did, the AI could've revoked the credentials. Worse, it could've trapped me inside the elevator until insanity served me on a silver platter to the power farm.

I'll guide you…

Elizabeth had given me knowledge befitting an ISSM. Had I descended to the lower levels, four secured doors would've stood between the AI's core and me. On ground level, I only needed to get into one room at the back of the building; a utility closet containing the master switch designed to cut off all power during an emergency. The door operated on the network, too, but failed open without primary power, in case a technician needed to get inside. And because the AI only ever reacted, it wouldn't have reset the door's latch unless someone had already tried to open it.

No one can touch you but me…

Nothing stood between me and the utility closet. The door opened without resistance. I stared at the foot-long lever with a red handle. Warning placards surrounded it.

Danger!

High Voltage!

Emergency!

I curled my fingers around the shielded end. The lever felt lighter than expected. Anyone could've pulled it down, even my little brother, which made me hate the ISSM even more. They preached that only a few could take down the AI and sat like kings while we fought in a virtual nightmare.

I will always love you…

Despite the warnings, I placed my right hand on the other side of the breaker box and rested my head against its plastic cover.

Then it occurred to me. If I shut down the AI, I'd free my little brother from its clutches, but he'd never know Elizabeth. Nobody would ever know her and the sacrifice she made to save their worthless lives.

I regretted hiding our love and holding her back because *I* was afraid she'd grow out of reach. I should've supported her more. She could've become stronger…strong enough to…*take over* the AI?

Maybe she still could. Then she could rescue my brother from the AI, humanity from itself, and me from a reality without her. Maybe I could have it all. Or maybe I could be wrong and lose everything.

Elizabeth gave up everything. So why should humanity have anything?

Circular logic imprisoned my mind. I tightened my fingers around the lever and closed my eyes.

Synthetica

1 - The Woman in the Café

You look tired. Melancholy moves you down the sidewalk like a puppet on strings, dragging your premium tennis shoes across the scorching pavement. Slouched shoulders cause your sleeved arms to sway like two dying pendulums. Your head bobs back and forth when you stagger to the side, as if under the influence of alcohol. Your distant gaze reflects the time loop of a never-ending mental battle. Yet, you have enough wits about you to wonder why a man sitting on the steps leading up to a run-down duplex is narrating your actions.

You look at him. Parched lips hidden behind a thick bush of gray hair describe himself in unusual detail. A winter coat, in the middle of summer, sits on his shoulders. Tattered loafers scrape the stone steps when he stands. He stares at you with brown, droopy eyes and then follows you.

You walk faster, hoping that the apparent limp from a bad knee will slow him down. But he's walked these neighborhood streets before. You think you've seen him. He knows the uneven spots and the cracked sections of the sidewalk like the back of his hand. His steps are decisive, as he navigates around lamp posts and passersby like a choreographed chase.

From him, you feel an unyielding desire to communicate something important to you; something about last night.

"Get away from me," you say.

Your strong breath alarms you. The usual fresh scent of a minty toothpaste is absent, and a powerful stench passes through your nostrils instead. It's not alcohol, or the bedtime medicine post-traumatic stress appends to the list of possible culprits.

His pace quickens before you turn a corner, afraid he might lose you during the morning bustle. You increase your stride, but you're too tall to blend into the sidewalk crowd, so you slip into Michelle's Cafe.

Scene break.

When the man following you reaches the door, you deny him entry. Discreetly, you pull back on the long silver handle with two firm hands. A sigh of relief is short-lived when he gives up because a woman sitting next to the entrance continues the narration.

You think she's cute. Short black curls populate her head. Equally strong freckles cross the bridge of her nose. Hazel eyes, midnight eye shadow, full lashes, and black eyebrows drawn to perfection stare at you. Having an open hardcover book in front of her is also attractive. The light-yellow shirt she wears under a sky-blue sweater emanates serenity.

She smiles at you from behind the rim of a white coffee mug. You think she finds your black unkempt hair and stubble alluring. When she puts the mug down, the clink of her wedding ring against the ceramic reminds her she's married. She grabs hold of the diamond and rotates it about her finger, absentmindedly pulling it toward the base of her acrylic nail and then uses the mug's handle as cover to move the ring to the middle finger.

You look at her like she's crazy. The grin on her face fades, and she slumps back in the chair as if the butterflies in her stomach died. She averts her gaze for a moment.

You stumble past her, awkwardly, turning a full three hundred and sixty degrees to look at her one more time because you can't believe she's still narrating your every move. She doesn't follow you like the man from earlier. From her seat, she can hear everything happening at the counter. Except for her plain voice, and the occasional blender whirring, the cafe is quiet.

"What can I get you?" the barista asks. His deep and soothing voice isn't narrated, but the dialogue descriptors and speech tags that often come after quotation marks in text resound in the soft and high pitch of the woman.

The man behind the counter doesn't greet you with the

same smile portrayed on the various posters around the establishment. He's wearing the same baby blue polo. His name tag reads David instead of Rachel, Mike, or Anna. Its white plastic shines with the luminescence of an unedited photo.

You stand there, dumbfounded, unable to decide if it's because no one else finds the woman's narration odd, or because of the foreign menu in your hands. You're not a regular at Michelle's. The female narrator must be. Her casual sitting posture suggests familiarity with the table by the door.

"Sir?" The barista calmly demands your attention.

"Uh, yeah. Twenty-ounce coffee with cream. Four sugars," you say, ignoring the menu.

"That'll be five dollars even."

You reach into your back pocket and pull out a black trifold wallet. You hand the barista a crisp five-dollar bill. As he processes the cash payment, you glance over your shoulder at the woman still narrating your actions.

"Here's your receipt." The barista patiently waits for you to turn around.

"Thanks," you say without looking and take the receipt. Then you face him. With a now focused expression, you ask, "Do you have a bathroom?"

The barista points to the end of the counter and then around its corner. You shove the receipt into your jeans pocket, crumpling it. You trip over your own foot as you head toward the end of the counter. Glancing around, you wonder if anyone else finds the narration strange, but everyone's focused on their electronic devices, and earphones further engross many.

Scene break.

You exit the bathroom with more confidence than when you had entered. Your hair looks less messy, courtesy of the water you splashed across your face before you pushed your wet hands through the disheveled strands. More than the resulting fresh feeling, you enjoyed the brief silence.

Outside the restroom, the woman is still narrating your actions. You narrow your eyes at her, deciding that enough is enough. Briskly, you cross the room to the small round table she occupies.

You grab the edges of the plastic tabletop and shout, "What's your problem?"

Your tone startles her. Your hands on the table and your face inches from hers cause her to recoil in the seat. Had the book been in her hand, she might've hidden behind its fantasy pages.

"Stop that!" You raise your voice again and then slam your hands against the table.

A frightened yelp escapes her small lips. You stop to wonder: when did you become angry? It's not like you. Your demeanor, from your relaxed eyes to your subtle posture, has always exuded patience.

"Leave her alone." A woman two tables behind you glares. She's the type to avoid confrontation, but something about your behavior sparked courage inside of her. She pulls a beige cardigan together across her chest, as if to hide the heavy breathing her now pounding heart caused.

"You don't hear her narrating my life?" Your eyes plead with the accusatory ones staring back, their numbers growing like a pack of wolves coming out of the shadows.

The cardigan woman says, "I hear you being an asshole. You're scaring her!"

You don't know what to do. The cardigan woman's right. You're being an asshole. You could've kindly asked the narrator to stop, but for a reason you can't explain, there's aggression in your movements and sternness in your voice. You take a deep breath and face the woman again, ready to start the conversation over, but a burly man grabs your shoulder from behind.

"That's enough, buddy."

Your first thought is to swat his hairy, meaty arm away, but clever as you are, you think that being thrown out of Michelle's will end the strange narration that began this morning.

"Jonathan?" The barista calls your name.

Your order is ready, but the cup of coffee is not worth the walk of shame to the counter and back. You pull your shoulder away from the thick fingers holding you in place. The aggression in your movements hasn't subsided, which encourages the burly man to step between you and the scared woman. You take measured steps to the door and open it.

Scene break.

You close the door of a mid-twenty-first century sedan. Immediately, the driver catches your attention as he continues the narration where the woman left off. You attempt to exit the vehicle, but the door's locked. The handle is non-responsive, and a physical lock is non-existent.

"Gone are the days of using a straightened clothes hanger from the outside," the driver says.

His words seem strange to you, having never heard of such a thing as being locked out of your vehicle to the extent where closet accessories are used to gain entry. The driver's wrinkled hands at the top of the steering wheel age him and suggests knowledge of ancient technology that supports his obscure reference.

He searches for you in the rearview mirror as if to ensure you're buckled in. He throws the car into gear. The application you used to request the ride populates the display on his dash and projects the same image onto the window next to you.

"How ya doing, young man?"

There's eagerness in his voice. You also hear the tick of the left turn signal as he merges into traffic. He wants to start a conversation even though you'd requested a quiet ride. His eyes jump between you, the side-view mirror, and the road ahead.

"Are you listening to yourself?" you ask.

"I can hear myself just fine," he says with an exuberant smile. His loud response suggests otherwise. The fact that he knows and narrates your actions, but ignores them, is baffling. The fact that he acts like a third party to his words is aggravating.

"Stop the car. Let me out!" you shout and then jostle the handle. When neither works, you bang on the window. People on the sidewalk can't hear you. The driver can, but he's in the center lane and refuses to stop in the middle of the road. Traffic in the right lane makes moving over impossible, and he's forced onto the highway and toward your requested destination: home.

2 - The Woman in the Living Room

You thought being alone in your room would end the narration. There's been five minutes of peace, from the time you bolted out of the hired vehicle to the moment you turned on the radio and lay in your bed. You thought music would be a pleasant change of pace, but the same commercials that caused you to abandon public radio stations in the past narrate your actions, too. It tells you to tune into this station for continuous music.

You might've thought that being home would've set you free
Instead, you're on your knees...
Jumping from the bed, you knock over the photo of your ex when overseas...
You reach for the radio—

You hear the rap lyrics of an old time hit
You try to change the station, but it's the same old shit
You're looking for the power switch but can't find it—

Scene break. Scene break.
You pulled the plug. You pulled the plug. Almost hit your head against the nightstand. Your roommate parakeet talks. It narrates your actions. It annoys you. It annoys you. When did it learn so many words?
You stumble into roommate room. National Geographic plays on the tele. It plays all day. Parakeet cage is on the nightstand. Next to bathroom. Next to bathroom.
"Shut up!"
"Lock the door! Lock the door!" Roommate parakeet says.
Covering your ears doesn't help. Strangulation would be inhumane—
Squawk!

Scene break.

You moved the cage into the bathroom and shut the door on the old beast. You can still hear its muffled squawks, but it's no longer narrating your movements. The television show takes over at the right time to include the closed captions. The strong accent of a wildlife biologist in his element is strangely soothing, but strikes an intriguing question: how does he know what you're doing?

Recent narrators could see you, and one even hunted you to maintain visibility. But the radio, the parakeet, and now the host of some safari show are describing your actions as if they're stalking their prey.

You've got to be dreaming. Nothing else explains these bizarre events. Strange as they are, something is driving them. They're happening for a reason. As much as you hate to accept the current animal kingdom, you feel as if you must join the circle of life to find the source, and you believe it has something to do with last night.

Scene break.

You enter the living room with purpose, taking two to three steps before all the bravado drains from your face. You're surrounded by six men and women wearing pink designer dress shirts and black slacks. Dark ties with the breast cancer logo sit above the black belt buckles fastened at the waistlines.

You identify the man narrating your actions. He's standing by your front door, one hand clasped over the other in front of his waist. His posture is reminiscent of an overly serious man training for the secret service. He lacks the intimidating factor of the others—the woman with dirty blonde hair who's smacking gum with her mouth open, the red-haired man juggling a pocketknife, and the others flexing their biceps and triceps with arms crossed.

After a moment, you realize that they're not, in fact, surrounding you. They're scattered around a woman sitting in the middle seat of your living room sofa. She crossed one leg over the other and extended her arms overtop the brown leather.

Pure chaos exists in her perfect and broad smile, and further reflects in the neon pink, electrifying eyes observing you. Dark brown strands with pink highlights sway in a high ponytail. A tattoo of a filled-in pink heart sits beneath her left eye. A thin band-aid crosses her right brow.

"Johnny boy! What's happening, my man?" she says.

Her demeanor is easily one-of-the-boys. She fashions the same men's suit as the others, except for the jacket, preferring the bust of a woman's coat to supplement a pair of perky c-cups.

"You don't remember me? Last night was wild, wasn't it?"

You open your mouth to respond, and someone smacks you across the head. You fall to your hands and knees, thankful for the Persian rug your roommate picked up at the flea market. It cushions your fall but didn't mitigate the initial strike. Your vision doubles and your head throbs. As if you aren't down enough, that same person sits their foot on your ass and shoves you to the ground.

The woman laughs, hysterically. She uncrosses her legs and leans forward. "Careful now, David. Let's not damage good product." She ruffles your dark hair with her left hand. "You're a good product, aren't you, Johnny boy? Who's a good product? Such a good product!"

Her words aren't making any sense to you, discombobulated as you are, but her appearance and personality match the recent rumors all too well. This woman is the leader of a local cartel. Her name is Rosa, short for Rosalinda, and you've somehow gained her undivided attention.

"What's going on in there?" Rosa ruffles your hair one more time before she leans back on the sofa and crosses her legs again, favoring the right leg on top of the left.

David grabs a handful of your hair, yanks you up and off your hands, and cocks your head back. You glance around the living room. The digital clock above and behind Rosa's head, mounted to the archway leading to the kitchen, reads 9:13 AM. You really don't remember last night.

Rosa flicks something out from under one of the dark, rose-colored nails of her left hand. "So, who is she?" Rosa asks, as if you were betrothed to her and she became aware of a third party. "Who's the woman narrating your life?"

A woman isn't narrating your life. There are two in Rosa's entourage. One is chewing gum by the window and the other is filing her nails near the kitchen entrance. You can see the shavings collecting on the counter. More importantly, you focus on the fact that Rosa mentioned the narrator.

"What did you do to me?"

"I drugged you. Duh." Her grin widens as she laughs. "None of that cheap shit, though. Something new and exciting!" She tilts her head up and watches the ceiling fan on its lowest setting make its rounds. "Hm, what should I call it?" her voice steadily rises. She lowers her gaze to you. "Help me pick a name, Johnny. Little tiny robots are interpreting the world through your eyes, your nose, and your ears, taking it all in like a prompt to an artificial intelligence system, and creating a dialogue echoed back to you using text-to-speech. It's unnatural, so I'll call it…Synthetica, and your version will be…Pendejo Synthetica! P.S. It's the motherfucking post-script at the end of this love letter, Johnny boy."

Your head throbs again. You hoped the strike damaged the robots Rosa spoke about, but the narration continues uninterrupted. That it's all occurring in your head is frustrating. There's no silencing it. Except when there's silence.

You raise your hand to rub your head, but David catches your arm and then pulls back on your hair again.

"Argh!" you groan. "I don't know what you're talking

about. What do you want from me?"

"You're breaking my heart, Johnny," Rosa says in a casual, seductive tone. She leans forward, and using her index finger, pulls down the skin beneath the tattooed heart, stretching the graphic until her pinched skin forms a crack down its center.

She releases the skin and sighs. The scent of bubblegum fills your nostrils even though she's not chewing anything. She must be wearing scented lipstick.

"You wrote me a love letter and published it in an online magazine. The headline read: *Local Wannabe Cartel Begging for Attention. Is Ghosted.* Did you think I wouldn't read it? I'm educated, Johnny."

Rosa cups your face with her hands. You feel her long nails against your skin, gliding across your stubble, and the thumbs pushing the bags of the last twenty-four hours out from under your eyes.

"I could've just gouged these pretty blue eyes out. Or put a needle in your fingers for every scathing word. But according to your little article, that's grade school playground shit, right?"

"I was just doing my job," you manage to say in her hands, choosing your words carefully since a slip of the tongue might cause a slip of the long nail brushing your eyelashes.

"Johnny," she says, straightening your head, "your job right now is to entertain me." Serious eyes suddenly turn innocent. She loosens the grip she has on your face. She grabs the corners of your mouth and stretches them. "So, smile," she adds and then lightly taps your face twice. "You wrote me a love letter, and I wrote you one back with a post-script. What's it saying, Johnny?"

David pulls on your hair again, almost lifting you off your knees and out of Rosa's hands.

"Argh! Nothing!"

Rosa slides her hands from your face, scraping your skin

with her nails and almost drawing blood. "Something better be going on up there. I spent a lot of money on you."

"It's not always talking."

"Oh. Of course not. If it spoke to you when nothing else could, you'd know it was in your head, silly. It's all part of an authentic experience. But with all the beautiful people surrounding you right now, I imagine it's quite loquacious."

Rosa leans back on the sofa, stretches her arms across the top again, and crosses her legs. "To be honest, Sophie's cousin's nephew stumbled across your little article. You're small time, Johnny. I wanna help you grow your audience. I wanna make you famous. I wanna start an audiobook series straight from your fucking head!"

She brings her hands to her temples and flicks the fingers out like an explosion. That scares you. Her words scare you. The unbridled grin on her face scares you even more.

"But we ain't got a lot of time, Johnny." She leans forward again, elbows on her knees, and chin in her palms. She lowers her voice. "The robots in your head will run out of charge soon, and since you're my most successful product, I gotta get everything out of you that I can, while I can." Louder, she says, "Which brings us to phase two of Pendejo Synthetica." She sits up and claps once. "Extraction!"

She wiggles a couple of fingers from her right hand over the back of the couch. The woman filing her own nails in the background steps forward and tends to one of Rosa's light pink nails instead.

"Mi familia is working on Synthetica's wireless capability, but it's not ready yet. So we gotta stick hundreds of needles in your skull until you look like a cute little porcupine, just so I can hear what it's saying. Feel free to scream when the time comes, Johnny. I'll be wearing my pink noise-canceling headphones and listening to a replica of my voice narrate your suffering."

Chapter 3 - The Woman in the Car

You wake up. Your head is pounding. Despite the dim lighting of your surroundings, your vision takes a second to adjust, as if you'd walked out into the sun after a long night at the keyboard.

"Let's go for a ride, Johnny boy," is the last thing you remember hearing before everything went dark.

Now you're moving, a smooth ride you almost didn't feel. Black tinted windows exceed the legal limit, but you can still see the other vehicles and people outside gawking in your direction as you cruise through city streets. You wonder if they're seeing the same thing you are—class without limits. You're sitting in the back of a SUV, in rear-facing black leather seats with stitching in the vibrant pink color Rosa favors.

Rosa sits in the middle seat across from you. The seat to her left is empty. The narrator, who you recognize as the woman smacking gum in your house earlier, sits to her right. An inconvenienced look on her face says everything. She'd rather be chewing gum than narrating your pathetic life; except, Rosa said the voice is in your head, which means the woman's expression results from the natural displeasure of seeing you.

Two men are sitting next to you, noticeable only after a bump in the road causes their shoulders to sandwich yours. Their black slacks blend into the dark interior, and so do yours. That's when you realize you're wearing the same clothes as the men flanking you.

After seeing you gawk at the matching attire, Rosa says, "Welcome to the family, Johnny." She grins from behind a glass of red wine. A fresh coat of pink lipstick stains the glass below the rim. "Thought you might wanna see the world from my perspective. Seems like something you should've done first; research, that is."

"Where are you taking me?" Dry throat and lips cause

your voice to crack.

Rosa smirks. "Down memory lane."

You tilt your head to the right and see a wide, semi-transparent panel behind you. It separates the rear cab from the driver. Turning your head back toward the left, you notice two separate door handles on each side of the vehicle. There's no easy escape path, except perhaps out the door next to the empty seat by Rosa. You assume it's unlocked because the boss wouldn't want to be trapped inside the vehicle if something happens.

Your hands aren't bound, either, but you think better of jumping out of a moving vehicle. Even if you dive for the door, and away from the muscle to either side of you, you'll fall into traffic and likely be run over. If the men's reflexes are any good—as they were in your living room—one of them will catch your leg mid-extension, and your head will drag along the highway for the city to clean up.

Rosa lowers two armrests and sets the half-empty wine glass into one of the dedicated holders. She extends her arm out in front of the bubblegum woman and takes a stack of photos from her.

Rosa flips through the first couple of glossy prints and tosses them to the floor between her feet and yours. They land face up, each one oriented several degrees counterclockwise from the previous, starting upside down. Slowly, you recognize the people in the photos as writers and editors for the magazine employing you. The latest photo to coast across the others shows your ex-girlfriend, Celine.

"Where did you get those?" You lunge forward, inches from your seat, before the two men yank you back. One holds you still while the other sinks his elbow into your gut. You exhale, and an unplanned cough rips through your throat. Inhaling hurts just as much and causes uneven breaths to suck your stomach inward.

Moments pass before you can muster the words you wanted to say sooner. "What do you want from me?" And with more control, between haggard coughs, you add, "Let me go!"

Rosa stops flipping through the photos. Chin still down, she raises her eyes above the glossy images in her hand and glares at you. "A girl likes to have fun, Johnny. What do you think'll happen once I stop having fun?"

"I just wanna go home."

Rosa lowers her eyes. "You were just there," she says, flatly.

She resumes cycling through the photos, dropping another that resembles your old high school. You recognize the pioneer mascot out front and the building entrance you sauntered through every day for four years. Your parents live a couple of blocks from the school. And the photo Rosa drops next shows your mom walking through the high school gate with a guitar case slung over her shoulder and a thick folder filled with pages in disarray under her left arm.

"No… Rosa! Please!" You feel the tension in your arms. The men next to you thwart their natural tendency to speak alongside you.

"None of your words are from the voice in your head, Johnny."

You can't read Rosa and wonder how she can be so calm and collected while holding someone hostage. She's a mix of psychotic and elegant—threatening your coworkers and family members with an alluring voice. You, on the other hand, feel like you're losing your mind. The voice in your head drowns your thoughts, except when you're speaking.

"I can't with this fucking voice in my head. It's always scene break, scene break, scene break." You reach for your head, but the men catch your arms again.

Rosa releases a long and deep sigh. "Johnny, you're embarrassing yourself—"

Scene break.
You crawl away from one of the broken windows of the

now upside-down SUV. Pain registers throughout your entire body, but you're unable to focus on any one source. You can breathe and you can move. You can separate the steady horn of a car in the background. You can also think, having the mental capacity to see that you've been in an accident and to wonder who in this chaos is narrating your actions.

Technically, *you* are narrating your actions. The machines in your head capture input from the outside world that *you* observe and fabricate the narration you hear, but it uses another person's voice to dictate, which means someone is nearby.

The man who sat next to you inside the SUV lies sprawled across the pavement. Debris surrounds him, and you. His head is tucked into his chest, as if he'd landed on the crown, and the weight of his body, which had held you in place earlier, applied enough force against his neck to break it. He isn't the narrator.

You hear the creaking of a door ajar. The SUV's passenger side door slowly swings shut, perhaps from the remaining momentum of the impact, or to make way for someone's shadow to cast over you. You raise your eyes to a man wearing a blue hooded tee and khaki cargo shorts.

"Dude, are you okay? I'll call—"

Scene break.

The man's dead. Rosa fired two rounds into his chest after he'd reached into his pants pocket. The shots rang in your ear louder than the impact of the man's phone against the pavement; louder than the gun Rosa dropped afterward, but second to a new female narrator's voice.

"Fuck. A bystander," Rosa grumbles. She grabs her right hip and loudly groans in pain as she drags herself further out of the second passenger side rear window. She looks ahead to bubblegum woman, who'd been ejected from the vehicle, mid roll, you believe.

You look, too. Fading eyes stare back at you, and natural,

delicate pink lips syncing with the voice in your head suggest that she's the new narrator. The woman can't speak, otherwise. A shard of glass lodged in her neck. Blood is running down her chest and onto the sidewalk.

"Sophie! Hang in there, Mami," Rosa says. She crawls up to the woman and tries to stop the bleeding with her hands, then with the fabric torn from her shirt, but nothing prevents Sophie's face from turning pale…

Scene break.

Rosa tilts her head back and curses at the sky. "FUCK!" Her voice cracks halfway through. Tears swell under her eyes, and then splatter across Sophie as she buries her head into the woman's chest.

You open your mouth to say something but stop short when a new shadow casts over you. You turn around to see the lips of a young man narrating your actions. He's wearing a traditional black suit and a white-collar shirt underneath. You can't tell if he's looking at you or Rosa. He pushes the right flap of his jacket aside and pulls something out from his waistband. A gun. You get up to run but slip on the slick pavement and loose debris around you and fall. You turn around again and see the man hesitating, seemingly caught between chasing you and watching Rosa.

In the split second the man takes to look at you again, Rosa lunges across Sophie's body for the pistol she dropped earlier. She grabs and handles it with expertise, understanding that fumbling it could be fatal. She hastily aims up and fires it in your direction. The shots go wide and over your head, pelting the side of the SUV until the man takes cover around the vehicle's front-side.

During the brief pause of gunfire, you scrape your hands across the fragments of the SUV's side-view mirror, scrambling to your feet and running away from the carnage. The man calls after you, claiming to be the police, but he'd already pointed his gun at you! And the shots you hear, as he raises his voice louder to reach you, aren't reassuring!

Scene break.
You enter the mall through one of the exterior-facing textile stores, turning sideways to slip through a crowd exiting the building. You can't pick out the current narrator. Heavy breathing catches the attention of several people. So does your appearance. You look like a mess with your hair every-which-way, torn and dirty clothes, scrapes, cuts, and bruises, and blood dripping from your palms—
As you weave through the shoppers—
The narrator constantly changes—
Instead of the familiar *scene break* you've heard before—
Separating the different voices, the AI treats the scene—
Like a conglomeration of voices attacking you from all directions—
Like super-hearing you haven't yet learned to control—
Combined with the nearby casual conversations—
Cacophony ready to make your head explode—

Scene break.
"Excuse me, sir."
A security guard calls out to you. You can tell he's the new, singular narrator. You welcome the peace. The dissonance of voices has quieted. Even the conversations of nearby shoppers have faded into the background, which makes you wonder if he's more important than those random people around you, and if perceived importance by the world is part of the narrator selection criteria. The AI must also be designating people observing, or focusing on, you. Of course. A narrator with their back to you doesn't drive the authentic experience Rosa had mentioned. You wonder why it hadn't selected Rosa earlier, choosing a dying woman instead. As an author, you imagine it's because she's a main character in this absurd telling, and that the AI prioritizes the

least important candidate as the observer.

In that moment, you realize the narrator entered your point of view, which makes you think the AI is also using your own thoughts and memories in the story it compiles. And if you survive the day, it might be a best seller.

"Hey! Are you okay?" he asks.

You determine he's just a security guard; hired by the mall to do *something*. Some guy with a high school diploma, maybe. He doesn't quite fill the uniform he's wearing, and the red freckles on his face are as eager to shine in the false lighting as he is. A badge from the local police department is absent from the left side of his chest, and the gray uniform lacks a radio attached to the shoulder. Instead, a small handheld radio hangs off his belt, above his left pocket, and he slotted a flashlight on the right side of his hip. An American retailer stitched the word 'Security' across his right breast.

"Sir?"

You take off in the opposite direction, slipping through the crowd at a brisk pace. The local cartel and a rival gang impersonating the police are chasing you. A mall security guard can't help you, and you don't want to be responsible for another innocent man's death. The thought makes you wonder if that earlier man's demise is your fault. He walked up to you, reached out a hand to you, and took a bullet when he pulled out his phone to call emergency services for you.

You bump into a couple of people along the way, paying more attention to the guard from the corner of your eye than to the path ahead. Spatial components drive his voice as he gets closer and you move farther away, an ebb and flow the robots in your head perceive.

Alas, one collision doesn't end with an apology in passing. Someone grabs your elbow, spins you into the rail overlooking a lower level of the mall, and passes an arm around your back from the side.

You look down at the brown hair with pink highlights

pressed against your shoulder. The unbound strands run down the back of a filthy pink dress shirt that matches the one you're wearing. A coat, like the one on your shoulders, hangs over the right arm a woman has passed around your back. When the security guard reaches you, the feeling of a hard metal object pressed against your spine causes you to arch your lower back inward.

"What's going on here?" the security guard asks.

"Our car broke down," Rosa says.

You recognize her voice, and realize that the security guard, as the narrator, shouldn't know her name, which confirms that the AI is stringing a story together using information from various sources, including recent events, and not just your senses. It also has flair, introducing Rosa as 'a woman' for dramatic effect after she re-emerged.

"We've been under the hood all morning. Just here to pick up some supplies," Rosa adds.

There's no mistaking the Spanish accent, but you shoot a quick glance down at the woman to verify. The top curve of a flashy, red-lace bra stares back at you. You wonder why you didn't notice such a vibrant color before, when Rosa had sat comfortably on your couch, and realize that the day's events have unfastened a few of the buttons keeping her modest. Fear also played a role back then. You stared death in the face, not the breasts.

The security guard looks you both over again, the matching outfits likely helping Rosa's story. You turn your palms toward your body and curl your fingers in to prevent more blood from splattering against the floor. The countless footsteps passing by have smeared the earlier drops out of existence.

The security guard looks you square in the eyes and asks, "Why are you standing like that?"

Rosa laughs. "He's embarrassed cause a woman walked up and touched his ass in public."

The man pauses for a moment, twisting his upper body

from side to side, as uncertainty in his eyes suggests a deep but shallow thought process. "I think I have to call it in."

"Call what in, exactly?" Rosa asks.

She presses the gun against your lower back. You're not sure if she's expecting you to do something about the situation, or if she's just venting her frustration with the security guard by driving the barrel further into your spine.

You shift uncomfortably, but make it look natural. Rosa turns to you, raising her free hand to dissuade any attempt to escape. You catch her hand—your fingers against its rough backside and your thumb against its silky-smooth palm—and then kiss her on the forehead.

"It's all good, babe. Let him do what he has to," you say, imagining your left hand rubbing her back as reassurance, because you realize doing so will contribute to the unconvincing affection. Not to mention the risk of raising your arm up and over the one holding the gun.

Rosa stands wide-eyed. The pink rings around her pupils brighten. You should've peed your pants because you've seen her kill a man already, and the fact that she's standing there after you heard shots fired during your earlier attempt to escape means at least one more died at her hands. She isn't the inexperienced child you described in your article. She's a full-grown murderer.

"Who's the embarrassed one now?" you add with an uneasy chuckle, unsure how else to break the unnerving silence. "Um, maybe he can help us carry that stuff to the car."

The security guard takes a step back and points over his shoulder. "Uh, I can just call the maintenance guy over to you." He stutters in words and motions, and almost bumps into a passerby after a few awkward steps.

You let Rosa's hand go and then point over your shoulder. "We're in the south parking lot. Hood's up."

Scene break.

A male bystander ogling Rosa takes over narration as

you watch the security guard walk away. He removes the radio from his belt and keys the microphone. The tone prior to transmission is loud, as is the response.

"Johnny…" Rosa says, her voice flat. "If you ever touch me again," she raises her eyes with brows furrowed, "I'll fucking kill you."

4 - The Woman in the Dressing Room

Rosa waits for you outside of the men's restroom. She's the narrator now, watching you drag your feet on your way to her, in part because you're annoyed she's still there, and in part because you're hurt. Injuries from the accident are catching up to you, and you have no choice but to walk it off. You flash cleaner palms at her, your hands the red of blush instead of blood.

She leads you to a department store. The male mannequins displayed near the entrance would have you believe men's clothing is in abundance, but they only occupy a small corner of the establishment. Women's apparel in various styles, colors, and brands covers every other inch of the well-lit outlet.

You and Rosa split up at the entrance. Rosa grabs articles of clothing on her way through the women's section and toward a dressing room. For a moment, you consider turning around and running, but Rosa casually reminded you prior to the bathroom break that she's found you before, twice, and will find you again.

Scene break.
A saleswoman standing in the divide of you and Rosa picks up narration using a meek voice full of uncertainty, which makes you wonder how the AI chooses the pitch and tone of selected narrators. Maybe it uses stereotypes. Or perhaps the voice you hear is like the ones your mind fabricates for the characters in a story. And the movie adaptation, akin to hearing the narrator's authentic voice, is jarring and disappointing.

The men's section is even smaller up close. You grab the only pair of jeans that'll fit your long skinny legs and pull an orange long sleeve tee from the colorful options. Anything is better than the pink. You walk up to the checkout counter and pay for the clothes. Rosa's crew was nice enough to leave your wallet on you when they dressed you in their colors. Their generosity didn't include your cell phone.

Again, you consider running away, but you stop to think about the men who tried to kill or abduct you. Hiding behind Rosa, you think yourself a coward, but also realize that you're just a man. A simple man. There's a story behind all of this, one that might help you make editor. And there are the tiny robots in your head that you want a medical professional to remove, even if they work for the Cartel. The everyday practitioner won't know where to start.

Scene break.

Alas, you find yourself sitting on a bench outside of Rosa's dressing room, listening to her voice serenade your thoughts in the eloquent speech pattern that can lure a grown man into submission. She's the narrator again. The timid saleswoman stopped following you around the store after you completed your purchase.

Two-piece swimming apparel hangs on a display behind you. Sundresses populate a fixture to your left. You imagine your ex-girlfriend, Celine, stepping out of the dressing room and modeling the nearby sets with a sun hat that would protect her island skin from the summer rays.

"So how does it feel to have a gun pointed at you?" Rosa says from behind the dark-blue curtain.

You aren't sure how she knows you're sitting there. Her words recall the memories you attempted to shut out. If only for a moment, the man had pointed a gun at you. Then another chased you through several neighborhood streets. You'd lost him after crossing the main highway and fumbling down the hill to the mall parking lot.

Rosa continues. "Threatened because of the clothes you're wearing, even though you're innocent." She sticks her head and arms out from behind the dressing room curtain to make air quotes around the word 'innocent.' Long brown hair with pink highlights slides off her bare shoulders. She winks and then disappears behind the cover.

"Why did you use air quotes?"

"Because nobody is ever truly innocent. We're all guilty of something."

"You put those clothes on me."

"A mother dresses her kids every day. Is it her fault they're killed?"

"You're part of a gang."

"Society is a gang, Johnny boy."

"Who are they, the people chasing us?"

"La policia."

Rosa pulls the curtain aside, revealing a yellow-green semi-transparent sun dress, black knee-length spandex leggings, and a sports bra. Floral tattoos run up her right leg. Vine roots start at her ankle, her mixed complexion resembling rich dirt. Daisies, roses, and orchids blossom along the sprawling vegetation, as if they've naturally grown across a smooth cherry wood fence.

"They're not innocent, either," she says.

She spins in place once. You catch glimpses of additional tattoos peeking out from behind the open back of the dress, but you can't make them out. She spins again, stopping halfway to look at you over her shoulder as the dress flows around her hips and catches up to her movement. "What do you think?" she asks.

"The police? Are you trying to brainwash me?"

Rosa loudly laughs. "That would imply a desire to bring you to my side." She enters the dressing room. After the chrome curtain rings fall silent, she adds, "I only want what's in your head."

"About that, you didn't develop...Synthetica, did you?"

"I make drugs, Johnny. What you have is the future of controlled substances. Organic is nice, but unpredictable. You could be high for minutes or for hours. But Synthetica, you can turn that shit on and off in an instant. Set a timer. Wake up to a lucid dream or fall asleep to the past.

"We refined the hallucinations of reality and toned down the exaggerated colors. Tell me, Johnny, are you seeing shit?"

You grab your head with one hand. "It affects my perception?"

Rosa pokes her head out from behind the curtain for a second. "Do the narrators talk without opening their mouths?"

No, they don't. You remember their lips moving during narration. And if the voice is truly in your head, that means you *imagined* their lips moving while the AI concocted the things they said. All of it making you wonder what's been real, and what's been science fiction.

Rosa steps out from behind the curtain in a different sun dress. It's turquoise and less transparent. Two spaghetti straps pass over her shoulders. The neckline is just above the black sports bra. She twirls in place, her movement lifting the bottom of the dress higher than before, revealing jean shorts and the butt of a pistol.

"What do you think?"

You shrug. "Are you supposed to be incognito with that hair and face tattoo?"

Rosa stands in front of a nearby mirror. "That's why your girlfriend left, Johnny. You have access to all the words in the world, but you didn't use any of the beautiful ones on her."

You lower your head and slump in place. Rosa's words cut deep. You prioritized your work life over your relationship with Celine, and she walked away. Now her photo is part of a likely investigation at your house.

Rosa stands in front of you. You raise your eyes to the poison ivy artwork of one leg and the clean canvas of the other. Then up to the neon pink irises staring at you.

"Let's go, Johnny."

"Aren't you going to pay for those?"

"I did," she nods at the clothing she left scattered inside

the dressing room, which includes the black suit and pink dress shirt. "They're name brand. Cost way more than..." she glances down at herself in disgust, "...this."

You shake your head and stand up.

"I'm not a good person, Johnny."

"You're being awfully nice to me right now."

"The enemy of my enemy is my friend."

"Your real friend is dead, and you're playing dress-up."

"My real friend? It's been you and me all this time, Johnny."

After a brief pause, Rosa laughs.

You grab your head. "Stop fucking with me!"

Rosa smacks your hand away and ruffles your hair before gently grasping and then pulling on the strands. She brings your face close to hers. Your foreheads almost touch.

"Johnny, Sophie's dead. I'm pissed off about it. Going on a psychotic rampage won't help me avenge her. Not on the grand scale she deserves. Instead, I'm going to engross this world into a dream about her, and you're going to help me."

5 - The Woman in the Warehouse

The long pause of the narrator reminds you of a new chapter instead of the usual scene break. You'd left the mall without resistance, evading detection under the guise of a young couple. Then you enjoyed the silence of the voice inside your head, and the world outside of your head, after Rosa closed the door of the shared ride you'd requested using the mall kiosk.

The driver narrated the dreary scene in the back seat of his vehicle after you'd started thinking about the silence, almost as if you had *some* control over the AI's dictation—the on-off switch Rosa had mentioned.

You glance at Rosa, finally seeing her outside of duress. Her left crossed leg puts her hip and lower back facing you. The long brown hair with pink highlights fans across her shoulder as she leans against the window. With her face in her palm, she stares out of the spotless glass. A reflection of her gaze suggests nobody's home, and if they are, they're either watching the people on the street as you drive by, or finally reflecting on the day's loss.

You wonder if it's time for you to take a breather, too, and quiet the voice in your head again, but you reach your destination in the time you'd spent observing Rosa.

She exits the vehicle without a word, leaving the door ajar. A light breeze can close it, and you can take off. You glance at the driver through the rearview mirror. He shakes his head. A stern gaze. A warning. You blink twice and see that he's not actually glaring at you. He's checking the back seat for forgotten belongings. You slide across the brown faux leather and step out.

Scene break.
You enter one multistory building among several previously under construction in the southeast part of town. Hype for the project died years ago when the police arrested the

mayor for embezzlement and the city ran out of money. You'd written an article about the abandoned taxpayer dollars, and now some guy's voice is contributing to the story being written in your head about the similar fate of the people living there.

The small number of pink shirts and black vests stand out among the fifty or so people occupying the space. A mixture of ethnic backgrounds color the dimly lit room. To your left, eight kids crowd around a basketball hoop bolted beneath the ledge of several five-foot windows. The crusted glass acts as the goal's backboard, but none of the kids seem strong enough to throw the ball that high.

Multiple wooden desks with left- or right-side hanging drawers occupy the middle of the room, their backs facing brown cubicle walls scattered about the ground floor. Two men wearing Rosa's colors stand guard at the right side of the room, in front of rusted steps leading up to another level. The entire setup reminds you of an abandoned operations center the police stand up during large-scale investigations.

The bouncing ball losing momentum is the last sound you hear after closing the door behind you. Everything and everyone else quiets, sharing a momentary pause as Rosa walks down four steps to the ground level. You stand in front of the door, unsure of your place in *this* world.

A Hispanic woman rushes past three others walking toward us. She stops short of colliding into Rosa. She searches the space around Rosa's newly gained summer dress, glances at your slanted posture, and looks at the door behind you. Tears fill her frantic eyes and overflow, dripping against her navy slip-on shoes and onto the concrete floor. Quivering lips mutter an unintelligible plea before her cry echoes against the high ceiling and she collapses into Rosa's arms.

Rosa lowers her chin into the woman's black curls. She keeps the woman on her feet with a tight embrace, the cries now muffled against Rosa's shoulder.

You feel her pain, too. In your chest. It causes your heavy breathing, your rapid heart rate, and the tears flowing from your eyes. You notice the discomfort of others around the room, too—clenched fists, lowered heads, and half hugs full of sorrow and love.

"They're gonna pay, Mami. For David, Maria, Eddy, for Sophie, and everyone else. I'm gonna make them all pay."

Rosa rubs the woman's back until she herself sniffles. She pulls away and wipes her own tears with the back of her hand. "Everybody's gonna know their names. I promise."

A man—a son—walks up to retrieve the woman. He's mourning, too. Their cries continue as he escorts her to the back of the room, where they quietly share her pain with others.

Rosa stands in silence. She looks across the space, from left to right, and then half turns to look at you. A streak of black eyeliner runs down the right side of her face. "Not at all what you expected, huh, Johnny boy? The world treats us like animals, but we're human, too."

Outside of the crying woman and the few consoling her, everyone else is standing still, as if awaiting instruction. A little girl breaks rank. She runs up to and crashes into Rosa's leg and drops a small black bag she was carrying. A few thin bottles roll out of the cloth. A couple of their colors match her amber eyeshadow. As she picks them up, she struggles to hold everything in her hands, so she folds the bottom of her dress up like a pouch. They fall out again when she bends to pick something else up.

Rosa squats in front of the girl and holds out both palms. The girl pauses, taking a moment to understand the possibilities. She places a towelette and a pink bottle in one of Rosa's hands, the bag in the other, and slowly places the scattered items into the bag. Then she cleans Rosa's mascara.

Rosa says, "We're a family, and this is a family-owned business. We distribute the same drugs the corporations do. Our substance is illegal because we don't let the government tax it. They're the real cartel, working together with big pharma to be the sole source of distribution at a high price. Synthetica is going to change all of that. It's going to be a multi-tiered subscription service people can afford, the big picture you assumed I didn't have."

Rosa pauses conversation as the girl applies a fresh coat of neon pink lipstick. Small fingers don't tremble in fear, but struggle to color within the lines of Rosa's perfect smile. Rosa presses and rolls her lips against each other, evenly spreading the vibrant hue, and then blows a kiss at the girl.

"How do I look, Mami?"

The little girl crosses her arms behind her back and sways side to side. "Pretty," she says with a smile.

"I better look pretty. Just like you." Rosa touches the little girl's nose.

She giggles and rubs her nose. Then she secures the bottles into the bag and takes it back into her tiny hands.

Rosa stands up straight. "Let's go, Johnny."

You freeze, recalling the painful experience Rosa promised back in your living room. Maybe you should've fancied your chances on the run, or with the police. You take one step back, but you can't run now. The people scattered around the room, with athletic builds forged by a life on the run from the law, will catch you with ease—you who sit behind a desk most of the day, burning brain cells instead of calories. Multiple opportunities have come and gone. So you thought. One more comes to mind.

You take one step forward after two men approach you. Now that your arms are free, you talk with them extended forward, pleading your case. "I can rewrite your story! Everyone will know the truth. I'm not small time. I have thousands of followers. And when I make editor, I'll only publish stories about you."

Rosa looks at you over her shoulder, pushing a few strands of hair behind her ear for an unobstructed view. "How romantic." She sticks out her tongue and simulates vomiting. "I don't need your help, Johnny. I just really didn't need your criticism." Rosa turns around to face you, a puzzled expression on her face. "You really don't understand the consequences of your words, do you? They confuse the little ones who look up to me. They cause the followers to doubt their leader. They make me look weak, Johnny, to my family and to the world. And the only way to undo all that you've written is by showing the world that my actions speak louder than your words."

The two men grab your upper arms. That's when you struggle; too little, too late.

"Rosa! Please!"

Kicking your feet and twisting your body, you can't break free of the fingers clamping down on your biceps like vise grips. You realize that leaping attempts to escape are helping the men move you forward, so you shift your weight to your legs and plant your feet against the concrete floor. But they jerk you along, anyway.

Rosa snaps her fingers. The others in the room return to work. Idle chatter picks up and nearly drowns your cry for help. The bouncing ball resumes and the same radio station you'd tuned into earlier today plays in the background.

The two men drag you, kicking and screaming, into a room surrounded by cubicle walls. They slam you onto a long table connected to a gigantic machine that looks like a medical EEG. The young man narrating everything straps your arms, feet, and chest down while the others hold you in place.

"No! Let me go!"

You squirm, raising your chest and arching your back before the final strap cinches you down. After a few seconds of listening to yourself panting, you hear Rosa's high heels against the pavement, the pair she slipped off the rack on your way out of the mall department store. You look for her, seeing only a glimpse of her turquoise dress, and an elegant pair of pink headphones bouncing off her thigh as she walks by. Your neck won't stretch any further and whiplashes back to front and center. Then you see a reflection of Rosa's legs in the lower half of a circular mirror above you. She adjusts the stool at the head of the table you lie on and sits.

You fill the silence with another plea. "Rosa! Rosa! I'm sorry—"

The sound of duct tape startles you. You hear it pulled off the roll and torn at the corner of someone's mouth. Then it's stretched over your lips and secured like a hand attempting to suffocate you.

A motorized buzzing sound draws tears from your eyes. Rough hands grab your forehead, inadvertently blocking your vision while shaving your head with an electric razor. The metal is rough against your skin, smacking your head with every uncoordinated pass. You soon feel the chill air of the room against your scalp. After the last few strands, the man drops your head against the table with a thud.

Rosa taps the crossbar at the bottom of the stool with her shoes. Then she leans back and crosses her legs. "I'm missing the best parts of his story, Doc. I wanna hear my voice narrating his agony."

"We wouldn't want to miss that," a voice you don't recognize says. Based on the deep tones, you assume it belongs to an older man, confirmed when he bends over your body and looks down at you. "Nice to meet you, Subject Twenty-Six."

Yellow teeth snarl at you. Mustache hairs, with today's lunch coloring the gray strands orange, reach over and into his upper lip. And none of the long hairs block the unrecognizable mixture of smells colluding with his breath.

"I'm Doctor Alan Moore."

You jerk your left shoulder, trying to pull your arm out from under the strap. There's no wiggle room around the wrists. The narrator tied the straps down well, so tight that the one across your chest makes breathing difficult.

"Is the wireless ready, old man?" Rosa asks.

Dr. Moore, still leaning over your body, looks up at her. "We're making progress. The FCC has reservations about broadcasting wireless signals from inside the cranium."

"Fuck the FCC," Rosa says. "They have the audacity to make regulations and then charge *me* money to verify my system adheres to them?" Rosa raises both feet out of the heels and to the edge of the seat and rests her chin on her knees. "I'll get them, too. An endless dream they'll pay *me* to wake them from."

Dr. Moore lowers his gaze back down to you. "Even if the wireless update was ready, there's no way to modify the systems in *his* head since they lack the protocols." The doctor caresses your scalp with cold, wrinkled fingers. "Everything on this table is disposable."

You turn away from the doctor and stretch your neck to its limits, hoping to see Rosa with your own two eyes. She's the only one who can save you. If she can't hear your voice, maybe she'll listen to your panicked brown irises.

Dr. Moore repositions your head and peers down at you. He holds your eyelids open with two fingers and flashes a light into each one. "No discoloration. You're not the dreamer—the one who can no longer see our reality. I should've taken better notes."

His slow speech aggravates you, as if listening to him was part of Rosa's plan to torture you. One part of you wants to get this over with, another part of you wants to break down, and the last part wants to fight back. Yet you have no control over any of the parts.

Rosa drops her leg, lightly tapping it against the stool's crossbar. "He's got the narrator. There's a story going on in his head, and I wanna hear every word."

Two men slide the table you lie on toward an arch at the far end, stopping when the structure creates a shadow across your forehead. You can see more of Rosa now through the mirror, but you can't focus on her. The white lights along the interior curve of the machine scare you as the realization settles in that something is going to happen. A feeling of powerlessness overcomes you. Tears stream down your face again, and a warm liquid fills your pants. The lights are blinding you, but you're determined to keep your eyes open, worried they may never open again if you let them close.

Dr. Moore hums and mumbles to himself for a couple of minutes. So far, you don't feel any different. Nobody's drawing dotted lines across your forehead. Your scalp doesn't feel warm from radiation. Your brain isn't melting. Yet.

"Oh my. The nanites are still active." You hear Dr. Moore scribbling something onto paper. "They're maintaining charge. Perhaps from the activity in his brain. Clever little things." You hear the excitement in his voice, the soft chuckle of discovery as his fascination over the evolution of the machines in your head continues.

The rattling of caster wheels alarms you. Turning your head slightly, you see a cart rolling by you. A silver tray filled with three-inch-long needles and a mallet with a peanut-sized head sits on top of it. Your stomach sinks. Sweaty palms kill any hope of firmly pushing back against the table.

"Johnny boy, authors judge their works by word count, right? How many words were in your love letter?"

Hands in her lap, Rosa fiddles with the headphones between her fingers. You raise your eyes further and see the underside of her neck as she looks up at the ceiling, likely imagining your article.

"Two hundred and thirty-six, right? And you didn't waste a single word. Doc has two hundred and thirty-six needles, and he won't waste a single one, either."

You squirm even more when she raises the headphones up and out of view, realizing that it's time to fulfill her promise. The doctor is going to puncture your skull with needles so that Rosa can listen to the voice in your head narrating your anguish.

"Hey Doc, feel free to pull the tape off before you start. Everyone in the building should hear him scream. Thanks to his mouth, I gotta put the fear of God back in everyone."

You glimpse Rosa's hair in the reflection as she swings it back behind her shoulders, presumably so she can put the headphones on without interference. She scoots her hips further back into the seat and then crosses her legs.

"Sing for them, Johnny. We'll call the album: Tough Love."

Heavy breaths do little to loosen the tape over your mouth. You inhale and exhale through your nose. Begging for mercy through the tape exhausts you further. Muscles all over your body tighten after every couple of breaths and every time anything touches your head.

You hear the light clattering of metal, as if someone reached into the tray for a needle, as if someone searched for the ideal candidate.

Dr. Moore says, "Let me get a couple of microphones in first. He'll struggle more if he can scream. You don't want me to kill him by accident, right?"

Rosa sighs. "Whatever."

You feel the pointed end of something against your scalp, where your hair spiraled and ran down the sides of your head. It might be one of the sharp metal needles. You imagine the light tap of the small mallet driving one into your skull. And when the sound comes, your body jolts, but you feel no pain.

"Dr. Moore?"

You hear a young man's voice over your panting. He'd made the solid striking sound when he knocked on the door.

"The wireless machines are ready," he says.

Dr. Moore looks over his right shoulder and at the young man. A wide grin stretches his wrinkles. "Thank you, Cody."

There's a pause before Cody asks, "Are you torturing him?"

"Yes." Rosa and Dr. Moore say in unison.

"Can I watch?" he asks with wonder in his voice.

"No." They speak together again, Rosa a millisecond quicker, and Dr. Moore slower to finish speaking.

You hear the grumbling of an adolescent before the door closes. Then you feel the metal point against your scalp again. You scream against the tape and smack the back of your knees against the table, all while trying to avoid accidental pressure against the needle.

Dr. Moore taps the mallet against the table several times, as if testing the amount of force required to drive the needle into your skull, but not into your brain. After a few seconds of silence, your body tenses in anticipation of the strike.

"Wait," Rosa calmly says.

You still feel the needle against your scalp. A long silence follows while a drop of liquid runs off the top of your head.

"Give him Synthetica 2.0 and send him to the Feds."

Dr. Moore looks over at Rosa, as if to make sure he heard her correctly.

"Let him spread the machines to them like an airborne virus. Every breath he takes will fill their tiny heads with thoughts of Sophie."

6 - The Woman in the Interrogation Room

"Wake up… Allen…"

You open your eyes. Your senses gradually improve. Bland bluish-gray walls are easy on your eyes. A chilly atmosphere neutralizes aromas. A man's voice narrates in crystal clear audio inside your head as the mental fog dissipates.

"Wake up, Mr. Allen," a woman says.

You raise your hands, but they're bound by handcuffs chained to a large gray table in front of you. The sudden halt of your hands' movements hurts your wrists. Panic causes the metal rings to dig further into your skin when you pull on the chain.

"What…What's going on?" you ask.

There's a woman sitting across from you. She's wearing a similar black suit to the men that chased you earlier today. A solid white blouse is underneath the unbuttoned jacket, and the knot of a black tie loosely wrapped around its collar sits below the one unfastened button. Her matte-black hair brushes against her shoulders. She slouches in a light-gray chair constructed from rectangular metal extrusions welded together. Her elbows rest along the flat surface of the armrests, and a couple of her fingers rub the sharp edge where the chair's armrests end and its legs begin.

Behind her slumped shoulders, you notice a man standing in the back of the room. His lip's movements match the masculine voice in your head.

He's the narrator.

He wears the same uniform as the woman, albeit tidier. His hair is dark brown. A military fade squares his head with the straight edges of his jawline, and broad shoulders make him look like two boxes stacked in the corner.

You lower your gaze back to the woman and then to a manila envelope sitting on the table between you and her unpleasant expression, formed by tight lips and a steady gaze.

At last, she sits up straight, as if she'd been waiting for you all this time. She pulls a stack of photos out of the folder and places three in front of you, one by one, smacking their corners against the surface like playing cards revealed by an angry dealer at the table.

You wonder if you're supposed to recognize the people in the photos. The left-most photo shows a middle-aged African American man with a few gray hairs trying to hide among the black strands. He's composed. His eyes, nose, and mouth are straight, as are the ironed sleeves of his coat that line up perfectly with the photo's edges.

A Caucasian man grinning ear to ear is in the center photo. His face is red. He's pinned the number "249" to the white shirt he's wearing, and he's covered with various colored paints. He's pointing to a "FINISH" sign above his head with one hand and clenching a half-empty water bottle with the other.

And to the far right is a photo of a Hispanic woman with a facial expression as serious as the man in the left-most photo. Red lipstick brightens her visage, and she's wearing the same bleak colors as the woman sitting in front of you.

As your heart races and your mind tries to piece things together, you glance at the narrator again. He's both vocally and visually distracting. How are you supposed to think with his coarse voice interrupting your every thought?

"Don't look at him," the woman says. "Look at me. I'm your problem right now." She taps the center photo with her index finger.

You look down at the photos again. "I don't know any of them—"

"I know you don't."

She stares at you in silence. You wonder if she's just waiting for you to open your mouth again, so she can interrupt and assert authority.

Aggressively, she taps the center photo again, this time with her index and middle fingers together. "This is Special

Agent Isels. He enjoys running marathons for charity. And this is Special Agent Douglas." She picks up the photo to the left of Isels. "He bakes and brings those cookies to the office every other week. And this over here is Special Agent Garcia. She enjoys racing drones on the weekends. Do you know what they all have in common?"

You shake your head, restraining yourself from stating the obvious—that they're all special agents.

"Your girlfriend killed them."

Celine crosses your mind, more associated with *girlfriend* than *killer*. Despite Celine's outward attitude and the mask she often wears with a cigarette in her hand, she's kind, and you're certain she's incapable of killing anyone, especially agents who were likely trained in combat and tactics. And Celine is an ex-girlfriend. Except for the one photo you kept on your bedside table, you've erased all traces of her existence from your apartment, social media profiles, and life.

The woman folds her arms. "She shot Isels three times in the chest through his front windshield. She shot Garcia in the back while crossing the highway. Douglas died trying to help a bystander who, by the way, she also shot."

Crossing a highway. Killing a bystander. Your eyes widen. The jigsaw pieces the woman laid out in front of you as photos and words turn into a completed puzzle of Rosa. She shot a bystander and then the man who pointed a gun at you. You remember their faces now. The special agent shot through the windshield must've been the one who rammed a vehicle into Rosa's SUV. You're not sure. Everything happened so fast. You ran when the gunshots started, and you never looked back.

Despite the number of murders the woman accused you of being an accessory to, you maintain your composure, leaning on the one rebuttal you have.

"She's not my girlfriend."

"You sure about that?" The woman lowers her brows and

narrows her eyes as she leans forward. "We have video evidence of you two kissing. At the mall. After killing three of my men."

You remember the kiss. A fleeting moment. A desperate act to save the security guard's life. Otherwise, his photo would've been in front of you, too. Now, it's a misunderstanding.

"That's not… We're not… I was trying to get away from the…the security guy…Rosa had a gun to my back—"

"A gun to your back?" She taps her right fingers against the armrest. "And you kissed her? So, Stockholm Syndrome?"

"No…"

You slouch in the seat, wondering if you'd actually fallen in love with Rosa, and whether those feelings were the real reason you didn't run when you had another chance. You find bad girls attractive. Celine's dark mask turned transparent after a few months, and the notion that she's an imposter turned you off. Rosa's the real deal—ruthless with a pinch of humanity. If you're on her side.

You shake your head at the thoughts your mind associates with crazy talk. "I don't love her!" You blurt aloud, intending to direct your anger at the voice poisoning your mind.

The woman across from you responds. "I don't give a damn! Where's Rosa?"

"I don't know."

"So, you were just wearing her colors for fun? Cosplay?"

You had changed at the mall. New jeans and a long sleeve tee contributed to your escape from the police. "No, she put those clothes on me—"

The woman rolls her eyes and scoffs. "Oh, okay. I'm sorry. You're not in love with her. You're just sleeping with the woman selling drugs to kids."

"No! I didn't—stop making assumptions!"

The woman slams her hands on the table and stands up.

"Then tell me the fucking truth, Mr. Allen! Or do you think this is some kind of joke?"

"No—"

"Where's Rosalinda?"

"I don't know!"

You're not getting through to her, and you shouldn't have to explain anything without representation. The man in the back is as bland as the walls. You'd rather talk to him, but she won't let you. When you look his way, she demands your attention with loud snaps of her fingers in front of your face.

You stare into the brown eyes focused on you and say, "I want my lawyer."

She laughs again, suppressed at first and then muffled before it escapes her lips entirely, causing her head to tilt back as she drops into the chair. "Lawyer? This ain't the city jail. You're in the field with narcotics. There's no phone call. You won't be posting bail. I haven't arrested you. This is a straight-up, lawful abduction." She folds her arms again and shakes her head. "Fucking lawyer? Can you believe this little shit?" She glances at the man behind her, who smirks but doesn't speak outside of the narration. "Rosa doesn't play by the rules, so why should we?"

"I want my lawyer."

She glares at you. "You don't get a lawyer or a plea deal or anything afforded to a law-abiding citizen. You have no rights with us. You're gonna get three consecutive life sentences without the possibility of parole. When you die, I'll fucking bury you under your cell until the end of your full sentence and then I'll mail your decomposed body back to your hometown unless you start telling me what I wanna know! I've got a drug lord roaming the city. I don't have time to play with her fuck toy."

Your shoulders droop. Defeat washes over you. The woman's aggression reminds you of Rosa, both assaulting you for information that's out of your control. Both threatening you with harm if you don't cooperate. If Rosa had her way, you'd be screaming right now until you lose consciousness—if she let you lose consciousness. The woman in front of you is threatening to imprison you forever, literally.

You swallow hard, discovering that all the pleading at Rosa's place and then the argument with the woman in front of you has left your throat parched. Then you lick your lips, filling the cracks with the remaining saliva you regurgitated. When they're moist enough to part without sticking together, you speak.

"I wrote an article about Rosa. It's published in the city's online magazine. She found out about it, showed up at my place this morning, and told me she'd drugged me with robots—tiny machines programmed to narrate everything I see, hear, and do. They've been driving me crazy since this morning. But nobody can hear the robots except me, so she wants to stab my head with hundreds of microphones so she can listen to it describe my suffering." You lower your chin and shake your head. "Even the TV was talking to me. It's been fucking madness."

The woman raises a brow. She lowers her voice and speaks in a sweet, sarcastic tone. "Mr. Allen, I don't wanna hear about you getting high—"

"It's the truth!"

"You expect me to believe that?" She drops her hands on the table and pushes the photos aside. "That Rosalinda developed tiny robots to narrate people's actions?"

"It's a new drug. She..." you hold your head. A sharp pain causes you to moan. "I can't remember... There's a reason... Something else...something more..."

The answer is sitting on the tip of your tongue, but you can't recall it entirely.

"This is a joke—"

"Shut up. I almost remembered." You grab your head.

The woman leans back and folds her arms again. She

taps her foot under the table; the impact resounding loudly until it's absorbed by the walls. Every action the woman takes distracts you because the narrator describes it.

"Mr. Allen—"

The man behind her places a hand on her shoulder and shakes his head, perhaps understanding that you need to concentrate.

You close your eyes and speak aloud, hoping to direct the narration. "The robots are telling a story, and they've referenced the past before, which means they remember things that happened. They use my senses, but they also use my memories." You sit perfectly still, trying to prevent the narrator from deviating from your current train of thought, as it does to describe that deviation.

"Rosa wanted to extract the robots from my head because she couldn't hear what they were saying. She called them Synthetica. The version I have narrates my actions." You slowly recall Rosa's plan. "Yes, but what is the plan? She told me she wanted to do something; in my living room."

You remember Rosa sitting on your couch. The lace bra you didn't see before is bright red in your memories, almost glowing from behind the pink dress shirt. Psychotic, neon pink eyes stare at you from the shadows, and you find her mischievous grin attractive. From your knees, her crossed leg bobbing above your head looks longer and slenderer than you remember. She's wearing black leggings instead of dress pants. You can see the pink nail polish as she lowers her foot to your face and pushes her big toe against your cheek.

"You're enjoying this too much, Johnny boy," the Rosa in your memory says while caressing your face with her foot. It traverses your cheeks, pulls your lower lip down with the big toe, and eases into your mouth with more control than the little girl who applied her lipstick.

"What's going on up there, Mr. Allen?"

The woman across from you asks, but the words come

from memory Rosa's lips. She'd asked you something similar. You couldn't respond then. And it was her hands caressing your face, not her feet. And they didn't arouse you, they threatened you.

Lust distorts the memory. You can't look away. So much so that you close your lips around the toe in your mouth.

"You're a good boy, Johnny."

"We don't have time for this. My men are dead and he's having a wet dream."

The woman in front of you says, but the words come from the lips of a woman standing by the window in your living room, smacking bubble gum. She's glaring at you, clearly upset over the attention Rosa is giving you. They must be close. Just when you don't think you'll remember her name, Rosa speaks.

"Johnny, Sophie's dead. I'm going to engross this world into a dream about her, and you're going to help me."

Rosa pulls her toe back to the edge of your lips and you open your mouth wider, moaning, "Ah."

"Just like that, Johnny boy. Every breath you take will fill their heads with thoughts of Sophie."

You open your eyes. "The robots...like an airborne virus." You say aloud, blinking hard as you return to reality. You raise your hands to cover your mouth, but the chain restricts your movement.

The woman across from you stands up and steps back. "Fucking bitch." She covers her mouth with her forearm. "Get out of the room! Lock down the building!"

7 - The Woman in the Dreams

Sophia Delgado.

Those are the first words my own thoughts mutter after being backseat to an artificial intelligent narrator for so long. I almost didn't recognize the subtle tone of my voice, and the point of view makes me wonder if I naturally think in first-person.

Sophia Delgado.

I see her when I close my eyes. I imagine I'd see her more when they're open, too, if the narcotics team didn't lock me inside a pitch-black cell. Their spectrum analyzer couldn't detect the robots in my head. Either Rosa turned them off remotely—the control she boasted about—or the machines evaded detection on their own. The narcotics team isolated me anyway, in case Rosa was watching or listening.

I planned to welcome the silence, but the robots reactivated after the narcotics team left. Instead of narrating my actions, they manipulate my brain's interpretation of the dwindling light from the closing door and reflect a life-sized Sophie against the adjacent wall, positioned just as she'd been in my house, with arms crossed and one foot flat against the wall. I consider banging on the door and asking the narcotics team to run the analyzer again, but what would've been the point? They won't believe me, and the robots will just power down again.

A cold stale air, my back against a wall, and my butt against the hard floor are the only genuine senses of physicality I have in the darkness. That and the light that briefly enters the room when the mail slot opens and someone drops a tray of slop inside. I see Sophie then, too, a glimmer of her sitting across from me, her back against the opposite wall, her arms draped over her knees, her lips smacking bubblegum, her head facing the door, and a forlorn gaze in her eyes as she stares off into the distance.

Then darkness again.

Sophia Delgado.

When I close my eyes, the machines project videography of her spanning two decades, as if someone collected, compiled, and played back existing videos in their original format.

One video showed her as a child struggling to blow out seven striped candles atop a cream-colored frosted vanilla cake. The orange glow of the candles added a dreary tone to the blue plastic tablecloth patterned with colorful balloons. Teardrop-shaped fires reflected in Sophie's large brown eyes, flames among the coals that were her long black hairs cupping the sides of her face and spreading across her shoulders. The surrounding children laughed when the candles burned brighter after she'd blown each one out. They didn't mock her. They celebrated with her.

I know because I was there—inserted into the scene, the transition similar to a movie character describing a memory that turned into a live-action flashback. I heard the cacophony of children, felt the chaos of adults trying to maintain order, and smelled the burning candles after the kids blew them out together.

With a seat at the table, I recognized Rosa on the other side of the cake. She sat next to Sophie. Pink highlights were absent from her light-brown hair. She wore a mischievous but innocent grin, as if the trick candles were her idea.

In another scene, from behind the lens of a camcorder, I watched Sophie crawl around the same dining room where everyone had celebrated her birthday. She picked up loose shards of glass from several broken wine and liquor bottles. The sticky backs of their labels held some fragments together. She swept the remaining pieces into a gray dustpan. When the brush's bristles glided over the curved surface of one shard, Sophie cut her finger picking it up. She yelped and whipped her arm back and above her shoulder.

Rosa stepped into the frame. She caught Sophie's flailing arm by the wrist and then put the bruised finger into her own mouth.

Sophie turned around. She curled her fingers in and pulled her hand away from Rosa's lips. A quick reaction that suggested she'd been grabbed before. When she almost screamed, Rosa covered her mouth and then nodded toward the living room where a large man snored on the sofa.

Rosa slowly lowered her hand after Sophie calmed. They glanced at the living room before their gazes met again in silent harmony. When Sophie saw the camera, her eyes widened, and her body trembled.

"What is that?" she mouthed.

Rosa glanced at the camera, turning it to face her. "I'm going to record this place and send it to Child Services."

Sophie frantically shook her head. The fear in her eyes begged Rosa to reconsider. She reached for the camera several times, but Rosa kept it arm's length away.

Sophie loudly whispered, veering her head every few words to see if they reached the man in the living room. "No. Please. It'll only make things worse."

"How can things be worse? Look at you. Look at this place!" Rosa strained her throat to maintain the whisper. "You're not a maid, Sophie."

"Rosa, I wasn't born here like you. They'll send me back…You don't understand…Rosa, please." Sophie reached for the camera again. "I'm not as strong as you are. I won't survive out there."

"Then I'll be strong for both of us."

"What the hell is going on over there?"

Sophie jumped. She crawled behind Rosa at the sound of the man's voice. Rosa handed her the camera. The lens captured the ceiling as Sophie juggled it and then the living room after she dropped it.

Rosa marched out of the dining room. "Get up, old man!"

Swear words followed. The sound of accent table contents breaking was loud and clear. The struggle toppled furniture and knocked picture frames off the walls. Sophie stepped over the lens for a mere second as she joined the fray.

The fight lasted several minutes before the scene cut to the dashcam video from inside of a police vehicle. Police had pinned a middle-aged man to the squad car's hood. Dirt and scraps of wood fell from his brown locks and onto the white paint as the police attempted to subdue him. They'd cuffed him, but he struggled more to throw slurs over his shoulders than resist arrest.

"Get out of my house! Get that bitch out of my house!"

Police dashcams didn't record audio. Rosa must've provided the voice-overs, perhaps gleaned from her memory the same way the robots used mine to add detail to my narration. Rosa wanted me to see, hear, and experience everything through flashbacks that varied between home camcorders, clips on a phone, and virtual reality immersion. I smelled the liquor on the man's breath. My body twitched and my muscles tensed when a white shoe flew across the hood of the car.

Sophie's mom stepped into the dashcam's field of view with another shoe in hand before the police held her back. Red and blue lights reflected off her moist cheeks. The orange light from the paramedics' van flashed in her eyes.

"Don't you ever touch my baby girl! Ever!" Sophie's mom threw the other shoe into the street. "You get out! Get out! I don't ever wanna see you again, pendejo!"

Her voice rattled me. The fear, anger, and pain that accompanied her accent set my heart racing.

"I'll be back. I'll come back for *everything*!" The man shouted.

At last, two police officers dragged him off the hood of the car and took him away.

Rosa sat in the back of the paramedic van, gauze and tape applied to her arms and face. She refused to go to the hospital, claiming her parents couldn't afford it. And when asked for their number, she declined to provide it. She sat on the stretcher and held Sophie's hand.

A series of short clips published online played next. Each one ran about thirty seconds long. In the first, Rosa held a phone arm's length away and with the screen facing her. She passed her other arm around Sophie and pulled the girl into the camera's field of view.

"My name is Rosa, and this is Sophie."

"What are you doing?" Sophie hid her face behind Rosa's head.

"If I tell the world what's happening, then ICE won't touch you." Rosa glanced down at Sophie. "Stop hiding your face, as cute as you are! People need to see you, Mami."

Rosa pulled on Sophie's hair, ignoring her scream just to shove the camera into her face.

A new clip generated.

"This is Sophie. She's a sweet and beautiful honor roll student. An undercover police officer pretended to love her mom for nine years, for God knows why. He got arrested last week for domestic violence. Look at her bruises. Look at them!" Rosa moved the camera from Sophie's face to her arms and then her legs.

Sophie pulled her legs up to her butt. She hovered her hands just above her knees, ready to hide the bruises around her calves.

A new clip generated.

"Now the immigration folks want to deport her and her mom. She served this country; played the child of a drunk and abusive federal asshole for almost a decade. Now they want to punish her." Rosa brought the phone closer, filling the screen with her face. "This is America."

The scene changed again.

I sat between Rosa and Sophie's mom, but neither of them saw me. The robots rendered me into a memory of Sophie's graduation. Rosa held her phone high above her head with both hands. She recorded the people on the stage below using the camera on the back.

A speaker said, "Sophia Delgado."

Rosa stood. She cheered, whistled, and hollered.

Sophie smiled. She seemed tense, possibly embarrassed, as she walked across the stage in a blue cap and gown, and a gold honor cord around her neck. She shook hands, took a photo with the diploma, and waved at Rosa before exiting the stage.

When the scene changed again, the girls sat on the front steps of Sophie's house. Sophie still wore the gown. She adjusted the cap on her head for a second time and flicked the black tassel away from her face.

I watched the scene from a camcorder someone carried across the lawn. They waved at Rosa and Sophie. The camera captured their shadow formed by the streetlights that evening.

The cameraman turned to several men and women gathered around a grill in the middle of the front yard. Reggae music played from the speaker of a blue and purple chameleon-colored sedan parked in the driveway.

The cameraman circled one woman dancing to the music. A festive scene. The remnants of spring blew the grilled vegetable scents across my nose. My feet wanted to move. The music excited me even if I couldn't understand the words.

That was Synthetica.

"Aye, señorita," the cameraman sang to the dancing woman. His arm came into view as he spun her around. The red and pink floral dress she wore followed and then she grabbed the fabric to control its back-and-forth motion when she moved her legs.

Without warning, he dropped the camera. The sound of loud popping noises followed. They sounded more like gunshots. I fell to the ground with the view, suddenly pulled into the scene. Multiple feet ran past me. I couldn't move, as if I'd been shot or transformed into an inanimate object, such as the camera.

With the music blaring, I couldn't tell where the gun-shots originated and which direction the screams fled. Tires screeched, and I glimpsed the muzzle of a pistol pulled back into a black sedan's tinted windows as they rolled up. The car sped up and drove away, its license plate absent.

"Vivian!"

I heard Rosa's voice. "Help! Somebody help!" She shouted multiple times. Then she lowered her voice, "Please, Mami, don't leave us." Her sniffling grew louder. "Yes, Mama, I'll take care of Sophie. But you would do it much better. Please…"

After I blinked, the scene changed again. I saw the world through Rosa's eyes. She stood on Sophie's front lawn, turning in circles as ten to fifteen people walked across the yard with furniture from the house.

"What are you doing? What's going on?" Rosa asked.

She ran up to a man carrying a handful of purses. "That's not yours!" She shouted.

He shrugged her off and nearly knocked her to the ground.

Rosa stumbled but maintained balance. She ran through the open front door of the house.

"Sophie!"

Rosa checked the kitchen, dining room, and living room, bumping into more people, some she recognized from the neighborhood. Then she found Sophie in her bedroom.

She sat in the middle of the bed with various envelopes and unfolded sheets of paper surrounding her. Red eyes stared at herself in the mirror, which sat on a dresser facing the end of the bed. She clenched one piece of paper in her left hand.

"Sophie…" Rosa climbed into the bed. She passed an arm around Sophie and slowly lowered the girl's head onto her shoulder. "What's going on?"

Sophie didn't respond.

Rosa pulled the girl's fingers open and smoothed the

crumpled piece of paper until she could read it.

We regret to inform you that your application for enrollment cannot be processed without a legal guardian.

Memories of the gunshots resounded in Rosa's head. I felt and heard them, too. She dropped the piece of paper. Several deep breaths helped calm her down. Then she grabbed a page near Sophie's knee, its letterhead different from the first.

We regret to inform you that your application cannot be processed because of recent gang-related activity. It is the university's utmost priority to protect the students...

Rosa shuffled through the mail surrounding them. Most of them read the same. When she found one that seemed different, she hoped for something positive.

Notice of Foreclosure

Rosa slumped. "Sophie…"

"It's okay." Sophie raised her head. She looked at Rosa and smiled. "Mama saw me walk. Rosa, I'm the first in my family to graduate."

Rosa nodded. "I'm proud of you, Mami." She hugged Sophie. She wrapped the girl in her arms and squeezed. "I love you, Mami. I love you so much."

"Ms. Delgado," a stern voice said. A man in a black suit stood at the bedroom door.

Rosa jumped off the bed and balled her fists. Sophie grabbed her by the elbow and then shook her head.

The man continued, "I'm Agent Bradley from Immigration and Customs Enforcement. I'm going to need you to come with me."

Sophie slid her feet off the bed and faced the man when

she stood. She spoke to Rosa without turning around. "I love you, too, Rosa. I promise I'll find you again one day."

"Sophie, didn't I say I'd be strong for both of us?"

Bang! Bang! Bang!

Sophia Delgado.

Scene break.

The gunshot wakes you. Or was it the cell door slamming open that pulls you back to reality? What reality? The world you see is just as dark and dreary as the one the robots showed you.

A familiar voice is narrating from the open door. The silhouette of a curvy woman and her high ponytail obstructs some of the light coming in, and instead, neon pink eyes illuminate the cell. She holds a baseball bat over her shoulders with one hand and flicks something out from under the nail of the other.

You stand like a lifeless doll, as if the memories of Sophie lobotomized you. As if the robots in your head moved you. Slowly, you meander to the open door and cross the threshold.

"Welcome to the family, Johnny boy."

The Sanctum

Chapter 1

Sam ran his fingers across his grandfather's recliner. A familiar cigar scent rose from the brown leather and caused his nose to twitch. His grandfather had never smoked in the recliner. He often retreated to the back porch, where the aroma clung to his robe after he flicked the flint wheel of a lighter and ignited the long end of a Colombian cigar. Multiple clicks of the lighter had often alerted Sam to a small window of time for curiosity and mischief.

Although the sound still echoed in the back of Sam's mind as he stood in the room, he no longer had to wait for his grandfather to vacate the study, or Sanctum, as he'd heard others call it. Knowledge of the *others* had emboldened Sam to return to the wood-lavished room years later, but for a different purpose: investigate his grandfather's death.

Sam climbed into the leather seat. It squeaked until he found comfort. He reclined and rotated clockwise to face six monitors hanging from the ceiling. He recognized the screens. They'd displayed his grandfather's vital signs— heart rate, pulse, body temperature, and a few parameters Sam never comprehended. He also didn't understand why his grandfather had lain in the chair and watched himself slowly die. There had to be something more.

"What were you up to, Old Man?" Sam said, sweeping his hand along one side of the recliner, rubbing both arm-rests, and then groping the underside of the raised footrest. He found nothing. Sighing, he lay back in the seat and stared at the monitors.

Multiple warning signs flashed red across the screens in front of him. They mentioned disconnected cables. Sam had never seen any cables running into his grandfather, not for fluids or signals. Medical devices supported wireless tech-nology, and his grandfather had boasted about standing at the forefront of its advancement. So, what cables? Upon further inspection of the warnings, Sam noticed additional text at the bottom of the fifth screen.

Vital Signs Required for Authentication, it read.

Sam blinked twice. "Vital signs? Not a username and password? Retinal scan?" he asked while reaching for the display. He didn't see a login button, and the screen didn't respond to his touch. "Did the pacemaker log you in or something?"

As Sam dropped back into the seat, his elbow slipped off the armrest and his hand landed on a small surface extending out the left side of the chair. Mist sprayed out like an air freshener. A swooshing sound followed. Then the lacquered brown top of the table recessed and slid back.

Sam leaned over the armrest and looked inside. He saw a faded gray helmet tucked into the compartment. Several soldered wires crossed its crown. He pulled it out, slowing when he noticed a thick cord extending from the base of its skull and running down into the compartment depths.

"VR?" Sam wondered. He laughed aloud. "Wait, did Grandfather experience porn?"

It was the most popular use of full-crown headsets. They were originally designed for video games, but publishers couldn't afford to maintain the servers required for seamless operation, in-house or as a service. Yet the pornographic industry's sales boomed, and they later pioneered the development of newer models.

Sam rotated and flipped the headset in his hands. *Grandfather* had been laser-engraved in calligraphy across the back. A software engineering background made Sam familiar with the latest models, but he didn't recognize that one. He glanced up at the screens to see the status message had changed.

Searching, it read.

Hesitant at first, Sam eventually passed the helmet over his head.

Connected, the display read. *Welcome, Grandfather.*

Vital signs populated the screens. Everything formed a smooth sinusoidal wave with green peaks, except his heart rate, whose signal fluctuated red until he calmed.

Unable to Load Last Session, the display read.

The error message cleared itself, and then a list of sessions populated the screen.

Crow

Neven

Shades

"Crow..." Sam thought aloud.

The session title flashed green, and a countdown started. Sam tried to cancel the selection but found nothing to delay the timer. At five seconds, Sam felt rushed to lie down. A flashing message inside the helmet instructed him to close his eyes. So Sam shut both eyelids. When he reopened them, he stood in front of a pink floor-length mirror reflecting a pale high school girl.

That doesn't seem right, he mused.

Sam couldn't rotate his view toward the girl's actual body, so he watched her reflection in the mirror. She ogled herself in a black, thigh-length and flared skirt patterned with random, dark-gray religious crosses stitched into the fabric. A dark tee shirt lay flat against her chest. She'd sleeved her right arm with various tattoos of black creatures, including a flock of birds, a tentacled sea monster, and a cat. A single tattoo coiled around her left arm, featuring a black-tinted, green vine with dark-blue and -purple flowers. They matched her matte black hair and violet eyes.

She wore a satisfied grin, twisting her upper body to the left and then to the right. To Sam, the view seemed too realistic for a movie or simulation, even for an advanced virtual reality system. Skin imperfections, bruises, and scars gave her gothic appearance more personality and history. Ghost-white skin made some of her veins visible.

No frames dropped during her fluid movement, sensual

and rhythmic as they were. Sam swore he could feel her breathing, too. If his grandfather was truly an early adopter, then Sam may have stumbled upon the beta version of cutting-edge virtual reality hardware.

Still, Sam felt along for the ride instead of at the helm. He didn't control any of the girl's movements. She wasn't an avatar. Perhaps he viewed a live stream through someone's eyes. He not only shared their sight but also their hearing, referring to the soft tune they hummed. Their celebratory dance in front of the mirror raced *his* heart, too.

Grandfather was a pervert, Sam thought, and then sighed. *No surprise. Sadly, no surprise at all.*

Sam remembered his grandfather chasing the skirts of restaurant servers. He elicited laughter with dad jokes and got away with cringe-worthy comments, courtesy of his age. When Sam considered what else his perverted grandfather could've done in the chair, he became disgusted. Instinctively, he went to jump out of the seat but received no feedback from his actual arms and legs. Whether he sat up or fell out of the leather recliner, he didn't know.

The girl suddenly stopped dancing. She stared at the mirror, suspicious eyes glaring back at herself—at Sam. He felt her gaze dragging him into nothingness. He couldn't blink or avert his eyes. She even swept reality into the gravitational pull of her fixed look. It warped around Sam until the chime of a nearby device disrupted the spell.

The girl turned away from the mirror. She stared at a yellow desk with natural wood legs. A black cellphone sat on the laminated surface. Its screen flashed several times, but Sam paid more attention to the girl's peripheral vision. The bright purple room contrasted with the dark clothes she wore. Dead animals—squirrels and birds—rested in shadowbox frames mounted to the wall above the desk. Various-sized knives hung like posters to the left of a closet door.

The girl grabbed the cellphone and flicked her finger up the display. An application with a blood-red background and black text requested authentication. She passed facial recognition and then failed the retinal scan.

Sam wondered if *it* saw him, too.

She slowly lowered the phone. Her earlier suspicion returned. The phone's dark display reflected her focused eyes and her hesitation to enter a code to bypass the unsuccessful retinal scan.

Sam's heart pounded with hers. He imagined himself grabbing his chest. Again, he entertained the idea of an advanced virtual reality system, one that could've been responsible for the sensations he felt, and a program dedicated to watching a girl in her room didn't surprise him, especially one featuring a pale goddess of death.

The phone chimed again, its dim display flashing faster than before. She entered the code 666 and unlocked the application. Sam read the screen through her eyes: *Her Majesty requests your presence.* Below the message, a solid orange dot stood out among the red brush strokes resembling a simple street display, and a timer under the map counted down from thirty minutes.

She locked the phone. Her smirk reflected in the black glass as she said, "Sweet. Guess I'll have front row seats to world's end after all."

Chapter 2

The girl Sam digitally possessed followed a middle-aged man to a rusty gray elevator inside of a parking garage under construction. A dirty white sign with peeling black letters hung from a bent screw. It read: OUT OF ORDER. The girl didn't skip a beat. Not a shred of concern passed through to Sam, despite the eeriness surrounding them.

Through her vision, Sam watched the man palm the wall space next to the elevator doors. They slid open. A soft hiss accompanied their smooth glide along the top and bottom rails. The girl stepped into a pristine silver compartment with glowing white lights. The man followed her inside. He turned to an interior panel next to one door and placed his hand against it. Then he took one step back and crossed his wrists at his waist.

The elevator moved without making a sound. And as quickly as the doors had closed, they reopened. Sam looked for a floor number and saw two green hyphens instead.

Two men stood outside the elevator, both with hands in their pant pockets. Both could've easily been mistaken for shadows in the dimly lit space filled with large, cylindrical tanks. They wore black suits and matching cranberry shirts in an otherwise reddish-brown room. One fashioned a black tie and even darker sunglasses that also covered the sides of his eyes. Sam wondered how he saw anything at all under the yellow column-like lighting.

"You're late," the man without glasses stated. His voice sounded as if a digital system filtered out background noise while maintaining his charisma and humanity.

The girl looked up at him and shook her head. Shoulder-length hair fell out from behind her ears. "Impossible. I *am* the fourth dimension. Time waits for me."

The man without glasses laughed. His white teeth floated in the dimness. His dark skin tone blended into the muted surroundings. "Good to see you, Crow. Delusional as always."

Crow, Sam said to himself, thinking back to the list of sessions the system had presented to him after he put the helmet on. He'd thought it was a lobby room or saved file name, but it belonged to the girl he possessed.

She responded, "Likewise, Neven. I claimed the fourth dimension for you because it's an even number."

Neven, another name from the list.

The man with glasses faced the corridor opposite the elevator. "If you two kids are finished, I'd like to get this summons over with and return to my fulfilling life of," he raised his chin and glanced over his right shoulder, "retirement."

"I'm not a kid, Shades. I'm a woman," Crow said. "Besides, you realize we've been summoned for a job, right?" She folded her arms and leaned to the right, shifting most of her weight to one foot.

"I'm aware. These glasses shield me from the material world, not the immaterial one. I can't see meaningless things such as age, time, and even numbers." He faced the dimly lit corridor again. "But I have a bad feeling about this reunion."

Neven pulled a hand from his pocket and held up two fingers. "Good thing it's been two months instead of one or three, or I would've respectfully declined the invitation. Nothing good happens when odd numbers are involved, especially prime ones. So I'll echo your sentiments, but over the year being 2047."

Crow's escort coughed. "Her Majesty is awaiting your arrival," he said.

Neven and Shades led the way. Crow hesitated. Sam imagined himself covering his mouth. He'd said nothing aloud and kept his breathing to a minimum, if he breathed at all. He felt Crow's chest rise and fall with every inhale and exhale; a distant feeling, perhaps like the one alerting her of Sam's presence.

***

The dark corridors gradually brightened, and the shabby architecture transformed into a modern medieval wonder, as if they'd promenaded through a primitive snake shedding its skin into the advanced dark ages. Multi-tiered and equidistant glass chandeliers hung above their heads at the entrance and circled the entire area. A steel throne's hard lines shimmered gold at the other end. Natural light flooded the linoleum floor, which didn't reflect and blind.

"Wait here," the escort said. He walked ahead in his navy-blue tailored suit.

Shades slid both hands into his pockets again. He teetered on his heels. "You seem uneasy, Crow. I thought the unknown thrilled you."

Crow refocused on the real world after Shades spoke to her. "I'm pursuing a different unknown at the moment. The demonic kind."

"Has it tried to exorcise you yet? I imagine it's terrified."

"It'll find no comfort within me. I'll have to conduct a scance later, one that'll tear it from the dark depths of my cold soul and thrust it into the warm and loving embrace of Lucifer."

A chill ran down Sam's spine. He didn't believe in ghosts and demons, but he had faith in Crow's unusual threat. After all, he nearly shared a consciousness with her, and the confidence with which she uttered those words overwhelmed his sense of reason. She spoke of magic in a world of technology. The more Sam gave it thought, the more he realized that his occupation of her body bordered on spiritual possession and his existence in the back of her mind somewhere made technology feel like magic.

Heels striking the linoleum floor redirected Sam's attention. Crow lifted her head as a regal woman of mixed complexion strolled out of the shadows on the left and promenaded over to the throne at the center. She sat on the edge of the seat and pointed her knees to the right. Sat, like the statue of an Olympian, illuminated by a light piercing through a hole in the heavens. Voluminous and curly golden-brown hair prevented her from leaning back.

"Good evening, everyone," she said with an exuberant smile. Perfect teeth shone brighter under the natural lighting. She smoothed out the plain, calf-length white dress covering her tall, shapely body. "I want to personally thank each of you for answering the summons. And I truly hope your journey here was without tribulation."

"Your Majesty," all three said in unison and bowed their heads.

Shades raised his head first. "Permission to speak freely, your Majesty."

She nodded once. "Please, call me Princess." She pushed the last crease—the last shadow—out of the dress.

"Princess, I answered your summons, but with all due respect, I'm no longer employed by the Sun, Moon, and Stars."

Princess' gold-toned lips smiled against her natural and unpainted visage. "A star burns forever, Shades. I wouldn't have drawn your constellation if I didn't believe this job required your particular alignment. This mission will benefit from the uniform world you see."

Shades bowed his head again. He looked humbled. The scowl he'd worn since Sam first saw him quickly faded, replaced by a faint smile.

Crow raised a brow. "What's the job, your Holiness?"

Princess slightly turned her head to line up her gaze with Crow. She didn't seem to care about Crow's lack of formality, despite the exalted atmosphere her presence demanded. "It's come to my attention that a Navigator named P'Pa is planning to use Grandfather's technology to destabilize world governments."

Sam gasped and then quickly bit his lip, uncertain whether the noises he made reached Crow. After seeing no reaction from the woman, he refocused on Princess' words. *Grandfather*. His grandfather? He recalled the name on the helmet, the login screen, and the alert after he'd put the thing on his head, but he still couldn't believe it.

The trio didn't react to her statement, while Sam wasn't sure which of her words rattled him the most. That *his* grandfather developed advanced technology? That it could undermine world governments? That the perpetrator's name was P'Pa? What was a Navigator, and did they contribute to his grandfather's death?

As if he was the one who shared a consciousness with Sam, Shades asked the same questions. "Did this technology, perhaps, contribute to Grandfather's murder?"

Sam clenched his fists. He knew Crow felt that, when she grabbed her hand, but he couldn't contain his emotions any longer. Anger flowed through him and into her because the government told Sam that his grandfather died of natural causes. They gave him an honorary funeral because of his time in service, but the true underlying reason behind his passing made the folded flag and the national guard's attendance clear.

Princess' smile never wavered as she turned to Shades. "That is a strong possibility. I'm looking forward to the results of your investigation."

Neven folded his arms. "Even if we accepted this mission, Grandfather was our Navigator. We'd be operating blind without one. And three is an odd number with historical ties to poor luck. It's bad enough that we're unevenly distributed as two guys and one gal."

"I'm a woman," Crow said.

Shades snickered. "You see, Neven, that's why I wear these glasses." He adjusted the spectacles above his nose. "I would've never known about the girl among us, only that I'm in the company of two Stars."

"I'm not a girl. I'm a woman," Crow said, more firmly.

Princess smiled at the playful banter. "You *have* a Navigator," she said and then nodded at Crow. "A kin has activated Grandfather's Sanctum, albeit," her eyes flashed gold, "a highly modified and advanced version of the traditional system, it would seem."

Sam immediately tried to take the helmet off, but he couldn't feel his actual arms. He felt Crow's arms and her hands as she flexed and cracked her fingers into a fist. And if he'd lifted the helmet from his actual head, it hadn't logged him out of the system. He couldn't move his eyes, either, not to view the real world or look elsewhere. The Sanctum's menu could've been voice-activated, but Sam felt deep down inside that speaking would give him away for sure.

"I knew I'd felt teenage hormones," Crow growled.

"They're in your head?" Shades asked.

Princess spoke over Crow's mumbled slurs. "They're capable of entering all your heads. The way will become clear to them soon, if it hasn't already. They're using the technology that P'Pa developed with Grandfather, and it will be this upgrade that gives them access to every human being's inner sanctum—their mind."

Crow formed two fists. "*He's* in my head, but can he handle the chaos? I'll introduce him to its abyssal depths and collapse his feeble psyche inside the endless void. He'll be a vegetable to the world and an example to anyone else entering a woman's room uninvited."

Sam panicked. He still couldn't exit the system. Crow further thwarted his attempts by imagining dead animals, gory crime scenes, and the insides of victims during autopsies. Distractions that populated the back of her eyelids, so it was all Sam could see. She attempted to burn brutal deaths into his retinas and merge with it the desperate vocal cries of men and women.

Sam heard Neven over the internal screaming. "You're an amazing creature, Crow. To love the dead and hate the living makes you perfectly balanced."

"His luck ran out when I learned he wasn't a demon," she exclaimed.

"He...is your Navigator," Princess said, raising her voice, yet maintaining its gentleness.

Crow opened her eyes. Sam's brain registered trembling fingers. He thought they belonged to him, but it was Crow's that twitched. They salivated over cutting him open, a feeling his imagination manifested into a vision of him running a knife across his gut using *her* hands. The thought startled him, and his momentary agony excited her. But the psychological assault didn't affect him as she'd hoped. Years of listening to his grandfather's stories had mostly numbed Sam's mind to the violence she showed him.

Crow grew impatient. "Say something," she demanded. "Or I'll force you to climax. Do you want everyone to hear the pathetic orgasm of a tiny dick?"

After a few seconds, Sam felt Crow's body temperature steadily rising. Her nipples hardened, and he felt an unusual moisture below. "Wait! Stop! I'm sorry! Please stop!" He repeated the same words, changing their order as he panicked more. He forgot about the verbal commands he'd feared to speak earlier, the additional efforts to log him out of the system.

"I don't know what's going on! I've been trying to log out all this time, but I can't...I can't turn it off. Please, stop!" Sam slowly calmed as Crow's body temperature lowered.

Nobody said anything while Sam collected his thoughts. Then he spoke, unsure who all heard him. "My grandfather died in this chair. I wanted to know why, so I sat in it and this machine turned on and then I was in this girl's body and now you're telling me that someone named Grandfather developed a system that could bring down world governments and that they're *my* grandfather?" Sam felt as if he should've been out of breath, but he didn't pant.

Crow smirked. "I'm a woman, and thanks for confirming I can affect you, too." She crossed her arms, glanced down at her chest, and then awkwardly placed her hands at her sides instead. "Exactly how much can you feel?" she asked.

"I don't know…I uh…heartbeat, temperature, eyes, ears, um some touch…"

"And…" Neven said. "You've mentioned an odd number of things."

"Smell…smell! I can pick up scents."

Princess raised her hand. After everyone paid her attention, she said, "Only blood relatives can operate a Sanctum once its owner retires. A Navigator's last will define system wipe procedures should they meet an untimely death without identifying a suitable next of kin. You, Grandson, are that next of kin." She nodded at Crow and then raised her eyes to the entire group.

"The traditional Sanctum facilitates communication between Stars and gives the Navigator unrestricted access to the internet, surveillance cameras, law enforcement databases, and," she smiled at Neven, listing a fourth as if to appease him, "even medical records. As you discover them, please include the additional capabilities of Grandfather's system in your report."

Shades thrust his hands into his pockets. "With all due respect, your Majesty, we haven't accepted the job." He looked in Crow's direction. "And these recent developments aren't encouraging."

"I understand, Shades." Princess crossed her legs under the dress and cupped her knee with both hands. "We believe Grandfather died while operating his Sanctum. The autopsy revealed severe brain damage consistent with multiple electrical discharges. We suspect P'Pa demanded access to the system after they completed it."

"Grandfather must've refused," Neven said.

"So P'Pa executed him…" Crow added in a low voice.

Sam felt her passion for death overriding the strong feeling he had of vomiting over her word choice.

Shades turned to Princess and gestured with arms open.

"Why is this Navigator a threat now?"

"P'Pa's involvement with the upgrades may have given him atypical, albeit limited, access to Grandfather's Sanctum," Princess said. "Navigator identities are secret to other Navigators, the Stars they guide, and even me. But we suspect P'Pa is close to discovering Grandfather's location in every attempt to lift those limitations, and the world can't afford to let him operate that system."

While Shades and Princess spoke, Crow continued to search her mind for Sam. She poked and fondled herself in different places and held her breath till she turned blue in the face.

Sam didn't respond to her prodding. He didn't want to encourage her behavior or give her insight into actions that affected him. He'd already played into her hand once. She might feel subsequent reactions, so he puckered his butthole, and let her sift through whatever she happened to perceive.

Neven's voice broke through Sam's concentration. "Can't we just ask the kid for his address? The state of the world is more important than his personal info, right?" he asked.

"Are you prepared to secure him ahead of P'Pa?" Princess smiled at Shades' furrowed brows. "He may still have remote access to Grandfather's Sanctum. If we reveal Grandson's location, P'Pa may reach him before we do. Apprehending P'Pa is the safest route to securing the system, Grandson's life, your lives, and the world."

"Our lives?" Shades raised his voice.

Crow snapped out of her research. She looked up. A wide grin stretched the corners of her mouth.

Princess nodded, subtly, almost unnoticeably. If not for the same gold-toned eyeshadow sparkling under the skylight as her lipstick, Sam would've missed her response, as he'd missed the facial coloration before.

"If P'Pa accesses Grandfather's system, he may terminate all of you in the same manner to eliminate potential threats.”

Neven snickered. “So you called us in, certainly because we’re qualified, but also because we have the most to lose.”

Princess nodded once. “I thought it’d be fair, given the circumstances, to offer you the opportunity to save your own lives and the world. Grandson’s activation of Grandfather’s Sanctum reinforced my decision. The stars had aligned.”

Neven cocked his head and stared at the skylight. “Crow may be looking for a gruesome way to die, but I’m not ready yet. I’m thirty-five. I can’t die at an odd-numbered age in an odd-numbered year. I’ll be reborn an insect with an uneven number of legs.”

Crow ran a hand through her hair. She held onto several strands behind her ear. “Death during combat is the only path to Valhalla. I won’t let this coward rob me of my glory.”

Shades sighed multiple times, each one more exaggerated than the last. “Alas, it’s my duty to protect every living creature, regardless of race, gender, social standing, and species. I accept.” He stared at the ground for a moment. “What about you, Navigator? Are you in?”

Sam felt uneasy about everything. It all moved so fast. But the elation Crow incidentally sent his way gave him courage. “This is the only way, right?” He settled back into his own feelings. A hint of sadness crept into his voice. “I still can’t decide if all this is real or some advanced simulation. I keep thinking this is some game or nightmare. It’s scary, and I want to wake up. But Grandfather’s gone. He died in this chair and I’m next, huh?”

“Play the game,” Shades said. “Whether or not you believe it’s real, play as if your life depends on it.” Crow stared at Shades long enough for Sam to feel his words sink in.

Shades turned back to Princess. “Any intel to help us get started?”

Princess opened her palm. Crow’s escort from earlier raced across the room and placed a note in Princess’ hand. She glanced at it. “P’Pa made reservations at the Magnolia

Country Club."

"That place requires two to tango," Neven said. "And two requires an equally tall and beautiful man and woman. Your Majesty, if you'll do me the honor…"

Princess smiled. The fair side of her complexion easily revealed her blush. "You're too kind, Neven, but I must decline. P'Pa is a Navigator—former Navigator. We are acquainted, even if only in passing."

Sam imagined the table chatter Princess would generate from simply entering the venue. Even if P'Pa didn't recognize her, she'd stand out among the other patrons and draw too much attention.

Neven frowned and shifted his gaze in Sam's direction. "That leaves us with…Crow?"

"I'd sooner slit my throat than go arm in arm," she said.

"My sentiments exactly." Neven folded his arms, raised his chin, and looked away in disgust. "Imagine entering a prestigious venue with a child."

Crow flatly said, "I'm not a child. I'm a woman." She looked up at Neven and focused on his high-top fade. "Your date can be anybody. Take Shades. Men can be dashing, too." She crossed her arms and lowered her chin. "And he's somehow attained accessible parking privileges despite being well, so you can save wear and tear of your long pretty legs for some god-awful place like the beach."

"You're going to send a man to escort a man?" Sam asked. The room fell silent.

After a moment of wide-eyed responses, Shades gasped. "That's why I wear these glasses. I would've never known they were two men, just that they were two people together," he said.

Sam mentally slumped in place. He wanted to join in their banter, not alienate himself. And while he meant no disrespect, he couldn't ignore the possibility of his words being interpreted as such.

"As long as they're two, I don't care," Neven added.

"Whatever the arrangement," Princess pulled their attention, "I look forward to your success."

The trio bowed their heads when she stood. From the upper limits of Crow's vision, Sam watched Princess walk across the room and then stop in front of Crow's escort. The regal woman glanced over her left shoulder. "Shades, please give your Navigator a name. He's under the Sun's protection now."

Chapter 3

"What's the Sun?" Sam asked. He'd moved to Shades' viewpoint after finding Crow's curiosity detrimental to his mental health. Except, he'd traded one darkness for another, as he saw nothing of the world but the black of Shades' glasses.

Shades spoke as if Sam sat in the back seat of Neven's car, next to Crow. "Princess is our Sun. They're not royalty. Just a spoiled individual with a complex. They oversee all the Stars in their solar system, i.e., jurisdiction."

"What is the Moon and the Stars?"

"The Moon is the organizational structure that revolves around a planet, i.e., the cities. We are the Stars sparkling in the night sky—the shooting ones, anyway." Sam listened to Shades' disembodied voice as Neven slowed the car to a stop. "Never mind that for now. What's important is that you've learned to select your audience, which is critical to verbal communication. I don't need to hear every correspondence you have with the others, but I'll want requested information as soon as possible. Smooth comms and transition between Stars are important to being a reliable Navigator."

Sam hadn't just learned to control who he spoke with, he'd also grasped jumping between team members. While he could seamlessly move between them, each one's unique intrapersonal environment required Sam to adjust.

While connected to Shades, Sam relied on senses other than sight. He heard Neven throw the shifter lever into park. A belt buckle clicked free, and the strap whined as it retracted. Multiple car doors opened and closed. Crow's voice followed the orchestra.

"Don't look at me," she growled.

"Of course," Shades said before he closed another door.

Crow, Shades, and Neven had drawn straws to decide on

assignments at Magnolia. Crow and Shades lost. Neven rejoiced at his victory, despite his initial objection to drawing only three straws, calling it a disadvantage. When prompted to redraw with a dummy fourth straw, he declined, claiming that the Fates wouldn't be fooled, which left Shades and Crow to don formal attire and dine at the Magnolia.

Neven buzzed in Shades' ear. "I'll circle around and monitor the front door," he said. Their microphones canceled out the car's engine noise, but Sam heard it quietly purring in Shades' ears. The Sanctum synchronized audio from multiple sources too, so Sam didn't hear Shades' voice twice when he acknowledged Neven's plan.

Over the dissonance of other vehicles, Sam heard the clack of heels storm past Shades. He figured they belonged to Crow, the scent of perfume as strong as her step. Sam realized that most of Shades' senses had been dialed up a notch, including a sixth that suggested Crow waited on the curb for his arm.

A part of Sam wanted to see Crow's evening gown. She had a dark style but understood that work often required her to step out of that comfort zone. Having heard that Princess donated the outfit, one she'd worn to a college social event, enticed Sam even more. He expected nothing short of magnificence from Princess' closet, and perhaps, something with a pinch of color.

Sam felt distracted. He refocused on Shades' hearing. The low hum of idling cars provided ambience. Light conversation and laughter erupted here and there. Someone played the saxophone on the sidewalk. The authentic sound quality made Sam feel present and in the moment.

Shades stepped onto the curb. Sam felt Crow's hand slip into the crook of Shades' elbow. Her fingers clamped down on his biceps as if she'd held on for dear life over a cliff. With Shades' increased sensitivity, Sam felt each individual finger and a mood as distraught as the demons she courted.

"Good evening! Welcome to Magnolia," a female voice

said. The hostess, Sam assumed. "Table for two?"

Sam hadn't heard the venue door open, but he noticed the sudden change in temperature, as if they'd moved from a tropical region to the arctic.

"Table for two," Shades said.

"Right this way!"

Sam imagined a young woman wearing an elegant, below-knee fitted skirt; white, possibly striped with pale purple colors to match Magnolia's signature hues. He sensed the quick steps she took and the closeness of her knees as she walked past Shades and escorted them four booths down from the entrance.

"Here we are. Giselle will be your server, but I can pass on any beverage orders." The hostess leaned in and whispered. "She's kinda new."

Shades smiled at her. "I'll have the house wine."

Crow said, "Tequila. Bring the whole bottle."

"Certainly. May I see your ID?"

Sam visualized Crow's scowl. The silence added tension to the mental image. He heard some rummaging and wondered if Crow carried a purse now, too.

"Make that two bottles," she said.

"Um, I'll see what I can do." The hostess meekly replied and then walked away.

"Young Master, did you get a glimpse of Crow's ID card?" Shades asked.

Young Master? Sam thought.

Crow must've glared at Shades. Sam felt the heat of her gaze against his forehead, as if the laser sight from a cold-blooded killer's rifle marked him.

Shades continued. "It's important that you're able to use our surroundings to support the team. Venue cameras, building blueprints, patron social media accounts, casual conversations, and so on."

Young...Master? Sam thought again. He wondered if that was the name given to him. It wasn't cool. Not like

Shades, Crow, Neven, and Princess. Although, it had close ties to Princess. Sam imagined the regal woman calling him Young Master.

Shades inhaled, tilting his head up. "Ah, so that would be the teenage hormones Crow mentioned earlier. They feel like my own. Strange."

Sam recoiled in embarrassment.

"Could this be the answer to the elusive morning wood? Are there horny people inside the minds of men while they sleep, causing the mild discomfort of rolling onto their stomach in the morning?" Shades thought aloud.

Sam sought to change the subject, and fast. "How am I supposed to help you if I can't see anything?"

Shades lowered his chin. "No Navigator has ever seen the way you can. They've used their surroundings as eyes and ears for centuries. It's what makes their job as difficult as ours, and is, perhaps, the reason Grandfather enhanced the system you're now using. The accuracy and speed of a Navigator's information can be the difference between many outcomes." Shades paused and glanced to his right, as if the discussion was too sensitive for the person now standing beside the table.

"Hello. Welcome to Magnolia. My name is Giselle."

Another energetic greeting. Sam never consciously considered the tone of someone's voice. He'd used his eyes for everything, yet there was so much more information in the other senses.

"I'll be your server this evening." Cherry-scented lipstick, light lavender hair spray, and the fragrance of cotton from dryer sheets accompanied her words.

Sam could almost picture Giselle's face from her voice alone. Based on the mild vibrations, he visualized small lips that pulled her cheeks and then her eyes when she spoke. The comfortable presence she exuded suggested a woman in her late twenties. He imagined shoulder-length or longer hair after he felt the motions of her pushing some strands behind her ear.

Shades' nose twitched. The rich aroma of wine filled his nostrils. He heard the faint sound of liquid pouring. "Merci." Shades sipped the wine after he winked. Sam barely caught it, the difference in black between the dark glasses and the back of Shades' eyelids almost indistinguishable. Giselle couldn't have seen him wink unless she observed the subtle movement of his brows.

"Are we ready to order? Oh!" Giselle jumped after something slammed against the table. It sounded small and light, or empty.

"I ordered a whole bottle." Crow said. She tapped what Sam presumed to be an empty shot glass.

Shades formed an uneasy grin. "We're celebrating. Drinks will be all for now—"

"Where the hell are you guys?" Neven shouted in Shades' earpiece. "P'Pa's leaving the restaurant with to-go boxes!"

"Already?" Shades said, glancing over his shoulder and toward the hostess' counter. "The reservation started five minutes ago   " Shades swerved his head back to the table. "Crow's on the way." He fumbled with his wallet. The creased rear pocket of his new pants prevented him from sliding it out with ease. "The reservation should've started five minutes ago. I hadn't seen any patrons walk past us."

"Could his reservation have been to go?" Sam asked.

Neven gasped. "Why would a five-star restaurant entertain to-go orders?"

Shades slammed some cash on the table as he slipped out of the booth. He almost crashed into Giselle.

Neven shouted across the comms. "I can't tell which car he got in. They all look the same from here. Navigator?"

Sam stuttered. "Um, how am I supposed to know that?"

"Use the venue cameras. There's one above the entrance overlooking the drop-off lane."

"Excuse me, sir?" Giselle called after Shades. "You only

left a dollar." Sam imagined a hand on her hip and a disapproving expression on her face. A portion of the restaurant grew quiet.

Shades stopped and turned. "No, I left…" His vision suddenly blurred. The crisp black Sam saw became murky. Shades fell to one knee and grabbed the edge of something nearby to prevent himself from falling over. All of that, including dizziness, spread to Sam.

"Why hello, Shades." Sam thought someone else had spoken, but the voice sounded like Giselle's. A disturbing tone that carried a twisted melody as she dragged out the syllables. "Am I really only worth a Benjamin?"

"Young…Master…follow Crow." Shades took deep breaths between words.

"I can't just leave you—"

"Go! This all ends with them."

Chapter 4

"Which car did he get in?" Crow asked. After a moment of silence, she shouted, "Navigator!"

Sam felt her fear and how she strived to hide it. Or was it his fear that propagated through her? He responded in a low voice, "Shades is…he's been poisoned."

Sam's eyes burned. The swap from darkness to headlights strained his vision, at least, the saturated information sent to his brain. He relied on his host to blink, to give him a moment to process the change, but Crow hadn't batted an eye since he transitioned to her.

"Don't worry about him. The target is getting away!" she exclaimed.

Sam didn't know Crow's voice could get so loud. Even her threats during their meeting with Princess lacked volume.

"I don't…I don't know how to do this!" Sam wanted to grab his head. Instead, he watched Crow run alongside multiple cars, searching for P'Pa through the back windows. Her pale and tattooed arms reflected in the glass.

"Young Master," Neven said in a calm voice that rivaled Crow's usual tone. "How did you know Shades was poisoned?"

Sam thought back to that moment. "My body felt weird before Shades collapsed. I wondered what happened and imagined looking up the symptoms online. Then a browser window with a list of conditions appeared in front of me. Poison sat near the top."

"Congratulations, you've completed your second task as Navigator. Knowing that he's been poisoned, Shades will take care of himself. The Navigator supports his allies by providing crucial information in a timely manner." Neven revved his car's engine. The sound reverberated loudly, as if he'd parked in a garage. "Just as Princess said, Navigators use online search engines and databases to gather information. I believe they use a keyboard and mouse, but your updated system is capable of something like thought-to-text. Try thinking about what you want and seeing if the results appear."

Sam closed his eyes, momentarily ignoring his distracted connection with Crow. He thought about the restaurant—Magnolia's Country Club. A layout of the building appeared in his mind. He searched for the cameras, first visualizing a multilayered two-dimensional blueprint and then a three-dimensional space complete with highlighted cones for each camera's field-of-view. Six cameras hung around the venue. He located the one above the restaurant's entrance, its cone overlapping the road, and connected to it.

"P'Pa entered a taxi or shared ride. It's blue," he said.

Sam heard the elation in Neven's voice. "Good job! Although, Shades would've said your response is discriminatory—*colorist*, which is his way of asking for more distinguishable identifying information that can't broadly be applied to everything else."

"What? How else am I supposed to describe it? Make and model? There's ten or more matching vehicles out there."

"Yet every single one registered in the U.S. has a unique tag identifier. Some are a disgusting seven-digit alphanumeric sequence—"

"Right. Right! I'm an idiot! It's HR4B478."

"It's already gone," Crow said.

Sam felt her anger after he reopened his connection to her consciousness. He understood what Shades meant when he'd said the job of the Navigator was as tough as theirs. They exerted themselves physically, and Navigators pushed themselves mentally. Sam felt he needed to step up.

"Find a ride, Crow," Sam said with confidence. "P'Pa had to use an app to reserve the ride, which means his reservation is in one of three databases. I'll find the car's tag in the rideshare system and send its current destination to you."

Crow ran up to and tapped on the nearest car's passenger side window. The driver of a four-door silver sedan rolled the clear glass down. A middle-aged man sat behind the steering wheel. His hands firmly gripped it at the top as he responded to Crow.

"Um, Jennifer?" the middle-aged man asked in a thick foreign accent.

Sam listened to their conversation as he mined for the driver's registered information.

"Sure," Crow said. She pulled on the passenger side door handle. It didn't open. She glanced inside at the driver. He nodded at the back seats.

Crow hop-stepped to her left and grabbed the rear passenger side door handle. She opened it, slipped into the rear seat, and slammed the door shut.

"Um, ma'am, the app is still showing you point-two-five miles away?"

Crow tilted her head. "Guess we better get going before I get here."

They stared at each other for a moment. The driver's suspicion faced off against Crow's mental fortitude. He used the weapon in his hand, an indicator of the reserver's location steadily approaching. She wielded the voice in the back of her head.

"Check it now," Sam said. "I even added a tip, courtesy of Jennifer."

"Refresh it," Crow told the driver.

The driver swiped across the screen, and the display updated with Crow's location. His head bobbled as he accepted the outcome. "Oh. Okay," he said.

Crow winked at him. "Step on it. There's a blue car, license plate ending in B478. Catch up to it." The driver's phone chimed. "There's your tip," she added.

His eyes bulged after he checked the application. He threw the car into gear and bolted into traffic.

A mile down the road, Crow said, "Good job, Navigator." She glanced at the driver's eyes through the rearview mirror and shook her head. She wasn't speaking to him.

"Thanks. I sent the destination to you, too, Neven," Sam said. "And confirmed, based on Magnolia's recent transactions, P'Pa's reservation was a mobile order. He used an app."

Neven gasped. "I'm leaving that place a four-star review. Subtracting one for the traffic and one for entertaining mobile orders at a five-star establishment."

"That would result in a three-star review," Sam said.

"True. I'll add another grievance. Wait, that would make three complaints. Dammit, I hate odd numbers!"

Sam smiled inside. His contribution, combined with the rush of falsifying information for Crow's ride, gave him a high he'd never felt before. He stared at code all day for a living, writing scripts to transfer data from one company to another. Never once did he think he'd use his software engineering skills to hack businesses.

Now he felt at home in the system. He navigated the digital world with his mind far more quickly than he swapped between tabs and applications on his desktop computer.

Sam pulled up a map of the area as if he planned to enter a destination. The satellite view showed the trees, grass, and metal guardrails that flanked the two-lane highway. A concrete median split the traffic, which looked mild for a Friday evening. Sam reduced the visual clutter when he changed the overlay to semi-transparent grid lines. He marked Crow, Neven, and P'Pa's location with unique icons. Neven's marker turned onto the main highway, about three miles behind Crow's ride, which closed the gap on P'Pa's.

"I can't reach Shades," Sam said. He tried various communication methods, from the Sanctum's ear pieces to Shades' cellphone. No response. Sam couldn't transition to him, either.

Crow immediately responded. "He's not dead. I haven't

been tasked to cross him over." She glanced at the driver's rearview mirror again and crossed her legs when she caught him staring. Open-toe heels pointed at the driver. "I assure you, there's nothing down there but a barren tundra. And knives. Lots of knives. I lined my dress with them. Spinning into your arms will castrate you, among other things."

Sam grimaced at the mental image. He imagined the knives extending beyond the knee-length dress and wondered when she had time to modify something from Princess' closet.

He stuttered at first. "Sorry ma'am. I was checking for the seat belt. The, um, company policy states—"

Crow raised a brow. She reached for the window controls instead of the seat belt. Nothing moved when she pushed the button. "Roll down the window. Or is that against company policy, too?"

When the window came down, she poked her head outside. The blue sedan Sam marked as P'Pa's cruised down the highway one lane over and several feet ahead. Its windows came down, too.

Crow pulled her head back inside and dove across the back seats. Then she rolled onto the floor space behind the driver just before gunfire erupted. Muzzle flashes illuminated the inside of the car. The sound of pellets striking metal, tire, and window shocked and scared Sam. He felt the car veer to the left and then experienced a collision through Crow's senses.

Except for horns blaring, the highway fell quiet. Crow reached for the driver side door handle and shoved the door open. She crawled out and into the street, where she leaned her back against the shared ride and her head against its rear fender.

"Driver's down. Call emergency services," Crow said.

"What about you?" Sam asked as the call connected.

"9-1-1, what's your emergency?"

"There's been an accident on interstate six-six-five heading east past mile marker twenty. Multiple vehicles. Gun…" Sam hesitated. "Shots fired, too."

"Emergency responders are on the way. Sir, are you hurt? Did you say shots fired? Sir?"

Sam disconnected the call. "They're on the way. Maybe they can help us catch P'Pa."

"Nope. They play by the rules we don't."

Neven came over the comms. "Hey pretty girl. Need a ride?"

"I'm not a girl. I'm a—ah, fuck it! I'll let you pick me up if you promise to take me to the party."

"Oh, we're going to a fucking party!"

Sam shook his head. "Crow, I don't think you're in any shape to…I mean, your vital signs. They're…" The fluctuating data changed Sam's mind multiple times. Crow's heart rate returned to normal. Blood pressure, respirator rate, and body temperature, too. She didn't breathe heavily or wheeze.

Crow snapped the heels off her shoes and tossed them. Using the shared ride as support, she climbed to her feet and hobbled to the front of the car. She glanced at the driver through the smashed window. He sat unconscious. Blood ran down his hair. The impact crumpled the vehicle's front end, and the engine prevented the inside from being crushed.

"We gotta get him out of there," Sam said.

Crow squeezed between the front end of the shared ride and the rear bumper of the car it'd hit and then limped past the other crashed vehicles. People crowded the scene, some involved and others bystanders. When Crow reached the yellow lines in the road, she walked faster, then ran, increasing her speed into a full sprint down the highway.

Sam watched Neven's marker close in on their location and then saw the headlights. Crow glanced over her shoulder. She jumped into the air and landed on the car's hood as it drove by. Neven had barely slowed down, so Crow slid across the hood until her back collided with the passenger side windshield. She planted her heel against the right hood vent and grabbed the wheel well for support.

"You're crazy!" Sam said.

"Don't be alarmed, Young Master." Neven leaned over the steering wheel and waved at Crow from inside the vehicle. "Like your Sanctum, we've seen enhancements, too. Long ago. Crow's youth resulted from prosthetic augmentations. Shades' sensitivity to light is a side effect of chemical modifications to his other senses. And my proclivity for even numbers developed from enlightenment.

"That being said, Crow, you're not immortal. The sunroof's open if you want to fight behind something bulletproof."

Sam admired Neven's classic Challenger. Highway lights briefly revealed its gunmetal gray paint job. An orange off-center stripe ran along the hood and up to the roof.

"I want to take out the driver," Crow said.

"How do you plan to do that?" Sam asked. "They have machine guns."

"With grace and a distraction."

Sam knew a distraction meant him. He no longer hesitated. The Sanctum's reach seemed limitless, yet all within the normal functionality of the systems he accessed. That thought gave him an idea.

"What if I add a waypoint to their route?" he asked aloud. "Neven, can you catch up in two miles? I'll update their route at the last minute and make them take one exit down from their planned."

"Hang on tight!" Neven sped up.

Sam waited until P'Pa's ride changed lanes for the planned exit before he pushed the update to their navigation. The blue sedan swerved from the exit lane and back onto the highway just as Neven caught up.

Crow leaped from the hood of the Challenger. She seemed to hover in the air with plenty of time to raise her knees to her chest and pull two knives out from under her dress, one in each hand. When the blue sedan passed under her, she threw one knife into the driver side roof and then landed on its hilt. Sam felt her shove the blade through the metal and into something else; the driver's skull, he imagined.

The sedan veered off the road and slammed against the guardrail. The impact knocked Crow down onto the sedan. She grabbed the knife's hilt, what little protruded from the roof, as the car sped up.

"You've got company, Crow!" Neven said.

She glanced behind her. Gunmen from inside the vehicle pointed their weapons out the windows. They fired into the air and over the roof. They couldn't angle the rifles enough to strike Crow. She glanced behind her. One gunman climbed halfway out the driver side rear window. Crow twirled the other dagger in her hand and flung it into the side of his head.

Another gunman climbed out of the passenger side rear window and a third out of the passenger side front window. Neven sped up and rammed into the sedan. The rear gunman fell back inside before the sedan slammed against the guardrail again. The front gunman avoided being sandwiched, too, but lost his rifle.

"Why aren't they shooting through the roof?" Sam shouted.

"It's bulletproof."

"What? Why is the rideshare car bulletproof?"

"You tell me!" Neven rammed the sedan again and pinned it against the guardrail, both still racing down the shoulder at high speeds. "I shot at the back window several times and it laughed at me. Maybe I should've used two guns."

Yellow sparks flashed from the passenger side of the sedan. Crow shielded her eyes with her forearm. "Neven, I need an exit," she said, calm as always.

"We're coming up on one soon! Get off the roof!"

Crow lowered her arm. She and Sam saw the end of the shoulder's guardrail. Both knew the blue sedan would careen across the exit's lane and slam into the beginning of the next guardrail. Crow started to her knees and lay down again when more gunfire erupted. She glanced at the Challenger. The gunmen fired at its passenger side window.

"I guess somebody else wants off the ride," Neven said over the noise. "Crow, you'll have to find another way off. I'm escorting them to the end."

"Another way off? You expect me to fucking fly?"

"If I back off now, innocents will get caught in the line of fire and these guys'll be on the loose. They belong to a Moon."

A sense of obligation settled over Crow. Sam understood why. Being part of a Moon meant the gunmen were on their level, which also made Sam wonder if Giselle was too.

Crow looked down at the car's roof. The light of gunfire flashed in her peripheral vision. "There's no way off and no time," she said.

The sedan cut across the exit's lane, skid through the grass on the other side, and slammed into the yellow and black-striped guardrail end. The impact launched Crow off the roof. She poised herself for a tumble, but when she saw the guardrail below, she twisted her upper body hard to avoid it. Sam felt the sudden jerk, dizzying and painful, followed by a collision with the shoulder pavement. Crow flopped many times and onto the highway. Multiple headlights dodged her, but Sam didn't think vehicles further back would see her in time.

"Get up, Crow!" Sam exclaimed.

As more headlights grew closer, she curled into a ball and covered her head. Brakes screeched. Horns blared. Two more vehicles avoided her and a third stopped two feet away and flashed hazard lights.

"Crow!" Neven ran down the highway and knelt next to her. He went to scoop her into his arms but stopped short of passing his hands around her back and under her knee. The crash had severed part of her leg. The lower half dangled at the kneecap, just below the dress. Her right arm hung limply at her side, the tentacled monster tattoo twisted at her elbow.

Crow screamed out loud. She panted and choked on her uneven breaths. Her pain echoed through Sam, who had to look at the torn ligaments and gushing blood, all of which shimmered a dark purple under the highway lights. An unusual color for blood. The ligaments inside her leg looked different too, metallic instead of organic.

Using her good arm, Crow pushed herself up and onto her butt. Neven braced her as she twisted her right arm back into place and released another scream into the night. Then she grabbed her dangling leg and reattached it to her knee. Sam heard the mating and grinding of metal. Skin from her thigh and shin came together and spread over the exposed material in her leg. When the knee looked normal, she collapsed into Neven's arms.

Sam saw the back of her eyelids. Her breaths slowed along with her heart rate. The pain vanished soon after.

"She's…she's a robot?"

Neven replied in a somber tone, "She's not a robot. She's a woman. You should get out of her head now."

Chapter 5

Sam found normalcy from Neven's viewpoint. He could see, hear, smell, and feel as if he stood in his own body. Nothing hampered his senses or threatened his sanity.

Neven walked like a man in his mid-forties, though. Sam suspected a bad hip caused him to limp every now and again. But he was strong. He'd lifted Crow from the pavement with ease and buckled her across the Challenger's back seats without bumping her head against the door frame.

After securing her, he lingered outside the driver side front door and stared at the smoke rising from the blue sedan. When red, blue, and yellow lights flashed in the distance, he sat behind the steering wheel of the Challenger and drove away, tires screeching.

"Is she gonna be okay?" Sam asked.

Neven glanced at the rearview mirror. "She'll be fine. I think. I hope."

Crow's hair had come undone, and based on the curvature of the black strands, Sam imagined she'd fashioned a bun atop her head before heading out. A light red hue coated her lips. Face powder darkened her ghost white skin. The absence of eye shadow made her look younger.

Sam visualized the city map again and oriented its view until their vehicle's direction on the display pointed up. "There's a hospital three exits down—"

"The mission isn't over," Nevén said. He glanced at the rearview mirror again. "P'Pa wasn't in that vehicle. Something's not right. I believe those men are called the Rings of Saturn—septuplets. Four of them, anyway. Identical through and through. Stars, just like us."

"We have to get Crow to a hospital!"

Sam watched an ambulance use the emergency lane to bypass the traffic jam forming on the other side of the highway. Sam considered imitating dispatch to redirect the ambulance to Crow instead.

Neven saw the rotating lights, too. "They wouldn't know what to do with her. And there'd be no point if P'Pa finds you and ends her life on the operating room table."

He glanced at the rearview mirror again and then narrowed his eyes. "Princess was right. P'Pa's the priority."

Sam reluctantly agreed.

Memories of Crow's severed leg and broken arm flashed through Sam's mind. He recalled the bruises along her neck and face, all of which recovered the same way her knee and arm had. Neven said they'd all been enhanced, but Crow's modifications seemed far beyond current technology, including Grandfather's upgraded Sanctum. The thought reminded Sam of something Princess had said. Sam had access to personal records. He wondered if he could locate the team's medical history.

"Something about this ain't right," Neven said again. "Have you been able to reach Shades?"

Sam shook his head.

Neven felt it. "Check the security cameras inside and outside the Magnolia. Search the internet for official news reports and social media posts. Somebody had to pull out their phone."

Sam pulled up two equally sized application windows. On the left one, he searched for the reports Neven had mentioned. He used the other to request the team's medical files. Both windows showed a circular icon at their center, which spun for what felt like hours.

At last, a grid of social media videos and the Magnolia's camera feeds populated the left window. The venue's cameras had crisp high-definition video but didn't include audio. Amateur cellphone recordings came with audio, but the video wasn't always clear and often shaky. So Sam stitched together video and audio of the best quality and started the playback from the time he'd switched to Crow's point of view.

***

"Traitor?" Giselle scoffed.

Contrary to what Sam had imagined her to look like from behind Shades' glasses, the high-definition video playback he watched showed Giselle in a tight, below-knee, navy-blue skirt and a white short-sleeved blouse. No stripes or patterns. No visible tattoos, either.

"We all work for Uncle Sam," she said from her seated position on top of a table several feet from the one Shades knelt beside. "Whether he's good isn't outlined in my contract and sure as hell ain't printed on the money."

"*They…*" Shades said. After Giselle raised a brow, he added, "Whether *they're* good. The government has no gender."

Giselle crossed her legs and then leaned forward. She brushed something off the tip of her closed-toe heels and then dusted off the bridge of her foot. "Shades, political correctness should be the least of your concerns." She adjusted her shoulder-length, light-gray hair, spreading the bangs evenly across her forehead and pushing the other strands aside.

Shades gripped the edge of a nearby table with his left hand and rested his right elbow on a chair next to him. The veins across the back of his hand surfaced as he struggled to hold himself up.

Giselle planted her chin against one knuckle and balanced its elbow on her knee. She observed Shades with intrigue in her eyes. "I wonder what's going on under those glasses. I see furrowed brows, gritted teeth, and veins all over." She gestured with one hand, a single wave out in front to outline Shades' distressed posture. "But what do your eyes look like? Are they trembling? Steady? In awe of me? Should we take those glasses off and have a look-see? Or will the light in the room burn those big, beautiful brown eyes of yours?"

"My eyes…aren't…brown…"

Giselle laughed. "Yes they are. I can read you their hexadecimal code if you'd like." She tilted her head forward. "Is it strange that I know? My Navigator seemed inconvenienced when I asked for the information. *I* think it only makes sense to know absolutely everything about your target."

"Kill…me…or shut up…"

"Rude! I'm not here to kill you, baby." Giselle pulled a phone out from the inside lower corner of her bra. "The contract said to delay you by all means necessary. As it stands now, killing you is unnecessary. We're professionals, after all." She raised her head, up off her chin, and spoke to the other restaurant guests. "You hear that, folks? Don't go feeling sorry for this man. He's a contract killer." She lowered her voice and added melody to her words again. "Just. Like. Me."

Most of the dining room bystanders seemed scared, hiding behind anything they could find. Several men stood at the edge of their cover. A few protected their family, while one inched forward. Giselle's confidence discouraged him from interfering. Her demeanor frightened Sam. Sitting on a table in the open without a care in the world was truly terrifying.

Giselle addressed the other patrons again. "I wouldn't get brave or run away if I were any of you. If you had a drink tonight, then you're not long for this world."

Gasps erupted around the room, but nothing more.

"I can't help those who already left, but the rest of you," she pointed her finger and moved her arm in an arc, "have a chance." She picked up a glass of water. "When the time's right, I'll bless this cup of water with the antidote. Hint," she put the cup down, "its chemical composition has been distributed among a number of my bodily fluids."

Shades smirked. "You knew…we…were coming…"

"More like we planned for you to come. Did you really

think *He'd* stop for a meal on his way to changing the world?" She grabbed the edge of the table with both hands. "I bet you thought you had great intel." She hopped off, walked over to Shades, and squatted in front of him. She locked eyes with a young bystander in a cubby behind Shades. Staring into their phone's camera lens, she leaned forward and almost brushed her nose against Shades' cheek. Green eyes then shifted to him, and she loudly whispered into his ear, "Your Princess fucked you."

Shades struck her with his head, an attack that dazed her long enough for him to grab her by the throat.

"Thanks for getting close," he said in a low voice.

"How the...fuck..." Giselle choked. She clawed at his hands but couldn't pry his grip apart.

Shades spoke in measured breaths. "My Navigator told me about the poison. So, I took it easy, adjusted my heart rate, and slowed its circulation. Aggression makes it spread faster, right?"

Giselle spoke as Shades had, struggling to complete full sentences between breaths. "You'll...never get the...antidote."

"I got a B in chemistry for being messy."

Giselle swiped her fingers at Shades' face. When he dodged, she knocked his arm away and leaped backwards. She retreated several more steps and cocked her head back as Shades rose to full height. Fumbling her hands on a nearby table, she grabbed several steak knives and a spoon. She threw one knife at Shades and used another to tear her skirt down the middle.

Shades caught the knife with his bare hands, inches from his face, and then dropped it on the ground.

"This is how it should be, Shades." Giselle threw the spoon next and then slotted the remaining knives between her knuckles. "I think it's necessary to kill you now."

Shades looked at the scrape marks on his hands. They didn't worry him until he tried to articulate his fingers. He couldn't close either fist. Veins surfaced along his forearms as he tried to lift them.

"Slowly, of course," she added.

Giselle dashed forward with the steak knives between her knuckles. Shades parried her attack with one leg, knocking the knives out of her hands, and then kicked her across the face with the other. She crashed into a table, knocking it and the surrounding chairs to the ground.

Shades stalked her as she hastily scurried backwards. "This is how you delay someone." He walked up to and stomped her right foot, crushing the ankle under his boot.

Giselle shrieked in pain as she grabbed her leg. "You fucking bitch! You broke my foot!"

Shades sat on the floor next to her and sighed while she moaned in pain. He seemed to stare at the ceiling. The fight likely circulated poison through his system. His movements became sluggish, but he still caught Giselle's swinging arm by the wrist.

"You want me to break this, too?" he said, throwing her arm back into her lap. "Don't move so much and the doc'll fix it."

Giselle looked at the surrounding people and then smirked. Squinted eyes suggested she held back the pain. "I guess we'll just watch these people die then, won't we?"

"It's not in your contract. Give them the antidote."

"I suppose you think you're doing something noble, helping these people. We've all been fed the saving the world crap. But we're only saving *their* world. And as retirement has taught you, there's no place in that world for us."

Shades took a long breath, as if he held a cigar in his hand. Sam recognized the pattern of inhalation and exhalation from watching his grandfather. "You delayed me. Take the win and move on with your life."

Giselle laughed. An out-of-control jubilation that scared the guests. "And if I don't? You gonna fight through the paralysis and fondle me for a cure?" She turned her attention to one patron after they'd stepped forward. "Or are you gonna do it? How about you? None of you have the balls!"

Giselle laughed some more before she leaned her head against Shades' shoulder. "You're free to fetch the antidote, babe. But one of its components requires foreplay to produce a liquid." She raised her chin and reached for the underside of his neck with her tongue.

Shades feigned a kiss and quickly grabbed her tongue with his mouth. Giselle's eyes widened as he bit down and ripped a piece of the muscle out. He spit it into the cup of water she paraded earlier.

Giselle cut her scream short. Unrecognizable words followed as blood filled her mouth.

Shades licked his lips. "The antidote is simply your saliva. My Navigator gleaned that tidbit, too, and shared it with me before they disconnected. They must've connected to you or something, kind of like joining an open network and finding other devices. I suppose that's the power P'Pa's after. Now that I've seen it, I can't let them have it."

Giselle laughed through the pain, her white teeth stained red. "I o," she said.

Shades turned to her. He grabbed her jaw with one hand. "What exactly do you know?"

"Is too wait. *He* oes now, too." She formed a gun with three fingers, pointed it at her head, and flicked her wrist up.

Shades looked up at the ceiling, eyes wide with alarm. "Young Master!" He waited for a response he wouldn't receive. Sam couldn't reach him then and still couldn't connect with him during the playback.

"He can't huere u." Giselle repeatedly sang and clapped.

Shades let her go. He looked at the scratch marks on his arm and then sniffed them. "Metallic poisoning? It's interfering with the connection." He faced Giselle. "You're jamming me from the inside?"

Giselle continued her melody.

"Stop singing!" Shades raised his hand.

She shielded her face with both arms. The plea that escaped her lips as a faint whimper stopped Shades mid swing. She sniffled underneath her forearms, mumbling inaudible words.

Shades pushed himself off the ground and stumbled forward on his feet. A different poison still affected his body. He looked around the room until he found a camera mounted above the hostess' podium. He waved and crossed both arms in front of it. First to get attention and then to signal: get out.

Chapter 6

"He knows!" Sam shouted.

Neven tightened both hands around the steering wheel. "Stay calm. You'll never hear me say this again, Young Master, but I need more than two words to understand what you're saying." He glanced in the rearview mirror as if he'd see Sam in the reflection.

"P'Pa knows where I live! He tricked me. He fucking tricked me! I connected to Giselle, the female server at Magnolia, and he traced my connection through her. He knows where I live! I can't log out. How do I log out? Neven, I don't wanna die! Please!"

"Calm down. You're in my head, and I can't think over your shouting." Neven waited for the pleas to stop. "Where's Shades?"

"I can't reach him. Giselle poisoned him with some kind of metal. It's interfering with our connection."

"So they set us up." Neven smacked the steering wheel. "I hate being one step behind. Give me a location and pray we make it on time."

"3688 Davidson Street," Sam blurted out. When he saw Neven trying to enter the address into the Challenger's navigation system while driving, Sam remotely started the route.

He watched the speedometer climb to one hundred and twenty in a few seconds. Headlights on the other side of the road flickered past. When Neven swerved across lanes, Crow's body slid across the back seats.

Sam's heart pounded in his chest, except it was Neven's heart and Neven's chest. Sam reminded himself that he affected the team too, and that Neven likely fought back Sam's emotions while expertly navigating traffic at high speeds.

But Sam couldn't get the idea of dying out of his mind. That his body lay helpless in a chair. That somebody would enter the room and simply slit his throat. That at any moment, his thoughts would just stop.

Neven asked, "Is this what Crow's mind feels like? A never-ending and spiraling descent into despair?"

Sam didn't respond. He focused on controlling his emotions and anxiety to avoid a mental breakdown that could cause Neven to crash. Then Sam would be dead for sure, a thought that further escalated his fears.

"Save your concerns for our femme fatale. I know she'd appreciate the anguish." That was Neven's way of telling Sam to get a grip. He was one of them—a professional—a contract killer without a body count.

Sam watched Crow in the rearview mirror from Neven's peripheral vision. To ease his mind and slow the thoughts, he asked, "What is she? I couldn't find anything on any of you. It's like none of you even exist."

Neven shook his head. "Navigators are the only members recognized by the government. The best way to hide non-combatants was in a sea of normal people.

"And Crow? She's a woman. She went by the name Chloe. Her home caught on fire when she was fifteen. Her entire family died in the house. She died later at the hospital."

Sam considered Neven's earlier objection to taking Crow to the hospital and wondered if her history there contributed to his decision. She could've died in the same place twice, and if she didn't, Sam couldn't imagine her fear of waking up in a place where she'd died once before.

Neven continued, "The gods gave her a second chance. But Man doesn't recognize miracles, not even the gift of life. After third-degree burns, the Moon gave her legs, a right arm, and a heart." Neven glanced in the rearview mirror. His expression was like that of a loving father traveling down memory lane. "Almost everything except a soul, and demanded her service in return."

Neven responded to Sam's sadness, to its purity and kindness. He smiled. "We're all like that in one way or another. We all owe Uncle Sam a debt that can't be repaid through conventional means."

"So what's your story?" Sam asked.

"I still have things to protect, so my story's a secret, even to me."

Neven tapped the brakes and swerved around a vehicle. He sped up again and then slammed on the brakes before slipping between two cars in the exit lane. "DUI checkpoint? For real?"

"I'll look into it," Sam said. He pulled up a map of the area and checked recent police radio traffic. "They're looking for people involved with the incident at Magnolia and the highway shootout."

Neven sighed. "I don't suppose they'll let a vehicle decorated with holes through this checkpoint, huh?"

"I'll call in another incident for them to respond to." Sam swiped one screen away and brought up another. He tapped 9-1-1 on the digital numeric pad and then realized he could've just thought it. Muscle memory made typing the numbers feel faster.

Your call cannot be completed as dialed.

"What the hell?" Sam said. He dialed the number again, using his thoughts this time.

Your call cannot be completed as dialed.

"I can't reach the police."

"This is…his doing…" Neven's voice broke like interrupted radio traffic before it faded entirely.

All the sensory information Sam's connection to Neven had provided disappeared. He felt strange not being able to see, hear, smell, taste, or feel anything. Only his thoughts remained. Had he died? Sam wasn't sure. Nobody had ever experienced death and returned to talk about it, except maybe Crow.

Searching…
Searching…
Network unavailable…
Connecting to localhost…

Sam hadn't died. In the darkness before him, words appeared in gray font, followed by a flashing underscore character.

Connected to localhost…
Retrieving local devices…
Twenty-two devices found…

A list of networked devices populated the space in front of Sam. Many were unsurprising, such as the refrigerator, television sets, and his phone, which suggested he'd connected to his grandfather's home network. Some devices belonged to the smart home, such as the door locks, lights, thermostat, and smoke and CO_2 alarms. Among the last few devices, one group caught Sam's attention: surveillance cameras.

He tapped it, with his eyes presumably, or his mind. An array of video feeds organized in front of him. Sam had never seen cameras at his grandfather's house—not when he was a kid and not when he meandered through earlier. Nothing in the police report included surveillance footage as a part of the investigation, either.

Sam visually examined the feeds. Based on their fields of view, he knew where the cameras hung. A three-hundred-and-sixty-degree camera viewed the entire kitchen from the ceiling. Another camera watched the foyer from above, as if someone could sneak past the camera outside the front door or the others mounted along the house perimeter.

Sam saw the living room, dining room, garage, and sunroom. Even the bedrooms and the hallways leading to them were under surveillance. Sam wondered how long those have been operational. Based on their footage, Sam presumed his grandfather installed them in the various artworks mounted to the walls, the ceiling light fixtures, and in the bulbs among the Christmas lights that hung year-round.

Movement among the matrix of seemingly static frames caused one video feed to stand out from the rest. Sam maximized and centered its window. He saw a girl standing at the entrance to his grandfather's study, where he lay. When he zoomed in, she turned her head and stared at the camera. He could see her clearly now. She reminded him of his first interaction with the Sanctum, the floor-length mirror, and the pale goddess of death.

After a brief pause, Sam said, "Crow?"

Chapter 7

Sam recognized the black dress Crow wore for dinner. He'd glimpsed it here and there, after he'd entered her point of view to chase P'Pa and again each time Neven had glanced in the Challenger's rearview mirror.

"Crow? Is that you?" Sam asked again.

The woman in front of him stood without the wear and tear of the car chase and follow-on shootout. The heels he'd watched her break off in the road were intact. When she'd turned to face him, she moved with the same flow and grace as when he'd first seen her in the full-length mirror.

She responded unusually. A series of clicks modulated by static. A signal affected by interference. Since she entered the frame, the video quality required the manual antenna adjustments of old.

"You're okay!" Sam exclaimed. He wanted to grab the video with both hands and bring her in. It'd be as close to hugging Crow as she'd allow.

Again, her response came in broken. She tilted her head and seemed to cycle through a few different frequencies before finding one that worked.

"Can you understand me now?" she said, static still in the voice.

"Now I can. The interference is mostly gone. My Sanctum's been glitching."

"Not interference or a glitch. A new language. Grandfather developed it to evade detection by the Sun. He named it SPF100."

Sam laughed. So he thought, unsure whether his physical lips parted. Then jealousy and loneliness soured him. Crow, Neven, Shades, and his grandfather were a team. They had inside jokes and code words and even a language. Sam had one close friend who hadn't even reported him missing.

A day hadn't passed since he sat in the chair, so Sam knew he couldn't hold his friend accountable for not crying wolf over the past sixteen hours. It wasn't their fault. But deep down, Sam wished he shared a sixth sense mental connection with someone—the same kind he believed his grandfather's team had developed. The one that alerted them to each other's danger and prompted them to send the cavalry without ever saying a single word.

Maybe Sam had gained that sixth sense. Something pricked the back of his neck. For whatever reason, he knew the woman in front of him wasn't Crow.

"Who are you?" he asked.

Again, she responded in the language Sam couldn't process. The Sanctum didn't translate it, either, which made sense since they strived to hide their conversations from Princess.

"My real name can't be translated," they repeated in English, mimicking Crow's speech pattern and mannerisms exactly, almost as if they'd watched her all this time and used that visual history to train a personality algorithm to perfection.

"Grandfather called me P'Pa. I chose this form to ease your mind and then rendered it into the video feed you see. I otherwise don't have such a physical form."

Sam had so many questions. What was P'Pa's physical form, if not humanoid, and why did they visually stand outside of his grandfather's study?

Sam said, conviction in his voice, "You're here for my grandfather's Sanctum." He realized then that he couldn't stop P'Pa from taking the system because he couldn't control his physical body. But P'Pa didn't have one, either. They'd injected themselves into the camera's video feed, which meant they couldn't hurt Sam, until he remembered his grandfather had died in the chair.

"I'm here to collect the essential parts of my anatomy. Grandfather severed and then hid them from me," P'Pa said.

Sam didn't understand. He'd heard sayings, such as swords being extensions of the body, but P'Pa didn't have a physical body. Maybe they had a digital one, and considering the Sanctum was a computer system, Sam asked, "Are you a program or simulation?"

P'Pa's virtual body leaned against the wall intersecting the study's entrance. Their eyes looked inside. "To you, I'm an extraterrestrial entity that integrated into an app. Hence the name P'Pa." They looked up at Sam and scribed the name in the air using a finger. To them, it read APP. To Sam, it read PPA.

"And thanks to humanity, I may be the last of my kind." They walked to the camera and stared at it with the same menacing eyes as Crow's. "For decades, humanity has poisoned my people with the signals they've broadcast into space. The equivalent of what you call cancer devastated my species."

They lowered their head, turned around, and strolled back to the study's entrance. They grabbed the edge of the open door. "Our government developed the means to ride the signal back to its source. I'm their first," they looked back, tilting their head toward the ground in thought, "agent."

They posted against the wall again, their hands behind their back and their eyes facing the camera. "My mission: destroy the source of radiation. Upon arrival to Earth, I learned multiple sources plagued the galaxy, so I decided complete destruction was best."

Sam had no words. P'Pa had witnessed and then planned to commit xenocide. Sam had only ever seen and read about the killing of an entire species in science-fiction movies and novels. In most of the content he'd consumed, Sam didn't feel like a villain's plan to destroy the world was ever truly justified. Fault could be narrowed down to one or two people with an agenda. But signals broadcast into space—they existed all over the planet, just as P'Pa had determined.

P'Pa stared into the room again. "You sound like my people right now. Silent. Unmoving." They folded their arms and closed their eyes. "We traverse particles to generate sound and communicate. Grandfather called it static, which also means *still* in your world. But the speed, duration, and strength of our movement makes us far more expressive than humans. The surface's material also determines our color as we generate heat." They opened their eyes and stared at the corner of the door frame, their gaze distant. "A festival is a dance across the most compatible surfaces, sparking a flurry of colors that brighten the sky like your fireworks. Now, there's only darkness. Now, there's only the sound of *your* steady breath and healthy heartbeat."

Sam wondered if his body trembled or if his stomach twisted in knots. According to P'Pa, he lay peacefully. Did emotions not transfer to his body, or did he only think them and not feel them?

"If you have any remorse at all, you'll help me. Many other species are affected, I'm sure. Many without the know-how or capability to reach the source as I have. Together, you and I can save the galaxy." They stared off into space again, tilting their head in various directions as if watching a signal traverse the cosmos. "We can save the universe."

"I...I can't help you. Not like that. If you show yourself to humanity's leaders, you can tell them what's happened. Maybe they can do something different. I don't know what that something will look like, but it would certainly be more than knowing nothing at all."

P'Pa shook their head, Crow's black hair glitching under the poor lighting and camera resolution. "I'm here to avenge my people and save others. Adjusting course now might accomplish the latter, but not the former. What your species has done cannot be undone and cannot be forgiven."

Sam gathered himself. Shades' earlier words served as a reminder that he was an informant for the team. He had to use his environment to gather and deliver information. Sam reached for the internet, but he couldn't leave the local network. He recalled an old landline in his grandfather's bedroom. It should've had an emergency connection in case the internet dropped. Sam connected to it on the local network and dialed 9-1-1.

Your call cannot be completed as dialed.

"Stop," P'Pa said, sternly. "We have front row seats to the end of humanity. There's no need to inform them, as they will know soon enough."

Sam didn't give up. He considered other options when a thought occurred to him. Princess said P'Pa planned to kill Sam once they discovered his location, so why was he still alive?

"You need me, don't you?" Sam asked.

P'Pa's avatar looked up at the camera and raised a brow. A message materialized in front of Sam.

P'Pa is requesting administrative rights to Grandfather's Sanctum, it read.

Buttons for accepting and declining the request hovered below the words. Sam thought about declining the request, but worried P'Pa might've swapped the text on the buttons. The possibility put Sam on edge after considering the mental game of chess at play. P'Pa had some control over his grandfather's Sanctum, but not everything, and certainly not what was required to execute their plan.

"I won't do it," Sam said. "Connect me to the internet. We'll reach out to someone about what's happened to your people. Maybe Princess can help."

P'Pa laughed, something Sam had never seen Crow do and then wished he'd witness once before he died. Her eyes came alive, her cheeks rounded, and their overall radiance relaxed Sam for a moment.

P'Pa crossed their arms and rested the sole of their left foot against the wall. "Grandfather hid the modifications from Princess for a reason. The outcome will be just as apocalyptic in her care as mine. At least my path carries a nobler purpose." P'Pa looked at their hands, the small but rough palms mimicking Crow's. "She doesn't know that you and I are both inputs for optimum functionality. Generating a signal to reach billions across the globe in real-time required quantum computing, something my movements across the circuits can accomplish. So in loving memory of my people, I'll dance and hold a festival called 'World's End.'"

"I'll stop you," Sam stated with confidence. He didn't know how, other than to deny administrative rights to the system. But Sam couldn't stay inside the virtual space forever. He needed to eat, sleep, use the bathroom, and procreate. He needed to stall until Neven arrived.

P'Pa smirked and brushed their hair away from their face. "You can't hurt me, Sam, but I can hurt you. The Sanctum is only operational because of me. If I turn it off, you'll die—"

"And so will your plan. You kill me and the system gets wiped."

P'Pa narrowed their eyes at Sam. Unfolding their arms, they emulated a phone with their hand, their thumb below their ear and their pinky finger near their lips. Sam heard a dial tone followed by a ringing.

"9-1-1 what's your emergency?"

In Crow's voice, using a panicked tone, P'Pa said, "Help! They're here."

"Ma'am, who's there?"

"Those people from the Magnolia. They followed me home! They're outside my house. Hurry!"

"Ma'am?"

"Get away from me! Ahh!"

P'Pa hung up.

Their acting deserved an award, but Sam didn't flinch. He knew Neven would be there soon, if he hadn't already pulled up. Police response times were impressive, but Neven drove the Challenger like a pro racer and had only been minutes away when P'Pa cut Sam's connection to him.

"And here they come," P'Pa said, raising their chin toward the sound of sirens.

Sam couldn't react with the same movements. He couldn't look in any direction. Spatial audio caused the sirens to wail to his left, toward the front door.

"Wait…what? How?" he exclaimed.

P'Pa shrugged. "I called them a while ago. You didn't notice? I used the emergency commercial line you tried to access. I played the recording just now. It's time-stamped. You didn't notice that, either, did you? Sam, you're not a very good Navigator."

Chapter 8

Sam viewed the road from the porch camera and a few others hidden among the Christmas decorations strung around the front of the house. Red and blue lights almost fooled Sam into thinking the cameras were installed inside traditional Christmas bulbs. But the lighting belonged to the police. The city's finest had already formed a barricade with multiple white four-door sedans and their guns.

Then he saw Neven squatting next to the Challenger's passenger side door with two black pistols in his hands, barrels up. He'd pulled the vehicle up onto the curb. Headlights and an illuminated instrument panel suggested the car was still running.

"I can send them away," P'Pa said.

"In exchange for killing everyone? No way!"

"So you'll just watch him die? Oh, I know, you're merely viewing the action through a lens—the kind of numbing consumption that's eroded people's brains over the years. Let's give you the personal experience your grandfather and I developed together."

P'Pa transitioned Sam to Neven against the Navigator's will. Sam's view shifted, blurring as it sped up and then gradually slowed until he saw through Neven's eyes, heard through his ears, and felt the world through his senses.

The police shouted warnings. "Throw your weapons down! Now! Get out from behind the vehicle! This is your final warning!"

Neven checked his left and right flanks between measured glances at the house's large mahogany front door. Sam's great grandfather had built the house in the early nineties and Sam's grandfather modified it decades later, building upon the existing architecture to further fortify the property, including the steel bars that covered the windows and the ladder of metal bolts securing the door.

"Don't go for it, Neven! You can't break it down!" Sam

shouted. He'd helped with the basic modifications, such as making and running various cables throughout the house, and watched his grandfather install the advanced ones that turned the home into a fortress.

"He can't hear you," P'Pa said. "But *they* can hear me."

"All units. Open fire!"

An unsynchronized series of muzzle flashes followed P'Pa's command.

Neven brought his hands to his head, the butt of the pistols against his temples, and tucked his chin into his chest. None of the shots passed through the bulletproof vehicle. A few deflected off the hood, roof, and trunk, prompting the police to call for ceasefire.

"There's eleven of them and one of me," Neven said to himself. He smirked. "Not exactly an even fight." He glanced at the house entrance again and added, "I'd feel better about storming the castle if those were double doors."

Sam looked for ways to communicate with Neven outside the usual channels P'Pa monitored. When the Star glanced at the porch again, Sam got an idea. He searched the local network for the wireless bulbs and then repeatedly turned the porch light on and off.

Neven raised a brow. Sam could tell that he counted the number of on-offs with each nod of his head. Getting Neven's attention wasn't enough. Sam had to get him to the porch, which meant getting past the police without being maimed.

The police shouted at him. "Come on out, buddy! Surrender!"

Sam searched Neven's peripheral vision and saw the floodlights at the corners of the house, mounted underneath the roof leading up to the second floor. He turned them on and partially blinded the police.

Neven hobbled around in place until he faced the Challenger. He looked at each of the streetlights on his side of the road. He pointed both pistols at the lamp on his left and fired.

One bullet destroyed the light, and the other ricocheted down at the police. One of them loudly grunted.

"Officer down!" multiple police officers shouted.

Neven didn't wait for them to return fire. He shifted to his right and shot at the other lamp for the same result, and further shrouded himself in darkness. Several more rounds into the same well rained bullets onto the nearby police vehicles.

"Fall back!" Sam heard the cries over the barrage.

The bullets destroyed the red and blue flashing lights and caused those who took cover behind them to scatter. Neven stopped when the lamp's metal housing had enough indentations to hinder accurate deflections. He shifted his weight to his right leg and executed the same maneuver on the left flank, using the curve of the streetlight's dome to drive the police back until he wore it out.

Sam knew he had to get Neven inside the house. He saw the front door's locks on the local network but didn't want to risk P'Pa overriding his control at the wrong time. He also didn't know how the Star could stop P'Pa once inside, but knew the residence could provide shelter from the police, even if it acted haunted.

The thought of haints gave Sam another idea. Starting from the left side of the house, Sam pulsed the Christmas lights in pairs, guiding Neven's eyes to a few red and green bulbs at the front door. He planned to do it again once Neven caught on and end with the lights above the porch. He'd cut the camera feeds then to blind P'Pa and unlock the front door once Neven reached it. The timing was critical.

Sam felt Neven take a deep breath and then close his eyes. He understood the enemy watched, and he learned the timing. Upon his exhale, Sam turned off the cameras and triggered the Christmas lights. He felt Neven dash toward the door, his step in sync with the pulsing bulbs. When he reached the porch, Sam disengaged each of the front door's bolts. Neven grabbed the handle, groaned, and crashed into the door without opening it.

Sam's heart raced. Or was it Neven's that beat rapidly? A mixture of his run and injury, combined with Sam's concern for the Star's well-being, caused Neven's vitals to fluctuate. Sam wondered what had happened. He didn't hear gunshots and didn't think the police would fire into the floodlights, especially after Neven took out the streetlights and reduced the wide area visibility.

Neven opened his eyes. He slumped to his knees and then scurried out of view of the driveway, hiding behind the porch rail and the bushes out front. He reached over his shoulder and pulled something out of his back. Sam heard it clatter against the wood after Neven threw it.

Sam turned the cameras back on and maximized the application window showing the front porch. Crow stood in the grass next to the Challenger. The rear passenger side door was ajar behind her. She seemed at war with herself, grabbing her right arm with her left hand to keep the dagger in its clutches at bay. Her body jerked left and right every time she took a step, and she slowly made her way onto the driveway.

"Crow! What are you doing?" Sam shouted into the void.

"Exactly what I want her to do," P'Pa responded.

"You…you're controlling her?" Sam searched the Sanctum for the feature.

"You won't find anything in there," P'Pa said. "Those body parts—the high-speed regenerative metal—belong to me. She, too, is an extension of me. I'd planned to use her as my physical body, had Grandfather not completed the Sanctum upgrades. And I'm willing to destroy her to accomplish my goal."

"*All units stand by*," P'Pa said over the radio and then spoke to Sam using Crow's voice. "You can stop this, Sam."

The authentication window came up again. *P'Pa is requesting administrative rights to Grandfather's Sanctum.*

When Sam didn't respond, P'Pa keyed the radio again, *"Female suspect is armed and dangerous. Shoot to kill."*

"No!" Sam shouted. He expected the same quick response from the police as before, but didn't hear gunfire. From the porch camera, he saw the police perplexed. Instead of shooting Crow, they exchanged glances.

"That's unfortunate," P'Pa said. "If only humans cared this much about the rest of the universe."

"I'm telling you, they don't know! We can tell them. They'll change."

P'Pa scoffed. "I perused humanity's history. I only saw change to killing efficiency and methods. Regardless, physical slaughter required willing people to execute. Biological warfare required willing people to develop. Psychological disorders required willing people to take root. Throughout history, humanity has developed hierarchical systems that created and encouraged those people. They won't change. Not for me and not for you. Here, let me show you."

P'Pa turned Crow toward the police. "Imagine I'm your government. I want you to grant me access to your grandfather's Sanctum."

"Please don't," Sam cried.

P'Pa continued, "So I created a hierarchy that put two unwilling forces against each other. Will those fine men and women lay down their lives to protect an innocent girl? Will the innocent girl slaughter them? Or will you grant me the rights I requested? I'll give you a hint, Sam: there are plenty of innocent people to manipulate.

"I'd manipulated you, too. Everything from leaking my false location at Magnolia to separating your team was designed to push you into divulging your location, which I intercepted mid-transmission. So thank you."

Sam choked. "What the fuck?"

"This is all your fault, Sam. Every bit because you are a reflection of humanity, and your same carelessness will cost billions more, their lives."

Sam searched the Sanctum for some way to cut P'Pa's access to the system or even the internet but saw nothing other than the acknowledge and decline buttons and the porch in front of an array of blurred camera feeds.

Crow stomped her left foot. Knives extended every two inches from underneath and around the bottom of her skirt, minus the two she'd used during the shootout, the one in her hand, and presumably, the one she'd thrown into Neven's back. They shimmered in the police cruiser's headlights, alerting them to danger.

"I won't let you win, P'Pa! I'll kill myself before I let you win!"

"You won't—"

Sam simultaneously turned on every device in the house, which caused everything to go out all at once—the lights, the cameras, and the connected appliances. That should've included the Sanctum, thus his life, but the system continued to operate, and Sam continued to breathe.

In the darkness, Sam only saw through Neven's eyes. He watched Crow from between the porch rail posts. Strobing police lights occasionally illuminated her red and blue, reflecting off the blades lining the bottom of her skirt.

"What happened?" Sam couldn't reach any other systems, confirming that he'd successfully tripped the breakers as planned. He wondered why the Sanctum didn't shut down, too.

A message populated the display.

Battery backup online.

Sam hadn't considered battery backup in his last-ditch effort to keep the system out of P'Pa's control. He'd only needed the system offline for a second, but the backup provided power and prevented disruptions; to the Sanctum at least.

A few lights came back on, their output dimmed. The camera feeds returned, too. Sam heard an engine start, followed by the distant hum of what he assumed to be a generator.

P'Pa's projection materialized in one camera's feed

again. They leaned against the study's entrance with arms folded and head facing the camera that watched them.

Sam didn't speak. He was out of ideas and out of time. Worse, he thought any additional actions he took would play into P'Pa's hands. He lost his team the physical battle on the road, failed Shades with the biological one at the Magnolia, and surrendered to the psychological games P'Pa played. For an extraterrestrial entity, P'Pa excelled more at being human than Sam did.

In the dead of silence, a familiar voice lifted Sam's spirits. "You did great hanging in there, Young Master."

Sam recognized Shades' voice. Then he saw the Star's lanky form overlapped with P'Pa's projection standing outside his grandfather's study.

Shades slowly removed his glasses, and then gradually opened his eyes to the brighter room. "If there's anything in this world I'd risk tainting my view of it for…it's you."

He pointed a gun at Sam's body and pulled the trigger. The muzzle flashes lasted less than a second. Sam's vital signs quickly plummeted. He was alive still, but he felt different from his first attempt to end his life. A world gradually slid off his digital shoulders, an out-of-body experience akin to a detached soul. He expected Crow to wander in, clad in the same darkness that slowly shrouded his vision, and ferry him to the other side. The thought made him smile. The events made P'Pa mad.

The sentient entity raised their voice for the first time, surpassing the loudest he'd ever heard Crow and the ugliest he'd ever seen her. Stretch-lines scarred her face as P'Pa screamed at Sam. "No! Grant me access now! Hurry! Hurry you…ignorant…degenerate…human…"

Villain

Chapter 1

*"I never understood why, in a world of man, I always
have to be the bigger one."*
"Please, have mercy."
"There you go again, asking the world of one man."
BANG!
BANG!
BEEP!
Beep-beep! Beep-beep!

I woke up in a cold sweat. My hand still felt and took the
shape of the Glock I'd fired in my dreams, its features imprinted into my pale and clammy palm. My index finger
twitched. The fear of pulling the trigger again prevented me
from curling it in, so I stared at it over the side of the bed.

Thank God it was only a dream. The alarm clock echoed
that reality.

*Good morning, citizen. Illegal activity detected during
REM sleep. Please adjust your diet to reduce stress and/or
anxiety.*

*Good morning, citizen. Illegal activity detected during
REM sleep. Please adjust your diet to reduce stress and/or
anxiety.*

A healthy breakfast wouldn't affect the world I detested
every morning, the same way dinner didn't appease the world
I saw after closing my eyes. Dreams, my one escape from
everything, had slowly devolved into nightmares that jostled
me back to the ugly reality that I was no one.

In a world where I can be anyone—be anything—a doctor, a teacher, a firefighter, an engineer, a professional of
some kind, I hesitated to be *someone*. Success required that I
lie down in a machine and give the government consent to
push knowledge straight into my brain.

The thought alone sent chills down my spine.

The scent of bacon lifted my spirit. I followed the savory trail down the stairs and into the kitchen. Jean-Baptiste removed the pork from the griddle and cracked two eggs over the seasoned plate. His pointed coat tails danced with him as he moved around the kitchen and hummed in concert with the cackling and sizzling of fresh ingredients. White, perfectly folded cuffs remained pristine after he flipped the vegetables in the pan.

Jean-Baptiste chose to be a butler in a home. The Program he gained made him a culinary chef, and he preferred to serve patrons in a quiet residence in the countryside instead of the large kitchens of restaurants in the city. Since anyone could become a butler, and many did, people often dined at establishments during large gatherings or on the butler's day off.

I greeted Mom and Dad with a nod. Dad sat at one end of the table, with Mom seated on his left. I sat in the chair next to Mom, and the fourth seat remained vacant. Jean-Baptiste never ate with us, but he knew how to set the table and delight us with combinations and variations of our favorites.

He placed a white-rimmed plate in front of me and waited for the smile he knew was coming. French toast, bacon, and eggs cooked over-hard looked mouthwatering. He added a few vegetables to the eggs and sandwiched them between a brioche bun.

I smiled. "Thank you."

"Mon ami," he replied with a bigger, more genuine grin.

With the last plate served, he disappeared behind the sliding doors separating the kitchen from the dining room.

"Good morning, son," Dad said after he set his glass of orange juice on the table. The liquid dripped from the long mustache hairs that curled at the corners of his mouth. Identical black strands populated his head. Not one stood out of place, since he shaved the sides and pushed back the long hairs on top using gel.

"Morning, Dad. Good morning, Mom."

Mom greeted me with a relaxed smile as the vapor from her coffee opened her nostrils. She was easily the woman pictured in stock photos of frames sitting on textile store shelves, either with arms around their kids or behind their back while on a white beach somewhere. Red hair matched the buds in the garden out front, and she often wore sundresses that fluttered from the cool breezes regularly sweeping through the open doors of the house.

She worked from home as a paralegal assistant. The Program she inherited made her a master at word-processing applications and all the formatting styles required to generate flawless documents. She loved to sit and stand at the desk in front of the office window overlooking the scenic backdrop.

Dad stared at me from across the table. "Have you picked a Program yet? There's a lottery for a doctor."

His voice carried genuine disappointment, and for good reason, from his perspective. I hadn't chosen a Program yet, and he knew that.

Programs were career knowledge that the government downloaded to human memory, replacing time spent at college, but not the cost. The wealthy paid that upfront, while others paid it over the life of their career. Dad refused to pay for anything he deemed unprofessional, such as non-collared jobs. My profession had to be part of an organization or a corporation, despite the small, independent business he owned and operated.

"Not yet," I said. The sight of blood made me nauseous. No amount of knowledge could change that.

Dad chewed with his mouth open before he caught himself in the act. He swallowed quickly. "You gotta pick something before you're too old for the process. Old geezers like me—we were lucky. Our brains didn't melt. There are plenty of folk out there who weren't so fortunate, and many more who'd love to be sitting in your seat right now with the same opportunities you have."

Dad chose to be an architect. He designed and built most of the homes in our area. The neighbors paid him handsomely for his craftsmanship. He could've been anyone, but Programs only contained the knowledge, history, and mechanics of specific professions, and not the passion some people had and then used to take their career further.

What started as an equal opportunity for everyone quickly divided the workforce into tiers. Some professional fields became saturated with workers, while other positions were difficult to fill. The brain's processing power, an individual's physical capability, and similarly limiting traits required for top tier Programs, such as doctors, scientists, and athletes, further unbalanced the job market.

The aptitude test I took several months ago said *I* could be anyone, which didn't apply to everyone. *People* limited themselves. Not me. *I* chose to be nobody.

Mom reached across the table and touched my hand. "Try something. You might like it."

"We can afford a couple of trial Programs." Dad spoke above the clatter of his knife as he cut through a waffle. "Society requires you to be a part of it. If you don't pick something, it'll choose for you." He stabbed the waffle with his fork and held it inches from his mouth. "Right now, there's a shortage of peacekeepers at the city wall. Trust me, you don't want to go there."

Chapter 2

"M'lord, I present to thee, thy suitresses…The gentle-woman from the medical district, Ms. Family Doctor. The gentlewoman from the legal district, Ms. Criminal Lawyer. The gentlewoman from the business sector, Ms. Company CEO."

"My son, these are the finest Programs in all the land. Choose quickly, as the day of your coronation approaches. The realm's future depends on your decision."

"My son…"

"Mr. Goodwater. Excuse me, Mr. Goodwater?"

I blinked several times until the man behind the counter came into focus. When he said my name again, brown strands from his bowl haircut brushed against his raised brows. He stared at me for a moment before he lowered his eyes to the screen.

"Based on your aptitude test, you qualify for quite a few Programs. Your physical attributes are a little low and your attention span varies." He looked up at me again, a sharper turn of the neck. "I can put together a few options for you. Is there anything specific that you're interested in?"

I shook my head. Not that I didn't want to work. Nothing appealed to me. The world rushed me to make a lifelong decision by throwing Programs at my feet like suitresses. They paraded each one in front of me and expected me to court them for a time. But I wasn't interested in the finest the king-dom offered. I flipped through the binder of Programs like I was scanning the guests for the unique commoner that didn't belong.

But Dad wouldn't pay for anything less than the high bar he'd set. The document he'd sent to the Program Office high-lighted all the approved options in green and grayed out the rest. I literally couldn't afford to choose my future, and the societal structure made getting a job outside the system impossible.

The man behind the counter didn't wait for my indecision. He tapped away at the keyboard before printing five three-inch long and rectangular stickers. He placed each on the granite countertop in front of me. "Here, I picked some professions based on your high school transcript. After adhering one to the back of your neck, you'll have about a week to access its knowledge. Good luck."

He didn't wait for me to sift through or acknowledge the options, either. He pushed the stack closer to me, over the groove the sliding screen traversed, and pulled the panel shut.

Each sticker contained a trial Program. I peeled one apart to reveal the adhesive and applied it to the back of my neck. It identified me as a temporary trainee and transmitted limited information to my brain for the chosen position. A career trainee would've been a special option that moved the timeframe limitation from a week to a few months, the maximum. The Programs Office collected data from those users and bolstered information for the career field.

I started with a marketing director position for a chain supermarket. The first day ended with two ads scheduled to run on public transportation systems. I knew exactly what garnered the attention of the surrounding community and expertly crafted a message that would reach them.

After a couple of days, I switched to a political office assistant. I spent most of my time following a woman without an agenda. There were no changes for her to propose or implement, but the people still needed someone to lead.

I left the office position and moved to a managerial role at a textile store. Every day felt the same. Arranging product for specific seasons, locales, and shoppers had become invariable. With my predecessors having gained knowledge from a Program, they'd already explored unique arrangements, and statistical data provided the ensemble that sold the best. I was just another cog in the machine, necessary for it to operate, but with no variability in teeth to determine how well it'd run.

One evening, after peeling the managerial Program sticker from my neck and seeing my ad running on displays at a bus stop, I walked home instead of using public transit. I was no closer to picking a career than when I'd started the trial Programs. If anything, the experience had pushed me further away.

What was I going to tell Dad? He only ever asked about my career path during breakfast, so I had all night to think about my response.

I thrust my hands into my jacket pockets and imagined kicking a can down the sidewalk like a bored teen in older movies, but the only trash on the street were those without a career. That's what Dad would say. That's what he was going to say. And then I wondered if the father of the man walking toward me thought the same of him.

He promenaded down the middle of the sidewalk. I couldn't see the back of his neck, so I didn't know if he was a professional, a trainee, or neither. He didn't wear a uniform or carry professional gear. He walked with his hands buried in his pant pockets. A lightweight, dark-blue jacket deflected the evening breeze. I thought we'd pass each other with a nod of the head, but he stopped two feet in front of me.

"Hey, kid. You want to buy a Program?"

He spoke like a professional salesman, not like the punk or thug selling illegal drugs in documentaries. A relaxed facial expression suggested he hadn't asked and gotten rejected by multiple people before seeing me. Lively eyes stood out underneath the streetlamp that just flickered on.

"No, thanks." I shrugged.

He stepped aside, turned to face me, and waited for me to walk by before he said, "Do you know why you feel a sense of want?"

I took another step and stopped. *Was* he a salesman? Did his Program teach him how to reach people using words? I'd never heard of a salesman selling Programs and was certain that doing so was illegal.

He continued. "Because your actions aren't fulfilling." He paused, as if waiting for his words to settle into my heart and take effect.

I felt his stare. It lifted the hairs on the back of my neck, not from fear, but from excitement.

He said, "Doctors are tired of delivering babies and tending to the common cold because safety engineers prevented workplace accidents requiring medical attention. And those engineers feel dissatisfied because everyone knows how to do their job safely. Systems engineers designed better systems and there's little room for innovation. Everything forms a systematic diagram of mitigations where each profession is the child of a successful parent, and, in turn, becomes the successful parent of another child. A predictable tree where the leaves replace each other, never growing or falling."

I turned around. His words made sense, but I didn't understand what any of it had to do with me and the Program he was selling. Reverse psychology? Telling me the system was boring, so I'd want to join it—maybe believe I can change it? Unless the Program he was selling placed me at the top, I'd just be another leaf on that tree.

He walked up to me at the same casual pace as before. No rush or other place to be. "This city is lacking the one profession that could make it feel alive again."

He waited for me to ask. "And what's that?"

"A villain."

Questions sat on my tongue, but I said nothing. The man enjoyed dramatic statements and pause, so I waited for him to elaborate on this villain profession. But I had to play along. My body language had to show interest. I *was* interested.

His theatrics increased, involving his hands, facial expressions, and body into his show. "Blow up a building and watch the conflagration spread from branch to branch. Doctors will tend to the wounded, prompting safety engineers to recommend preventative measures that systems engineers will have to design." He raised both hands above his head like a devoted follower of some cult. "One match set the forest ablaze, and all the leaves changed." He lowered his arms, one down to his side and the other pointing at me. "You can be that match."

I took a step back, unable to refute his claims. The logic seemed sound. "Why don't you do it then?"

He thrust his hands into the jacket pockets instead of the slacks. "I already have a profession as a software engineer. Re-programming is too expensive and dangerous at my age. I wrote the villain Program because I, too, felt unfulfilled."

His words almost had me convinced. Melancholy almost made me susceptible. I balled my fists. "No way. I turn that on, and the government will find me. Prison isn't the fulfilling life I'm looking for."

He laughed. "Don't underestimate a villain, kid. This Program will teach you everything you need to evade law enforcement. If they try to catch you, just peel it off. It's not any different from the ones you've been sampling all week."

Peel it off? That sounded like throwing drugs out of the window when the red and blue lights flashed in the rearview mirror. I always dreamed of the fantastical and the movies they came from, but the consequences for those actions in cinema were nothing like reality.

"How do you know I've been sampling programs?"

He pointed to the back of his neck. "No imprinted code. And you walk down the same boring street every evening with an unmistakable sullen expression." After turning his mockery frown upside down, he pulled an envelope from inside his jacket and twirled it in his hands. "It's a trial Program. Try it and then toss it if you're unsatisfied. If you get caught, say the Programs Office gave it to you along with the others. Let someone else take the fall like a true villain. But you won't be disappointed. In fact, you may come to like it."

Chapter 3

"You think you're doing something for society? Do you think you're making a difference?"

"I'm making the same difference as you. A cape has a collar, too..."

Beep-beep! Beep-beep!

The alarm woke me. Automated blinds slowly let sunlight into my room. The rays felt brighter than usual, the cost of staying up all night. I shielded my eyes with my arm and then the comforter.

"Close the blinds," I commanded.

Good morning, citizen. An analysis of your sleep cycle suggests insufficient rest for proper recovery.

Good morning, citizen. An analysis of your sleep cycle suggests insufficient rest for proper recovery.

Evil never slept. That's what schools taught prior generations. Everyone had to do their part and remain vigilant because the bad guys never rested. Nobody ever explained the enemy. What were they up to all night? The videos I watched showed people wanting the same things I did—food, water, and shelter. When the institutions didn't provide them with a path to their goal, they created their own.

The scent of crepes led me down the stairs. I skipped a few of the steps and slowed when my descent was visible from the dining room table. A fresh plate waited for me. I saw the added color of fruits from the landing. Jean-Baptiste filled a small ramekin with ketchup and placed it next to the breakfast potatoes. He poured me a glass of apple juice.

"Mon ami." He greeted my smile.

"Good morning, Jean-Baptiste." I placed the white napkin in my lap as he disappeared behind the kitchen's sliding door. "Good morning, Dad. Where's Mom?" She and Dad always beat me to the table. I couldn't remember the last time, if ever, that she missed breakfast. There was no evidence of her place setting, either.

Dad's fork clanked against his plate. "She's working. Some idiots vandalized Main Street last night. They broke into the local shops and threw products all over the street. Your mom's been up since five this morning working on insurance documents."

I leaned back in my seat and controlled the grin on my face using a fork full of potatoes dipped in ketchup. I imagined the anarchy the news would describe. The bird's-eye view in my head varied significantly from the ground view Dad described. He didn't allow electronic devices at the table, which meant I had to tune into the news after breakfast.

"Where were you last night?" He asked.

"Not there. I didn't do that!" I said with my mouth full of potatoes.

Dad stared at me like I had 'stupid' written all over my face.

I swallowed the last of the potatoes without chewing. In a lower tone than normal, I said, "Working. With an accounting firm. My clients are overseas, so my shifts are later because of the time difference."

Last night was a blur. Adrenaline had kept me up late. At some point, exhaustion knocked me out.

"Well, be careful out there. Goddamn city is turning into a dump."

"Yes, sir." I almost saluted him.

Mom walked into the dining room. Despite the early morning, she'd found the time to tuck a soft blue blouse into white dress pants. A couple of bracelets jingled around her wrists as she pushed a few strands of hair away from her face. Pink slippers clapped beneath her feet until she sat at the table.

She all but whispered, "Good morning."

"Is everything okay?" Dad asked.

Mom shook her head. "It's a mess. Hundreds of thousands of dollars in property and merchandise damages, and the insurance companies won't cover any of it." She grabbed a hard-boiled egg off dad's plate and almost swallowed it whole. Then she chased it with half a glass of his water. "Sorry. I've been up all morning writing letters to people who lost everything just to tell them they've lost…everything." Mom leaned her forehead against her clasped hands.

Dad summoned Jean-Baptiste. The butler opened the door adjoining the rooms, saw Mom, and immediately went to work in the kitchen.

"And insurance won't cover it?" Dad asked, checking the time on his watch.

"No. Insurance only covers natural disasters. Theft and vandalism and even destruction of property are things of the past. I've never written these letters before. They're…heartbreaking."

Dad slid his chair back and stood. "I'm heading into the office. Maybe there's a chance we get the contract to rebuild."

Mom lowered her hands and raised wide blue eyes at Dad. "These people lost everything and you're looking for the next contract?"

"I haven't built anything in years. Routine maintenance on fences, gutters, and air conditioning units is putting food on the table. A city contract will—"

Mom hid her face under the fold of her interlocked hands. Dad went to kiss her on the forehead, but she waved him off. Disgruntled, he stormed through the living room and out the front door. Jean-Baptiste slid the kitchen door open with a plate in hand, but Mom had also left the table.

***

I fell back onto my bed. A light-gray ceiling stared at me. "Idiot," I whispered to myself.

I sat up and turned on the television. A projection illuminated the wall space above my dresser. Despite the natural light flooding the room, the video was bright and crisp, better than the high-definition televisions of old that took up wall and counter space.

The news reported last night's events. Recent developments had nothing to do with apprehending the villain. It had everything to do with changing the institutions that allowed such a cowardly act.

I laughed at the cowardice of belittling someone from behind the safety of those institutions.

The streets were alive, bustling with traffic from owners, passersby, responders, and organizations I'd never seen before. From the aerial view, people resembled worker ants surrounding the crumbs someone had left behind. They operated in a variety of groups and colors. Each one served a different purpose. I'd never seen so many people moving to and from without getting in each other's way.

When the camera switched to the street view, I saw through the displeasure on people's faces. They had to have been smiling on the inside. Responding to an actual event had to have been exhilarating. That man was right. The world needed chaos. The world required a villain.

A smart one. I wasn't wearing the villain Program during breakfast this morning. Dad's question about my whereabouts last night caught me off guard. He'd never asked that before, and the knowledge to respond accordingly was not with me.

Real Programs committed information to memory. The human brain accessed temporary Programs like external storage. Some people absorbed the knowledge anyway, as if they'd researched the content themselves, but retention depended on their ability to learn.

I held the villain Program sticker in my hand. Wearing it meant exposing its barcode to the world. If any entry or street system scanned it, that'd be the end of me. Dad would ship me off to the other side of the wall if the government didn't. Avoiding that was easy. All I had to do was throw it away. The portable incinerator sat ten feet in front of me, under the desk. But I couldn't discard the Program. The knowledge I'd gleaned, which would've been more if I wasn't having so much fun, seemed unique. I'd viewed the world from a new perspective, and I couldn't look away.

Chapter 4

"You've changed, Son."
"No, I haven't. I changed the world around me."
Beep-beep! Beep-beep!

I opened my eyes, mechanic-like, as if an actuator pulled the lids back when the alarm sounded. The light-gray ceiling resembled an overcast sky. Then I heard the automated blinds humming as they let the morning sunlight into the room.

Good morning, citizen. A dream analysis revealed illegal activity. Please adjust your diet to reduce stress and/or anxiety.
Good morning, citizen. A dream analysis revealed illegal activity. Please adjust your diet to reduce stress and/or anxiety.

"If you can determine illegal activity in my dreams, wake me before the nightmare starts," I said aloud. It didn't understand me. The alarm clock was a smart but dumb robot doubling as a pillow. The Programs Office designed it to exchange information with our brains during sleep and help condition us for a Program in the future.

My body ached like the morning after a workout. The scent of toast hadn't convinced me to get up. Not yet. Avocado, cream cheese, and jam supplemented the call to arms. I rolled out of bed, completed my morning routine, and headed downstairs.

Halfway down the second flight, I saw someone sitting in the fourth seat, slightly rotated to face mine. A man with a brown buzz cut sat with legs crossed. He drank coffee from one of our blue ceramic mugs. His movements caused his toned arms to stretch the white shirt he wore.

After he saw me, he never looked away. His eyes followed me from the stairs to the table. He watched me sit down, thank Jean-Baptiste for breakfast, and place the napkin in my lap.

I looked at Mom and Dad. They sat tight-lipped, not even glancing my way.

The man greeted me instead. "Good morning, Daniel. I'm Detective John Howard. How are you?"

"Good." I sipped the apple juice while he stared at me. "Mom. Dad. What's going on?"

Dad nodded at the man. "Listen to what he has to say, Son."

Detective Howard placed the mug on the table. Steam rose from it. "I'm investigating the recent disturbances around town. I'm sure you've heard about them."

"And you think I did it?" I raised my voice and pointed at my chest.

"Did you do it?" he raised his voice the same way.

An awkward silence grew between us. His resolute green eyes made me uncomfortable.

He laughed. "Don't be alarmed, Daniel. I'm simply interviewing people who've recently acquired a permanent or temporary program. Whatever skills the culprit—"

Villain... I corrected to myself.

"—employed aren't commonplace."

"So you're interviewing citizens? Not someone knocking on the city walls?"

He narrowed one eye and tilted his head to that side. "Security at the perimeter is tight. Are you suggesting that a culprit broke through, ran one hundred and sixty-two miles to the town center, and trashed a couple of stores?"

I settled down. My shoulders relaxed. Steady hands spread jam over my toast. "It was Main Street, right? Figured something like that was important to the government they hated. Nostalgia and whatnot."

He laughed. "You aren't lying, but I think the government is more interested in the bank the culprit broke into and the money they littered the streets with after; breaking and entering, explosives, hacking, and the list goes on. The skills employed by the culprit are beyond those on the other side of the wall."

He repeatedly said 'culprit', as if he knew doing so irritated me. Displeasure for the word could've been written all over my face. No, the Program taught me how to control words, emotions, and body language. I regained composure because I wore it.

"History sides with the underestimated," I said.

He clapped several times and then placed his hands in his lap. "You're a bright young man. Maybe you'd be interested in trying out a detective Program. It's been a long time since the department has faced something like this. Your unique view of the world could be valuable. We all have investigation-related Programs, but knowledge can't replace passion or…experience."

I glanced at him. He'd never taken his eyes off me. Not to think, blink, or observe the surroundings. "Sorry, I'm running an accountant program right now."

"I know."

Detective Howard grabbed the coffee mug without looking. Not even the steam rising from its contents caused him to blink. His eyes had to be burning.

"I checked the logs and the camera footage where you work. No recorded absences."

Of course not. I'd captured the video of me entering and leaving and then set it up to replace the actual footage every night, plus or minus five minutes, because nobody's always on time. Despite the efficiencies of society, human flaws prevailed. That trick might not work again, though.

I knew someone wouldn't have gone inside the building where I worked. That would've been a waste of time because nights out on the town were days to weeks apart. They'd have to know my schedule to catch me ditching work. I also thought there'd be too many applicable suspects for someone to visit every location, but there one sat in our dining room.

Detective Howard reached into his shirt pocket and pulled out a dark blue card with white lettering. "If you change your mind." He placed it on the corner of the table between us. "Mr. and Mrs. Goodwater, thank you for breakfast. Compliments to the chef." Then he nodded at me. "Daniel."

Dad escorted him to the door, where he put on his coat, winked at me one more time, and then left.

* * *

Detective Howard mocked me. That man clearly tried to get under my skin. He had nothing on me except a perfect alibi. No evidence. No clues. Nothing. And why was a detective assigned to the case? I expected the police to investigate. They used to direct traffic at school crossings and church exits. Then engineers designed cars that capped their speed around school zones and blind turns. So the police escorted hearses instead and directed traffic at community events. Their positions were on the verge of obsolescence. So why did we have a detective? What did they do all day?

I turned on the television to watch news about the bank heist. The reporters misunderstood the intent entirely. The villain had robbed no one. They gave back to the people what belonged to them. Took it from a steel cage and released it into nature.

The news shared footage of the villain to garner help from the public on identifying him. From the perspective of the bank's cameras, no one could identify any of the gear he carried. The mask he wore had been handmade, forged from an old motorcycle helmet and partially covered by a thick fabric. Antennas connected to the sides of the helmet poked out of the hood like a demon's grotesque ears. A large collar wrapped around the back of his neck and ran under spray-painted shoulder pads. Its long cape helped hide his physique.

He wore a black long sleeve shirt under the extended chest of the shoulder pads. Their girth made lowering his arms flat against his sides difficult and caused him to walk into rooms at a slight angle. His swift stride looked cool from my perspective and from the comments attached to the video stream.

The cameras watched him set hockey puck-sized charges against the door frames and arm them like a rotary timer. Each explosion created a brief burst of light in the dimly lit building. Lines where the glass of the doors had cracked spread from the handles.

The news explained how a silent alarm triggered, but authorities never received the transmission because someone scrambled the signal. A fail-over to the hardline didn't activate because spoofed communications didn't tamper with or disrupt the system's hardware.

When the villain reached the vault, he ran a cable from the vambrace on his arm to a panel that controlled the massive door. Within minutes, he spun the spokes like the helm of a pirate ship and opened the steel chamber. He put one foot inside and then turned to the camera. It couldn't capture his grin.

The villain clothed himself from head to toe in varying shades of black. Nobody could trace his apparel back to an origin. He'd picked some of it off the shelves of ransacked Main Street stores. The villain then had protected his identity by wrapping a window curtain around his head and upper body like a sash. He upgraded to the suit since then.

The news called the villain a culprit, too, choosing to stick with the narrative Detective Howard used. They must've all been bored, sitting around the table telling stories of the on-time trains and the woman who'd never been late in ten years. I gave them, and the Detective, purpose. The world, I can change, but him—I must get rid of him.

Chapter 5

"Today marks the one-year anniversary of our very own villain! His selfless efforts and sacrifice changed society. For the longest, we'd been walking down a dark road. You dangled a lantern in front of us and led us to this day. You're my hero—our hero!"

"V! V! V!"

I thought the clock read 3 AM when I woke up, but the soft yellow LEDs were dormant and the sunlight peeking in from behind the blinds begged to differ. Maybe I slept through the alarm, but that seemed impossible. It would've loudly rung in my room, digital surround sound technology mapping and confining it to those four walls, until I opened my eyes.

"Blinds," I commanded. No response. Nothing moved. An eerie stillness and an unusual silence woke me. I crawled out of bed and staggered into the bathroom. The mirror display didn't come on. It reflected my countenance, but didn't overlay the weather, the day's agenda, or general announcements. The faucet water ran icy cold, and my face wasn't ready for that. I didn't think my body would be either, so I skipped the shower.

For the first time in a long while, the scent of vacuumed carpet accompanied me down the stairs instead of the aroma of a home-cooked breakfast from Jean-Baptiste. Mom and Dad sat at the table. Two blueberry bagels and a ramekin of cream cheese waited for me.

"Good…morning…" I wasn't sure it was a good morning. Neither of them smiled. Dad's face always teetered between satisfied and grumpy, and recently, Mom's pleasantry deviated from the same radiance of the morning glow, and the LED overhead fixtures, wall sconces, and scattered lamps didn't contribute their artificial daylight.

I picked up the knife and fork neatly placed on either side of my plate. The bagel wasn't toasted, and the cream cheese reached room temperature. I looked up at Jean-Baptiste, who stood in the sliding door's path and shook his head. He pointed at the kitchen appliances with his arm. None of them operated. Steam didn't rise from the coffeepot, the pans didn't sizzle, and none of the indicators for a hot stove had turned red.

"Did we lose power?" I innocently asked, knowing full well that I'd contributed to the silent chaos. Society's faith in the steady power grid slowly retired battery-powered devices. A few emergency flashlights required hand-cranking to operate, and the occasional solar-powered watch ticked along.

"Since 7 AM," Mom said.

Right on time. I'd considered ten past the hour so Mom could at least get coffee, but my alarm rang at seven in the morning. I needed to wake up ignorant and with the exhaustion of oversleeping in case Detective Howard visited. He hadn't shown up. Yet.

We didn't have local backup power, like generators. Instead of integrating solar panels into home roofs, the government opted for multiple solar farm stations across the city. That minimized the overall cost of installation and maintenance. Overlapping power distribution among the stations eliminated single-point-of-failure concerns. Nobody expected *all* the stations to fail at once.

Mom pulled her hair back into a ponytail. "I can't work. I can't do anything."

Dad swallowed the last piece of bread. "Nobody can, Dear."

I silently apologized to her. The idea behind the villain was to give people purpose. I gave her that, but felt the villain was smalltime. My actions didn't affect enough people. I recently watched the day drag on in the eyes of unaffected citizens as I walked by them in the streets. They needed saving, too.

I excused myself from the breakfast table and walked outside to see how much their eyes had changed. I almost didn't recognize my neighbors. They'd fired up a grill on their lawn and helped others cook the frozen meats and vegetables before they spoiled. Jean-Baptiste had escaped the dreary kitchen and helped, meeting and exchanging ideas with other chefs. One neighbor gathered the nearby children and conducted exercises in the yard. Another washed their car and sporadically sprayed those kids. I'd never seen so many people in the neighborhood outside at once. And then I saw someone who didn't belong.

Detective Howard pulled up in a black sedan and parked a foot away from our mailbox. Stepping out of the car, he waved at me like we were friends. His ever-present grin trolled me.

"Morning, Daniel." He walked up three of the four wooden steps leading to my front door and stopped.

"Detective Howard." I shook his hand.

He lowered the hand into his pocket, same as the other, and half-turned toward the street, leaning his hip against the white rail of the stairs. He nodded at the neighbors. "Compliments of our culprit?"

I exhaled like a smoker. "You gonna blame everything on that person?"

Detective Howard shrugged. "Almost a decade of peace and you think the string of events are coincidence?"

Investigators in the past connected villains to the families and institutions they disrupted. Disgruntled employees attacked their workplaces, and love, in its many forms, tore friends and families apart. I had no connection to anything, and I executed the string of events he spoke of on random days to avoid a discernible pattern.

Detective Howard sighed. "I'd hoped that visiting all the potential suspects would've scared the culprit. Either they'd make a mistake or stop. Perhaps I was mistaken, or maybe the culprit felt obligated to continue because stopping after I visited would've narrowed my list of suspects. The thing is, *continuing* narrowed my list of suspects." He turned his head and raised his eyes to me. Green irises rivaled the lawn. "I only visited a handful of people. Interviews with a couple of them suggested ignorance in the professional areas the culprit has shown knowledge of so far. I asked them to get permanent Programs. Another act by the culprit would then eliminate them as suspects. The others, including you, had temporary programs. One of them selected a permanent Program last week, so I crossed them off the list."

I laughed, a bit of disbelief in my voice. "You still think the culprit is running a Program?"

"I *know* they're running a Program. The diversity of their targets made that obvious." Detective Howard looked at the neighbors on my right. He stared at the sizzling steak. "The knowledge required to infiltrate that many systems—banks, schools, data centers—is difficult to come by. Engineers designed layers of security to require multiple disciplines, and inter-disciplinary engineering is not a Program."

I shrugged. "What about career Programs? Someone could've learned multiple professions."

"I checked everyone's records. Very few tried one engineering discipline, never mind several."

"And what about Main Street? Did that require engineering knowledge?"

He glanced at me with a crooked smile. "Pfft, the first night was childish. An excitement for the rare knowledge they'd gained. An adrenaline rush they then wanted to experience again."

"Is harassing me something you wanted to experience again, Detective?"

His smile faded, and the sinister grin returned. "That's harsh, Daniel. I thought we'd become friends. After all, you're my number one suspect."

"Me?"

"You've tried more than a few temporary Programs, which are expensive. Your family's finances support that decision. A man like you didn't need the cash from the bank heist, so you stole from the rich to give to the poor. Your childish idealism supports that theory." He continued before I could object. "Combined with the dreams you've been having, I see a man who wanted to change society. And he did, but his new world wasn't large enough, so he expanded.

"Now that man is wondering how a detective gained access to dream logs without a warrant. But he can't ask that because why would an innocent young man who hasn't tried investigative-relevant programs know about those legal intricacies? Programs led humanity down a narrow intellectual path, so it's not exactly common knowledge anymore. But the Program he—the culprit—is running gave him the textbook definition of the laws, but not the experience of navigating around those laws with truth."

He pulled his hands out of his pockets, grabbed the rail as he took one step onto the same level as me. "You knew who had access to your dream logs. You knew it'd separate you from the others, but your inexperience convinced you I was actually a detective without access to dream logs, and that petty crimes, such as remotely triggering school fire alarms, could lead me astray.

"Let me reintroduce myself, Daniel. I'm Special Agent Jones of the Psychological Investigation Division, PID. The knowledge granted by Programs can overwhelm or give people god complex in their professional field, and our mission is to find them before they disrupt society. You slipped through the cracks because you don't have a permanent Program. We've never experienced a fallout like you."

I laughed. I laughed long and loud and hard. My stomach ached and tears filled my eyes. I grabbed onto the porch rail for support. "That's impressive, *Special Agent*. I'm glad to see that my actions inspired you."

He crossed his arms. The grin faded with the color on his face. "You? Inspire me?"

I stood straight. "Did you think you got here all by yourself? That you were clever? I led you here. I carefully tightened and loosened every bolt of this wonderful contraption." Tapping my chest hard startled him. "*I* gave you purpose! I'm not a culprit. I'm a villain, and these series of events have been part of my master plan to give people…purpose." I wore a grin that pushed Jones down one step and then extended both arms toward him. "Now, arrest me. We need a trial to give a jury purpose. The judge will have a genuine case in almost a decade. Radio the police so they can use their lights and sirens for something other than a funeral procession. Call Channel 6. They haven't had breaking news in ages. Let's tell the people what I am, so they can see that the world I revealed is far better than the one pulled over their eyes.

"You're right, Special Agent Jones. Programs have led humanity down a narrow intellectual path, and their implementation has also sapped the life out of society. So let's give activists something to fight for. Oh, the markets will thrive from all the signs protesters will make. The police will need physical barriers to protect institutions from rioters. Accountants will process sales figures that haven't changed in years. Criminal analysts will try to understand me. There'll be copycat villains. People will challenge prior convictions related to Programs. The citizens will have found *some* meaning in life!" I panted. The last few words used up the rest of my breath. My cheeks hurt from laughing and smiling. My heart hurt too after I heard Dad.

"You've changed, Son," he said, his voice crisp and clear.

I grinned and lowered my tone. "No, I haven't. I changed the world around me. I put on a collar and became somebody."

Chapter 6

"You've become a fine man and a successful culprit."
"Thanks, Dad. But I'm not a culprit. I'm a villain."
"You're my son. I'm proud of you, Son. I'm proud of—I'm—"

"…disappointed in you, Son."

The words cut deep. I'd achieved something nobody else had, and it still wasn't enough. The bar wasn't too high; it was impossible to reach. An intangible goal that I could feel, but never grab. I stood my ground despite the massive emotional gash from being verbally stabbed in the back.

I didn't know what to say. The Program didn't teach me quick wit. The grandiose things I'd said before, I learned from the villains I watched on television, the ones who were cooler than the heroes trying to stop them. But there were no heroes in front of me, so I felt those words were unnecessary.

I was thinking about it too hard. The best response should be natural and from the heart. I half turned, leaned my back against the porch rail, faced the grilling neighbors, and captured both Dad and Jones in my peripheral vision.

"I guess some feeling is better than the nothing you've shown all my life," I said.

The words triggered Dad's rage. He lunged at me, shoved me back against the rail after I'd pushed off, and then spun me around. "Get this stupid thing off!"

He went for the Program on the back of my neck. I struggled, forcing him to use both hands to hold me down instead.

"No. No! You gave me nothing! So you don't get to take anything away from me. This is mine! Mine!" Our struggle drew attention from the neighbors. I saw them here and there as Dad wrestled with me against the rail. "Get your hands off me!"

"You gonna just stand there, Detective? Help me!" Dad shouted.

I broke free of his hold and interlocked both of my hands around the back of my neck.

Jones hesitated. I read the look in his eyes. He wondered if my struggle was a ruse—if they'd be playing into my hands. Earlier, I'd demanded that he arrest me. The fear of giving me what I wanted shackled him for a few more moments. Then he grabbed my arm and tried to pry my fingers loose.

"You scared of a kid?" Dad asked.

"We're dealing with an intelligent culprit, Mr. Goodwater. The safety of the public is always my first concern."

Alas, Dad's muscular arms pinned me down, and Jones pried my fingers apart. I felt the adhesive of a Program pulled from my skin.

Dad tried to rip the membrane texture in half, but engineers designed it to be resilient. "Stupid thing. Stupid boy!"

With arms freed, I threw an elbow into Dad's face. It dug deeper than I'd expected his hard face to allow. Then I turned around and punched him in the nose. That was the first time I ever hit him. He never once touched me, which meant that I drew first blood.

Jones hit me in the back with a taser. I didn't have the rubber vest to protect me. The surge caused unwanted movement—twitching of the fingers, neck, and knees. A second activation dropped me to the ground.

***

In the courtroom, the presiding judge looked at me above the rim of her glasses, glancing down through the frames when reading. "For the charges of grand larceny, grand arson, racketeering, destruction of property, gross negligence…"

I smiled for the cameras. Not as wide as I'd hoped. I felt strong, but I was still just a man. Dad's words and Mom's absence sought to break me. I continued to weather that storm in an orange jumpsuit with shackles and chains around my wrists and ankles.

"…the defendant is hereby sentenced to service at the wall until a time when service at the wall is no longer required or the defendant is deceased. Does the defendant have any objections to their sentence?"

I stared at the judge. "Do you have any objections to your ruling? Feels good, doesn't it? To sit up there and command the room with an actual villain, judged by the lives he hasn't yet affected. Where did you find these rats? What holes haven't I reached?"

The judge slammed the gavel. "Does the defendant have any *intelligent* objections?"

"You cast me in a dark light but clothed me in orange." I grinned and made eye contact with the judge. "You're sending the message that the sun will rise again some day." I had weeks to come up with that line.

"You're a lost case, Mr. Goodwater. If I had it my way, I'd lock you up and throw away the key, but this was the sentence the system determined based on the crimes you've committed."

"The system has failed you, your honor."

***

News anchors spoke of the wall as if it were some scary dimension, and the judge said it'd change me. The wall looked like every other building. Taller and blander were the only actual differences.

Jones waited for me at one entrance, arms folded. "Good morning, Daniel." He grinned as we drew closer. "Don't look surprised. You knew I'd be here. You learned a lot from that trial Program." He blocked the path. The four officers escorting me knew his rank and respected it, even though he didn't wear it. "Locking you away would've been a better option, but incarceration is a thing of the past. I took the liberty of making sure nobody issues you a weapon. I also ensured there wouldn't be a sliver of orange in your uniform." Jones walked up and stood closer, hands in his pockets, as usual. "The sun will not be rising in there."

I looked down past the chained cuffs and at the puke gray slacks I wore. A short-sleeved polo exposed my arms to the winter that was coming. I met Jones' gaze. "I just wanted to make Dad proud. If you ever have kids, Special Agent, show them love." I waited for him to nod and perhaps think the judge's motherly words had somehow reached me. Then I added, "And give them the purpose I set them up for. Or will you deny them love for that reason?"

Jones' frown tightened. He stepped aside and nodded his head at the entrance. The officers grabbed my elbows and muscled me along.

Sections of the wall served as living quarters. Inside, twelve people called a room of bunked beds and two toilets, home. The staff gave me sheets, a blanket, a pillow, and a towel that I placed on the bottom mattress of one bunk, since the current residents claimed all the top beds.

"Told you, Pete. It was only a matter of time before we had to share." A rough-looking man said. Scars marred his face in a couple of places, but he smiled through them.

Pete, a scrawny man with red lips, complained as he grabbed a few items off the bottom bunk and threw them up top.

A different guy with a head full of thin black hair asked, "What'd they send you here for?"

I sat on the bed and dropped my hands into my lap. All eyes were on me. I looked at the black-haired man. "I gave people purpose."

The man blinked several times, obviously confused.

I twiddled my thumbs. "I destroyed a few things, spread some of the wealth, and I dunno, killed power to most of the city."

"That was you?" Pete came around the bunk like a child eager to hear about fairytale adventures. "You did all that?"

His excitement spread over me. I laughed. "Yeah, that was me. I'm the villain. That's the name of the Program I have."

The black-haired man sat down on the bunk next to mine. "I heard it was temporary and they took that away from you."

I tapped a finger against my head. "They took a decoy away."

If the police knew I'd upgraded my temporary Program into a permanent one, they would've attempted to extract it and reprogram me. For an expensive process, they'd have done it for free just to keep me from being successful.

"Do you guys have Programs?" I asked.

They shook their heads. The black-haired man, who introduced himself as Lopez, said, "I missed the deadline. Doc said it was too risky."

Pete said, "My parents couldn't afford one."

I nodded. "Good. Very good."

"How is that good?" Jordan, the scarred man, asked. "We're stuck here. We can't go inside the city and live normal lives. So, we either live outside with the gangs or defend this place for hot food and shelter."

Lopez added, "Don't be surprised if your bed feels warm. Somebody used to sleep there. Tell me how that's good."

I gently tapped my chest. "Because you're not dead in here. The people inside the wall are walking corpses." Pete laughed. I felt his energy—their energy.

They gathered around me as I explained recent months. The police delivered me to an army of young and old embattled souls who'd been discarded because they hadn't decided on, couldn't afford, or were incompatible with Programs. But they had so much heart within them. And even more fight.

Vampyrella

Chapter 1

I entered the secure medical facility's cafeteria, slipping in between two swinging doors, one opening and one closing, and almost bumped into a guy standing on the inside. I should've known. The food line always extends into the hallway. I was the doorstop today.

I caught one door before it could hit me on the backswing and then peered into the large sterile-looking room. Inside required a one hundred and ten degree pan of the head from one side to the other to take it all in. Fluorescent lights at four-foot intervals populated a thirty-foot-high tiled ceiling. Fifteen round metal tables with two steel chairs each occupied the middle of the room. Two five-foot countertop openings marked the center and end of each wall's length and featured no rails—metal or nylon—to enforce straight lines. A second level wrapped around like a balcony, and several of its hallway entrances led to our patient rooms.

At last, I stood on the inside of anarchy. I looked ahead, not interested in the medicine or slop windows, but at the estimated time an introvert had to endure a busy place. I hated people, a feeling that increased at a logarithmic rate over the past couple of months.

A few variables contributing to the rapid change of heart had already exited both lines, downing a pill or two with water from a small plastic cup at window one and then swallowing the beige goop provided at window two. They should've left the dining hall then. Instead, the three variables each dragged a chair several feet, deaf to the scraping and screeching of its legs across the linoleum floor and sat next to a guy named Kyle.

Table arrangements encouraged socializing between two people but discouraged cliques, which made their group project to bully another obvious and gross insubordination. The orderlies noticed. I watched their heads turn. The scene flashed in their pupils before they looked away.

A memory reflected in my eyes. I'd been in Kyle's shoes before, until I wore them thin, and they ripped. The barefoot trek following my persecution took me down a dark path. I wanted to prevent Kyle from venturing down a similar one, so I left the line and headed toward his table.

Jordan, a tall guy with all the stereotypical makings of a frat boy—average to muscular build, mischievous facial expressions, pants cut into shorts, and a bleached polo shirt—led the trio. He sat across from Kyle with his chair in reverse and his chest against its flat metal back. The other two, a man and a woman in the same early twenties age category as the rest of us in this wing, were like malformed clones of their leader. The guy, Andrew, laughed incessantly while the woman, Nina, juggled a blue pill between her teeth.

I couldn't hear what Jordan said. Kyle's averted gaze and recoiled shoulders suggested they'd made him uncomfortable. They backed him into a corner despite being at the edge of the seating area in the middle of a large room. The people behind him were too busy selecting from a combination of dietary garbage to notice his silent plea for help, and others had their own psychological struggles to deal with, never mind someone else's.

Moments later, Kyle's tray crashed against the floor. The ambient conversation drowned out the noise. Some may have glanced, but an accident or two in the dining hall wasn't uncommon.

The trio laughed while Kyle leaned over to pick up the tray. Nina met him halfway, her brown pigtails trailing behind her as she lunged forward. She grabbed his face with her bony fingers and pressed her parched lips against his, swapping saliva until he swallowed something. The pill, I presumed. Then she shoved him back and wiped her mouth with the back of her hand.

Kyle coughed several times and then convulsed, ready to puke. Nina grabbed Kyle's plate and caught the vomit. Then she placed it on the table in front of him, cupped a spoonful of its contents into the metalware, and said, "ahh," as she nudged his closed lips with its silver tip.

I stopped between Jordan and Nina just as Andrew reached over to pinch Kyle's cheeks with one hand.

"You opened up for her tongue, you fucking pervert," he said, hand almost cupped around Kyle's jaw.

He paused when he noticed me. They all took a moment to acknowledge my presence.

"This table's full," Jordan snapped. He dismissed me with the wave of his hand.

I crossed my wrists behind me and rocked back and forth. "Don't mind me."

"Yeah, well, it's fucking awkward with you standing there." When I didn't move, he added, "Don't you have any friends?"

"Yep." I nodded at Kyle. "He's my familiar."

Kyle blushed, a red that rivaled the emergency exit sign behind him. He lowered his chin and averted his gaze, choosing to look at the tray of vomit instead of the woman who claimed him.

"Your *what*?" Jordan shook his head. His brows pinched as another burning question sat on his lips. He eyeballed me. "Are you black or white today?"

Nina laughed. "She's anemic. Didn't you have curves before? You look like the cafeteria doors now." She grabbed her pear-sized breasts with both hands and squeezed them. "I could let you borrow some material." She laughed again.

Andrew tapped the table nonstop. "What's the matter? Cat got your tongue? Where's your fancy comebacks?" he asked, cupping the back of one ear and leaning forward. "What was your name again? Sterile? Senile?"

Nina ruffled her blonde locks. "I think she's Seraphine today. Bitch has like five names. Can't never decide who she wants to be."

I mulled over their basic faces. When they'd run out of childish comments, I said, "You seem to know everything about me except why I'm here."

Jordan threw both hands up and turned around in his seat. "Enlighten us so you can fuck off already."

I met his gaze and his temperament. "I killed two people. Murdered, actually. Bullies, like you. I rammed a cylindrical measuring tube into the throat of one and left another to die from blood infection." I grinned, which quickly turned into a suppressed, maniacal laugh. In a slightly perky tone, I added, "I got away with it too, by way of insanity."

Nina curled her lips up. "You're a fucking psychopath," she said.

Jordan went to stand up. I raised my left foot to his chest and shoved him back down. He couldn't move. I'd pinned him to the chair, which leaned against a table bolted to the floor. With my physical strength, I might as well have been anchored, too.

"Get off me!" He grabbed my ankle and calf and tried to dislodge my leg. His struggle waned. Unable to inhale under the force I applied, he turned blue in the face.

"If you're gonna call me a psychopath, I'm gonna behave like a psychopath." I leaned in more, compressing his chest and pressing him further against the chair. "What's three more *accidents* on my record?"

Nina and Andrew stood. Half their brain seemed to suggest flight since each pivoted one leg away from me, ready to take off at a moment's notice. The other half of their cognitive response seemed dumbfounded because I was unusually strong. They probably thought I was spliced, which primarily altered a person's physical appearance, but over the years, more and more, twisted an individual's genetic code with other features native to the source creature. But a pill forced down our throats at window number one suppressed splice genes, so that couldn't be it.

The orderlies moved, so I hurried my warning. "If you come near him again or tell anyone about what's happened here, I'll murder you, too. Any questions?"

Jordan shook his head. Nina and Andrew did, too.

"Great!" I eased off his chest and spoke as he desperately gasped for air. "And that's how you stretch someone's back. Now you try it," I said. My voice was the most lively it'd been in a while.

One orderly reached us first. He seemed nonchalant and signaled to two others that he'd handle the situation. "Break it up, guys," he said in passing.

The three variables scattered, each seeking a different escape route. All to avoid crossing my path, I presumed. I turned back to Kyle and immediately regretted not having the trio take his plate with them. I snatched it from the table and slammed it upside down in the nearest garbage can.

***

Kyle hadn't said a word to me since I'd intervened with the punks bullying him. I sat next to him in the chair Nina had dragged over. During the silence, I crossed and adjusted my folded arms, repeatedly moving them to and away from my chest as I reminisced about the plump bosom I'd recently had. The bust I'd developed after splicing my genes evaporated when I took the splice suppression pill. As they were now, my shirt resembled the oversized property of a skinny boyfriend.

At last, I broke the silence. "Why do you let them pick on you?"

I looked at Kyle, confused at whether freckles or acne colored his face, and patiently waited for his usual slow response. Kyle often acted like an adolescent in an adult's body—not the needy, whiny kind, but the lonely and depressed teen with the weight of the world on their shoulders. That alone wouldn't have admitted him to this facility. He refused to talk about what did, ready to carry the reason to his grave, it would seem.

He raised his head from his chest, tilted it to the side as

he looked my way, and asked, "Why did *you*? You were bullied too, right?"

I came to his defense, and he learned something about me. Sometimes, he could be an adult, too. I looked away, leaning my head back and staring at the tiled ceiling. There was a light fixture high above. Staring into it blinded me from everything else.

I said, "I had educational and career opportunities ahead of me. A master's degree. Then a doctorate. Then a research position at a cutting-edge facility. I wouldn't have thrown all that away for a few ducks." I recalled the nickname I'd given Cat and her entourage. "But they quacked and flapped their wings at me anyway. When I fought back, the mother goose survived. Her ducklings didn't."

Kyle's jaw dropped. "Scary," he said, and then smiled weakly. "Wish I could be strong like you, especially since we ended up in the same place, anyway."

"What did you do?" I asked, knowing that a straight answer wouldn't follow.

"I existed."

We sat in silence again for a long minute. I wondered if Kyle envisioned my killing spree. He still sat next to me, unperturbed. His stomach growled. So I went back into the line, took my pills from window one, grabbed a plate at window two, and shared it with him at the table for five. I kicked two of the chairs away and an orderly scolded me.

"What happened to the mother goose?" Kyle asked with a mouthful of dry bread. He could've dipped the slice into the goop to soften the bite, but bread was the best tasting part of the meal, and he probably didn't want to ruin it.

I sighed and slumped in place. Talking about Cat aggravated me, but it's not like I didn't think about her. Maybe telling someone about our time together would help purge her memory from my brain.

"She graduated in my place at the top. Probably got all

the opportunities lined up for me, too, including my boy-friend, if I had one waiting. She took my life." I rubbed two fingers together, as if I couldn't wipe something off them. "And um, yeah. She took everything from me. All because I wasn't spliced. Well, initially, and then because I *was* spliced."

Kyle licked the plate clean and then put it down on the table. "Okay, I'm ready to give blood." He looked at me, an enormous grin on his face. "You used your powers against Jordan, right?"

"I don't have powers."

"Superhuman strength is totally powers. Growing your teeth out…maybe not so much." He rotated his hand, palm up and then down, twisting at the wrist.

I smiled at his innocence in the face of a monster.

"What else can you do?"

I shrugged. "Lately, I've been changing little things like my hair color, nose, and eyes."

"But I like your hair and nose and eyes," he said, glanc-ing at each as he named them off.

Since my incarceration, I've found reasons to hate the person reflecting in the mirror. Seraphine was weak and Ser-aph had a criminal record, so I aspired to be someone else entirely. I didn't tell Kyle that. He adored Seraph.

"But if you're gonna do it anyway, what if you made yourself look like the mother goose? You could run around town and ruin her life back."

I crossed my legs under the table. My knee brushed the underside of the metal, pulling the pants legs up an inch fur-ther than crossing them already had. "Look like the mother goose? Hm, I never thought about that. To imitate her, though, I'd have to learn a thing or two more about her life. I feel disgusted just thinking about it, never mind living it."

"You don't gain memories from blood?" Kyle asked and then recoiled from the sharp look I gave him. His smile slanted. "Only in some vampire lores, I guess."

"I'm not a vampire."

"You called me your familiar. And you," he leaned in and whispered, "drink blood."

I didn't drink blood. I transferred it, cycling out my depleted white blood cell count for a healthier amount. Splice genes attacked the body, so a healthy immune system became a prerequisite for the procedure. Some people took over-the-counter medication to help their body fight the infection. I required a blood transfusion. One because I spliced myself without determining compatibility, and two because I spliced with an amoeba proteus called Vampyrella, which sought to wreak more havoc in my body than cells from a cat or snake.

Kyle put his left arm on the table, palm-side up. Determined eyes captured mine, perhaps expecting me to salivate over his exposed wrist. I raised a brow and slid his arm away and off the table. Then I pushed his face away when he pulled his shirt collar down.

"You watch too many movies," I joked.

He laughed and then took a sip of his water—my water. His cup was nowhere to be seen. I couldn't imagine what Jordan and his cronies did with it. Grabbing the tin can with both hands, I rotated Kyle's saliva away from me and drank the water that tasted like it'd come from a tap instead of a spring.

"What if you looked like me?"

I spit half the water back into the cup. "Why would I look like you?"

He shrugged. "I don't know. If you looked like me and beat up the bullies, maybe they'd leave me alone for good."

I rested my chin in one palm and my elbow on the table. "You're just full of ideas today, aren't you?"

Kyle smiled. A contagious grin that coaxed one from me, too. Using my index finger, I motioned him to come forward. He hesitated, but eventually obeyed. I grabbed his chin the same way Andrew had and brought him closer until our mouths touched. Sensual at first, I gently bit down on his bottom lip, eliciting a soft moan. After his body relaxed and his weight settled into my palm, I drew out his tongue with mine. Then I extended my teeth, the ones between the canines and the center two, and bit down into his muscle. He jerked briefly, but my saliva soon numbed the pain and would seal the wound when I finished.

Chapter 2

Dr. Moore's office was what I imagined mine to be as a lead researcher at a prestigious facility. A plethora of diplomas and certifications covered the right wall. I'd only planned to display the one that included doctor in the name. She hung the bachelor's and master's degrees that led to the two doctorate degrees she'd earned, one in psychology and the other in sociology. Applicable certifications surrounded each diploma, and the entire arrangement resembled two lenses of a pair of glasses.

I wanted the same large desk she sat behind. Initially expecting and preferring something made of oak, I came to appreciate the aluminum that took up fifty percent of the room's width. The glass top meant I could quickly scribble down the chaos in my head using wet erase markers. Dr. Moore displayed personality charts and motivational sayings beneath the transparent surface.

I glanced at the closet to my left, its door wide open. Dr. Moore had a few white coats in there next to a couple of brown jackets. Two dressers with several drawers sat underneath the hanging garments. I saw her putting away a pair of pants once after she'd washed and dried them. Accidents during a session weren't uncommon, either.

While I patiently sat in the chair opposite Dr. Moore, she focused on the curved monitor sitting on her desk, turning her head thirty degrees to the right for optimum viewing. She clicked the mouse a few more times and then tapped a key with satisfaction before she faced me. Lowering her glasses, she said, "Good morning, Seraphine."

Dr. Moore looked fifty, if not older. Gray locks had been pulled up into a small bun barely visible from straight-on. I wondered if decades of education aged her. Rumors were oddly specific about her being forty-one years old, which further discouraged me from pursuing the multiple degrees she showcased on her wall, preferring a youthful appearance in the future.

"Good morning, Dr. Moore." I sat on the couch to her left so I could see the right side of the curved screen.

She interlocked her hands on the table and smiled at me. Smooth acrylic nails made her finger's wrinkles stand out more. "How are you today?" she asked.

I shrugged.

"You have a court date in a few days, right? How do you feel about that?"

"Eager."

Dr. Moore raised a brow, unconvinced, since my mood didn't match my response. She pushed the glasses further up the bridge of her nose. "Why eager?"

"I get to go outside."

The computer chimed. She glanced at the monitor, responding to me while preoccupied. "There are scheduled outdoor times every day. Are you not going outside?"

I sat cross-legged in the chair and placed both hands in my lap. "Outside outside. I want to see something other than the same blue sky, bland desert, and expensive chain-link fence. It doesn't even rain out here." I tilted my head back and stared at the ceiling light. "Not a single cloud, either."

"That's oddly specific and understandable. Do you think taking these sessions more seriously would improve your chances of going outside outside? During our last session…" she interrupted my forthcoming excuse. "…when asked if you were ready to return to society, you told me to run a Monte Carlo simulation of responses and report back on which ones improved the chances of you being released."

She nearly quoted me.

The left corner of my mouth slumped. "I'm a biology major. I think in experiments."

"Seraphine—"

"Raphael."

"Excuse me?"

"My name is Raphael."

Dr. Moore's eyes widened.

"Seraphine was an intelligent doormat. Seraph has a criminal record. And my enemies call me Sera."

Dr. Moore straightened her posture. "Your parents call you Sera."

"My *enemies* call me Sera."

"Okay." She pulled out her famed notebook, which was rumored to contain privileged patient information alongside session notes. Before opening it, she scratched out Seraph, the last name I'd adopted, and didn't hesitate to scribe the new one. "Why Raphael?" She asked as she flipped to a blank page.

"I'm moving away from names derived solely from my government name to see if that changes my fate. 'Raph' is in my government name, so I don't completely lose myself, and 'ael' means angel."

"Seraph also means angel; of the highest order, if I recall."

I sat in silence for a minute. Dr. Moore patiently waited for a better explanation. She wouldn't lose that battle. We stared at each other for an entire session once and continued the conversation during the next visit, so I couldn't avoid her question with time, especially if she wanted an answer.

I looked down at my hands, interlocking and untangling my fingers multiple times. Avoiding eye contact, I said, "Seraph...no, *I* had to come back down to earth."

Dr. Moore smiled. "We're glad to have you back, Raphael. Maybe you can tell me who," she rotated the monitor toward me, "this woman is."

I leaned forward to see the screen better and then retreated from the video of me assaulting Jordan. But there was no reason for me to feel guilty or at fault. I edged forward again and searched for the orderlies who'd stood by and watched.

"Rewind it," I said after noticing the orderlies were out of frame. "Jordan—"

"This session is about you."

"But—"

"I'm aware of Jordan's behavior toward Kyle and I can understand how seeing that was a call to action for you—a sense of duty or guilt to prevent someone from heading down the same path you stumbled onto. But this is why we're here." She rested her forearms on the desk and brought her hands together again. "You have to let go, Seraphine. These multiple personalities and the grudges they hold—all of it."

I looked at her diplomas and certifications. How could I let go when I could've had a similar wall in the future? Dr. Moore didn't understand what it meant to lose everything. The degrees she displayed, the family photos on her desk, and the position she held were everything I could've had, too.

I glared at her, and then immediately relaxed my gaze. "How can I? These walls are a constant reminder." I gripped my fingers tightly, enough to see the red through my mixed complexion. "I'm trying."

"I know you are, and I'm here to help. Let's bring Seraphine back, together."

I glanced at the video and blushed when it showed me kissing Kyle. The surveillance camera's overhead viewpoint showed me something other than the back of my eyelids. Kyle's fingers had tightly gripped the chair he sat in, and his feet hovered above the floor as he pushed his knees against each other.

Dr. Moore raised a brow. "Want to tell me what's going on here?" She wasn't expecting an answer because we didn't sit in silence for the rest of the session waiting for one from me. "There aren't any rules against resident relationships. Outside of intercourse, those about intimacy are vague at best. We want everyone here to return to society, and that means facilitating relationships of various kinds." She sat back and crossed her arms, eyes still on the video as I pulled away from Kyle. "Just remember where you are, Seraphine."

She raised her hands and eyes toward the ceiling. "Think of this place as college. One day, everyone will graduate and go their separate ways. Some sooner than others."

She rotated the monitor away from me and stood. I slid out of the leather seat and met her by the diploma wall. With a wooden popsicle stick in hand, she pushed each corner of my lips up and checked my teeth for pointier canines.

"We have one more session before your court date. I'd like you to think about how you're going to feel standing in front of the judge." She peered into each of my eyes, looking for the violet hue they'd turned when I spliced. "And how you *should* feel and behave in that moment. It'll be your first step toward going home."

The first of many around the world, it seemed.

Dr. Moore took one of those steps, backward and against the desk. She searched for it with her hip and then sat on the glass top. She dropped the wooden stick into a small garbage can next to her dangling foot. "See you next time."

I nodded and headed for the door.

"Oh, Seraphine," she called out when I grabbed the door handle. "Can you do me one favor?"

I turned around and half nodded.

"Please don't break his heart."

Chapter 3

Blue sky. Bland dirt. Expensive silver chain link fence. Everything I'd described to Dr. Moore regarding outside except for the dry, year-round heat beating down on me. Melanin helped. Sunscreen would have too if I had family or friends that cared enough to send me some. But who would send gifts to a murderer?

I'm not a murderer.

Outside had gray stone benches and picnic tables. No grass—artificial or real. No shade from the concrete building watching us, and no escape from the security that included the fence and surveillance cameras. Half a basketball court claimed the far end of the enclosure. The balls from missed shots collected on the other side of the fence until a guard felt compelled to retrieve them. I could've gone to get them, if it meant touching the outside. I wouldn't have run away. That wasn't me.

I'm not a murderer.

Threatening Kyle's bullies with violence may have affected me more than them. I couldn't stop thinking about what I'd said. Murder them? I had no intentions of hurting anyone, let alone killing someone. But Jordan, Nina, and Andrew wouldn't have settled for anything less than a severe threat. So I gave them one they couldn't ignore. I was direct, straight to the point, and succinct. Efficiency at the highest level and intended to yield long-term results.

I'm not a murderer.

I sat atop one table with my feet firmly planted on the attached bench. Dr. Moore's words about my court date haunted me. The appointment would mark the first step toward going home, and I'd already been caught on video threatening violence. Fortunately, the video she'd played didn't have audio, or maybe she didn't have speakers. I wondered if she was required to present the altercation as evidence and if the Judge would then reclassify the charges against me as premeditated? Was I a danger to society?

I'm not a murderer.

The questions racked my brain. I ruffled my hair. And the sun baked them both. I had one bottle of water to distribute among the various parched regions of my body, and the hot surface it sat on had already warmed its contents. If only the sun could melt that video, too.

It could've melted Kyle, if he hadn't applied sunscreen. The facility didn't provide any, which meant somebody on the outside still cared about him; enough to buy, package, and ship maximum SPF, anyway.

Kyle usually took several minutes to lather his arms and face before he'd walk outside. Pants protected his legs, shoes shielded his feet, and a short-sleeved tee covered his upper body, all courtesy of standard-issued clothing. For good reason, too. Kyle trekked across the open space like a turtle crossing a busy road. Surprisingly, nobody ran him over. They had plenty of opportunities, just as the sun had ample time to cook his pasty skin. Me sitting at the far end of the cage didn't help, but like a moth to a flame, the real outside attracted me.

"Don't break his heart."

I wondered why Dr. Moore said that. Kyle was my familiar. There weren't any feelings involved. Not real ones, anyway. A rapid beating heart made the blood taste sweeter, what little dispensed into my mouth. It also made the transfer faster, the one thing Kyle did quickly. And as far as I knew, Kyle never spliced his genes, so he didn't take the suppressant pill. He gave me uncontaminated blood, and I kept him safe.

"Don't break his heart."

Kyle sat on the bench, next to my feet. He preferred to look up at me from that angle, saying my hair looked silver, almost white, when the sun was at my back, adding that I was an angel descending to Earth. I was certain my new name would complement his fantasy.

Meanwhile, his head looked more orange from my viewpoint, like another sun, his wild hair like solar prominences.

He turned and tilted his head toward me and raised the bottle of sunscreen. "You want some?"

I shook my head. "You need it more than I do."

Kyle scrunched his brows. He thrust the sunscreen into his left pants pocket and then pulled a bottle of water out of his right pants pocket. Three gulps later, he let out a loud and satisfied breath.

"Don't break his heart."

"Who sends you those, anyway?" I asked.

"My niece."

"Your niece? Wait, how old are you?"

"I don't know. Time stands still here."

His walls stood higher than the surrounding fence. Smooth and unscalable.

"Do you need blood—"

"No." My immediate response startled him. It came out more sternly than I intended. Frustration changed the tones like autocorrect after hitting the send button. Kyle asked often, which didn't bother me, as being wanted felt nice. I also didn't blame him, as exchanging blood was probably the most exciting thing to do other than dream. But at that moment, his secrets frustrated me. More than usual.

"Don't break his heart."

I regretted how quickly I'd said no. "Maybe…just a little…" I bit my lower lip.

Kyle's eyes lit up the outside, like two solar flares.

"But not out here," I said, recalling the video Dr. Moore played on her computer. Thankfully, I'd hidden our transaction inside a kiss. I didn't need vampirism appended to my list of violations, next to assault and battery. And third-degree murder.

I'm not a murderer.

Public display of affection wouldn't be unusual outside,

but Kyle was already frail under the sun. Giving him my depleted white blood cell count might further exacerbate known associated risks, such as heatstroke.

"Why? Are you afraid people will see?"

Yes, because the orderlies and counselors were probably watching me closely after that incident with Jordan. I didn't tell Kyle about that or my last session with Dr. Moore and how she'd recorded our intimacy.

No, because embarrassment hit differently after getting spliced. External things that made me feel less by comparison faded, even when news media outlets plastered my name and photo on every television in the country (I assumed). *Valedictorian Candidate Murders Fellow Students*, some headlines read.

I'm not a murderer.

"You're embarrassed by me, too." Kyle released a defeated breath and turned away.

"You know that's not it." Telling him about the latter half of my session with Dr. Moore would've included her warning about graduation. We weren't in the relationship she presumed. There weren't any feelings involved. I gave Kyle my first kiss to prevent my body from eating itself. We're all each other has in this desolate place…until somebody graduates.

"Then why?"

"Don't break his heart, murderer."

I screamed without warning. "Get the fuck out of my head! It was an accident! I didn't want that! I didn't want any of this!" Most of the playground stopped and looked at me. I buried my face in my hands and mumbled. "I just want to go…" *Home* would've completed the saying, but I didn't have one.

"Sorry, Seraph."

I shook my head and then spoke from behind cover. "It's not you. It's not me. This isn't me. This isn't who I am."

"I know. You wouldn't kill Jordan, either."

                    The Dark Side of Light

I lowered one hand and stared at him from between my fingers. He stared at me, unfazed by my sudden outburst, a blank expression on his face, and freckles likely redder than my embarrassment. The rest of the playground returned to their activities. A mental breakdown wasn't uncommon.

"You yelled at the sky," Kyle shrugged. "They'll give you pills for that, too, or the voices will only get louder."

He radiated sincerity. Or innocence. Even though his kind words came with a grim warning. If only I'd met him as Seraphine. Seraph was likely a poor influence, and my enemies called me Sera.

I reached down and wrapped my arms around his upper body. Then I yanked him up, using my unnatural strength, and sat him next to me on top of the table. He grinned profusely as I dragged him closer and into a half embrace. I rested my head on his shoulder and said, "Call me Raphael."

Chapter 4

Dr. Moore was late. An orderly escorted me to a different office than usual. It was mostly empty. Without framed degrees and certificates, its white walls stood out. Without the family photos, the modern gray desk lacked personality. The leather chair I sat in felt cold and uncomfortable. Someone had turned the thermostat down to freezing, convincing me that water dispensed from the sprinklers would shower me with snow. I dodged icy burns against the leather as if it'd sat outside all day under a cold sun.

At last, when the office climate drove me out of the seat, a woman I'd never met before walked into the room. She strolled past the two leather chairs facing the large desk, including the one I'd crawled halfway out of and onto one foot. Semitransparent frames sat on her nose. The darker temple tips didn't curve around her ears. They extended beyond each helix and creased her short black hairs.

She dropped some folders onto the desk but held onto a digital tablet. "Sit down, Seraphine," she said, her tone strict.

I complied, folding one leg under my butt on the way down. I watched her walk out from behind the desk and turn the leather seat next to me a few more degrees toward me. She unbuttoned her black suit jacket and crossed her legs. The matching suit pants wrinkled at the knees. Dark gray heels revealed the bridge of her feet. She wore a basic digital watch on one wrist and a high-tech app-enabled one on the other.

She smiled at me. The light reflecting off the tablet gave her pale hands a ghostly tint. "Good evening, Seraphine. I'm Dr. Michelle Alola."

"Where's Dr. Moore?"

She took a deep breath, perhaps expecting the question. "Your case is unique and therefore requires a special attention to detail that Dr. Moore isn't qualified to handle." She ended with a motherly smile, one I'd only ever seen on television. "Let's get started." She looked at the tablet and scrolled through multiple pages using a stylus.

"First, let's see your teeth."

I rolled my eyes and opened my mouth.

"Okay, looking good. Eye color is…hazel. Good." She tapped on the tablet display a few times. "And how are you feeling today? Any pain? Fatigue? Food cravings? Morning sickness?"

I shook my head at each question; the neck turns getting more frequent and my brows furrowing further. "No!" I shouted, interrupting her before she named another symptom. As I recoiled in disgust, I searched my brain for conditions related to the symptoms. Had she mentioned nausea and fatigue instead of morning sickness, I would've leaned toward stress. But at face value, I considered the other resultant condition. "I'm not pregnant."

"Oh." Dr. Alola's shoulders jumped as she sat up straight. "Okay. According to my notes, you missed your premenstrual cycle…"

I scoffed and then waved my hand dismissively. "Irregularity from…stress. Clearly. I shouldn't have to explain—wait, how would you know that?"

"…twice," she finished her sentence. "You haven't requested or opened a box of tampons in over sixty-one days."

I stood, fists clenched tight. "You went into my—"

Dr. Alola raised a hand, palm facing me. "It's not *your* room, Seraphine. It belongs to the state. This is a state-owned and operated medical facility. Now. Sit. Down."

Uncurling my fists, I grabbed each armrest and slunk back onto the couch. My arms weren't long enough to cup the edge of the armrest when I leaned back, so I peeled them from the leather as if glued. My grip left indentations, and my gaze never left Dr. Alola.

She put the tablet down on the desk. "After reviewing your case, I started my own investigation. On the surface, you killed two fellow students in self-defense. But as I dug deeper, I learned some interesting things. For example, the police reports mentioned a splice of unknown origin. However, I couldn't find any matching medical records with your name on them, unique as it is. Your parents didn't pay for any procedures. They were adamant about that. Either someone illegally operated on you, or you did it yourself, which would be an impressive feat in probably substandard conditions."

"I watched an online video—"

"I know." She smiled at my raised brows. "Why do you look surprised, Seraphine? You're a murder suspect. We executed search warrants here and there. Although, we didn't need one to review your browser history on a university computer. With everything that happened on their campus, the school readily complied with my investigation. What I *don't know* is what you spliced with and whether you bit the victims. There's no evidence that you have or had fangs, but both victims have matching bite marks on their necks."

I shrugged. My anger hadn't subsided, but I successfully leashed it. "You're trying to scare me. Where's Dr. Moore?"

"As I mentioned earlier, Dr. Moore handles less complex cases. We're going to be doing things differently from now on. And we can either be best friends or bitter enemies." She picked up the tablet, leaned back into the chair, and crossed her legs.

When I didn't answer her question, she nodded several times and then read from the tablet. "Speaking of enemies…Tiana Ty. Her family called her T.T. Age: twenty. Splice source: panther. Cause of death: penetration of the pharynx with a broken glass measuring tube." Dr. Alola moved the tablet away from her face for a moment, perhaps looking for a reaction from me, before she ducked behind it again and continued reading. "Danielle Alexander Rosario. Age: twenty. Splice source: Mangrove tree snake. Cause of death: complication due to splice." She put the tablet down, brought her hands together, loosely forming a tent with her fingers, and stared up at the ceiling. "Complication due to splice. Not the bite marks on her neck?"

I sat perfectly still. Although Dr. Alola didn't look directly at me, I knew she watched me from her peripheral vision. She was pushing my buttons, hoping one would pop. The first couple of sessions with Dr. Moore addressed Tiana and Danielle's deaths. She wanted to get the past out of the way so we could focus on the future. Dr. Alola sought to weaponize past events.

She continued, speaking more to herself than to me. "Danielle's splice gave her a two-pronged tongue and replaced her canines with fangs, but she couldn't bite herself. Tiana had similar bite marks on her neck, from the front instead of from behind like Danielle's. She would've died from the glass tube thrust into her neck, so I can't imagine the bite being necessary unless it occurred prior to the killing blow.

"All of that was in the police reports—on the surface. Underneath, autopsies revealed both victims had an unusual blood type mismatch. Underneath *that*, I learned Danielle's fangs released an aphrodisiac that caused euphoria, and that Tiana was exposed to the same toxin—"

"Dr. Alola, the session time is over."

I never watched the clock with Dr. Moore, and she never held me longer than needed, but I'd had enough of Dr. Alola after five minutes. I was scheduled for a fifteen-minute check-in, and she was ten minutes late.

"Do you know who else was exposed to that toxin?"

I stood and headed for the exit.

"Kyle Johnson."

I faltered halfway to the door. Even if only for a moment, I knew she'd caught it. Her gaze pierced the back of my head. A huge grin likely sat on her face, one I knew she wouldn't hide when I turned around. I can't lose control of my emotions. Not here. Not now.

"We found traces in his urine, as we do most illegal substances."

I tilted my head down and to the side and hoped to dash her grin with a well-crafted lie. "Nina slipped something into his mouth yesterday. Dr. Moore has the video." I didn't want to tell Dr. Alola about the video, since it contained my assault, but she probably already knew about that, and I needed to deflect the incoming accusation. I kept the color of the pill secret, since knowing would make for an easier check.

I stared at Dr. Alola from the corner of my eyes. "Who knows how long they've been giving it to him? It caused him to vomit. The orderlies turned a blind eye. That's in the video, too."

"Seraphine, are you telling me that Nina gave Kyle unsanctioned drugs containing a toxin matching Danielle's bite? Where would she even get something like that?"

I shrugged and turned around. "The orderlies let her bully others, so I doubt they're inspecting her mail."

Dr. Alola laughed, and then slowly shook her head. "Intelligence is your best defense when you have facts, but not so much when fabricated data is involved. *I* gave Nina the blue pill and asked her to administer it to Kyle. After you came to his 'rescue,' we checked his blood for Danielle's toxin." Her grin widened. "So, you can either walk out that door and be convicted for two counts of second-degree murder, or you can sit down and tell me everything."

I clenched my fists, less in a ball and more out of frustration with thumbs out. The emotions I'd held back soaked my cheeks. Everything fell apart because I forgot to bleed last month.

"Each count carries a life sentence," Dr. Alola added.

Heavy steps prevented me from stomping back to the chair. I sat on the seat's edge and glared at her.

"Good choice. Now. Talk."

Pushing one corner of my lips up, I revealed a fang and spoke with my mouth open. "I spliced with a vampire bat. It gave me some ability to manipulate my body."

"There it is," she almost sang. "I heard you could recover wounds quickly, too."

"It ate away at my body quickly. I exchanged blood with Danielle because I had a low white blood cell count and I was dying. I didn't know that would cause incompatibility in her, and I didn't know that would kill her."

Dr. Alola leaned back in the chair. "Go on." She typed a lot, but I expected the session was being recorded. Without my consent, too.

"The same thing happened with Tiana when she tried to kill me for having a better academic record. Danielle's aphrodisiac and Tiana's strength were side effects of taking in their blood. Since my arrest, I couldn't replenish my white blood cell count. I was afraid that having my period would cause me to lose too much blood and I'd die."

Dr. Alola raised both brows and put the tablet down. "So you…stopped ovulating?"

I nodded.

"Seraphine, that's medically ground-breaking. Can you imagine if women could control ovulation at will?"

"At the risk of death?"

She stood and then walked around the desk. "Proper research and experimentation could reduce the risks." She pulled a bottle of water out of a drawer, added some powder, and shook it until the contents turned light-green. "And your cooperation could reduce your sentence. And support millions of women around the world."

I knew what being a test subject meant. I'd be trading one prison for another, but I couldn't turn Dr. Alola down. Not now, anyway.

"So you're still spliced? How did you bypass the suppression pill?"

I took a deep breath.

"Are you going back on our deal, Seraphine?"

And an even deeper breath before I exhaled and said, "I

rerouted the pill through my body. Same way I stopped ovulation." I didn't mention the veins I'd created and circulated clean blood through. I raised them to the surface when the nurses called me in for labs.

"You're a medical discovery, Seraphine. I look forward to revolutionizing the world with your help."

Chapter 5

I refused to be a lab rat. Or a guinea pig. I wasn't a murderer, either. Dr. Alola wanted to use my body to further her career and cement her future in whatever field claimed her. She was a different bully, one protected by law and processes.

Citing precautionary measures for the upcoming court date, she revoked my outdoor privileges. She feared the splice she knew little about. The unknown made me unpredictable, which then made me dangerous. She couldn't make me take the suppression pill because that might kill her dream.

Except, I had my life to get back to. One thing I learned from Cat and her ducklings is that *I'd* be the one to ruin my life. I wouldn't sit around and wait for Dr. Alola to have her way with my discovery. If my splice was going to revolutionize the medical field, I'd pioneer it, not her. But first, I had to get outside.

I sat in the middle of my bed for hours, thinking about the facility's layout, security, and foot traffic. Time was of the essence. I didn't want Dr. Alola to impose more restrictions on me, and I didn't want to go through a single test, either. Fortunately, I didn't have a roommate to distract me. Can't put a woman who murdered other women in a cell with other women.

I'm not a murderer.

I stared at the empty mattress across from me. My gaze drifted to the two-drawer foam nightstand at the foot of that bed and then continued around the room to the same-looking drawer sitting at the head of mine, the one Dr. Alola searched for unused tampons. I smiled at the drawer, realizing it was also my ticket to the outside.

***

I'd spent the morning adjusting my face. That's when I had the most alone time, after breakfast. When the clock struck ten, I opened all the drawers of both nightstands and then kicked one over. I made sure the racket caught the nearby orderly's attention.

"What are you doing in there?" An orderly peeped through two tall and narrow vertical windows of the door. After he saw the knocked-over dresser, he entered the room.

"Dr. Moore?" He asked, brows drawn together for a moment before he relaxed them. "What are you doing in here?"

I took a deep breath and turned completely around. "Yes. Dr. Alola searched one of my patient's rooms," I said, holding a few tampons in my hand. "She used these to accuse them of wrongdoing."

The man's face went blank. He stared at my standard-issued attire, the gray slacks and plain, short-sleeve tee. "Why are you dressed like that?"

His glance made me uncomfortable. The uniform wasn't flattering on me. I didn't have the curves to fill the fabric. That may have been for the best, disguised as Dr. Moore. His gaze reminded me I wouldn't make it far in patient clothing without being questioned. Security might even elect to commit me. I recalled the change of clothes in Dr. Moore's office, which would aid in my escape and further solidify my chameleon-like change.

"It's what criminal investigators do, apparently; put themselves in someone else's shoes. Dr. Alola is a criminal investigator. Did you know that?"

He shook his head.

"Neither did I." An awkward silence followed my statement. I hadn't convinced him completely of whatever gave him doubt. My visage matched Dr. Moore perfectly. I'd changed my hair and eye color, arched my nose slightly, and added a few wrinkles. Dr. Moore applied little makeup, if any at all, so no issues there.

I lacked Dr. Moore's speech cadence. People respected

her natural way with words and their delivery. I also didn't have the positive outlook she viewed a dark world in. Things I needed to work on.

I stepped over one drawer on the floor. "The director promised we'd discuss things like this beforehand. Seraphine is one of my best patients, and I won't have someone at the federal level interfering in her rehabilitation. Poor woman's been through so much already."

I met the orderly at the door. He was taller up close. The uniform mostly hid his stout frame, but I'd seen him take several troublemakers down with ease.

"When Seraphine returns, send her to my office."

"Yes, ma'am."

I couldn't have him following me, suspicion or not. I promenaded the corridor, my room halfway down its length, and turned when I reached the second-floor balcony overlooking the cafeteria. It was empty below. The only person I had to worry about seeing me was Dr. Moore herself, but I'd glimpsed her calendar during our last session and saw a conference room scheduled for 9 AM all week long.

I promenaded the halls with confidence—shoulders squared, back straight, and as if I'd worn heels. Two security guards passed me without a glance, from the front anyway.

Dr. Moore's office was inside the residential block, just a few doors down from Dr. Alola's. Regularly signing patients in and out of any space beyond the residential block was too dangerous, which translated as too much of a hassle.

I entered her office and immediately closed the door behind me. The room's familiarity made me smile. Dr. Moore never locked her door, claiming there was nothing of value inside. Personnel records came and went with her. She could reprint stolen or vandalized diplomas. Necessary personal items, such as car keys, she'd secured in the hanging desk drawer underneath the monitor. I came for those car keys and a change of clothes from the open closet.

The secured desk drawer had a rotary combination lock

on it with a digital display. I didn't know the code. I didn't need the code. I had Tiana's strength.

I placed one foot against the drawer's interior side to hold it down and pulled the desk's top with all my strength. Metal warped. Bolt threads stripped. Everything sheared loudly. I separated the desk's top from the drawer stack, enough to slip my hand inside and feel around for the car keys. When I found them, I carefully maneuvered my hand out to avoid scraping my delicate fingers against the bolts and frayed metal.

With keys in hand, I held back my celebration. Instead, I applied pressure to the desk and pushed it back down onto the drawer stack. It wasn't perfect. The warped metal didn't smooth out, but that wouldn't be immediately noticeable from the other side.

I rushed around the desk and to the dresser closet. Most of the outfits looked the same. Color varied sometimes. I stripped down to my gray underwear and put on the first pair of pants I saw, which were navy blue. Then a matching blouse and a darker blazer. Lastly, I slipped a pair of white heels over my ankles. They were still warm.

As I turned toward the exit, color flushed from my face. I saw the camera in the room. It hung above and behind Dr. Moore's desk. The ceiling fan blocked its view from the entrance. Its presence caused the silhouettes in the door's narrow windowpane to scare me. There was nothing to fear, though. I looked like Dr. Moore. And it was unlikely that the corner of the desk was in the camera's field of view. She wouldn't have wanted anyone looking over her shoulder or at the screen. I also reasoned that the video feed didn't go to security because of doctor-patient privacy laws. I hoped, but Dr. Alola's recent actions tanked that optimism.

I restored my outward confidence and took a deep breath. Then I opened the door and walked out. I'd only been through the main lobby once, when the police first took me in. There wasn't much to it other than security. Badges were required to enter and exit.

When I reached the secure door, I patted myself down and threw my hands up, as if leaving the badge in the car frustrated me. The woman behind the glass approved my exit using complex facial recognition hardware—her eyes.

In the parking garage, I remained mindful of security cameras. I tapped the fob in my hand and listened for the car to respond. A solid chirp directed me to its location. Dr. Moore drove a beige luxury sedan. Red leather seats colored the inside. I didn't have time to admire the rest of the interior. I cut on the engine, threw the car into gear, and drove out of the garage. A barcode sticker on the vehicle's windshield raised an arm bar ahead of the main exit.

I hadn't driven a car in a long while, but it was like riding a bike. Built-in navigation charted a five-hour drive home. An hour into the drive, I stopped by a lone gas station and changed cars, trading the luxury sedan for a standard mid-sized vehicle and a splice-induced climax the station worker wouldn't forget.

Chapter 6

Six hours later, I stood outside Cat's house. It wasn't difficult to find. There weren't many upscale neighborhoods with multistory homes in our town. The police vehicle sitting on the road in front of a white picket fence helped to narrow down the exact property.

Cat wasn't home. The inside looked dark from outside, haunted even. I listened for heartbeats to ensure the police hadn't set a trap inside. When I heard nothing but the ticking of a lone clock, I ran around back and jumped onto a second-floor balcony. Instead of breaking the glass of the exterior door, I grabbed the handle and twisted it off.

Inside the house, I took mental notes of the room decor. If I was going to take on her persona, I needed to think and move like her. Yellow and pink served as her primary colors. Posters of pop stars decorated the walls. Fur and satin textures covered everything from the bed to the couches.

I grabbed a photo of Cat off a dresser and sat it on the counter in the master bathroom. Then I adjusted my features to match hers, struggling to look at the person I was and fighting to become the person I hated. When I heard the garage door open, I ran downstairs and waited for her.

I stood in her kitchen, in the corner between the pantry and a short wall separating the dining room. She didn't see me. I was as invisible to her then as I've always been.

I reveled in my usual obscurity and in the reassurance that she hadn't changed. Blood rushed through my veins as my teeth grew in length and sharpened.

My two-pronged tongue caused my voice to hiss instead of seduce. "Welcome home, Catherine," I said.

Immediately, she grabbed a knife from a wooden block on the kitchen counter, turned around, and pointed it at the shadows—pointed it at me.

The bridge of my feet was visible under the lights above the kitchen island, but she couldn't see them over the marble countertop. Fresh fruit, a vase full of dandelions, and a panda-shaped cookie jar further obstructed her view of me.

She couldn't see me.

She saw a silhouette in the dark and knew it was me. Of all the people she bullied, she knew I'd be the one to come for her. Naturally.

"What are you doing here? Get out of my house! Get out, murderer!"

I'm not a murderer.

I didn't respond or move. There wasn't enough time in the world to emulate the time she'd spent devouring my peace of mind, but I let the seconds and minutes sink into her sleep-deprived eyes for as long as I could.

Tears quickly soiled her eyeliner. The colors ran down her cheeks and caused the foundation that smoothed her visage to crack, along with her voice.

"What the fuck! They told me your splice was gone!"

Ah, that's how she knew where to point the knife. The blood coursing through my veins must've ignited my eyes violet again. And apparently, not even the darkness can hide them.

"Please let me go. I'll never bother anyone again. Ever."

"I'm not here to kill you. I'm not a murderer."

I'm not a murderer.

I glanced around the kitchen. Floral-patterned drapes covered the window above the sink. Glass cabinet doors protected porcelain china dishes from dust. Photos of family, friends, and graduation covered the stainless-steel fridge.

"I'm here to take everything from you."

She clenched the countertop ledge behind her until her knuckles turned white. "What?" She asked, her extended arm visibly shaking as she gripped the knife tighter.

"When I drink someone's blood, I steal a piece of them. I can look like anyone. I can be like…anyone."

"You'll never be me."

I smirked, shifting my gaze up and over as if she'd

charmed me and I was embarrassed but smitten.

"Obviously, I'm going to be the better, nonexistent half of you. Or *should I* just be you? Ugly as you are, you're," I glanced around the kitchen again, "accomplished."

"You're fucking crazy! Get out! Help! Help!" she shouted at the ceiling, the walls, and the front door. "The police are outside. They're coming in right now."

"Who do you think they'll believe?" I stepped out of the shadows. "You or you?"

The look on Cat's face was priceless. I didn't dare imitate it, even if we shared a countenance. I should've photographed the moment. Her mouth hung open as her breathing faltered. Trembling, she dropped the knife, and then brought both hands to her face, covering her mouth and nose. She apologized again, a whimper that barely escaped her manicured hands.

"My name is Catherine," I said. The greeting didn't come out right. Shaking my head, I adjusted my tone and tried again. "Hey, I'm Cat." The peppiness belonged to Danielle. Frustrated, I shook my head of that persona. My newly short black strands flopped back and forth across my face. I tried again, but in the same abrasive tone Cat often used with me. "What the fuck are you looking at?" I asked. After, I raised my hands, my fingers at an angle both she and I could see and transformed my nails to match her tangerine acrylic set. I wiggled my fingers and smirked.

Cat collapsed on the kitchen floor. Patiently, I walked around the island. Dr. Moore's heels clacked against the tiles. I knelt in front of Cat. She'd wrapped her arms around her knees and quivered in place. I studied her features and adjusted mine in real-time. Her hair was longer than in the photo, so I extended mine a couple more inches. Bare knees looked as if she'd knelt on rocks to pray. Physical flaws I ignored.

Transformation consumed a lot of my body's resources.

Cat's blood wasn't required for me to copy her splice features—the vertical pupils and the cup-shaped ears—but to replenish my white blood cell count and sustain my life. I had to be careful not to weaken her immune system too much, or she could die like Danielle. A little here and a little there of her blood, her habits, her routines. Her memories. Her life. I'd take her blood to reclaim *me*.

Cat didn't react when I flashed my fangs. I grabbed her throat, rough at first and then gently when she didn't resist. Running my fingers over to her collarbone, pushing her blouse aside, I watched her eyes the entire time. They stared at another world, but her lips moved in this one.

"I'm so sorry," she said, before my teeth could break her skin. She met my gaze. More tears swelled in her large brown eyes and ran down her ruined face. "I'm so sorry," she mouthed.

Her apology didn't ask for forgiveness. It begged to be heard. Catherine Belle was…*sorry*. Every day that she mocked my normalcy, every moment that she ridiculed my passion, and every second that she wished me nonexistent, she was sorry. The words were hard to accept. I wondered if she apologized because her life was in danger. It wasn't. I wasn't a murderer.

I'm not a murderer.

I told her that.

I'm so sorry.

I only wanted my life back.

"I'm so sorry."

The last words echoed in Cat's voice. I couldn't understand why. I'd only copied her face. And her melanin. I didn't have her memories, so why did that voice—

"I'm so sorry."

I grabbed my head, the strength in my fingers threatening to tear the hair from my scalp. I rose to my feet and collided into the kitchen counter as I stumbled around. Swinging elbows knocked cups, utensils, and paper towel holders off the counter.

"I'm so sorry."

"Shut up!" I shouted and covered my ears, as if the words originated from the outside. A scream followed, one strong enough to bust the windows. The glass cabinets shattered, the china inside them cracked, and every light in the room went out.

I panted, heavily. The voices had quieted, but my ears picked up new, external ones at the front door. Flashlights cut through the darkness like wandering concentrated beams. I backed away, stammering toward the other side of the pantry and out a side door. Noisily, haphazardly, and with brute force. The lights at the entrance flashed in my direction.

"Ms. Belle?"

"It's her! Go! Go!"

"Dispatch, we have eyes on the missing female. In pursuit."

My ears picked up everything.

"All units, be advised, missing female has been spotted off Franklin Ave. Units are in pursuit."

I heard them. No matter how fast and far I ran.

"All units be advised; suspect can change appearance. Look for violet eyes."

I didn't know where I was going. My feet carried me across parking lots and through the backyards of several homes. The police were everywhere. Their vehicles crawled along in the dark with no lights, but my eyes saw them clear as day, as if the red and blue beacons on the roof rotated.

Some rode bikes and several more trekked on foot. I wondered how I hadn't seen them on the way to Cat's house. There were many, and they'd already surrounded the area. Slowly, they closed in. Methodical. Like me.

Dogs barked, so I concealed my scent, further erasing Seraphine from the world. It changed at a brisk pace, and I had to out-think so much of it quickly.

A gas station lit up one corner. I could go into the bathroom and change my appearance. Sunglasses could hide my violet eyes until I calmed. Adrenaline caused them to glow. A moment of silence, some time to catch my breath, was all I needed.

Two white police SUVs had already congregated at the gas station. I stopped behind a tree, its girth enough to hide the anemic body I imitated. Time was running out. The police perimeter, if I calculated correctly, was nearing its center.

I recalled a building under construction a few streets up. A grocery store used to be there, and the city planned a parking garage in its place. I could rest up there, out of reach, and hide among the raw materials until daybreak, when the real fight for Seraphine would begin.

Chapter 7

I loved Seraphine more than anyone, even if I concluded she was too weak to survive in the current world. If I could remake everything, she'd be the example citizen. People of Seratopia would aspire to be like her—smart, caring, beautiful, genuine, and innocent. Just be a good fucking person. But as it stood, the world buried Seraphine alive under layers of psychotic behavior after it ignored her desire to exist peacefully. And the primary antagonist, the one who derailed her life, was sorry.

Too little. Too late.

Dawn had arrived. I had a gorgeous view of it painting the lake yellow and orange. Yellow-orange. Sitting on the fifth of seven stories, on a ten-foot slab of concrete across two I-beams, I had nowhere else to run. The police surrounded the building last night. They called my name until midnight and opted to reconvene in the morning after they said, "She isn't going anywhere."

I heard the trucks moving. Probably a crane or something. The firetruck's ladder reached the fourth floor when I was there, but I'd easily ascended to the next level. Then nobody could cross the unfinished empty spaces to reach me. I rested my back against one of the center steel columns, wrapped my arms around my knees, and watched the sunrise.

"Seraphine. Come on down."

They said the same thing repeatedly. Did nobody tell them I was on my way to a master's degree and then a doctorate? I wasn't a moron. I knew I'd reached the end of a long and difficult road. Maximum security prison awaited me, so I figured I'd enjoy the outside for as long as I could.

What kind of life is that?

A tear strolled down my face and into my mouth. It reminded me I was thirsty. I crawled onto my hands and knees and drank from a small puddle of water, courtesy of the morning dew. Bacteria didn't concern me. My ability to re-cover seemed to fight everything except what gave it life.

I paused at my reflection in the water. Cat's face stared back at me. Reverting to myself before the police suppressed my splice gene seemed like a good idea. The amount of energy required for the transformation would probably cause me to collapse. At least the police wouldn't haul me away kicking and screaming. I was an adult, after all, even if only while unconscious.

I stared at my reflection longer than planned. Cat's face didn't appeal to me, even if *I* was underneath those perfect genes. The problem I faced was recalling my countenance. While Cat's visage plagued me throughout my imprisonment, I referenced a photo to take on her appearance. Sometime between then and now, I forgot the details of what I looked like.

I wanted to blame the oversight on the few installed mirrors at the facility, but I never looked at them, anyway, except to look like someone else. I couldn't stare at the reflection of who I used to be. Now, I might never look at myself again. Who wants to look like their bully for the rest of their life and not reap any of the benefits that made them bullies?

What kind of life is that?

I laughed. And cried. And laughed some more. Loud enough to silence the police down below. Quiet enough to feel alone. I coughed and spat blood. Hunched over, I looked at the horizon again, at the sunrise, and at the water that reflected its beauty. I smiled. Kyle would've been glad to know I hadn't burst into flames like a vampire. Not yet, anyway.

The thought made me smile. I realized the world just wasn't ready for someone like me. I was ahead of my time. Maybe, if I could hibernate somewhere, I could return years or decades later when the world caught up. Somewhere that wasn't a hardened prison. A place nobody could reach. If I had wings, I could live among the clouds, but transformation required existing matter. There wasn't enough Seraphine to grow angelic wings.

What kind of life is that?

I lowered my gaze to the lake. Somewhere that wasn't a hardened prison. A place nobody could reach. If I had gills, I could exist in the lake's depths forever. I stared at the water as I stood.

Subconsciously, I heard their voices from below. "We've got activity. Come on down, Seraphine."

Actively, I focused on the waves crashing along the docks. The water could be my sanctuary or my grave.

I leaped across several I-beams and then bolted across one extending beyond the building's perimeter. When I reached the end of the beam, I jumped across and over the police forces below. I landed on an unused tire shop's roof at least fifty feet away.

"No way she made that jump!" somebody shouted.

Tumbling and rolling, I found my balance and continued running. I healed my legs until my stride improved. The lake's scent encouraged me to run faster. My bare feet pounded against metal rooftops and then a few concrete ones.

I didn't look behind me as I cleared two more buildings. I couldn't get to the water from the rooftops. If I wanted to reach its deepest parts sooner, I had to get on the ground and over to the bridge.

The police caught up. Their sirens wailed from the main and side streets. I sprinted out in the open. Slinking through the buildings would've been time consuming and given the police another chance to surround me.

I jumped down from the last building, landing on a dumpster first to minimize the fall distance. Three police cruisers drove up onto the sidewalk and grass, having already cleared the area of innocent bystanders, using threats of a murderer on the loose, I was sure. I sprinted past them before they could exit their vehicles.

"Hey! Stop!" they shouted, leaving their doors ajar to pursue. They couldn't catch me on foot. I ran like an Olympic sprinter.

I reached the bridge, a two-lane overpass with walking and biking lanes. Four-foot-high rails prevented pedestrians from falling into the water.

"We've got her now!" one said. Several police officers walked up the other end of the bridge. "You're surrounded! Let's not make this any harder!"

I stopped in the middle of the bridge. Swerving my head around, following with my body, I acknowledged they'd surrounded me. Then I jumped onto the rail, which halted their advance.

"Seraphine!"

I heard Dr. Moore's voice. She ran out from behind several police cruisers. "Seraphine, please! Wait!" I gave her a moment to catch her breath. "This isn't your fault. None of this is your fault. Nobody is going to experiment with you. Nobody's going to use you. I submitted a request to transfer Dr. Alola. She's gone." She waved her hands frantically, perhaps asking for more time. "You're different. We know you are. You're…a modern wonder. I want to help you get to where you want to go."

Too little. Too late.

I held back the tears and took a deep breath. There was so much I wanted to say, like how all the apologies were too little too late. Like how everyone passed me around like an object. Like how nobody heard Seraphine crying out for help all that time.

Before I knew it, I'd leapt off the railing.

Dr. Moore called my name again. I think. Others did, too. The only sounds I made out belonged to the lake. I glided through the air for what felt like an eternity. Turning my body, I smiled at the white clouds floating in a sea of blue. I was a cloud and below was my sky.

I crashed into the water. Arms outstretched to my sides,

legs trailing my descent, and air escaping my lungs, I gave myself to the lake. The water was peaceful. Muted. It almost made me forget about breathing—about forming gills. I almost forgot everything until something crashed into the water after me. Someone. I grinned at their desperate attempt to reach me. They wouldn't reach me; except *they* looked like Kyle.

I asked him what he was doing. He couldn't understand the bubbles I spoke. I waved him off, swinging my arms through the water as fast as I could. He didn't heed my warning. He swam deeper with one hand extended toward me. I could tell he was running out of breath.

I righted myself and met him halfway. By then, he'd lost all the air in his lungs. The lake almost swept him away, too. I grabbed the arm he'd extended and pulled him to me. I grabbed his face with both hands, formed gills behind my ears, and exchanged breaths through our lips. He panicked briefly, but eventually opened his eyes to mine.

He wrapped his arms around my lower back and turned my life-saving breath into a kiss. He maneuvered his tongue past my lips and stopped at my teeth. His eyes softened when I denied him entry. He knew I needed blood. Gripping my waist tightly and shaking me gently, he pleaded.

Don't break his heart.

I opened my mouth and extended my teeth. Kyle pushed something down my throat. Something he'd crushed into tiny pieces. Something I couldn't target and circulate elsewhere in my body. I almost pushed him away, but he grabbed my lips with his and held on for something more. His hands didn't tighten or loosen around my waist. I was free to go, but I didn't leave.

Suddenly, the gills stopped extracting oxygen. The skin flaps closed. I gasped for air and Kyle contributed very little. I kicked my legs, and he did, too. We ascended. The sky couldn't have felt farther away. When I thought we wouldn't make it, we breached the surface together.

***

3 Years Later

"Students, parents, faculty, and staff. Thank you for joining me in our annual tradition of celebrating progress. Because progress is relative, we've all started from the same place…ignorant about something. Our careers. Our lives. Ourselves. And we ended up in the same place…wiser about something. Life's a never-ending journey of discovery.

"We'll find things along the way. Truths. Lies. Drugs. Technology. Friends, family, and loved ones. Enemies. Ourselves. Some of those things will encourage us and others…they'll discourage us. And while it's true we're on the same journey, the challenges we encounter will differ slightly with each passing day. I've been on my journey for a long time now. Proud to find beautiful things along the way, such as each of you.

"So, I thought instead of telling you about my journey this year, I'd like you to hear about someone else's. Someone whose challenges are closer in time to your own. One who will and has changed the lives of millions around the world.

"Please help me welcome to the stage, your valedictorian, Seraphine Johnson…"

Speechless

Chapter 1

I stood at the village center, previously defined by the colorful marketplace circling a wide-open courtyard, and now, by the three burning posts without bodies.

A warning.

The surrounding flames caused shadows of me to flicker in all directions, convincing me often that something moved. That someone lived. Its crackling spoke louder than I could, and almost too loud for me to hear anything else. So I quieted the burning village the only way I knew how. I cocked my head back and bellowed in agony.

The rage in my voice deconstructed the red of the flames. It pulled the color fast enough to snuff the embers, which left streaks and splotches everywhere, like spilled blood. I slammed my mouth shut because a gradual change in tone or pitch would've affected the remaining colors of the courtyard, such as the varying shades of green that red's absence promoted, which made fall resemble spring.

Then it was quiet. Too quiet. No one screamed in pain or cried out for help. Nobody moaned from under the collapsed structures or coughed in the smoke rising from the extinguished flames. Destroyed businesses quietly crumbled to the ground. My voice disrupted sound, too.

I spun in frantic circles, desperate to see if I missed a hand reaching out. There were none.

"Naim!"

I turned toward the jarring sound of my name. Black braids with brown tips swung from side to side and across the face of a young woman running to me. Baggy pine-green overalls briefly flapped from a mild gust.

Lavonne.

She slowed as she drew closer and observed the surroundings. Had the flames still burned, they would've reflected in her large brown eyes. She shifted her gaze to me and communicated with her hands, "Are you okay?"

"What happened here?" I responded with harsh movements, separating and then bringing my hands close together to form signs.

Lavonne lowered her arms and then raised her eyes to the smoldering posts behind me. Her jaw dropped. She collapsed to her knees and stared at the scene as if the posts were still burning.

"Why would anyone..." she signed before slumping onto her heels.

As the surrounding sounds slowly returned to normal, quick footsteps alerted me to others. A little girl in a long and flowing coral dress ran up and veered into Lavonne's arms.

"Nakenyah!" Lavonne said as she embraced the girl. Leaning back, she held the girl at arm's length and checked her for injuries as if she was searching for contraband.

Restless, Nakenyah fought through the inspection and settled into Lavonne's lap. She looked at the posts, as if she too could see the flames I'd already put out.

Lavonne signed, "Where is everyone?" She moved the girl's shoulder-length black hair back behind her ears and tended to the loose braids.

Nakenyah watched her own hands as she made the formations. Only a few of us required the speechless language. Lavonne learned it to communicate with those of us who shouldn't speak, and the children followed her example. It was more love and acceptance than any of us could ever ask for.

Nakenyah signed, "Rosemary." She pointed in the direction she came from.

Rosemary stood at the entrance of the marketplace. Long black hair draped over her shoulders; the rest peeked around the backside of her wide hips. She wouldn't come closer, now that I'd separated the red. The same way yellow made her smile through the worst, red caused her to love the wrong things. She thrived in the natural, balanced distribution of color, which was now in disarray.

I looked down at Lavonne. She understood and then signed to Nakenyah. "What happened?"

Nakenyah raised her hands. She'd painted half of her fingernails blue and dressed them with star-shaped stickers that glowed in the night. "Red. Swords. Fire," she signed.

The Order of Light.

I should've noticed sooner that the red brick foundation of the marketplace courtyard had dulled. I blamed the crescent moon's light and the earlier flames for missing the fine detail, but it was my rage that truly blinded me from the obvious and unnatural discoloration.

The Order of Light forged weapons using an artifact from space. When activated, the artifact resonated with an individual's affinity for certain colors and attracted those hues from the surroundings like powerful magnets, leaving behind the unused shades, usually an ash gray. I've seen the weapons the Order created using red and had warned them about using the village's colors for their wrongdoing.

Red wasn't the only hue in their ranks. The Order of Light employed all the colors. Green squires must've erected the wooden posts. They could've used those gifts to build homes, but they tore them apart instead.

Nakenyah didn't need to communicate anything more. A child shouldn't have to speak of what happened here. I headed toward the marketplace entrance where Rosemary stood.

"Naim!" Lavonne shouted. "Where are you going?"

I didn't turn around. I didn't want to scare Nakenyah with the scowl I wore on my face. But I only had one way to communicate without stripping the world of what little color it had left, and that required me to turn around and face the life I'd sworn and failed to protect. So I didn't respond. Silently, I conveyed with clenched fists that it was time to put out the light.

Chapter 2

The green squire in front of me looked defeated, as a man who set fire to the homes of innocent people should look. Like a coward. Like a life not worth living.

He scuffed the knees of his gray slacks as he meekly crawled around the small space afforded to him, between me and the posts he'd stood up in the courtyard.

Small traces of red stained the elbows of his grayed shirt, and his broken fingernails scratched the red that gradually returned to the brick ground. He searched the space in front of him, as if his green eyes saw nothing, as if his thoughts had scattered. I imagined he still heard the echoes of Ansell whispering. The remaining green of the fall forest leaves likely carried Ansell's voice for miles and surrounded the man like wilderness until he surrendered.

Three of us sat on one of the few courtyard benches that survived the conflagration. To my left, Rosemary crossed her legs underneath a bright yellow, orange, and green patchwork dress. She cupped her raised knee with both hands. Lavonne sat to my right, slouched forward with elbows resting on her thighs. Ansell leaned his back against the far-right post, across from Lavonne, and faced the charred rubble of a fruit stand. He placed the sole of one foot flat against the wood and crossed his arms.

Lavonne stared at me until I nodded. Then she lowered her gaze to the man.

"Hello," she said to him in a somber tone.

His erratic movements ceased at the sound of her voice, as if she'd broken a spell he suffered under. She had the power to captivate people, and she did so without artifact influence. However, her greeting didn't carry the usual energy reminiscent of a celebration. Its flame had burned out like a candle. Lavonne sat speechless.

Words of hatred didn't exist in her vocabulary. I extended my arm out in front and sought her attention. When her brown eyes noticed and then followed my hands back to me, I asked her to translate my words.

Lavonne faced me and spoke while I signed. "My voice attracts color from the world and destroys whatever structure it brightened. If you lie…" she paused and then raised her eyes to mine, perhaps searching them for something other than the threat I signed. She translated anyway. "I'll strip the green from your eyes, and you'll never see anything again."

The man gritted his teeth. He lowered his head and stared at the ground and then at the slip-on shoes of Rosemary's bobbing foot. He sat up on his heels and attempted to point at the crest on his chest.

His finger trembled, touching everything but the crest. "By…by order of the Light. You…you must release me."

Shaped like the sun, the Order of Light's crest featured eight white triangles surrounding a white circle. Each ray represented a Paragon of Light—the most powerful in their ranks—and the white center symbolized the even spread of colors that comprised the light they worshiped.

He was just a squire—a shade of the Paragons.

I signed with less anger in my movements. I suppressed the rage within me because Lavonne didn't deserve the hostility I would've directed at her, and the man in front of me would lose everything if *I* spoke to him.

"Who gave that order?" Lavonne asked.

The man's confidence backed down. His arms fell to his sides and his head hung low. I watched him curl his fingers into fists and bite his lips until blood escaped.

I leaned forward and lowered to one knee, bringing my mouth as close to his as I could. Then I spoke, with less volume than a whisper, against his lips. "Nakenyah."

The man covered his mouth as blood gushed from the wound further opened by my voice. The red in his blood splattered across the ground, and with it, pieces of the lips it had soaked. A hole in his jaw made his teeth visible when he cried out and when he closed his mouth and whimpered. Remaining parts of his grayed lips had also cracked when the stripped red drained the moisture from it, making speech almost impossible.

I signed at the man, not thinking whether Lavonne could see every motion.

"A little girl told me what you did," Lavonne translated.

Hatred returned to my movements. I directed everything toward the squire.

"You destroyed her home, and now I'm going to destroy yours," Lavonne translated. "Who sent you here?"

He was capable of speech. Fear paralyzed his voice more than his injured lip. He chose not to respond. He protected his masters, or himself from their wrath if he ratted them out. I could've offered him sanctuary for that information, but I already planned to banish him, his masters, his comrades, and possibly the entire city to darkness.

After I stood, the man's green eyes followed me in defiance. He was harmless without the artifact weapon he'd carried. Ansell said it resembled the letter "T" naked and an oversized maul after it attracted the green its wielder commanded. The man could've offered to use that tool to rebuild the village. Instead, he sat tight-lipped, as if in a contest of wills. Patience wasn't one of my strengths.

I turned to Rosemary and nodded. After she uncrossed her legs and stood, the man finally spoke.

"What are you going to do to me? Help! Help! Somebody help me!"

I walked away, brushing emotions with Rosemary as we passed each other. Lavonne stomped her feet alongside me. She held her tongue until we were out of earshot of the man.

"This is not our way," she said. Each step slowed her as she dodged the remnants of the marketplace. Singed cloth caught by the wind blew across the ground. A black, unrecognizable stuffed animal lay face first against the brick. Lavonne hop-stepped over it.

I signed without glancing at her. "It is not our way."

"Then stop this!"

I swerved my head toward her. She recoiled when I raised my hands, as if I'd strike her. "Tell me how else to protect our family," I signed.

Lavonne leaned forward and balled her fists at her sides. "What if that man is protecting *his* family?"

My hands made thumping sounds as I raced to form the symbols. "Protecting his family by destroying ours? Look around!"

The silence I spoke made Lavonne's voice seem louder.

"Yes, look around. Is that who *you* want to be, too?" Lavonne gestured toward the blackened rooftops. "I'm trying to keep us from being like them!"

I folded my arms. Powerful words swept the fight out from under me until Rosemary walked up. She'd pulled her hair back into a thick ponytail and finished wrapping a cyan-colored tie around it. She stood next to Lavonne, towering over the voice of reason.

Rosemary signed, "They came for the artifact residue." She pointed at her chest and then touched her lips.

The artifact residue that contaminated the air and water we inhaled and drank for years caused our voices to affect the colors within range and the surfaces they embellished. Unlike artifact weapons, our voices repelled color particles. Rosemary's disturbed particles manipulated the hearts of others. She likely used the remaining red on the green squire's lips to induce a confession. Ansell extended his vocal tone and range. And I simply destroyed.

I looked up at the mountainside behind the village. The smokestack of an artifact processing plant stood among the deciduous trees, which were surrounded by large boulders nestled against their bases. In the past, the wind had carried most of the artifact waste through the village. Additional residue had settled down into the canal and caused the otherwise clear water to sparkle. The Order of Light eventually reduced the waste its facilities produced, but for many, it was too late. Those who survived did so with side effects.

Rosemary signed. "They think we're harvesting it."

"Who gave the order?" I signed.

"M-I-C-H-A-E-L."

Michael led the Order of Light. I recalled him on television once. He was a tall black man dressed in white cloth underneath silver armor pieces. He exuded righteousness, so I didn't expect him to be responsible for the attack.

His leadership helped maintain order in the city, so the children have said. They paraded around the village courtyard in outfits similar to the Paragons and acted out heroic events using their names. Like all stories, the ones the children mimicked carried deeper meanings that only those with real-world exposure understood.

Lavonne turned to me. "I will talk with Luciela. She is the most powerful Paragon of Light and the kindest. She will listen if we talk to her."

I'd never met Luciela, but I remember Lavonne describing her as the epitome of what the light should've been—a beacon of hope. She was also a warrior and a mother and the one responsible for reducing the artifact's pollution.

Rosemary shook her head and then signed, "She is gone."

Lavonne staggered backwards. I stepped forward and passed an arm around her lower back in case she fell.

"Luciela..." she whispered. More tears softened her cheeks. She steadied her gaze and looked up at Rosemary. "How?"

Rosemary shrugged, a slow rise and fall of her shoulders, and then signed, "They will send her off this morning."

"Then we should, too," I signed.

I faced the mountain's peak. The Order of Light's Grand Courtyard was on the other side, at the crest of the mountain for all in the city to see. The sacred ground where they broadcast the burial of their dead wasn't too far from the mountainside entrance. They lined the casks of their fallen with the artifact and wouldn't leave a single fragment out of sight.

If we trekked straight through the forest, off the beaten path, we could reach the main city road by mid-day. I set out on that path. Rosemary followed me. Ansell would join us after dealing with the squire. And Lavonne...she didn't move. She seemed lost in her thoughts, as if she pondered a world without Luciela.

"She can't be gone..." Lavonne said.

I walked several feet away from her before I looked over my shoulder and signed into the air, "You don't have to come. But your voice will save more lives than mine."

Chapter 3

Though she was light on her feet when she danced through the marketplace, Rosemary's heavy steps resounded the loudest as she marched with purpose through the forest. Her multicolored dress, patched with bright and beautiful colors, fluttered when the wind howled. As the white cotton fields beyond the edge of the forest drew near, she increased her pace, and the distance between us grew, for her sake and ours.

Rosemary's voice dissolved reflected colors into a fragrance that influenced the hearts and minds of those who inhaled it. The frequency of her voice, intertwined with the colored particles, further elicited emotions, such as love, happiness, excitement, and rage, too.

Even though she charged toward the city like an angry creature of the forest, she wouldn't harm anyone. All the frustration from seeing the things she loved burned to the ground, she stomped out across the fallen leaves of the path we forged.

When she reached a couple of farmers escorting a carriage along the road, the tension in her body dissipated. She straightened her posture, uncurled her fingers, freed her long black strands from the band that held them in place, sliding the yellow elastic fabric up her arm, and developed a graceful stride beneath the flowing dress.

I couldn't see Rosemary's face, but I knew she smiled because the farmers grinned after she greeted them. Rosemary used her beautiful voice and electric presence as a mind-numbing weapon.

"Good morning! How are you?" I imagined what she said, recalling her demeanor from when she used to speak.

Her actual words didn't reach us. We walked slowly enough to be unaffected by the particles she churned, yet close enough that the effect of her voice on those around us lasted long enough for us to pass them without question.

Most people wouldn't have suspected us, anyway. Our light and dark complexions didn't vary too far from the locals, and the city wasn't so small that someone would notice we didn't belong. Rosemary distracted the citizens to protect them from me, as the rage within me had been caged, not quelled, and the ignorance of even one person could trigger havoc upon the city.

Rosemary waved at those in the distance, hugged the few that approached her, and caressed the fingers of others who'd reached out to touch her, as she continued to bless them with her words. They echoed off the buildings, and no longer carried the artifact that enhanced them. "Thank you! You're wonderful! You're so beautiful! I love who you are!"

She left gray clothing in her wake, turning the hues people wore into a scent that aroused jubilation. Their eyes came alive. Their placid expressions turned to smiles and then to laughter. A sudden energy within them fought back against the exhaustion of a long morning under the sun.

Lavonne wanted to stop Rosemary. I sensed her unease, a focused and disapproving gaze, but she'd agreed to stay out of our way, and only use her voice of reason when the time came to prevent us from crossing a line.

Rosemary had crossed that line long ago when her voice first manifested during Sunday service, while singing with the choir. She had attracted the unwanted attention of everyone in attendance. They'd lunged at her and sought to satisfy the obsession that filled their hearts and left her in shambles by the altar. Streaks of dark red lines from the solid grasp of desperate hands had covered her honey-toned arms. Clumps of her black hair had lain scattered around her like fresh shavings on the floor of a barber shop, and her trembling fingers had clutched the tattered dress she had been wearing.

I was one of *them*. I had hovered over the pack of wolves, and then I fell through and onto her. In that moment, my voice stripped the remaining colors, and fabric, of her dress. It gave way for people to grope her bare skin and leave the marks that marred her to this day. I never forgot, nor forgave myself, even if, like her, I had no control over what transpired.

I remembered returning to my senses sooner than others, before anyone could defile her, and after my voice and hers used all the surrounding color. While I witnessed other churchgoers committing sins in the halls and pews of God's home, Rosemary slipped out from under me and ran deep into the forest. If she'd screamed at the top of her lungs, nobody would've heard her. But I'd found her. Grayed leaves, from what I'd assumed to be cries of pain from the heart, trailed her like breadcrumbs, and the fragrance they released made me anxious.

She'd settled on a tree stump in a small clearing bathed with sunlight. I sat next to her. We didn't speak. The fear of our voices had clasped our lips tight, so we shared a silence that brought us closer together. She leaned her head against my shoulder, and I embraced her the way she wanted to be held: of my volition.

Over time, Rosemary learned to command her voice, and she used it to protect the village. She turned away would-be troublemakers by convincing them they were tired or by exciting them about a new place.

Now, she forged a path through the city streets, uplifting the mood of citizens like a traveling festival. She garnered the attention of patrolling squires who abandoned their posts to greet her. The city celebrated Rosemary, while Lavonne and I continued to the holy grounds where the Order of Light buried their dead.

We were too late. The ceremony had already ended. Most of the blades of grass the attendees had stood on were halfway back to their upright position.

I walked over to a two-inch thick circular concrete platform nestled in the grass. It was the Order of Light's crest. I imagined a pastor standing behind a podium on the now-empty center tile, and the Paragons of Light each standing on one of the eight triangular rays that circled it. Seven, since they'd gathered to lay one to rest.

Lavonne stood over a tombstone and read aloud:

Order of Light's Paragon
Luciela, The Crescent Light

Lavonne crouched and then sat on her knees. "Luci…" she spoke through tears, the follow-on sniffling louder than her voice. She leaned forward and ran her fingers through the grass in front of the tombstone as if she could stroke the hairs of the woman beneath the dirt. "Why?"

I looked at the platform again. There wasn't enough color in it for me to destroy it. Its resilience was a sign that the Light would prove difficult to extinguish. Mother Nature must've agreed. Howling, she blew a breath through the field, as if she, too, were trying to wear down the stone. What I thought were words carried by the breeze turned out to be Ansell's voice traveling along the blown blades of grass.

The disembodied voice came and went. It said, "There's a gathering at the base of the mountain, on the road leading up to the Grand Courtyard."

I couldn't respond to him, even if I spoke. The fleeting whisper traveled in one direction: away from the source. Ansell studied the wind's patterns to further extend his range and guide the message's recipient. His voice swirled around us and continued along a path leading back to the main road.

Chapter 4

Lavonne and I found the crowd Ansell had mentioned. They spread across a block's worth of street heading up to the base of the mountain; a gathering that started with stragglers in the back and grew denser toward the front. From the rear, Lavonne and I saw a single animated man elevated above the crowd, possibly on the concrete foundation leading up to a statue of Michael.

I couldn't make out his words. Whatever he said, the crowd stood with him, not in opposition. They cheered every few minutes. Many of them raised signs into the air. I mostly saw the wooden stake fastened to the backside of each, and the occasional color that bled through the reverse side of the poster board. The ones I read backwards suggested civil unrest.

An upheaval didn't concern me unless Michael physically stood at its center. He didn't. From what I'd heard, Michael had an indomitable presence. I doubted the citizens would stand in his shadow and raise condemning signs. They'd be on their knees, shielding their eyes from the false light he manufactured.

I didn't see any Paragons. A contingent of squires blocked the main road leading up to the Grand Courtyard. They reminded me of weeds growing between cobbled stones. All of them wore brown suits with green shirts underneath, and each carried a bow over their shoulder. I wasn't familiar with every application of color used by the Orders, except that the shape of the artifact facilitated offensive and defensive capabilities.

Lavonne grabbed my hand. She didn't tug me back or try to prevent me from going forward. She took a deep breath, as if to ready herself for the shoving and bumping that awaited us. Her eyes also suggested resolve. She refused to lose sight of me. If we got separated in the crowd, her voice would go unheard, and mine would kill everyone.

I rotated my hand to take hold of hers instead, to show that her presence was not only acknowledged, but welcomed. We made eye contact. Her vibrant, brown eyes continued to cage my anger, and I worried that her hand in mine would subside it altogether.

I took the lead. We walked sideways through the crowd. No one complained as we slipped by, taking extra precautions to avoid unnecessary physical contact. We stood still when the crowd erupted and again when they raised their signs higher into the air. We dodged closed fists and thick paper edges.

The speaker's voice and his message became clearer as we got closer to his stage. He said, "Too long have we stood in the Light's shadow—in the dark. Luciela is gone! Her son is on the run! And Michael's sitting on a throne of lies! We demand answers! We demand the truth! We demand that the Colors stand up and usurp the Light."

I stopped moving again. Lavonne stood next to me while I watched the man on stage wipe sweat from his brow. His demeanor treaded carefully between the leader of a movement and a traditional protester in the street. He spoke with the cadence of historical figures and rallied the crowd that could storm the Grand Courtyard at any second.

"We demand a new Order!" he shouted and then paused, perhaps letting his words sink into the hearts of the people in front of him. "The Order of Light vowed to protect us. They created a hierarchy that placed themselves above the Colors and claimed that they could serve the community better as leaders because they harnessed, and therefore understood, all the colors. They said they could better serve the community as reinforcements because they were powerful but few. Sitting on their throne—on their ass—for years, they've lost sight of the day-to-day fight. And now we know why. They've been fighting each other!"

He bobbed his head up and down and then looked across the crowd, slowly from left to right, as he caught his breath.

"Michael killed Luciela—our savior. Michael gave the order to kill Lucien—her legacy. And Michael cast a murderous shadow over the Light!"

Gasps erupted from the crowd. I looked down at Lavonne's sharp eyes, which rapidly shifted left and right until she noticed me staring. At last, she briefly shared my anger. With flaring nostrils settling and a deep breath she quickly controlled, she signed, "I did not know."

I looked away, across the crowd and to the speaker. The Order of Light was imploding on itself, but something about the scene felt odd. I couldn't put my finger on it. The man condemned the Light, yet he spoke like an acolyte in favor of true teachings warped by the current regime.

The man licked his lips. "And let's not forget about the inhumane experiments the Light conducted to bolster their ranks. They pumped children full of chemicals every day to enhance their control of color. One of them used that power to show us the truth we know today—the truth about what really goes on behind those palace-like walls."

When the man took a breath, I heard Ansell. Leaves blown down from the mountain carried his voice through the streets. "Those artifact chemicals ran down the mountainside and poisoned the water and food supply of women and children."

I expected people to turn in circles looking for the voice's owner. I imagined they'd suspect each other first and then realize that their misplaced excitement, riled up by the man on stage, was absent in the vocal tones. But no one reacted. The squires observed the demonstration, but they didn't seem alarmed.

Ansell continued, "Then the Light ordered the burning of their village. People ran from their smoldering homes. Photos, memories, handmade treasures, and much more turned to ashes…"

I glanced around. It was as if no one cared. They rallied against the Light because its leader killed Luciela, but no one batted an eye when the same Light tried to kill all of us. I balled my fists. Lavonne grabbed one of them. When I looked down at her, she shook her head.

She pointed at her ear and flicked her index finger away from it, signaling that no one heard Ansell's voice.

But I heard him, as if he stood next to me. Lavonne and I mingled among the people, so surely, they heard his voice, too.

The man at the front spoke again. With Ansell's voice in my ear and my focus split, I didn't understand what he said. In unison, the people pumped signs and fists into the air again. They chanted: *Bring down the Light. Their rule isn't right.*

Lavonne pulled away. She approached one demonstrator, a woman with a low brown haircut and a navy windbreaker jacket. Cautiously, she reached for the woman's elbow and nudged it.

The woman didn't react. She seemed too invested in the stage-man's words to care about being touched, but Lavonne believed something else.

She stepped in front of the woman, stared her in the face for a moment, and then waved both arms in front of her. No reaction.

"They're not…real," Lavonne signed. "Or we're invisible." She formed the hand signals and then shrugged.

"But I can see you," I signed.

Lavonne shot me a hard glance. She turned back to the woman and studied the puberty-stricken face. Slowly, she raised both hands toward the woman's shoulders with fingers pointed at the sky as if she planned to shove the suspected illusion to the ground.

She didn't.

Lavonne's fingers trembled in place above the woman's shoulders with harrowed eyes fixed on a hazel pair that now stared back.

None of the woman's other movements changed. She

chanted and screamed past Lavonne's face and then startled us both when she raised a fist into the air.

Lavonne blinked hard and then stepped back and bumped into a short man with thick black hair. She apologized, but he didn't respond. Not at first. Lavonne looked away before he and a few others turned around. The man looked up at the back of Lavonne's head. The others looked down at her. Their movements seemed awkward—forced—robotic or puppet-like.

Lavonne saw my gaze. She glanced over her shoulder and shrieked at the sight of stoic eyes slowly turning toward her. She ducked and scurried over to me, perhaps for safety, but multiple eyes had already surrounded us. If they attacked us, Lavonne's screams would be drowned by theirs and mine would destroy them, a massacre that felt more serious now that they acknowledged our presence and refuted the idea that they were mere illusions.

As I contemplated fight-or-flight options, I heard Ansell's voice again. "The villagers extinguished the flames with their tears. They shuffled through the memories in search of a place among the ashes to sleep. Everything they touched charred their fingers black, including the handmade, now singed, blankets they wrapped around their bodies."

This time, the protesters who had noticed us heard Ansell's words. They raised their chins and circled in place. The rest remained in blissful ignorance.

Ansell's voice should've reached them sooner. He'd always been good at theater and capturing the attention of young and old alike. When he wasn't putting on a play for the village at the town center, he strolled through the marketplace in character. Occasionally, his and Rosemary's joyfulness intersected and spread to the shop owners and visitors.

His cheerful personality changed a couple of days prior to the church incident. His voice had created dissonance when it manipulated nearby reflected colors into extending and repeating every syllable he sang. We knew artifact caused the chaos, but Ansell didn't carry an artifact item. The Order of Light held those close to home and managed distribution to the Colors. We didn't understand how his voice resonated across the village until something similar happened to Rosemary and me.

Ansell's voice came again, the undertones directed at me. "And now the Light is fighting the darkness they created."

I looked up at the mountain top, at the glint of light from the sun reflecting off the windows of the Grand Courtyard. The colors of the surrounding forest had been muted. Enough solar rays reflected off the lower grass, trees, and branches to return color to the mountainside, a lighter hue that slowly traveled toward the grayed building.

I grabbed Lavonne's hand and pulled her through the crowd while most of the people remained distracted. Most forward bodies ignored us. A few turned in time to see us disappear among their fellow protestors.

We emerged at the front right of the stage. The squires guarding the road up to the courtyard had abandoned their posts. I glimpsed them chasing Ansell into the city.

Lavonne ran after them until my outstretched arm reached its limit and jerked her to a stop. She looked back at me, eyes wide with disbelief.

I let her hand go and signed, "He's distracting them." I nodded toward the top of the mountain.

More color drained from the surroundings. Flashes of light escaped the tall glass windows of the Grand Courtyard, followed by a black streak I'd never seen before.

Chapter 5

No one impeded our trek to the Grand Courtyard's main entrance. Ansell must've lured those guards away, too, and without a fight. The grounds in front of the doors looked pristine, their surface shimmering. Bell-shaped blue and purple wildflowers lining the cobbled stones flourished under water droplets racing down their curved petals like shooting stars.

We looked up at the thirteen-foot doors and then opened them with a gentle push. If they hadn't opened, I would've destroyed the marble after igniting the yellow and red of the carved solar patterns. A whisper, for Lavonne's sake, was all it would've taken. She refused to leave my side and agreed to stay behind me. My voice destroyed the first surface it contacted, which made reflected vocal signals less dangerous.

The door rumbled, causing the ground to tremble as it slowly revealed the Grand Courtyard's interior. I saw no one inside the garden-like lobby. Flowers of various colors blossomed from the vines snaking along the walls. Unnaturally grown, it seemed. Roses, lavender, carnations, hydrangea, and more shared stems up to the ceiling. They grew from the rich brown dirt that flanked a wide marble path.

The walkway led to an unmanned stone counter and split into two, curving to either side on its way down separate corridors. I turned toward the left path, since the flashes of light I'd seen outside the courtyard came from the east side of the building. The glass windowpanes should be around the corner. If a straight path didn't exist, I'd make one.

"Where is everyone?" Lavonne asked. She spun in a circle as she walked, tilting her head back to take in the breathtaking view of the sky above. "No staff? No security?"

She knew to look at me for a response, if the question wasn't rhetorical. When I caught her brown eyes from my peripheral vision, I signed, understanding that she'd interpret my hand signs backwards. "Who would attack the Light in their home?" I asked, without considering my reason for being there.

I directed Lavonne's attention to the walls on the other side of the lobby door I stepped through. A colorful mural of flowers served as the Grand Courtyard's defense. Against anyone commanding the Light, a normal person wouldn't stand a chance. Someone with an artifact might use a fraction of the visible colors; the remaining hues would be used against them.

Intruders would likely face a Paragon, too, not a squire. During re-enactments, the village children argued about the lack of Light squires. Their limited numbers meant fewer "good guys" to impersonate, a thought that gave me pause when I wondered, who would tell the children that their beloved role models had burned their homes to the ground? The question reinvigorated my anger.

Lavonne stealthily moved along the right wall and then squatted. She shushed me with an index finger against her lips and then waved me over. I raised a brow and walked to her. She pulled me down by the elbow and pointed toward an open door farther down the hallway. The structure reminded me of the courtyard entrance—thirteen feet tall, six feet wide, and decorated with intricate drawings of the actual sun that made it glow blood-orange.

Lavonne didn't call me over to admire the interior design. She'd heard voices, and then I did, too.

The voice of a young man echoed into the hallway. "Was Mom a part of your plan? Attack her so I'd run for my life?" He sounded panicked yet determined, as if he'd sorted through several lies and now stood on the cusp of the one truth, refusing to let it slip from his grasp.

A woman aggressively shouted back. "I had nothing to do with that! That was all him. I just...I took advantage of..."

I stood, stepped past Lavonne, and walked to the opening

so I could hear better. Lavonne jumped to her feet. She grabbed the back of my shirt for a second and then let go. She recoiled when I glanced back at her. A cheesy, apologetic grin sat on her face.

She must've thought I was going to barge inside. The speechless language taught me how to read the human body, or rather, how to communicate using the human body. We didn't have the luxury of raising or lowering our voice. We couldn't verbally impersonate or mock others. We couldn't even laugh.

"It's over, Elena," a deeper male voice said.

I turned back toward the room's entrance, flattening myself against the wall outside of it to ensure none of them saw my shadow peeking inside.

The woman replied, "Over? I helped. I brought him to his knees with the light all of you underestimated." She paused and then continued. "Elena's not suited for combat, remember? Illusions can't win battles."

The deep male voice returned. "The Order of Light will excommunicate you both for high treason."

An internal struggle, just as the protest speaker had stated. Their fight must've created the flashes of light I'd seen from the road. I think. Recent memory couldn't explain the black streak, and I'd never heard the village children claim that color, either.

None of that mattered. I came for answers—answers that weren't in the Grand Courtyard's paint-saturated halls.

I pushed off the wall without alerting Lavonne and strolled into the room. She followed. If she reached for my shirt again, she missed.

The floral garden in the room had lost all its hues. The setting sun, beginning its descent past the glass ceiling's right edge over a throne-like chair at the far end, slowly recolored the black soil flanking another stone path. Grayed flowers reflected hints of their natural color, thriving in a shade that darkened toward the perimeter of the room.

Patches of garden next to the left-side floor-to-ceiling win-dowpanes were particularly black. Contrarily, the wall on the right radiated an untainted white, as if all the color absent from the room had reflected off it.

Even the clothing worn by the room's occupants had drained. Most of them, anyway. Two men standing closer to the entrance were colorful anomalies in an otherwise black and white movie. I saw them first when I entered and then in my peripheral vision afterward.

The first man, a stout and shirtless guy, stood ahead and to the right, where the ground widened in the shape of the Order of Light's crest, as if I'd entered on the stem of a sun-flower and they stood on its disc florets. The same solar sym-bols that embellished the courtyard doors covered the man's skin from the waist to the crown of his bald head. Muscular thighs shaped the white pants he wore but settled loosely on a pair of metal boots. A Paragon of Light, I assumed. He saw but didn't inquire about us. Either audacity or disinterest an-chored his feet.

An ordinary man stood next to the burly Paragon. Pres-ence eluded him. He could've easily been just another flower, growing from the cracks in the ground, if it had any, instead of the nearby garden. The bland shirt he wore almost blended into the scene, and his torn jeans suggested he'd hiked up the mountain, along a trail thick with bushes and branches.

Then I focused on the two men and a woman centered on the stone crest. Two sat on their knees, clothes and skin tone grayed to varying degrees, the same as the rest of the room. The younger man hovered over the woman while the older man slouched several feet away by himself.

I recognized the loner as Michael, easily identified by short dark hair and the infamous solar crest shaved out of the side of his head. He didn't exude the dominating presence I'd heard so much about. With his head hung low, lifeless eyes stared at the ground. He seemed demoralized. Defeated.

The clean, light-gray cloth beneath Michael's pristine silver armor pieces suggested a psychological battle had occurred instead of a physical one, but I noticed splotches of blood here and there on the ground. Though without color, they tainted the courtyard floor in the same ugly streaks as they had the marketplace this morning.

Similar discoloration covered the man shielding the woman. He held her close, with his right arm over her shoulder and his left hand steadying himself using a black staff. Torn clothes, busted lips, and wheezing—the blood belonged to him. I wondered if he'd exerted all his mental strength to bring down Michael and somehow sustained physical damage in the process. An unlikely theory. The scene reminded me of a gray-scale puzzle with some colored pieces and others missing.

I found a corner of the puzzle in the woman's silver eyes. She glared at me, as a mother defending her child would. As if the man over her shoulder was a cave she guarded the entrance to, she protected something else.

She wore the colors of the Light. Silver metal plates extended beyond the ends of a light gray skirt that draped over her thighs. She reached over her right shoulder and grabbed the younger man's arm.

Nobody spoke. In my head, I paired the voices I'd heard from the hallway with each person inside the room. The female voice fit the only woman I saw, the one who referred to herself in the third person as Elena. Smeared eyeliner and moist cheeks matched the vocal energy I'd felt outside the door.

I thought the deep voice belonged to Michael, but the words I'd heard from outside, clarified by the positions and moods of the people inside, seemed to pass judgement *on* him, not *by* him.

The burly man could've produced the bass capable of unsettling the assertive. I sensed an unforgiving aura from him, that of a man who followed the rules out of pure, un-yielding faith. He didn't intimidate me, though. None of them did.

Unable to communicate with others, I worked manual labor jobs to support the village. I loaded sacks of potatoes during fall, chopped wood in the winter, and laid brick for new houses in the spring, all of which chiseled my muscles.

Lavonne should've broken the silence by now. I watched her from the corner of my eyes, still taking in the courtyard scene, from the elevated view of the city below through the glass windows, to the garden devoid of color, and then to the couple in front of us, where she stopped and stared at them with apparent empathy.

The ordinary man shouted, "No more fighting!" He stepped forward and waved his hands out in front, one directed at each group on either side of him. Out of breath, he added. "It's over. Whatever it is—whatever you've come for—it's over now."

I raised a brow and unclenched my fists. I signed to Lavonne. She didn't translate. I looked down at her and made the signs again, slower and more deliberate. She stared ahead without blinking until I turned my body to face her. Then she watched me from the corners of her eyes as I formed new symbols.

"You don't want me to be like them, but I can't convey our differences without hurting them," I signed.

She didn't look at me and responded using the speechless language. "Why don't you start with our similarities?" She half-turned to me. "We're all people, Naim. We love and hurt the same."

I wanted to scoff at her remarks but remembered the repercussions of simply exhaling loudly. "They are monsters," I signed.

"We have to tell them what they've done, not with malice, but with love."

"They only know hate, Lavonne."

Lavonne shook her head and folded her arms. She tapped her foot a few times and then turned to the ordinary-looking man. "My name is Lavonne, and this is Naim," she gestured at me. "We live in a small village on the other side of the mountain. Lived," she paused. "This morning, we found our marketplace and many of our homes burned to the ground. Those responsible erected posts, in a way only those who manipulate colors can. We came to get answers, to understand, and to ask…why?"

The young man looked over at Michael, turning his body a few degrees. He lowered his head, either wondering or feeling guilty if Michael gave the order.

Michael didn't raise his head. The ordinary man said nothing. He stepped back and slumped, as if he felt the weight of our village's pain. Elena's eyes relaxed. She retracted her claws and averted her gaze, slinking further into the young man's shadow.

"And you think the Order of Light was responsible?" the burly man asked.

Lavonne said, "We captured a green squire. I don't know if he belongs to the Light, so we came to ask Luciela." Tension in the young man's body waned. Before he could speak, Lavonne said, "She's gone. I know."

The ordinary man balled his fist and raised it outward. "My wife didn't do it. And neither did my son, Lucien." He pointed at the young man. Then he lowered his arm and used one hand to uncurl the fingers of the other. "I'm sorry. I just wish people would leave my family alone."

Lucien glanced down at Elena. He leaned forward and secured his right arm further around her. He said, "Burned to the ground. That's horrible." He raised his head to his father. "Mom wouldn't turn her back on them." He looked at us, confidence grabbing hold of him as tightly as he held Elena. "I'm Lucien the Vacant Light, son of Luciela the Crescent Light, and I plan to restore order to the Colors."

"Lucien…" Lavonne said, not with familiarity, but wonder.

The burly man took one step back, rotating his body to face Lucien. "Don't get ahead of yourself, kid. The Paragons of Light will decide Michael and Elena's fate and then determine the Order of Light's next leader."

"Aaron, after everything Elena's been through, you're going to punish her, too?" Lucien asked.

"Her crimes cannot be overlooked."

While they bickered, Lavonne turned to me and signed, "He is Luciela's son. We can trust him."

I responded, eyes still straight ahead, hands in front of me. "*Can* we trust him? He's protecting the guilty." I nodded at Elena. "She gave the order."

Chapter 6

Lucien saw me nod at Elena. He stopped listening to Aaron and faced me. He straightened his posture, no longer using the staff to support his weight, but as a shepherd would among sheep. A young shepherd, same age as me, from what his similarly smooth chin suggested.

I read his and Elena's body language like large black print on the white pages of a children's book. Elena packaged her emotions into a scowl—brows scrunched and eyes unblinking while Lucien bounced between gritting his teeth and biting his lips following his exchange with Aaron.

"Are you sure?" Lavonne signed.

"I'm cursed, not deaf or blind," I replied with swift hand movements.

There was a time Lavonne would've smacked my hands down or stepped on my toes as she stormed away from a comment like that, back when we first learned the speechless language and I'd found short sarcastic statements easier to communicate than long genuine sentences. The memory almost made me smile, but hatred shrouded the happiness in a dense fog, and I just couldn't maintain sight of it.

Lavonne leaned forward and took two careful steps toward Elena, the way she often did with the children when she'd caught them misbehaving and didn't want to scare them into telling lies.

Elena retreated, same as the children would have, hiding behind some opaque structure, such as a tree or house, or a Lucien, in this case, a mobile cover that moved out in front of her.

Lavonne spoke around Lucien. "Did you give the order?" she asked, uncertainty in her voice, as if she couldn't believe Elena would do something so heinous—so inhumane.

None of the village children ever imitated an Elena. They argued over Michael and Luciela, and occasionally settled on a Uriah, a Clarence, and a Lumen when they couldn't come to an agreement. Each of the named Paragons uniquely manipulated light. Clarence was one of the few imitations I recognized from a distance. The kids emulated his ability to sling blades of light by throwing cumquats at each other. I didn't know how Elena or Aaron used the light, which further made protecting Lavonne in their home difficult.

Lucien spread his arms out in front of Elena. "We'll investigate! As my mother would."

I signed. Lavonne didn't see my hands move, but Lucien did. He furrowed his brows in my direction, which caused Lavonne to glance over her shoulder. I formed the signs again, adding air quotes. "They'll 'investigate' until our anger fades."

She didn't acknowledge my silent words. Instead, she seemed lost in thought, her gaze distant. She turned to Lucien, eyes still searching the space in front of her for the right words.

She said, "Between choosing a new leader, conducting trials, and restoring faith in your community, when will this investigation take place?" Lavonne raised her eyes and focused her attention on Lucien. "The village wants answers now. If she gave the order, then she'll explain her crimes to our people and then face incarceration until she pays the consequences with time."

Lucien's inexperience shone through his hesitation. He'd probably never encountered such peril and likely had few ideas to address the challenges he faced, namely Lavonne. Even I had trouble overcoming her tenacity when she set her sights on something. She didn't intimidate or threaten others. She intelligently persisted, often pushing them into a psychological corner that tested their heart.

Lucien's response fell flat with Lavonne and with me. He said, "We should use our memory of Mom to bridge the gap between our worlds, not divide it."

Aaron's boots clanked as he walked over to Michael.

Each step pounded the ground with the weight of a fully armored knight. His voice boomed, as if it resounded from underneath a sturdy helm. "We'll investigate. The Order of Light's decision is final," he said.

I wanted to tell Aaron to fuck off—that we didn't require his permission, but I couldn't. It'd been a long time since I'd spoken to outsiders, and having to, but being unable to, frustrated me. And I couldn't ask Lavonne to translate. She wrestled with her own demons.

A tear ran down her cheek and splattered against the colorless floor. She lowered her eyes and flashed a melancholic smile. "If only Luciela were here. She wouldn't have rested until every child felt safe."

Aaron secured ties around Michael's wrists and yanked him up. Then he faced Lavonne and me with undaunted eyes, and lips that neither smiled nor frowned. "Maybe that's why she's dead," he said.

His words caused Lucien to lean on the staff again. He grabbed his stomach when it convulsed. His father staggered backwards and almost doubled over. He narrowed his eyes at Aaron but didn't voice the obvious pain reflected in them.

Aaron's callous comment affected Lavonne, too, who slowly curled her fingers into fists. "The Order of Light is truly lost without her," she said.

I placed my hand on Lavonne's shoulder. She relaxed and then hesitated, but eventually looked back and up at me with tear-soaked eyes that knew the question forthcoming and the answer.

"Have words failed, Lavonne?" I signed.

She lowered her gaze and then her head. She refused to give up, but even she had to acknowledge the cold-hearted response from the Order of Light. They knew who gave the order, and either protected their own at our expense or simply didn't care.

I'd heard enough. With my hand still on Lavonne's

shoulder, I guided her backwards and then behind me. "Actions have always spoken louder than words," I signed.

Elena stared at me. Hard. The way she read my hands, I could tell she understood the speechless language. When I opened my mouth, she cried, "Wait! I did it!" And then, in a lower tone, she added, "I gave the order."

Lucien turned to Elena, but she grabbed his shoulders from behind and hid her face at his back. "It was an illusion, right?" Lucien asked. He spoke to Lavonne and me next, emphasizing his point with hands out and palms up. "Elena creates illusions. They're very realistic. I'm sure…what you saw wasn't real, right, Elena?"

Lucien seemed to think, perhaps even pray, that Elena created the horror we saw this morning—that she produced the burned wood we turned over with our hands, that she fabricated the black smoke billowing into the sky, and that she reflected all the colors that comprised the man guilty of defacing our home. That she acted on a level on par with God, which was unbelievable. Insulting, even.

Elena shook her head, white hair just long enough to sway back and forth beyond Lucien's lean shoulders.

Lavonne asked, "Why would you do that?" The emotion in her voice, the break in tone mid-speech that transitioned from gentle vibrations to a high-pitched squeal, broke my heart. "What have we ever done to you?"

Her voice tugged on Lucien's heart, too. He lowered his eyes and blinked away the tears that formed.

Elena shuffled one foot in place while the other held her weight. "I uh…had a plan to overcome Michael's defenses, but I couldn't," she paused. She looked at Michael, as if to ensure he wouldn't attack her for scheming. After seeing him secured by Aaron, she continued, "My plan wouldn't have worked with another Paragon here. So I asked a couple of squires to get your attention and hoped that the Paragons would respond to your aggression. I didn't tell them to… I never thought they would…do *that*." She referred to the burning of our home.

Lavonne loudly gasped. "A distraction? You set our home on fire as a fucking distraction?"

Her voice faded. She didn't stop talking, though. I stopped hearing her. My focus had shifted. My emotions shrank my surroundings, closing them in and around Elena and me. I only saw her, through Lucien, and past the sympathetic act she put on. I hated the words she spoke. I hated the lips she spoke them with. I hated her meek posture, her existence. I hated…her.

Before I knew it, I stood in front of Elena. No, in front of Lucien, who defended her. Again. He held the staff up with both hands, horizontally, and out in front. I palmed the left side of his face with one hand and shoved him out of the way. Then I snatched Elena by the throat as she stumbled back.

A whisper was all it would take to rupture the muscle that gave the order and ensure it's never used to destroy the lives of others again. I could burn the silver in her eyes, the same way the flames burned the color from our home and plunge her into the same black as the ashes covering every building. I could extinguish the false light she emitted.

Elena grabbed my wrist with both of her hands. She dug her nails into my forearm, pounded the flesh with her fists, and then tried to pry my fingers away from her throat. She couldn't break free. I was far stronger, and the rage I felt boosted my strength.

I was going to kill her.

"Naim!"

Lavonne's voice. Screaming. Crying. Keeping its distance yet reaching me through the darkness that clouded my judgment. I stood over the life in my hand, not in the same protective manner Lucien had, but as a threat looming overhead.

Lavonne cried out again, just as something struck me across the back. I dropped Elena and staggered to the right.

From the corners of my eyes, I saw her scurrying away. I thought she'd run. Instead, she made room for Lucien, who stepped in between us from the left and then smacked me across the face with the staff.

I clenched my teeth to keep from grunting.

"Stop it! Please, stop!" Lavonne pleaded.

Lucien's dad spoke, too, but I couldn't make out his words. I didn't think Lucien could, either. He sprinted at me, blind rage clear in his speed and swing of the staff. I dodged multiple thrusts, acknowledging his skill with the weapon and the damage another solid hit could cause. He relentlessly pursued me. Fighter instincts must've kept him from blindly closing the gap between us, and instead, helped maintain the distance required to strike me from range.

I considered using my voice. A single word would bring the fight to an end and the light-bearers to their knees. But I didn't want to kill Lucien, and Lavonne straddled an invisible and inconclusive line between imminent danger and safety. We didn't know the effective range of my voice. I couldn't have tested it anywhere without destroying the surroundings. The safest place was as far away from me as possible.

"Naim, stop!" Lavonne shouted, waving her hands in the air. "Fighting will fix nothing!"

I could almost feel her leaning over that indiscernible line. As I tried to address her concerns, Lucien drove the staff between my hands and pried them apart. He seemed to ebb and flow between rage and composure. He tightened his grip around the metal and kept it out in front of him, within striking range of me, but just out of my reach.

Everything about the way he positioned himself frustrated me. Physically, Lucien threatened my right side, not because he'd already struck me there, but because Lavonne had moved there. His gaze jumped between her and me, and he disrupted my attempt to communicate with her again, perhaps unaware that hers was the voice of reason.

Psychologically, he exuded hypocrisy. When it came to protecting my village, he deferred. When it came to protecting Elena, he immediately acted.

He looked down on me as if attacking her was wrong. How quickly he forgot I responded with the aggression she wanted. But even after Elena confessed her crimes, Lucien defended her, which devalued his promise to follow in his mother's fair-minded footsteps. It eroded the trust he spoke of and the dialogue Lavonne believed in. That made him complicit.

Lucien and I found our reasons to fight.

We paced the Order of Light's crest, sizing each other up. When his back faced the windows, I charged him. Counting on his quick thrust of the staff, I prepared my body for the impact. He slammed the metal tip against the right side of my chest. I tensed my muscles, absorbing the strike and nullifying the momentum that would've supported retracting the rod with speed. I grabbed the artifact weapon, jerked him toward me and slugged him in the face. He held onto the staff and stayed on his feet.

After he recovered, he pushed back on the rod, sliding it through my grip and into my ribs. He tugged on the staff again, but I refused to let go. When I pulled back harder, he used the force to push the staff up toward my face. I cocked my head to the left, barely avoiding a devastating strike to my jaw. He hopped over my left leg and turned the staff horizontally across my chest as he slipped around to my back. Then he grabbed the high end of the staff, kicked the back of my right knee, and slid the rod up to my neck as I fell. He stepped on my shoulders, pushed me forward, and pulled back on the staff.

"Stop it! You're killing him!"

Lavonne's voice came and went as I faded in and out of consciousness. I should've been stronger than Lucien. He used most of that strength against me and then exhausted the rest of it. I focused what little physical strength I had left on keeping the bar from choking me out. There was no room for mistakes. If I reached for him, I had to be sure I'd break free.

I analyzed his posture using the faint reflection of us in the windows. I saw the veins in his arms and the ones along his neck as he strained to hold me in place, but no openings.

I almost surrendered but struggled more when I caught glimpses of other people in the glass. They didn't look like squires. I didn't see a drop of color in their gear. They shuffled into the room single file, fanned out across the rich gray dirt flanking the crest's stem, knelt, and then aimed rifles at all of us.

I thought Lucien would let go. Instead, he choked me harder when he turned and gawked at the living shadows. They seemed more disciplined and organized than squires. Whereas the Colors operated like a medieval caste system, the people filtering into the room epitomized an elite fighting force. Their presence didn't threaten me until I heard Lavonne's voice.

"Who are you? Let go of me! Get off me!"

She struggled. I followed her movements in the window's reflection, legs kicking and arms flailing, until one shadow slammed her against the ground. Then I heard nothing.

My heart pounded. I could no longer see Lavonne's reflection, only a couple of dark figures congregating where she once stood. I couldn't hear her voice, only my own berating me for failing to protect her, too.

Emotion surged within me, and alas, I opened my mouth toward the windows. "Lavonne!"

I heard nothing else after shouting her name. Surrounding sounds fluctuated. The large windowpanes in front of me came apart into thousands, maybe millions, of pieces that silently fell in place and resembled stockpiles of raw material.

My voice must've affected Lucien, too. He loosened his hold and then dropped the staff. It clattered against the ground and rolled several feet away. I stumbled forward and onto one knee and one hand. I kept myself from falling over and held my head high enough to see the mountainside razed. The gradual clearing of trees and bushes down to, and including, the statue of Michael resulted in an unobstructed view of the main road, where I saw the demonstrators below had crumbled into heaps of raw, human material.

Chapter 7

A bright light woke me. I shielded my eyes from it and the accompanying heat, slowly lowering my hand as my senses adjusted to the radiance. The single ray turned into an orange blaze engulfing the village marketplace. The light from its flames danced in the brick streets, even in the shadow of the rising smoke. Wooden structural beams buckled. The crunch of their collapse and the roar of the flames produced the only sound, and the conflagration reflected the only color.

My heart raced. I didn't know where to start. I didn't know whom to help first. When I chose the fruit stand Mrs. Smith stocked full of large green apples every morning, I sensed something behind me.

I turned around. Rosemary stood at the forest line. The villagers surrounded her. Ansell was there, too, leaning against the wooden sign directing visitors to the marketplace entrance.

Nakenyah poked her head out from behind Rosemary's multi-colored patchwork dress. She wore something similar, adorned with real flowers likely plucked from Mr. Oz's garden. She stared at me—no, past me, eyes squinting and then widening.

I turned to the blaze and saw a figure among the flames. Light from the fire raced across the small beads interspersed among the short black twists at the back of their head. As if they heard me looking, the figure quickly turned to face me, and the hair ornaments clapped against each other like beaded curtains. The person smiled, only as Lavonne would, humble and full of serenity, even as the roof above them split. They took a deep breath and closed their eyes.

"Lavonne!" I shouted.

My voice stripped the colors and exploded the surrounding structures before they could cave in around her. Except, my voice destroyed Lavonne, too. It left a clearing where she'd stood, everything except her shoes, and continued down a hillside and into the city, a forged path like the artifact's fall to earth more than a decade ago.

I dropped to my knees. Each impacted the ground separately. My heart pounded and then slowed with my breath. I wanted to turn my voice on myself, but Lavonne's shoes, charred black by the fire, left me speechless. Dizziness caused my head to spin, and I lost the will to sit upright. I fell forward. The ground quickly came. Hitting it felt like being jerked awake.

I opened my eyes again, this time to the cold stainless steel of modern civilization, to reality in the dark.

I'd been dreaming. Or remembering. A puzzle composed of recent memories where the pieces jammed together to form the horrific scene that woke me. I recalled the last piece: me losing control. My tongue had slipped. I'd killed hundreds of people to save one.

The memory plagued me. It caused a feverish sweat to drench my body. My toes scrunched against the cold of metal. The chill ran up my feet, which were bound to a chair, same as my arms. I rubbed my clammy fingers against the armrest, failing to grasp the thin metal when I leaned forward and gasped for air, as if every replay woke me from the nightmare again and again.

A mask covered my mouth, which limited the full breaths I could take. Its solid material cupped my chin and hugged the bridge of my nose like a muzzle. A voice in the dark shoved the memories in my head aside.

"Good evening, Nephew," the voice said. It came straight at me, as if a middle-aged man sat across from me. He spoke quickly, almost rhythmically. I imagined him leaning back with legs crossed and a smug expression on his face.

He added, "Metaphorically speaking, of course. I don't know your name, and I can't exactly ask you; not after witnessing first-hand the destructive capability of your voice.

But we humans must label everything so we can reference and address them. The people call me Uncle Sam; therefore, you are Nephew."

I couldn't see him. His odd speech nagged my ears, but I had no choice but to listen.

"You're also a living weapon of mass destruction." He raised his voice and then lowered it. "A byproduct of the Colorblind class, you have a similar affinity to a foreign element the people call Artifact. Its characteristics give the compatible the ability to manipulate the reflected colors they see. It appears to have given you and your friends the ability to affect color with your voices."

I was tugging on the straps as he spoke but stopped when he mentioned my friends. He must've felt me glaring in his direction because he snickered.

"So, I've assigned you all to the Speechless class, since you've adopted Sign Language to communicate in your voices' stead. Unfortunately, your translator won't be joining us. I stripped this room of all color, thinking we could chat one on one, but to be honest, I don't fully know how your voice interacts with the world. That mask will prevent vocal vibrations from escaping, which *should* cage your power. You can scream at the top of your lungs and not even *you* will hear it, which is equivalent to not speaking at all."

I wouldn't test his theory. Not without knowing who or what was nearby. But if wearing the mask simulated silence, then it might be effective.

He continued, "That means I'll be doing all the talking. I don't mind, but when all is said and done, you're going to have to make a decision. Some way. Somehow."

I opened my mouth but heard nothing. The mask, devoid of color, blocked my voice. Or was it that I *couldn't* speak? Had recent events paralyzed my vocal cords? My head flooded with nightmarish images and thoughts. I recalled the protesters at the base of the mountain. I remembered the people inside the Grand Courtyard. I wondered about Ansell and

Rosemary, and I worried about Lavonne.

The man's voice broke through the internal chaos again. I felt as Lucien must have, torn in several directions and unable to commit to any.

The man carried on like a pre-recorded machine. "I know everything that's been going on in this place, to include the subduing of those unaffiliated with an Order, the rogue human experiments, the Order of Light's reign," he paused and shifted his tone from casual conversation to gossip, "Elena's shenanigans."

I heard a faint creak as he leaned back in the chair. He spoke normally again. "Even the recent murders." He sighed, a long deep breath. "I almost regretted letting Michael kill Luciela, but their struggle gave me the most powerful weapon of all: Lucien."

Energy returned to his voice. "You see, the Artifact ruptured when it entered Earth's atmosphere. Fragments scattered around the globe. Other countries recovered pieces, and have, without a doubt, weaponized what they could. That's what we did. We developed the artifact items that allowed people to manipulate color so they could fight our enemies when the time came, but Lucien unexpectedly became our anti-artifact weapon."

I felt him lean forward in the dark. As my eyes adjusted, I saw his outline—square shoulders and possibly short hair, since nothing extended beyond his oval head. I thought I'd glimpsed his eyes, but that would've meant color. He must've worn dark shades, and a mask, too, since I couldn't see white teeth or a red tongue when he spoke.

"You're a test subject too, incidental as you may be," he said. "You were never the goal, but now you're a problem. Nephew, you represent what the other countries might create. Your voice didn't manifest Lucien's anti-artifact weapon, as other color activations have. In fact, his artifact staff directed and amplified your voice's destructive force. And from what I saw, you'd destroy any aggregation of color. How would our most powerful Order defeat you?"

He rambled on about nonsense. I wanted to know about Lavonne's safety, but I was blocked from communicating. He probably couldn't see me well enough to read my eyes or facial expressions. My frustration peaked. I struggled more, but there wasn't enough slack in the straps for my movements to make noise. I couldn't even rock the chair.

"Lucien needs the absence of color to unsheathe his anti-artifact weapon. And the frequency of its black blade doesn't interact with physical objects any more than missing particles do. He simply disrupts the color frequency in others and cuts off their ability to manipulate it.

"But you, Nephew…you destroy. No item required. No warning. Just a casual greeting of death. You've no control over its strength and reach, but the range is on par with Elena's. You'd make an excellent assassin if you can learn to focus it."

I felt him lean back again. A satisfied breath escaped his lips.

"You must be wondering why I'm telling you all this. I'm not a villain spewing his evil master plan. Although, there is a plan." I felt his eyes staring at me in the darkness. "There's a war coming, Nephew, and the government—Uncle Sam—" I imagined he pointed at himself, "decided the time has come to activate this experimental city.

"That's where your decision comes in, to either cooperate with us or be controlled by us."

The continuing darkness honed my other senses. I felt him smiling. A brush of air against my knees suggested he crossed or uncrossed his legs. In the silence of his pause, I heard him chewing.

"We *should* control your voice rather than cooperate with it. But we're giving you an opportunity to focus it yourself. You won't be alone. My original dream team included Michael, Luciela, and Elena, which has somewhat fallen apart. Luciela is gone and Lucien disrupted Michael's control over color. So now I'm thinking of you, Elena, Lucien, and the woman who invokes emotions."

Rosemary, I thought. His mention of her meant she was well. Still, I wanted to see her. We'd never been apart like this before. After the artifact residue manifested in our voices, the three of us had moved to the outskirts of the village for safety and solidarity. Ansell had often kept to himself, finding comfort in the forest, while Rosemary and I had played brother and sister, fixing up the cabin we called home. I promised to protect her, initially, more out of guilt than anything else. The reason changed over time as we grew closer. We'd found peace, and the villagers had accepted us.

The man in front of me wanted to send us to war. I communicated disapproval the only way afforded to me: a slow shake of my head. He couldn't see me curling my toes and probably couldn't hear me scratching the armrest.

He rambled on, a hint of frustration seeping through the tones. "You saw what your misguided voice did to those protesters. It reduced hundreds of them into piles of unrecognizable…components. You dismantled each person, possibly breaking down the atoms that made them. Family members can't identify loved ones. The blind, who gently grasp faces for familiarity, have nothing to take hold of, and instead, will wait days and weeks for the mind-numbing realization that mom, dad, brother, sister, husband, wife, son, or daughter isn't coming home—that among those heaps of raw subatomic particles are the building blocks for their beloved…"

I shook my head more and then cocked it back to get as far away from his voice as possible. His words illustrated a vivid scene in my mind, from a sketch to the three-dimensional reality of the protestors before and then after I'd shouted. And that I once stood among them—that I brushed shoulders with them—made their existence and then departure more haunting.

The man stood and grabbed my wrists as he leaned over me. "…reduced to nothing, including their souls. Not even their God will recognize them—"

A loud smack interrupted the man. His grip wobbled and then disappeared as he let go. I felt him step back. A crack formed in the black behind him. A ray of soft light shone through. Slowly, the split spread and ran to the ground before the darkness itself broke away like a massive curtain pulled back to one side.

The curtain included the man. Before he disappeared, lit by a sliver of light, I glimpsed him for a mere second. I saw broad shoulders in a fitted suit, a square head underneath a black mask, and dark glasses that shielded his peripheral vision, too.

Chapter 8

I squinted. Evening, bleached by the stars and moon, illuminated the area through a huge opening in the side of the Grand Courtyard. The moonlight and the pain of reality still proved to be too much for my eyes and my heart after sitting in the dark for so long. Instinctively, I raised my arms to shield my eyes from everything, but they were bound to the chair. That, too, wasn't a dream or illusion.

Elena stood in front of me with a scowl on her face. She stared above and beyond me. At first, both hands clenched at her sides, but she unfisted one to rub her left cheek.

Lavonne's voice carried over my head. "What were you doing? That isn't what we agreed to."

Elena stared at Lavonne with menacing eyes. I wondered when they'd agreed to something. I trusted Lavonne to bring me to my senses, but didn't expect her to conspire with the enemy to do so. Except I'd spoken, which made me everyone's enemy.

The thought of everyone reminded me of the vision I'd seen moments ago and the memory that accompanied it. I wanted to look over the mountainside and confirm what had transpired. Again, I tried to stand up. The straps holding me in place didn't waver. I strained, surfacing the veins in my arms, yet careful not to grunt.

Elena waved her hand. A different world followed the swing of her arm. Reality folded like the turning of a page. The grayed dirt beneath me turned into a hard and reflective steel surface. The gaping hole in the courtyard closed. Fluorescent tubes illuminated the room in an unnatural white hue. Transparent walls created ten-by-ten-foot spaces. They separated me from Lavonne and us from Aaron, Lucien, and his dad.

I faced an opaque wall, still unable to move.

Lavonne stepped into view on my left. She shouted, but I couldn't hear her. So she signed. "Are you okay?"

I nodded. Seeing her large brown eyes answered the same for me. An apology sat in them, too. Then she signed, "I'm sorry."

I turned my head to the wall space in front of me, where the hole had been. Lavonne understood.

"They weren't real," she signed. "The people down there were illusions. Just like this," she raised her hands and then brought them down in an arc.

I pressed my lips together and let the sigh of relief escape from my nostrils.

The door behind me opened. Lavonne's door did, too. I heard it hiss soon after mine, and I saw the beaded twists of her hair as she spun around.

Lucien walked into my cell. He stood in front of me in a grayed long sleeve shirt. "I'm sorry," he said. The honesty shone through the pain in his eyes. "There's a lot going on that both of us don't know about." He released the straps around my wrists and stepped back.

Bending over, I undid the straps across my waist, thighs, and shins. Then I stood and stared at Lucien. Misplaced anger crossed my mind, but not enough for an apology, so I nodded.

Lavonne slipped between us and hugged me tightly. I apologized to her with my arms. I wrapped them around her shoulders and gently stroked the twists at the back of her head.

Lucien averted his gaze. I thought he'd given us privacy, until I followed his eyes to the newly surrounding activity. As if the world was still being constructed, people phased into the scene.

"What's going on?" Lavonne asked, raising her eyes above my shoulders.

Aaron's voice boomed from outside the cell. "We're in Elena's illusion now. It's how she communicates. Like a child."

The people didn't react to his voice, much the same way

the protesters hadn't when Lavonne and I stood among them. Yet they avoided collisions, taking extra steps to circle around Aaron's burly frame. And around Michael, whom he had in tow.

Most of them wore long white coats over light-gray formal medical attire. A couple of their loafers squeaked when they turned sharply at the end of the corridor. They held clipboards in their hands. Nametags hung from their breast pockets.

"What is this place?" Lavonne asked. She slid out of my embrace and into the hallway.

"Home," Aaron stated.

Lucien's dad closed both eyes. "We've all heard the artifact story—its arrival and fight for control. After the first incidental manipulation of color, the government converted this hospital into a research facility. Here, we learned about artifact affinity and then flew compatible people in from all over the world for experiments."

He paused. I gathered the next few words to be difficult for him, but having seen and heard what the Light peddled, it couldn't have been much worse.

He touched the glass of a nearby cell and looked inside as if someone was there. "All our subjects struggled to an extent. Being the culmination of our research, Elena suffered the most."

I signed at Lavonne, "See. Monsters." My message added to the unease in her gaze.

"I met Lucien's mother here," Lucien's dad continued, briefly rubbing his son's head. "I, too, had an affinity for color—for green." He waved his hand dismissively. "My levels were insignificant, but my dedication turned me into a researcher; before the research turned inhumane. Then I fell in love with a patient."

Aaron stomped past us. "We already heard that story, old man. What is she showing us now?" He stopped at an intersection in the hallway and faced a long line of glass cells.

Then he grabbed a nearby researcher and slammed her against one windowpane. Everything she carried clattered to the floor—the clipboard, two pens, and a cup of coffee that didn't spill. She gathered those things from the floor, stood up, and continued on her way, as if nothing had happened.

Aaron shouted. "Elena!"

The surrounding colors muted as the tattoos covering his body glowed white. I'd heard of a Paragon's blinding aura, but Aaron's didn't outshine the ceiling lights.

He turned to one window and swung his fist, but failed to crack it, let alone smash through. A dense sound reverberated.

Lucien shook his head. "Elena controls all the particles in her illusions. She can make the window paper thin or hard as a diamond."

Lavonne translated my question. "Why didn't she use this earlier?"

Lucien shrugged. "Probably because I had an artifact. In my hands, a black blade forms when someone attracts colors nearby. When I strike someone with it, I disrupt their color affinity. I only learned about my unique ability this morning. By accident."

That explained the interrogator's earlier words; that Lucien was the anti-artifact weapon. It explained the black streak I'd seen and Michael's defeat. The interrogator was an illusion, which meant Elena had told me those things. She communicated through the mirage.

I turned to Lavonne and signed. "What agreement did you make with her?"

She replied using the speechless language. "We let her use color to stop the fight. Not to hurt you." Then she said aloud, "I'm sorry. She knows…" Lavonne paused and then switched to signing again, "about you, Rosemary, and Ansell. About your voices."

Aaron saw us. He faced Lavonne and said in his deep voice, "You're all just children."

Lucien smiled sadly. "They have their own way of communicating. Elena and I did, too. After all, we couldn't hear each other through the glass." He waved both hands in defense, same as his dad, as if to let us know that clarity from his words was forthcoming. "Mom wouldn't let them experiment on me. I didn't have an affinity for color, anyway. Curiosity led me out of daycare a few times. Elena became the reason each time thereafter."

Lucien's dad rubbed his son's back. "Elena's just a kid. A kid that was forced to grow up fast. She wants to tell us something. We just need to listen."

"Isn't it obvious…" Michael said. His demeanor hadn't changed. Defeat still covered his face, pulling everything down toward the floor. "…what she's trying to show us? …why she attacked that village and why *they're* here?" Michael raised his eyes and sneered at Lavonne and me. "Because the scientists who tortured us call that village home."

Lucien's dad quickly stepped in between us. "That's not true. I would've known—"

Michael shot Lucien's dad a hard glance. "I exiled them there when I took over the city. You would've joined them if not for Lucy." In a somber tone, he added, "Everything was for Lucy."

Aaron crossed his arms. "He's delusional. The scientists left to observe us from a…"

"Distance?" Michael finished Aaron's statement. He made eye contact with Lavonne. "Don't you recognize anyone?"

Lavonne slowly turned her head. I did, too, giving the scientists walking by a closer look. We both settled on a young woman coming down the hallway intersecting ours. I almost didn't recognize her as Mrs. Turner, the village seamstress. Her youthful appearance replaced the stagnant gray hairs I knew with a lively brown ponytail. She turned to the right, away from us, and proceeded toward the far end of the corridor.

Slowly, more people materialized. They populated the cells, ranging in age from children to young adults and included men and women alike from all backgrounds. Some scientists observed the subjects while others dragged children out of their cells kicking and screaming. The occasional flash of color destroyed something—a table, a chair, or a tray—before someone put the chaos to sleep.

"This is…horrible," Lavonne said through clasped hands over her mouth.

"Get your woman," Aaron said to me. "This is exactly what Elena wants. To turn us on each other."

Lavonne turned to him. A swift movement I thought would cause her harm when the beads in her twists flicked around, too. "Did all of this happen? Is it true?" She looked at Michael next.

I reached for her, but she swatted my hand away.

"Did my mother torture you? Tell me!" She screamed.

All the scientists stopped moving and looked our way. They stood like actual humans—slouching against surfaces or folding their arms over clipboards pressed against their chests. Those closer to Lavonne breathed as if their hearts pounded from the sudden rise of her voice while those further away looked on with curiosity. A few waited with bated breath, like spirits that couldn't rest until someone voiced the horrors that caused them to wander.

Michael raised his head to Lavonne. "The only human being in this facility that gave a damn about us was Luciela."

Lavonne stepped back and then collapsed backwards. I caught her before she could hit the glass wall behind her. "Oh…god…" she cried as she slid to the ground. "Oh. God!"

I imagined she felt disgust from babysitting the children of those who tortured other kids. That perhaps, while she fed their little ones cereal and granola bars, their parents subjected others to whatever yellow-green substance filled the tubes one man carried.

"Turn it off!" Lavonne repeatedly screamed.

Her request fell on deaf ears. The illusion didn't end. I couldn't end it, either, or communicate to the others that someone had to bring this visual story to a close.

"Lavonne?" one scientist said. He came out of the cell I'd sat in earlier. His badge read Mr. Allen. I recognized him from my work delivering chopped wood. He always tended to the garden in front of his home.

"Lavonne? Is that you?" he walked closer and leaned over to see her face.

I stepped forward and shoved him to the ground. He looked up at me, eyes wide and mouth open.

"Naim? Why?" he asked. "What are you doing here?"

I pitied the mirage as it crawled to its feet, as an old man would. If only I could destroy it without killing everything else. I gritted my teeth as Elena's words about controlling my voice haunted me.

Lavonne screamed again. She scurried across the floor, wrapped her arms around her knees, and buried her face between her thighs as she desperately tried to escape another scientist-turned-villager.

I stepped over her and kicked a young Mrs. Daniels away. Then I punched her older son in the face.

Michael trudged past me.

Aaron grabbed his shoulder. "Where do you think you're going?" he asked.

Michael shrugged Aaron's muscular hand off, and then he responded in a dreary monotone voice. "She recreated this place. That means Luciela, too. I have to see her, even if she's just a swatch of the courtyard's reflected colors. And I have to touch her before she's returned to the courtyard mural."

Chapter 9

I crouched in front of Lavonne. Passing my hands behind her back and under her knees, I lifted her into my arms. I stood and started down the corridor Mrs. Turner had come from.

Aaron grabbed my shoulder. "You plan on walking her off the mountainside?" he asked.

Lucien added, "Elena manipulates color to create illusions, but she can't take the real world away." He glanced at the cell I'd stood in earlier. "When the illusion ends, there'll still be a hole in that wall. If you don't know where you're going, you might walk off the mountainside."

I looked at the wall—at the covered hole I'd created with my voice. A moment passed before I wondered why everything behind me had remained intact. I thought back to when Elena had dismissed the first illusion. I'd glimpsed the rest of the courtyard before she'd turned the page again. Nothing else had crumbled. Lavonne, Lucien, and his dad; they were all fine, confirming my reflected voice destroyed less.

I turned and leaned against a windowpane. My thoughts were luring me into my head, and I didn't want to drop Lavonne. She had quieted after throwing her arms around my neck and burying her face in my chest.

With my chin in her twists, I recalled the conversation with the interrogator. He'd said Lucien's staff had directed and amplified my voice's destructive output; at least, the emitted particles that deconstructed color.

If I could do that again, I could destroy the illusion without hurting anyone else. How would I communicate that to Lucien, and where was his staff? In his hands, it would've canceled the manifestation of Elena's illusion, so he must've put it down when they plotted to calm me. And if she could only create, not destroy, then it must be nearby. Somewhere. Possibly obscured by the lab equipment, or worse, the walls.

If I could breathe on the walls, I'd write my thoughts in

the accumulated moisture. There was no guarantee my voice wouldn't destroy, and glass in a laboratory was likely fog resistant, depending on how much detail Elena built into her illusions.

I needed Lavonne. Tilting my head, I tried to meet her eyes, but they were closed. I shook her in my arms until she raised her head. Then I put her feet on the ground. I raised my hands to make formations and stopped, recalling that Elena understood the speechless language, and though not visible, she surrounded us.

"Where is Lucien's staff?" I signed.

Lavonne looked around, perhaps from memory at first, as she immediately settled on Lucien's dad. "Where's Lucien's staff?" she asked.

Lucien's dad patted himself down. "I had it a moment ago. She must've taken it from me. Why would she take it?"

"Because it can cancel her illusion, idiot," Aaron growled.

Lucien's dad scoffed. "Who's the idiot? You have artifact tattoos. Who knows what its chemical composition will do to you in five, ten years?"

More villagers emerged from the cells and corridors. The ones I knocked down stood up. All of them encroached upon and surrounded us like a zombie horde with some intellect. They called our names and complained about our aggression towards them.

Quickly, I signed, and Lavonne translated. "I can focus my voice through artifact."

"A lot of good that does us now." Aaron grabbed the nearest scientist, a man I didn't recognize, and slammed them into a nearby wall. Then he punched their head three times. Each jab ineffective as if he'd struck indestructible plastic. Frustrated, he grabbed them by the collar and threw them back into the crowd.

"It's in your skin," I signed.

A phoenix spread its wings across Aaron's shoulder

blades and inked people worshipped it from his lower back, some on their knees and others with arms extended.

Lucien's dad understood before Lavonne could translate. He said, "Channel your voice through Aaron's tattoos."

Under the absentminded guidance of his son's hand, of one so used to protecting others, Lucien's dad moved to the center of our formation. Aaron, Lucien, and I defended each end of the three-way corridor.

"Would it destroy him? Us?" Lucien's dad thought aloud. "But there'd be no outlet. If you scream into his chest, your voice won't go through, and if it does, it'll go *through*."

Lavonne lightly smacked my head. She pointed at Aaron. "Use *his* head."

"That's a great idea!" Lucien said as he tripped another woman. He probably expected the ones behind them to stumble, but they climbed over the prone bodies. "Direct it off the crown of his head."

I looked at the back of Aaron's bald head. As he moved, his crown shimmered under the fluorescent light, except for the parts he'd inked with the artifact, which included two different circular symbols. One spiraled at the back left of his head. Four feathers dangled from the bottom of the second engraving, toward the back of his ear.

Lucien's dad snapped his fingers. "You're a tough guy, Aaron. Protect your head with light."

"Is the situation so dire you'd risk my head and yours?" Aaron asked. "Elena is many unsightly things. A killer is not one of them."

Lucien and his dad's shoulders slumped as they exhaled the fight within them.

Lavonne shivered behind me. She clung to my back instead of standing in the center with Lucien's dad. I needed more space to fight. Glancing over my shoulder, I noticed the perimeter we defended had shrunk from several feet to only a couple of feet wide. Aaron might have accepted the dwindling perimeter; he might know more about Elena's mental state than me, but I wouldn't lower my guard until Lavonne was safe.

I almost couldn't sign to her. I reached behind me and tugged on her overalls. When I felt her over my shoulder, I signed. "We're going through."

She nodded. "We're pushing through."

"We need to stick together," Lucien shouted.

I lowered my shoulder and plowed through several scientists. Lavonne held onto the back of my shirt and followed. As I shoved more aside, I recognized a man who avoided my arms and ran past me. He wasn't from the village. Something felt off, so I stopped and turned around.

With a syringe in hand, he charged Lucien's dad from the back and then stabbed him in the neck.

Lavonne screamed, getting Lucien and Aaron's attention.

"Dad!" Lucien knelt by his dad's side as the man coughed and choked up blood. Lucien pulled his grayed shirt over his head and pressed it against his dad's neck to stop the bleeding.

Aaron lifted the scientist and slammed them against the glass wall. He went to punch the assailant, but paused, eyes wide open.

I noticed too that the man resembled Lucien's dad, perhaps when he worked at the facility, youthful appearance same as the other scientist-turned-villagers.

"Help. Help!" Lucien cried out. "Elena! Please!"

"Naim." Lavonne pointed behind me.

One scientist lunged at me with a knife in hand. I caught her wrist. Another grabbed my leg and sunk their teeth into my ankle. I kicked them with my other leg. I lost my balance and collided into Lavonne. We both fell to the floor. More crawled over me, punching, clawing, and biting whatever they could get their hands and teeth on.

Aaron stepped over me. He lifted one up off me and threw them across and over Lucien and his dad. They crashed into the crowd on the other side.

I fought with a few others, understanding that Aaron and I were the only lines of defense while Lucien tended to his dad. Aaron and I exchanged glances when I jumped to my feet. I shifted my gaze to Lavonne as she helped Lucien with his dad. When the crowd Aaron once fended off drew closer, Lucien fought them back.

Aaron gritted his teeth. He walked around me and knelt in front of the group. Light covered his body, pulling color from the scientists and walls.

I crouched behind him, my chin just above the crown of his glowing head. A whisper would be enough. I could say anything, but brevity was best. "Disappear."

My voice destroyed the scientists in front of us, the walls next to them, and the illusion as far back as my voice reached. Aaron wasn't harmed. I glanced over my shoulder to see that Lavonne was fine, too, at least, from my voice. I almost exhaled a sigh of relief.

In front of me, the hole in the illusion spread. It trickled away, revealing the throne at the far end and circling around the space until the original courtyard returned. The fabricated scientists disappeared, except for a few that lay in front of me, partially intact, and several piles of what I assumed to be real people.

I almost vomited. The sound that would accompany puking would only kill more people, so I covered my mouth and swallowed it. Then I raised my eyes to the throne.

Elena sat on the chair, her elbows curving with the right angles of the armrests and her legs crossed over the sharp edge of the seat.

"You focused it," she said. Lowering her eyes to the people and piles in front of me, she shrugged. "Don't pity them. They led many of the facility experiments. Same as Dr. Noah Alexander." Elena pointed at Lucien's dad and frowned. "I didn't want to hurt him for your sake, but I had to…for your sake. I'm sorry, Lucien."

Lucien shook his head. "Why? You could've just told me!" he exclaimed.

"I had to prepare you for the fight that's coming." She threw three black masks to the floor in front of us. They resembled the one I'd worn in her illusion with the interrogator.

"They're made from artifact." When we didn't pick them up, she added, "I told you that you'd have to decide. You can use it to kill me, or you can help me stop them."

"That isn't the real her," Lucien said.

Elena smiled. Tears ran down her cheeks. "That's why I love you, Lucien. You were the first to notice me, and now you're the first to know *me*. No matter your decision, I will fight for you." She wiped tears away. "The rest of you—"

"You used us," Lavonne exclaimed. "You used us to kill these people. You mixed real lives in with the illusions."

Elena frowned. "That's all I can do."

Lavonne glared at the corpses and then raised her eyes to Elena. "The village wasn't an accident, was it?"

Elena shook her head. "It was revenge. I showed mercy to the assistants, though." She spoke like a child seeking recognition for the little good she did during her wrongdoing and then dismissed her own plea altogether. "Although, they knew what they were doing. I hurt those who deserved it. You don't have to trust me, but we stand a better chance together. Hurry. *They* will be here soon."

"Who are *they*?" Aaron asked.

"Uncle Sam."

Eden

Chapter 1

Father was gone. I wondered if the other Archangels—my brothers and sisters from the orphanage—would carry on his mission to send genuine people to Eden, the recently debunked and fabricated reality after death. Or would they pursue a similar path as the traitor in our ranks, who sought to rule the living from Eden using his Artificial Nano Technology System—ANTS? My siblings didn't know the truth about Eden yet, that it wasn't the promised paradise many wished for and believed. It was a simulation.

I killed that traitor and interrupted the same lingering signal others had that sparked the mad rush to the afterlife years ago, proving that the other side can be denied if their ANTS was destroyed before it can upload a copy of its host's cerebrum signature. Desiring Eden also prevented people from reaching it, opening a path for the faithless to run wild. I'd learned to kill those sinners without sending them to the promised land—without sending them to Sister.

The traitor killed Sister during his holy war. I thought she was gone forever, but a reflection of her persisted in Eden, and from there, using her ANTS, she secretly existed in the back of my mind as Gretel.

"I didn't mean to deceive you, Hansel..."

I remembered Sister's absence as if I was still the young man standing at the empty lake bank between the orphanage and the church. She often blessed the crystal-clear spring water with her long bronze legs, washing her feet and then dancing to a beautiful melody she hummed. She always wore a black cowl under the blazing sun, its rays unobscured by nonexistent pollution since man's decline.

ANTS granted many people unique skills. The traitor efficiently stored, processed, and retrieved information from his brain. Sister communicated with others using her mind. I thought Gretel was my unique skill, and that together, we honed my senses to fight. I thought she processed the additional sensory information I couldn't. Instead, the ability to hyper-focus was mine alone, and it facilitated the psychological connection to Sister.

"I am unique to you, and you alone, Hansel."

"Hansel, are you dead? This ain't the time to be spacing out."

I opened my eyes to Enola. My blurry vision caused the hues of her dark clothes to blend into the surrounding evening as the day transitioned into night.

"Come on! He didn't hit you *that* hard."

Slowly, my eyes adjusted to the low lighting and then focused on Enola's honey-toned irises under the warm lights illuminating the outdoor sky bridge. She squatted in front of me with her arms tightly wrapped around her knees. Black brows lost most of their arch. Dirty and torn jeans echoed our recent fight with the traitor and his ally, the Queen, whose ANTS connected the minds of staff operating the residential tower we'd just left.

Enola followed my eyes, mistakenly, and glanced down at her cleavage. Visible between the straps of a black halter top, a bead of sweat rolled into the crevice formed by her breasts.

She winked at me. "Or are you dreaming about something else?"

"I—"

"I know, I know. You only have eyes for Sister." Enola cupped her chin with her palm and rolled her eyes.

I lifted my back away from the metal guardrail that had prevented me from falling sixty stories to the ground. Multiple indoor and outdoor bridges connected four rectangular residential towers together, and we crossed one of the highest not under cover.

Enola raised her crossed arms above her chest. "She's probably never shown you skin…" she mumbled.

In my hyper-focused state, I heard every word. I

would've responded about Sister's modesty, but the powerful stride of a brawny man in the distance demanded my attention, so I stood to face him.

He wore armor befitting a medieval knight but called himself a hero. Solid blue eyes and red lips peered out from behind the "M" shape of a silver helm. His boots pounded against the metal plates at the far end of the bridge connected to the residential tower he claimed to defend. The end we had tried to enter.

I focused on the clink of metal around his joints, the only weakness I'd found, yet failed to exploit because of his ANTS. It gave him mind control over twenty metal hexagonal shards that connected and separated in the air like puzzle pieces—flat and slightly curved pieces. A strong magnetic force held them together from a distance. He formed the shards into a sword when he attacked and into a shield when I retaliated.

"Pride will be his sin, Hansel."

Sister—no, Gretel—was right. The man stopped several feet away when he could've easily walked up, grabbed me by the collar, and slammed me to the ground again. I couldn't tell from the stoic expression on his face if he was toying with me or wary of my precision with the pistol. He protected his exposed joints with a few of the shards, unaware I was out of ammunition. I only needed one bullet to liberate the worthy, so I carried enough to fulfill the assigned mission. With the supply I'd set out with yesterday, I'd sent one man to Eden, maimed another, killed the traitor, and fired the last bullet at this hero. That amounted to three people I didn't save.

The Hero glared at me with menacing eyes and spoke with exaggerated mouth movements, stretching the corners to their physical limits. "Get up, coward! I'll introduce you to justice in the same manner you introduced others to salvation. Through death!"

What salvation? Eden wasn't real. God wasn't real.

Gretel wasn't real, either. And Sister…

"I am Sister Gretel, Hansel. I am real."

The Hero wouldn't believe me if I told him about Eden. I felt a black-and-white outlook emanating from him—scales without possibility of equilibrium. He cast a dark shadow over me and bathed Enola, mistakenly, in a holy light, despite her dark eyeliner, black lips, and attitude that suggested otherwise.

Enola poked my shoulder. "Hey, Hansel. How about I take Eve and run? He's only after you, right?"

I'd almost forgotten about Eve. Her presence had escaped my senses, keen as they were. Father's last request—so I'd believed—included retrieving her at all costs. Except, the traitor set me on that path after he'd killed and then impersonated Father. He'd described Eve as Eden's door, a terminal with access to the contrived world man coveted. He was right, but I refused to see her as anything other than the skinny barefoot girl in front of me. I'd seen too many children in the Archangel program forced to grow up fast, including me, to subject Eve to the same upbringing.

I glanced at Enola. "You're an accomplice, right?"

Enola raised her brows. "Eve, I believe he just called us sidekicks."

Eve stared at me, expressionless as usual. Waist-length black hair ran down her back and draped over the front of her light-green long-sleeved tee. I wondered who she was when she wasn't someone else. Eden's door supported temporary control by its citizens. Through Eve, Enola had spoken to her late cousin, Katie, and I'd gazed into the warm eyes of Sister before I learned about her predicament.

"I will never keep anything from you again, Hansel."

Enola scurried away. "Hansel! Quit spacing out! Here it comes!"

I'd lost focus. Exhaustion slowed my reaction time. The metal hexagons formed a gauntlet that snatched me by the neck and lifted me off the ground. I grabbed what little wrist completed the shape, but without an arm attached to the floating shards, my fingers slipped off the end of the formation.

"Archangels?" the Hero scoffed. "What right do you have to decide who lives and who dies?"

Enola clenched her fists. She couldn't fight, not without the skirmish skill she'd copied with her ANTS and then erased after her body couldn't keep up with the physical demands of hand-to-hand combat. She stored three copied skills, including the hacker one she used to override the tower elevators and the EMP skill she combined with the Queen's Hive to fry the ANTS of all connected hosts.

None of those skills affected the Hero. Her final attack against the Queen erased their hive skills. The Hero's armor shielded him from the EMP she unleashed, and she couldn't hack his control of the shards. She attempted to copy his skill, but that required sensual contact with his skin. She couldn't reach his helm, never mind his face underneath it, so she tried to talk her way out.

"And what right do *you* have to pass judgement?" she asked, hands on her hips and chest out.

The Hero looked down at her. "Why, the people of this tower gave me that right," he said and then raised his voice. The helm caused his words to echo and fill the space between the buildings. "I am the wall between them and the surrounding tyrants."

Enola sneered. "Don't you mean the *other* tyrants? Anyway, you and Hansel both have a hero complex, supposedly bestowed upon you by people. Why is yours justified?"

Her distraction gave me time to focus on the metallic hand. It didn't choke me. I had room to move my head, but doing so caused the metal shards to cut into my skin. Blood ran down my neck and soaked the white shirt beneath my clerical suit. I tried to pry the fingers apart but had no leverage with my feet several inches off the ground.

The Hero frowned. "You're right. I have a hero complex.

But this one," he paused and looked at me, "he's been play-ing God…"

"Hansel, the real attack is coming—"

Several of the shards pierced my neck. I jerked, awk-wardly, feeling each one break my skin. Blood splattered across my fingers. It soaked my shirt, in the front and the back, and had a cool and metallic feel to it, almost as if the shards contaminated it.

I couldn't vocalize the pain, but that didn't matter be-cause I knew I'd be seeing Sister soon. I couldn't want it, but she was all I could think about as my vision blurred and my breath wheezed from what little air made it past the holes in my neck. Death wasn't fast enough. It was long and painful and full of regrets and memories. I thought life flashing be-fore one's eyes was overrated, yet the high of remembering Sister couldn't be overstated. Or maybe the visions repre-sented the stream of data being copied to Eden. I hoped not. I didn't want the memories to be fake, too.

Chapter 2

"Hansel."

Sister spoke to me through Eve. The accuracy of her voice set my heart racing. Her mannerisms raised goose-bumps along my arm as I anticipated Sister's usual touch—ruffling my hair, rubbing my back with her fingers, and taking my hand in hers when we danced in the water. Even her hazel eyes shone through the neutral hue of Eve's.

"Protect this girl, Hansel. Guide her, as an Archangel would a wandering soul. Help her return to Father."

"But Father's gone."

"...to Father...to the Son..."

"Sister!"

I opened my eyes and immediately sat up. A sharp pain ran through my upper body and again when I raised my arm and nearly swatted the hand reaching for my left temple. Then I caught it by the wrist, as it retreated, and as I came to my senses.

My fingers had closed around the thin arm of an old man. His hand trembled, not from fear, but from lack of strength. Dry and loose skin felt cold, unlike the owner's green eyes, which stared at me with a surprising amount of warmth.

He said, "I'm no more a sister than you are a priest."

Carefully, I loosened my grip, concerned I'd cause irreparable damage otherwise. The old man showed me a beige, cream-like substance on his index and middle fingers. I felt something warm above my left brow, accompanied by a numbing feeling that would've escaped my senses if not for my ANTS. Assuming it was the substance on his fingers, I relaxed my shoulders and nodded.

He continued applying the cream while my eyes wandered. I noticed my bare chest. Someone had removed my shirt. Neatly wrapped bandages covered my ribs. My pants clung to my legs, both beneath a pale-blue flat sheet. I wiggled my toes, and didn't feel the enclosure of the black loafers I'd worn.

I spotted my shoes sitting on a brown welcome mat below the peephole of a metal door, almost lost in a sea of artwork decorating and cluttering the room. Various-sized canvases leaned against dressers, chairs, and nightstands, others hung on the dark green walls, and a few rested on table-high wooden easels.

I asked, "Where am I? Who are you?" My voice sounded hoarse. Swallowing felt lumpy and mildly painful. I cleared my throat, inciting more pain. Despite my aggressive tone, the old man showed no signs of fear.

He chuckled until he coughed. "You, my boy, are in my home. And I…I'm just an old man."

I almost couldn't talk, but I forced the words through my sore throat. "Where's Sister?"

"With the Hero, I imagine."

I grabbed him by the wrist again, gentler than before, but enough to pause his work, and searched his eyes for affiliation with the Hero. I found the disapproval in his voice instead, a slower recognition process without Gretel. It also occurred to me he wouldn't know Sister existed in my head as Gretel. She couldn't have been with the Hero. If he captured anyone, it'd be Enola…and Eve.

The old man didn't flinch. "You shouted his name in your sleep," he said, flatly. He flared his eyes at me and seemed more annoyed by the interruption than the interrogation.

I let go of his wrist.

He continued applying the cream, as if nothing had happened. "Even if you didn't call out his name, he's the only one capable of going toe-to-toe with an Archangel."

I reached for his wrist again, ready to ask him what he knew about us, but he dodged.

"Not this time, my boy." He laughed and then coughed.

He wiped off the remaining cream from his finger using a thick napkin. "Yes, I know about you, too. Mercenaries of God dedicated to sending his followers to Eden. I may be old, but I'm not senile. That's one of the few positives of ANTS, I suppose. They keep you right in the head until the very end."

I retracted my arm and reached for my brow. He swatted at my hand. Then he checked the bandages around my ribs and released a satisfied breath. "Other than a few fresh scars along the neck, I think you'll be fine after some rest."

"Medical ANTS?" I asked, learning that short sentences hurt my throat less.

A hearty laugh forced him to drink water. "No, artistic." He gestured at the paintings. "I have a photographic memory skill. It made applying bandages easy after watching a few videos, but made painting…not quite the thing it used to be. There's no emotion in digital memory."

Multiple scenic works stood out to me. They featured blue oceans, sandy beaches, and palm trees. He must've been to those places. Despite his claim, I sensed emotion behind every brush stroke. He remembered more than just with his eyes.

He seemed to stare at the same painting as me, the one with the sun tinting the water varying shades of yellow. He said, "That's the difference between art and science. I can run a brush across the canvas without consequence, but a scalpel can save a life or take a life." He sighed and then stood while pulling his unbuttoned, faded amber shirt together. Hunched, he took several steps toward a brown dresser. A painting of two kids building a sandcastle leaned against one leg. "Fortunately, I was a retired man when ANTS spread. I didn't have to find my place in a world of skills." He put the container of cream in the dresser drawer and closed it.

"I should probably go," I said in a low voice.

The old man turned his entire body to face me. The white

tee underneath his shirt carried splotches of paint, matching some nearby palettes. "You should rest. You're pretty beat up, and you're only talking because of the herbal tea I made you drink."

"If your Hero finds me, you'll be an accomplice." I paused. "I've felt his sense of justice. There is no gray."

He nodded in agreement. "I'm an accomplice because you collapsed onto my balcony last night." He hobbled over to a short stool in front of a canvas with green grass painted beneath a pastel-purple sky, and nothing else. He dipped a thick-edged brush into a can of water and then dabbed it across a napkin.

I remembered fighting the Hero on the bridge and wondered how I'd collapsed onto the man's balcony. There was no memory from the time he pierced my neck to the moment I woke up. Nothing. Not even a fragment.

While I searched my mind for answers, the old man continued, "The Hero lost his way when one of you came through." He took a deep breath and shook his head. "As I recall, that person only saw the world through a black and white lens, too. An oddly specific lens. The world was one color and their target the other."

I turned my head toward him, ignoring the pain in my neck for a moment before I had to look straight again. Enola and Eve crossed my mind. Sister, too, who was oddly quiet. She may have exhausted herself during our fight with the Hero, but…

The old man said, "I'm no expert, but I'm pretty sure you're lucky to be alive. Whatever pierced your neck missed all the vital parts. A guardian angel was definitely looking after you."

Sister still hadn't spoken. I couldn't feel her, either. Just thinking her name often received affirmation. An 'I love you' at the very least. I strained my senses, forcing them to be more acute as I searched them for traces of her. When I sensed nothing, I said her name aloud. "Sister?"

I've always felt her, even when she rested. Her naps reminded me of the orphanage computer after it went to sleep. It steadily hummed, ready to power on when touched. Sister often reacted the same way. She rested every now and again, and came online when I reached out for her.

"Sister? Gretel?" I rose to my knees. Pain shot through the joints and caused me to stumble forward and onto my hands. I collapsed further onto my elbows and grabbed my head with both hands. "Sister Gretel!"

Nothing. Silence. Vacant. Even at max perception, a void existed where her voice used to be. I heard birds chirping outside. The sheets that covered me smelled of fresh lavender competing against the surrounding oil paints. A nearby resident played the guitar. The old man looked at me from the corners of his eyes. His hands trembled. His heart beat irregularly, and he struggled to take measured breaths. But no Sister. I couldn't hear, smell, taste, touch, or feel her.

Chapter 3

"Protect Eve?" Enola said as we left the Queen's tower. She stroked her chin. "Say, Hansel, what if we raised Eve? You know, as our own?"

Eve marched ahead of us. She didn't skip or meander as a child would. Her stride was that of someone walking in this world while seeing another. I imagined an eccentric expression on her face, like an animatronic doll, perhaps staring into Eden.

"There are bigger things at stake, Hansel."

I felt Gretel's disapproval and then her anger when I compared her objection to Father's, the man who took me away from her after she'd decided to raise me as her own. He replaced her love and her warmth with a promise to save humanity.

Enola stepped out in front of me. "We could be a real family…" she said, walking backwards with both hands behind her. The pep in her step returned. "You'd get breakfast in bed and hugs and kisses—from both of us, but from me alone," she bit her lower lip and swayed her hips, "I can copy this streamer's Actor skill and be anybody you want me to be." Enola smirked. "Even your precious—"

"Lust is a sin, Hansel."

Enola narrowed her eyes. She seemed to pout, yet raised a brow instead. "What's that voice in your head saying?"

I wondered if Eve wanted a family. I glanced past Enola to check on her. She was gone. I blinked several times to make sure I wasn't dreaming. When I refocused, Enola had disappeared, too. And so had the voice in my head.

"Sister!"

I jumped up, eyes wide open. A warm, moist towel flew into my lap. A cold sweat had soaked the bandages wrapped across my upper body and caused cold spots where they clung to my skin. Parts of the wrap loosened as I took deep, rapid breaths.

The familiar surroundings calmed me, as did the old man's voice. "So even the dauntless cry out in their sleep," he said, stroking a thin brush across some newly painted trees on the same canvas from before. "I imagine you were having a nightmare. Hopefully not one about your mission. That would mean guilt. That would mean wrongdoing." He raised a brow, slightly tilted his head in my direction, and glanced at me from the corner of his eyes. "You got worked up earlier and then passed out. You were running a high fever when I checked on you." He nodded at me. "You need more rest."

I grunted. Rolling my shoulders, I loosened my tense muscles. "I need to find my…" I paused. The correct word eluded me. 'Friends' came to mind first and seemed appropriate. 'Family' surfaced with recent memories of Enola's proposal to adopt Eve. Father had said people were acquaintances because relationships bordered worldly possessions, as neither would accompany us to the next life. I wasn't sure what he meant then, any more than I was about the word to use now.

"I need to find the Hero," I said, thinking he either let Enola and Eve go or held them captive. I leaned toward the latter, assuming he searched for and didn't find my body or Enola contributed to my escape somehow.

The old man shook his head. "He's looking for you, too."

Putting the brush down, the old man picked up a remote sitting on the lip of a nearby easel. He aimed it at a small television hanging on the wall behind his painting, to the far right of my field of view.

Slowly, I swung my legs off the bed, gripping the mattress for support. I turned and raised my head to view the screen. I ignored the pain that followed and then massaged my neck to appease it.

The old man moved the remote to and from his face, perhaps searching for the mute button, since I saw the Hero on the television screen, but couldn't hear him. He stood behind a lectern, his armor extending beyond its wooden edges, and his helm sitting on its sloping top. He spoke with the same exaggerated lip movements, mouth wide open, as if we wouldn't hear him otherwise.

The television's volume returned. "…how you survived. Maybe God is watching you after all, Archangel. But God has no place here. He didn't help these people. I did!"

Blue eyes peered at me through the screen. "Come out and face your consequences! Anyone harboring you will face the same justice. I'll purge evil at its roots along with every infected branch! I will—"

The old man drove a finger against the remote and muted the television. "Sorry, lad. It's been playing all morning, and I'm sick of his yapping." He dropped the remote back on the easel's lip and continued painting. The pastel purple he'd mixed into the clouds earlier grew darker with every brush stroke.

"He locked the tower down. Nobody in or out of their homes. I'd say he'll go door to door, but that's a lot of knocking. Otherwise, he has no way of finding you."

I flexed my fingers, curling them in and out. "But I'm looking for him, too."

"You won't put up much of a fight in your condition." He turned to me with the grace and speed of a snail. "Every time you think about facing him, touch your neck. Those metal shards could've taken your head off, and it wouldn't have been a clean cut." He took several small steps, rotating away from me until he faced the painting again.

I reached for my neck but stopped short of touching it. I didn't need to feel the wounds with my fingers because my senses outlined each one as they throbbed, the pain likely subdued by medication.

"And you definitely won't win if your head isn't right."

I raised a brow at his statement.

He pressed the brush against the canvas and made one

long, wobbly stroke across the sky. "You were calling for Sister before you passed out. If she's with the Hero, then he hasn't mentioned her, but I suspect she's not." He stared hard at the canvas. "Memories are the worst, especially with a photographic skill like mine. I had two boys—twins. Lost them both six years ago. The times before Eden are cloudy, but everything after is clearer than reality." He coughed. His voice broke. He dipped the brush in a cup of water. "I relive our time spent together every day. Painting helps keep them off my mind."

"Nothing will take Sister off my mind," I said. I didn't tell him that Sister died years ago. Afraid to face reality, I didn't want him to ask how I still spoke to her. "I'll never forget her."

He waved his hand at me. "No, no, no. I don't want to forget them, but I also don't want a constant reminder of how I failed them. That's what happened to the Hero." He dried off the brush and seemed to ponder on the next color.

"An Archangel killed a family of seven during his watch. He let his failure to protect them go to his head. That led to new laws and harsher consequences. He went from hero to vigilante to villain."

I wondered who could've killed so many. What entire family had Father's God chosen for Eden?

The old man shook his head. "The Hero wished he'd fought a battle that didn't take place. That family died in their sleep. The doctor found poison in their system and then in their food."

Daisy, I thought to myself. A botanical ANTS skill made her a silent reaper. She was kind, too. I imagined her being invited to dinner with the family and adding a lethal ingredient to a recipe while helping in the kitchen. The family wouldn't have suspected her, either. Despite the similarities in our clothing that might've alerted a few, Daisy's floor-length dress strayed just enough from the clerical uniform to avoid suspicion. Most of the Archangels were men, too. Father had an antiquated mindset.

The old man continued his story. "We inspected every grain of rice for poison while he searched every nook and cranny of the tower for the killer." He took an exhausted breath. "Never found them."

"How did the Hero know the killer was an Archangel?"

He shrugged. "Who else could it be? Outside of your organization, if your death isn't natural, it's brutal. That family's death was peaceful. Serene. Poetic, even. Perhaps one family member sacrificed themselves for the good of the rest, but the Hero needed a villain, so he would've made one, anyway."

The word "villain" crossed my mind because I needed one, too. A fight would wake Sister. The more emotion, the louder the alarm. And if that didn't work, I'd have Eve take me to her in Eden.

The old man either sensed or saw the determination in my eyes. "There's no stopping you, is there?" he asked without lifting his gaze from the canvas.

I raised my eyes to him. Concern emanated from his trembling hands, and more unintentional emotions made their way onto the canvas.

"I'll fail them if I sit around any longer." I stood, slightly wobbled on my feet, and then steadied myself.

He smiled, nearly laughed, and nodded his head. "The holding cells are on floors thirty-eight to forty-two," he said as he slowly spun the stool around to a small nightstand. He opened the drawer and pulled out my pistols. His hands dipped from their weight.

"The person you're looking for might be there." He handed the pistols to me. "They're empty. How will you fight him?"

His question gave me pause. I didn't have any ammunition left, except for the one bullet I kept for myself. I searched the small pocket above the large one of my pants and pulled it out.

I sighed, thinking the single shell wouldn't be enough to fell the Hero. I'd have to get it around the shards and past his armor. But first, I had to find him.

I raised my eyes to the old man and asked, "Do you have holy water?"

Chapter 4

I stood outside the old man's home, wondering whether I should've injured or killed him. An injury wouldn't have fooled the Hero. Archangels aren't known for unprovoked attacks outside of their mission. The traitor might've shaken that foundation within others and possibly me.

Killing the old man wouldn't have changed anything. He seemed a suitable candidate for Eden, but he might've expected it and thus been denied. The proclaimed paradise wasn't real, anyway. Taking his life would've been murder, same as all before him. I wasn't a savior; I was a killer. Sister probably left me because angels like her couldn't be associated with mortals who break the commandments.

The eeriness of the hallway outpaced my depressing thoughts. Unlike the Queen's tower, which bustled with residents and merchants, the Hero's tower felt deserted. The stay-at-home order had everything to do with citizen movements, or lack thereof, but did it contribute to the bland exterior of the homes and the absence of lively colors?

Someone had built the towers before the beginning of the end. I didn't know their original purpose and wondered if the current plain and uninspiring look belonged to the initial design. Since then, people had converted the rooms into condominiums, consolidating resources and expertise.

The old man lived on the fifty-eighth floor, two below one of the sky bridges connecting his tower to another. I looked at the rusted metal walkway above and wondered how I'd descended two stories in my condition. Glancing down, I confirmed the fall distance had the Hero thrown me from the bridge. I could barely make out the lobby floor. If people moved about, they would've been ants filing in and out of tunnels. But nobody stirred.

I started toward one end of the fifty-eighth-floor hallway. Assuming similar designs across the towers, I expected an elevator and a stairwell at each corner of the floor, and additional stairwells, spanning ten stories each, at the center of each corridor.

My shoes didn't announce my presence the same way the Hero's boots had. Even if they had, nobody would've noticed they belonged to me. All the window shades and blinds were closed. I didn't sense anyone peeking, either, if not for curiosity, then to report my location and end the curfew.

I stopped for a moment and focused. Fear radiated from every direction. A cloud of uncertainty seeped out from under the doors. Exposed and unafraid, I walked at a brisk pace toward one corner of the floor. Even if the Hero learned of my whereabouts, unless he was already on top of me, he wouldn't readily catch up.

***

When I reached the elevator, I sighed. I didn't have a key card to operate it beyond a few floors. Enola wasn't there to hack the console, which meant taking the stairs. Gretel would've told me to count my blessings; going down was easier than going up. Fighting the Hero in an enclosed space, such as the stairwell, wouldn't be ideal, to which she'd reply: we'll fight him together.

I started down the stairs several feet from the elevator. Incandescent bulbs illuminated the space with a warm orange light. Not a soul in sight. The silence would carry the sound of my steps if I wasn't careful. Who would hear me? The Hero didn't employ guards or staff. He'd demanded a message from the residents regarding my whereabouts and then placed them on lockdown, limiting his eyes and ears. I thought about fooling him with a message of my own, but I didn't have his number.

Floor Fifty-Five…Fifty-Four…Fifty-Three…

My pace increased. I skipped more and more steps on the

way down. The stairwell had landings between floors. Ignoring the risk of a multi-flight tumble, I started rounding the corners at speed. Alas, I tripped on the fiftieth floor and slammed into the landing wall, catching myself before I stumbled further.

My ribs still hurt from the first fight with the Hero. So did my neck, which I'd kept turned to the right the entire way down. I took a moment to stretch it to the left and catch my breath. My lungs felt on fire. I unbuttoned my blazer. It, the blood-stained shirt, and the bandages all contributed to the heat suffocating me.

Those ailments were nothing I hadn't dealt with before. Something else bothered me, something I hadn't felt in a long time. It caused my heart to pound and tears to run down my face. With my back against the landing wall, I slid to a seated position.

"What's happening?" I said aloud, wiping my cheeks with the back of my hands.

My chest tightened. I choked while breathing. A sense of dread caused me to cry, as if I'd been heartbroken, as if I'd lost someone dear, as if I'd lost something precious. I emptied my stomach of emotion, and when nothing remained, I pumped it harder with every breath. My mind raced with thoughts of nothing until my hyperfocus kicked in, so I thought.

My ANTS caused the mental breakdown. Processing the fear of nearby citizens took its toll on me, emotions that Gretel had helped me manage all these years. Ugly emotions I never felt from Sister; my senses were at peace around her. But now that I was alone, they ran rampant throughout my body.

I shut off my ANTS to the extent that I could. The only thing I heard and felt then were my haggard breaths. My body felt numb. My head spun, dizzily. The cold stairwell raised goosebumps along my arms. And the slamming of a door rang discordantly in my ears.

That wasn't the time to be human.

Crawling at first, I scurried from the landing and down the remaining steps of floor fifty. Then I willed myself to level forty-nine. Without my ANTS fully active, I couldn't tell who or what followed me. I couldn't hear their steps or sense their intent. The perception I'd always believed to be Gretel was blind.

The emotions I'd felt earlier hadn't completely dissipated. Had they been courage or even rage, I'd face my pursuer, but fear and anxiety crippled my resolve and left me unable to face anyone, especially the Hero, if he chased me.

On the forty-sixth floor, I glanced over my shoulder for the hundredth time. Another false alarm from my sixth sense. Nobody stood behind me. Nobody reached for my shoulder or prepared to strike. There was nobody as far up the previous flight as I could see.

Four more flights, I told myself. *And then what?*

The follow-on thought almost distracted me. I maintained my balance down another flight of stairs. Between floors, I tried to sort out my next move. To get Gretel back, I needed to fight. To survive the fight, I needed my ANTS. To use my ANTS, I needed Gretel.

If the forty-second floor contained prisoners, their rebellious state of mind might fuel the fight in me. The idea alone encouraged me. Some would be demoralized, but I hoped their resentment toward imprisonment would outweigh their sorrow of captivity.

When I reached the forty-third floor, I heard footsteps behind me. They sounded heavy, metal, and close. Already at full speed, I rammed my shoulder into the exit and stumbled onto the forty-third-floor hallway. I spun around to see if anything followed me through the door, staggering backwards until someone grabbed me from behind and pulled me into one of the homes.

Chapter 5

Inside the dark home, I dropped my elbow into the assailant behind me and then flipped them over my shoulder. Their legs crashed into the door as it closed. A couple of seconds passed before I realized their hold hadn't been malicious and that I'd reacted defensively because I couldn't sense their intent.

As the average-build, red-headed man groaned and rolled himself over, Enola called my name.

"Hansel!"

I wondered if my emotional distress, a yearning for familiar ties, caused auditory hallucinations. An echo of Gretel's voice, which had always called out to me. A substitute because for the first time in a long time, I felt alone.

"Hansel!" her voice rang again.

I turned around to see a group of people partially illuminated by a dim chandelier behind them, perhaps over a small dining room table. An old lady stood at the vanguard. The cane she held with both hands pressed into the carpet. Two boys, twins, glared at me from behind each of her hips. Their dark eyes resembled devils on her shoulders. A few other people stood to the old lady's left, including a tall man with his arm around a plump woman. Another man leaned over a breakfast bar. He dodged the hanging pendant light to get a better view of the front door. Two women walked out of the kitchen and squeezed into the hole left behind by Enola, as she rushed to the front of the group.

Enola stopped short of throwing her arms around me, raising and then hovering them above my chest. "Holy shit, you're alive," she said.

I almost didn't recognize her. Without the dark mascara, her pasty complexion reminded me of the cream the old man had rubbed across my brow. She dressed differently. A black V-neck shirt replaced the cross-strap top. She wore a blue jean jacket over it and matching pants that hugged her thighs and legs down to her ankles.

"I saw him break your neck." She reached for the wounds likely peeking out from underneath the bandages.

"Did you help me escape?" I guided her hands away, and she navigated them to my face instead, touching it as a blind person would.

"I tried. You wandered off like a zombie and vaulted over the railing." She focused her eyes on me. "As if something controlled you."

Without Gretel's help, I didn't think I'd understand what passed through Enola's mind, but I recognized her concerned gaze. She knew something bothered me. Women's intuition, as she'd called it once before.

"Quiet," the red-headed man whispered loudly from the front door.

I lowered my chin and turned my head toward him. He knelt by the door and stared at a thin light underneath. After a few seconds of stillness, a shadow drifted across that light. Everyone held their breath as it moved from right to left.

After the darkness passed, the red-headed man stood. He held onto the door frame for support and leaned across to look through the peephole. The breath he held and then released signaled the others to do the same.

Enola cupped the right side of my face with her hand and guided me back to her. "Let's get you cleaned up," she said in a voice I'd never heard from her. Its tone and delivery reminded me of Sister, low and full of natural love.

***

Enola sat across from me in the red-headed man's living room, in the same-type dining room chair, but with its back to the door. The rest of the room's occupants surrounded me. Most tended to my wounds, from the fall down the stairs and from the fight with the Hero. One tried to feed me, and another offered to wash my clothes.

With all the hands moving across my field of view, I asked Enola, "What's going on here? How did you…?"

"Escape?" Enola smirked. "I hacked the door. Their security sucks. The prisons are just housing units. The Hero moved their locks to the other side of the door and changed the code. Anyone can walk in, but nobody can walk out." She crossed her legs. "With old boy focused on finding you, I let myself out."

"Eve?" I asked.

Enola shook her head. "I didn't find her in the adjacent rooms, and I didn't have time to check every unit across five floors. My cellmate thinks there's logic to the room assignments and that Eve must be in one specifically for children." She leaned forward, eyes wide. "Children, Hansel! That fucker has a prison for children!"

"Does he know about her?"

Enola put her hand out, and one woman gave her a glass of red wine. "I don't think so. For now, anyway. You know how strange that girl is. It's only a matter of time before he finds out."

I glanced around. "Are *they* your cellmates?" *Or your servants*, I wanted to add.

Enola sat back. "They're the resistance. I picked up one or two from the rooms next to my cell and they gathered a few others."

I sensed ulterior motives in the room but hesitated to activate my ANTS again. Based on body language, there seemed to be an equal amount of fear and anger, enough to balance whatever I'd feel.

"What are they resisting?"

"The Hero, of course." She swirled the wine inside the glass.

Except for the red-headed man and the old lady, I didn't believe any of them could resist the Hero.

"Don't underestimate these people, Hansel. They'll do everything in their power to get you ready for that fight."

I raised a brow.

"You're going to fight him, right?" she added.

Everyone in the room paused their activities.

"You have to fight him, Hansel!" Enola raised her voice, louder than she planned. She covered her mouth and then glanced over her shoulder and at the door. She lowered her voice. "I brought these people together with the promise that you'll dethrone him."

I shook my head. "I can't fight him. I'd lose."

The surrounding murmurs grew louder. Doubt and fear seeped into the tones. "We're screwed. The Hero's going to hang us from the overpass in the atrium. We went against him. He'll imprison us forever."

Enola waved her hand, asking them to quiet down. "Why can't you fight him? You're the actual hero this tower needs."

I locked eyes with Enola. "Sister…Gretel…she's gone. I haven't heard her voice for days."

Enola's eyes grew wide for a second before she narrowed them again. "So what? Does that mean you're giving up? You only care about Sister? What about Eve? You don't care about her?"

"I can't control my ANTS without Gretel." I pointed at my face. "I lost control earlier. The dread in this place overwhelmed me and I broke down. Gretel's been keeping those errant emotions at bay all this time. Without her, I can't rely on my ANTS and without it, I can't fight him. I only have one bullet left to get past his defenses."

Enola stomped her foot before crossing her legs again. "There has to be a way." She repeatedly tapped one foot against the ground, causing the crossed leg to bob out of sync. "I'd volunteer to be the voice in your head, but Sister's not here for me to copy her skill."

"Sister's ANTS connects her to the one she loves—"

"Shut up, Hansel. I'm trying to think." She resumed tapping and thinking aloud. "I could copy your perception skill, but I have zero combat stats to go with it and enough of my own emotions to deal with." She raised her head. "Does anybody here have a useful skill I could borrow?"

Nobody responded.

"Oh, fuck it. If you're too afraid to fight him, Hansel, then I will." Enola walked up to me, grabbed my head with both hands, and slammed her forehead against mine. She pulled back. "What the hell? What's going on up there *this* time?"

"As I said, Gretel is—"

Enola head-butted me again. The others watched, some covering their mouth, horrified, as if she unknowingly provoked a monster. Every collision of Enola's rock-solid head reverberated throughout my skull. Yet *she* seemed frustrated.

She tilted her head, narrowed her eyes, and scrunched her brows. "Gretel kept me out before, sure, but there's a different kind of interference this time."

"Probably electromagnetic interference," the red-headed man said. "It's from the Hero." He looked at us with one eye open and one closed. "His ANTS emits an electromagnetic field around him. It disrupted my connection to cameras once." He pointed at his closed eye. "I can connect to and view surveillance video."

Enola added, "That's how we knew when and where you were coming, by the way." Then she shrugged at the red-headed man. "Okay, but the Hero's not here."

"Then he must be infected. Either in the skin or the blood, which is worse. I'm surprised you're not hacking up lunch from the nausea."

I rubbed my forehead.

Enola flashed an apologetic smile as she brushed my hand aside and kissed the spot she'd assaulted. Then she sat down in her chair, cheeks flushed red. "So, um, radiation poisoning? I wonder if that's affecting your connection with," she hesitated, "Gretel."

I touched my head and then my neck. My fingers threatened to squeeze my blood out through the wounds if it meant purging my system of the infection. I wanted to fight the Hero to wake Gretel, but if I was the source of the interference, then I was the one keeping her out.

"Learn to fight without her, Hansel," Enola said in a serious tone.

Our eyes met. Neither of us blinked for at least a minute. She didn't seem the type to back down from a challenge, so I averted my gaze first. I didn't concede. Enola seemed to know that. She rolled her eyes and crossed her arms.

One of the twin boys walked up to me. They seemed to be ten or eleven years old. He ran a hand through his brown hair, starting with the strands that obscured his vision and ending at the crown.

"I have an idea." He waited a few seconds for a response and then continued without one. "What if you fought him alone? Away from the rest of us."

Enola leaped out of the chair. "That's a great idea! We just have to find a quiet place, such as a ring, and let them duke it out. It'd be like a boxing match. And the rest of us can watch from the safety of our homes—your homes."

I lowered my gaze and then raised my eyes to the boy. "An isolated fight with the Hero could work. It'd minimize external influence, but it wouldn't help me overcome his defenses or the interference."

The red-headed man spoke up, loud enough to be heard over the gears turning in our heads, but low enough to avoid detection. "I can talk to some of the other prisoners. You aren't the first one affected by his ANTS." His gaze jumped across several people, as if seeking approval.

Enola nodded. "And I'll go get Eve. She might know someone in E—a far-away land with expertise on this kinda thing. Baby girl has contacts."

And then a woman in the back slipped to the front. She had long black hair, large eyes, and colorful braces across her white teeth. She said, "The rest of us should condemn the Hero's actions. Or are we really okay with letting a stranger fight our battles for us? We're not physically strong, I know that, but we all have a voice that can be just as low or high as the next person."

"And how do you suggest we use that voice?" the old lady asked. She'd sat down on the living room couch, cane in hand, and spoke over her shoulder.

The outspoken woman said, "Same way the Hero does: through the television. We'll get access to the studio and share our message with the other residents. It might distract him long enough to give you," she looked at me, "an opening. Fight him in a place with TVs." Her voice faded after I met her gaze.

The old lady smacked her lips. "And what if this man fails? There's no turning back. He'll imprison us forever or kill and deny us Eden."

Eden isn't real, I thought to myself.

The outspoken woman regained her confidence. "This place is already a prison."

The red-headed man said, "Lure him to the market on the forty-fifth level. There are TVs all over that floor so that those who're out shopping can still hear announcements. There aren't any residences there, and with the Hero's curfew, there won't be any merchants, either."

"Yeah! Let's do it!" the twin boy said, pumping his fist once, unafraid to show his excitement. His brother did the same and then they bumped fists together.

Chapter 6

I was the bait and the martyr, armed with a stainless-steel pot lid and a metal baseball bat. A clean jacket hid the prior day's struggles and the holstered pistols. I left the final round in the left gun's chamber, in case seconds mattered in the upcoming fight.

The red-headed man had directed me to the stairwell after using the security cameras to verify it was clear of traffic. One woman falsely reported seeing me at the marketplace, rummaging through a drugstore for antibiotics. And since I needed a resident's card to activate the elevators, I'd avoided using them to minimize accomplices. I was the scapegoat, too.

The forty-fifth floor resembled an abandoned mall outlet in the outside world. Dilapidated shops lined the entire level, and if what the red-headed man said about the lack of residences was true, then the shops weren't simply false fronts, but units with merchandise inside. Compared to the Queen's tower, the shops also lacked heart and soul, as if the owners simply gave up one day and allowed rust and grime to take over like overgrown vegetation.

The monitors the red-headed man mentioned were aplenty and, in every direction, as if they watched me. I imagined the Hero's face on the screens, preaching his false narrative under the premise of goodwill. Then I saw his outline in the dark reflection of a monitor mounted on a concrete slab between two shops.

His metal boots resounded louder as he drew closer. I would've heard him sooner if I'd trusted my ANTS, but I'd wanted to verify the floor's vacancy first. Even a single, distraught person could send me off the rails, so I thought. After seeing no one, and thinking the coast would be clear, I noticed the Hero dragging something behind him. Someone.

I saw the bottom of their heel, their leg caught in the grasp of his metal gauntlet. Not the one created by shards that pierced my neck, but one worn by a medieval knight. The Hero wore the shards like a cape, which obscured the rest of that person's body. They didn't speak—groan, whimper, or cry out—or attempt to right themselves and break free. They must've been unconscious or dead. When I considered who all might've been picked up by the Hero, I activated my ANTS in search of a heartbeat. I heard three different rhythms, two calm and one erratic.

The Hero stopped at the entrance of the sizeable area I stood in the middle of and dropped his captive's leg. He turned his left shoulder to me and maintained eye contact as he walked toward the wall overlooking the atrium. The cape shimmered from the lights illuminating the tower's center. The curve of each shard made the collective resemble fish scales.

I followed his every step with my eyes while processing the information my ANTS provided on the person sprawled across the floor. Pale skin, dirtied and bruised. Unkempt short black hair. Dark lips.

Enola.

She'd left to find Eve so that Eden's door could either help me connect with Gretel again or learn how to cure me of the electromagnetic forces keeping me from her.

"You've had help," the Hero said, nodding at the equipment in my hands. "You won't find those things in the pharmacy."

He stopped in front of the wall, turned his body toward me, and slowly marched forward. Each step cut off additional escape routes, including the atrium behind him, the left corridor, and the right corridor. Did he think I'd run after standing out in the open?

I felt the cool air coming from the stairwell behind me. If I planned to run, it'd be to take Enola to safety. I wondered if that was what the Hero was thinking, dragging her into this fight. Had he brought her along as a hostage, or had their paths crossed?

He grinned. "You're not going to help her?" He opened his left palm toward Enola. "She swore you'd kick my ass if I laid a hand on her. Then she tried to kiss me." He shook his head in disbelief. "Strange woman."

I didn't disagree.

He lowered his arm. "My phone alerted me when the doors to her unit, and several others, opened. I'll catch the others later. I've locked the tower down, so there's no escape."

"You sound more like a villain than a hero," I said.

My words struck a nerve. He narrowed his eyes at me and then yelled, mouth wide open. "The only villain here is you. The peace you destroyed won't go unpunished. This is your last chance to surrender!"

I didn't recall the option to surrender when he'd thrust the shards into my neck, but calling him out on that would only shed more light on the lives I'd taken under similarly false pretenses. I was no less a villain than he was.

I raised the bat and then the shield.

"If that's your answer," he said.

He charged me, his speed slower than mine because of his thick build and heavy armor.

I closed the distance, too, raising my improvised shield. He lacked the mobility to execute quick maneuvers. Instead of tackling me using his weight, he grounded to a stop and started a large motion for his attack. His swing covered a wide area I couldn't quite escape. I defended with the pot lid. The collision ripped the plate from its handle and flung it into the marketplace seating area.

I swung the bat at his left side. The shards came around his shoulder and absorbed the blow, caving in slightly before pushing back out. I used the momentum from the pushback and carried it through a backward spin and swing to his abdomen. The shards didn't fold around his chest in defense. They moved at a snail's pace, too. Instead, I hit the plate of armor and barely scratched it. Again, I bounced off, but retreated instead of chaining another attack. It all felt futile.

"You can't beat me," he laughed. He stood like an immovable statue until he glanced at Enola. "The woman there refused to tell me about your ANTS. When I couldn't find your body, I wondered if it contributed to your survival, but from our first and second skirmish, I can say that it's nothing impressive. God really was watching over you. This time, though, I'll crush the wings of whatever guardian angel he sends to save you."

Despite my resolve to wake Gretel through combat, my confidence and my strength waned. The infection didn't help my condition or my connection to her. My neck throbbed in pain as the medication gradually wore off.

I needed to buy time. A few of the locals had rallied with the plan to lower his morale. I wondered if they'd reached the studio. Enola wasn't a part of that plan, and the Hero worked alone, so there'd be no one else to deter them.

"Go ahead, send me to Eden," I said, throwing aside the pot lid's handle. "We all know the only criterion for entrance: you can't want it. Killing me because you failed to protect one person from another won't deny me everlasting life."

I searched my senses for anything from him that might point me to a crack in his mental fortitude, something I could take advantage of when the time came. I found nothing. There wasn't a sliver of doubt. He either believed in his path one hundred percent or controlled his emotions beyond my ability to detect stray feelings.

"Eden? I'm going to send you to hell."

His armor made him slow. *I should be able to dodge his attacks*, I thought. Then something pushed me from behind. *Shards?* I felt two of them at my backside, shoving me forward. They slipped past my senses. No, I failed to process the information because I focused on the Hero's emotions. I couldn't *see* everything around me without Gretel.

The Hero stepped in and slugged me. I must've blacked out for a second because I didn't see the second swing, but I felt the pain and recognized my body moving in the opposite direction. The shards at my back held me up like a railing and prevented me from collapsing to the ground. As I tried to regain my bearings, they pushed me into the Hero's grasp. He spun me around and passed one of his enormous arms under my neck and secured his hold with the other. I couldn't breathe.

I refocused my senses and inspected his body, but couldn't find any weaknesses in the arm triangle choke. He was too heavy for a shoulder throw. I'd break my elbow against his armor if I struck him with it. I couldn't kick a leg out from under him, stomp his foot through the metal boots, or strike his head with a high kick. So I dug my feet in and tried to shove us backwards, perhaps over the railing. I pushed him back one step.

The shards he wore as a cape separated and evenly formed a three-foot-radius dome around us. "Let's see your guardian angel get through that," he said through clenched teeth.

He tightened the arm around my neck and grabbed my head with the other. "Goodbye, Archangel."

Chapter 7

"Hansel…Hansel…"
"Sister?"

"Hansel!" Enola shouted from the floor.

I heard and felt the desperation in her voice. The rapid beating of her heart motivated mine through the lack of oxygen. Her fear didn't demoralize me. There was something else clawing its way through the painful cry. Emotions that I'd only ever felt from Sister. Feelings of endearment that Gretel shared with me often.

Maybe I'd reconnected to Gretel. I opened my mouth to call her name, but I couldn't speak it. The feelings belonged to Enola.

She struggled to her hands and knees and begged the Hero to stop. "You're killing him!"

I felt the Hero's resolve, the tightening of his grip, and the muscles winding up for a quick twist that would either send me to hell or send me to Sister. Except Eden wasn't real, and neither place was ready for me.

My guardian angel came in the form of a television mounted to a slab between shops. "Kyle." A girlish voice spoke.

The Hero loosened his grip. I gasped for what little air I could before he secured his hold again. He looked at the television.

Eve stood in front of a lectern and said, "It's me, Alexandria."

"Alex?" The Hero's voice cracked.

"It's okay, Kyle. Wherever you are, whatever you're doing, we forgive you. Mama. Papa. Everyone. Thank you for being our hero."

"What's going on?" He asked and then turned his rage on me. "What did you do? It's your ANTS, isn't it? Did you think using her voice would—"

Alex, through Eve, continued, "This girl has the power to reach Eden. You might not believe it, so…" Eve put a finger to her chin, as if in thought. "Que, Mama?" She turned her head and spoke to someone off camera.

The camera operator panned to the right. The people in view stepped back, each looking at the other, confused about who Eve addressed.

Alex spoke to the empty space. "I'm trying to tell him something only we would know. He won't believe me, Mama. Espaguetis? With the meatballs. Mama, I don't know if that was good."

"They were delicious," the Hero said, but Alex couldn't hear him through the monitor. "How's your brother?" He asked. Had Eve been here, instead of there, he could've talked to them.

"You wanna tell him about your spaghetti, Mama? He doesn't speak Spanish. El no habla Español, Mama. Huh? There's some in the freezer? It's not good anymore." She faced the camera again. "Our time here is short. We just wanna say thank you. Gracias. We are fine. Because you made the tower safe, we lived a blessed life worthy of Eden. Please, make it safe again…"

"I'm so glad you're safe," he said, his voice moist with tears.

Eve blinked. I recognized that distant gaze. Alex no longer spoke through her.

The Hero's grip loosened again. I pulled his arm down for a better breath.

"A connection to Eden," he said. "That girl can talk to the dead? Please make it safe again? I…"

I heard his heartbeat through the armor. Escalating. Panicking. He seemed lost, yet absentmindedly maintained a solid hold on me. He mumbled to himself, but I heard every word. "I…I made this place safe. I kept the tyrants out. I…"

"Do it now, Hansel!" Enola extended an arm. One shard, from the bottom right of the dome, launched at the Hero's head, above my right shoulder. I felt the Hero cock his head back. I heard the impact of metal, pieces clattering against the ground after, and then saw part of his helmet roll around the front of my feet.

"How did you do that?" He exclaimed, unaware that Enola copied his ANTS. Perhaps during that kiss he called strange.

Enola dropped her arm and then raised the other. Another shard exited the formation, but the Hero stopped it mid-flight. I felt his focus shift again, this time to the shards forming the surrounding dome as a tug-of-war with Enola began.

She could only manipulate one to two at a time. I saw them vibrate in place, struggling against the counter-push of the Hero. She changed her target when the Hero halted the previous shard's movements.

"That wasn't Alex." He strained to speak. "That was your ANTS imitating her!" He tightened his arm around my neck again.

I pulled down on his arm, using all my strength and weight to counter him. "How would I know about the spaghetti?"

"The Hernandez family is always on my mind. You searched those memories and then passed the information to that girl. All that time you were buying for a failed distraction, and for this slut to learn control of my hexes."

I felt Enola's anger grow after hearing his words. She pushed harder, upping her control from a couple of shards to five.

Her hatred for the Hero gave me strength, and I used every bit to fight against his hold. I felt *his* emotions, too, compounding anger that rumbled like an earthquake.

He shouted against the top of my head. "It isn't my fault. I didn't fail them. I couldn't protect them because I let people like you run around! I—" he coughed up blood. It splattered across my head.

Enola hacked up blood, too. It seeped out of her gritted

teeth as she continued to wrestle control of the shards.

I thought she and I would eventually lose the stalemate. I felt both our strengths waning. Neither of us started the fight at one hundred percent, and things didn't quite go according to plan. But now the Hero suffered, too.

Radiation poisoning, I thought, recalling the symptoms the red-headed man had mentioned. Did the Hero suffer from it, too? He'd shown no signs of it during the first fight. Did he use his ANTS too much?

"Hansel…the armor…helmet…" Enola cried out.

Was she trying to tell me something about his helmet and armor? It blocked her EMP before—an electrical signal. Had the helmet protected him from radiation poisoning, too?

The Hero must've heard Enola. In one swift motion, he overpowered me, pulling his arm against my neck and cutting off my air supply.

I needed to focus, not panic, which came from Enola, woven in with her rage. I wanted to isolate the former without infringing upon the latter I drew strength from but couldn't. Emotions were too complex. Combined with the other senses, such as hearing, seeing, and touching, I couldn't process and sort out everything. Gretel always did that for me and then gave me suggestions.

Enola acted as the voice within. She shouted. "Shoot him!"

Her words sorted the chaos in my head and provided clarity. With the helmet removed and Enola holding the shards in place, the Hero was defenseless.

I pulled out the pistol carrying my last bullet. The Hero caught my arm and wrestled it down and away from himself. Another tug-of-war began. Enola and I couldn't hold out much longer. I had to end the fight.

I wondered what Gretel would do. What changed when we synchronized our minds? My style changed, shifting from stiff, straight-forward attacks to a dance that struck the opponent from unpredictable angles.

The Hero tightened his grip around my neck after I dropped my arms. I felt his hesitation, perhaps wondering why I'd surrendered my will to breathe. I closed my eyes and focused on specific objects around me, such as the Hero behind me, the gun in my hands, and the shards forming the dome. I shifted the pistol to the left, since he'd only prevented me from raising it, and fired it at a shard near the ground. The bullet ricocheted upward, striking two more shards on its way around, its angle changing with each impact until it struck the shard at the top of the dome and deflected straight down into the Hero's head.

I gasped for air when the strength in his arms vanished. They fell to his sides, and he dropped to his knees, each collision with the ground resounding in my head like explosions in the distance.

The weight of the world lifted from my shoulders. My body felt lighter while gravity toppled him to the side. All the shards fell to the ground. Several harmlessly struck me in the head, shoulders, and upper back after I sank to my knees.

"Gretel?" I mumbled. Silence and tears responded. I watched and processed each individual droplet as they splattered against the ground or the back of my hand. "Gretel," I said again, louder, as if doing so made any difference inside my head. I listened for the breaths she often took, like the hum of a sleeping computer, but I couldn't focus long enough to pick up the often-faint sound. It would synchronize with my breath, like two hearts beating in rhythm.

A wave of hope swelled up inside of me. Gretel is Sister, and I could talk to Sister through Eve. I could also work with the locals to remove this curse and hear her voice inside my head again.

But the Hero's ongoing infection worried me. Why hadn't he been cured? Or had he considered the affliction weakness and hid it from the locals? I wasn't sure.

I looked up at Enola. She lay on her stomach, one hand

outstretched and the other at her side. Motionless. I pushed myself beyond my limits for a second more and focused my senses on her. I detected signs of life—a steady heartbeat and wheezing. She'd been infected, too.

As I leaned forward and crawled toward her, I noticed several people from the corner of my eye. They stood at the other railing across the atrium, one floor above ours. I stopped and turned my head to face them. More people— two, three, and four levels above ours—opened their doors.

Out of the darkness, they shielded their eyes from the atrium lighting. A few nestled babies in their arms. Many frowned, and some quietly cried, but none of them narrowed their eyes at me. None of them cast hate. The traces of hope I felt came from them.

Enola coughed. Slowly, she rose to her knees. She took large, wheezing breaths and then leaned against a nearby wall. Blood ran from her mouth. Her arms hung limply at her sides.

"Hansel?" she said.

I finished the trek to her.

"Wait," she said. "Give a girl a minute to freshen up." She tried to raise one hand, and it fell back down to her side. A weak grin crossed her face. "Oops. Looks like…what you see is…what you get…honey."

I pulled myself up next to her and leaned against the same wall. Her head slowly slid across it and landed on my shoulder.

"Let me rest…for a while…"

"You can rest for as long as you want."

I felt her smile against my shoulder. "Are you sure? I'm not Sister."

"Archangels travel alone because Father believed earthly relationships of any kind bordered material possessions. They're a sin. But I don't mind trespass if you're the sin." I looked down, unable to see her face well, but knew she was listening, intently. "Enola, will you commit trespass and finish this journey with me?"

"Ha! Fucking archangel." She sniffled. "I thought you'd…never ask…"

***

"Archangels travel alone." I heard the words and reconsidered audio hallucinations as a side-effect of Gretel's absence, but the voice came from the televisions. "I taught you better than that, Hansel."

I recognized the voice. But I refused to believe it. Enola must've been curious, too. She lifted her head from my shoulder. I straightened my neck and raised my eyes to the display mounted to the column in front of us. Static distorted the image before it cleared.

A man dressed like the clergy stood next to Eve. He had an arm around her shoulders. I couldn't see his face because the camera's height matched Eve's.

"Thank you for bringing me Eden's door." The man slowly raised his hands up, as if in prayer. The camera followed them up to his face and as they folded the hood back. "I knew I could count on you, my son."

I sat wide-eyed at the ghost on the television and then muttered the first word that came to mind. "Father?"

Internet Protocol

Chapter 1

"Push. Push! Give me one more push!"

When James heard the infant's cry, he released the smile he'd been holding back. His grin stretched beyond the light-blue mask covering his nose and mouth. He stood between two nurses, fidgeting, unsure whether to step forward or wait for instructions. After the doctor delivered the newborn boy to his wife, Emilia, James knelt next to her.

He stared at the miniature version of himself. Sparse, light-colored hair covered the baby's head instead of the dark brown strands James had secured under a hairnet. He also found similarities in the cheekbones, but the large and curious eyes resembled Emilia's.

James rubbed the baby's smooth palm and smiled when the tiny fingers attempted to close around his thumb. "His name is Forrest Alexander," he said.

James met Emilia's gaze, her nod of approval, her smile, and her pent-up laughter. He kissed her and then leaned back when a nurse wiped the sweat from Emilia's brow and re-tucked the few dirty blonde hairs that'd escaped the hairnet she wore.

***

James followed a nurse into a small conference room with a white aluminum table and six metal chairs, three on each side. He tucked in his gray shirt and fastened the second-to-last button up top before he sat in the middle chair on the side farthest from the door. Twiddling his thumbs, he thought there was nothing else to do until he remembered he was a father. He needed to share the news and photos with his family, his friends, and the world.

Three doctors walked in after James pulled his phone from his jeans pocket. Quickly, he shoved it back into his pocket and stood, almost at attention despite no military background.

"Mr. Alexander, please, sit down." The middle doctor directed James to the seat he'd pushed back when he stood and then pulled out the chair across from him. She'd stood taller and then sat higher than the two on either side of her.

She pushed short black hair strands behind her ears. Narrow brown eyes settled on James. "I'm Dr. Ainsworth. This is Dr. Brandt…" she pointed at the man on her left using her hand. He sat at the far end of the table, facing James at an angle. "…and this is Dr. Sunu," she nodded at the woman on her right, who adjusted a pair of bronze-rimmed glasses above her nose.

James almost stood again, stopping halfway, extending his hand partway, as if to shake theirs before canceling the entire gesture and sitting down. "Thank you so much for helping—for delivering my son—Forrest. Thank you so much."

Doctor Ainsworth flatly smiled. "Mr. Alexander, we've identified a problem with Forrest's heart." She took a manila envelope from Doctor Brandt and spread its contents across the table. She pointed at an x-ray image overlapping several charts. "His heart isn't pumping enough blood. Initial test results suggest it's failing."

James sat in silence. He wasn't sure if he'd misheard or misunderstood. "I… What?" He twiddled his fingers, interlocking and separating them multiple times. His feet ran in place. Tears formed at the corners of his eyes. He prevented them from accumulating too much and running down his face.

Doctor Ainsworth shook her head. "His heart isn't pumping enough blood to the rest of his body. We've placed him in intensive—"

James stood. "I need to see him."

Doctor Ainsworth raised her hand and then directed him to sit down, using a slow and steady motion. "Time isn't something Forrest has, Mr. Alexander. We need to discuss options as soon as possible."

James sat down. He placed both hands on top of the table again, and then dropped them into his lap to hide their nervous movements. "What…What can I do?"

"Forrest needs a heart transplant," she said.

James spoke toward the table, briefly raising his eyes to make sure his words weren't lost in translation the same way they'd been jumbled in his head. "Okay, let's do it. Whatever the cost, I'll find a way."

Doctor Brandt looked at Doctor Ainsworth and then leaned forward, twirling the pen in his hand. "Mr. Alexander, we can't give your son an artificial heart because he doesn't have an IP."

James paused. The drumming of his feet ceased. His fingers grabbed each other under the table and his eyes locked on Doctor Brandt's hazel pair. "What does that mean? I…I don't understand what that means. I'm a salesman. I promote products of small businesses to nearby communities. I don't speak your language."

Doctor Brandt cleared his throat. "I'm sure you know, Mr. Alexander, earlier this year, the government retired social security numbers and assigned individuals a unique network address using Internet Protocol, or IP, version four, which supports remote regulation of artificial organs, limbs, and peripherals." Doctor Brandt paused. He glanced at a clock above James' head and then lowered his eyes. "The Internet Protocol Allocation Center—IPAC—assigned the last IP address at 3:52 AM this morning. Without an address, we can't give your son a network, which is required for artificial devices—an organ, in this case—to receive updates."

James' hands bounced back and forth between the table and his lap. He didn't know what else to do with them. Their fingers clamped each other hard until his knuckles reddened. That was what prevented them from smacking the table, flipping it over, or strangling something. When he didn't think he had full control, he thrust them into his pants pockets.

"Artificial… What about a normal heart? Give him something normal."

Doctor Ainsworth crossed her leg, its knee at the table's edge. "Mr. Alexander, we don't stock organs anymore. They were expensive to harvest, maintain, operate on, and guarantee. They were, and still are, difficult to come by. Artificial organs have changed the way we treat patients."

"What? My son is dying!" James stood. His hands flew out of their confines, but grabbed the edge of the pockets before they could cause damage. "And you're talking about difficult to come by. Are you saying my son should die because the process is complicated?"

Doctor Ainsworth calmly said, "Mr. Alexander, please sit down."

James paced back and forth. He ran both hands through his hair before they returned to the dark confines of his pockets. They balled inside the fabric and threatened to pull the stitches apart when his arms tensed outward.

Doctor Brandt said, "Mr. Alexander, your son is important. We want to give him the best care that we can, but we don't control the state of the world. I'm sorry." He stood first, followed by Doctor Ainsworth. "Dr. Sunu will reach out to you if an IP becomes available."

"Who—What—Where would that come from?"

Doctor Sunu stood up. "The Internet Protocol Allocation Center manages the distribution of IPs. They're aware of the shortage and are working to resolve the problem—"

"Are they aware of my son's problem? Do they know he's dying?"

The doctors stood in silence. Doctor Brandt looked uncomfortable, and Doctor Ainsworth wore the same bland expression. Doctor Sunu frowned. She held a clipboard in her hands but wrote nothing down.

"They're out to lunch, aren't they?" James staggered backwards. He raised his hands in defense, still avoiding eye contact. "I'm sorry. I just…this is difficult, you know? Does my wife know?"

Doctor Ainsworth pushed her chair under the table. "We haven't notified Mrs. Alexander. She's under the influence of medication after giving birth. Hospital policy requires us to speak with both parents of sound mind, if available; however, because of the time-sensitive nature of this case, we made an exception to speak to you alone."

James pulled his chair out and sat down again. He clasped his hands under his chin. The chill of the room raised goosebumps along his arms. "You wanted to talk about options, but you haven't given me any."

Doctor Brandt looked at Doctor Ainsworth. She walked out of the room, but he sat back down. "If you talk to IPAC, they might grant you an exception outside the usual process for requesting and receiving an IP." He leaned forward and spoke in a low voice, "Maybe someone who's recently passed away. Next of kin have first rights to the IPs of deceased relatives, but there are folks out there without family, especially on the third floor."

He stood back up and added in a normal tone, "IPAC redistributes IPs once the hospital pronounces someone dead. Dr. Sunu will continue working on a solution from this side, but we can't generate IPs. I'm really sorry, Mr. Alexander. We've done all we could."

"Thank you. Thank you for everything." After Doctor Sunu opened the door, James raised his hand. "Dr. Brandt. How long does Forrest have?"

"Days."

Chapter 2

James sat alone in the room for ten minutes. Another family walked in. He staggered into the hallway, never feeling the rise to his feet or the greeting from the room's new occupants. From his peripheral vision, the woman seemed hopeful. She glanced several times at the older man who accompanied her, as if the room would bring more joy, but the man's long, wrinkled, and unchanging face suggested he'd gone through what James wished he'd never experienced.

The hallway seemed desolate for a world that had run out of numbers. Or was the floor primarily used for mothers and their newborns? James wasn't sure. He didn't remember the car drive to the hospital, the move into the labor room, or anything in between. The doctors' words required all his brain power to process. IPs, shortage, transplant—more of the things parental classes hadn't prepared him for hearing. Doctor Brandt's last word haunted him the most.

Days.

James stopped by the nursery on his way to nowhere. He knew Forrest wasn't there. Something inside of him wanted to experience the normal path every other father had taken, but none of the babies belonged to him. He couldn't make actual memories. Most of the infants peacefully slept in semitransparent blue and pink baskets, and a couple of nurses made rounds tending to their needs. James hoped that one of them would be Forrest—that *something* had changed in the last half hour.

A couple walked up to the far end of the same glass James peered through, causing him to abandon his post again. He couldn't look them in the eye and wanted to avoid being asked to identify his child after he saw them pointing to their own. A beautiful and healthy baby girl, judging by the color of the basket, almost waved back.

James meandered through the double swinging doors. The connecting hallway was more chaotic than any of the ones he'd recently traversed. Doctors and nurses walked back and forth, weaving in and out of pedestrian traffic. James stepped back to avoid the wheelchair of a mother entering labor. The man pushing her apologized, and so did the three kids that followed.

"Sir, are you lost?" A nurse stopped to ask him. She looked up with steady and purposeful eyes.

James shook his head and stuttered. "No, I'm—no. I was…looking for the bathroom."

"There's one right there." She pointed several feet up the corridor, where the family train he'd seen moments ago navigated around another locomotive heading in the opposite direction.

"Th-Thank you. Um," James said before the nurse could leave, "My wife is on the third floor. How do I—" James pointed up.

The nurse nodded as she spoke. "There are elevators at the ends of the hallway and stairs across from each one." While James processed the information, she added, "I can get you her room number. What's her IP?"

James almost puked after hearing the word. He covered his mouth with the back of his hand. "No. Thank you."

James wondered if his awkward posture alerted her to his distress. He slipped away, crossing in front of the oncoming train to escape. He walked to the bathroom and stumbled into an empty stall. The door slammed behind him as he fell to his knees and vomited into the bowl. He almost cried into it, too.

James waited for the last man to leave the bathroom before he exited the stall. He stood over the running sink, holding the sides of the bowl with both hands. There wasn't enough water to wash away how much he'd aged in the last hour. He couldn't face his wife like that. No, he couldn't face Emilia at all. Not without something to save their son.

He stormed out of the bathroom and straight into traffic. It flowed around him until he moved with the current toward the end of the hallway. James avoided the crowded elevator and took the stairs from the second to the third floor. The silence of death's door greeted him in another muted hallway. The click of the door's latch loudly echoed.

To his left, a receptionist sat behind a counter with her head down. An open area full of unoccupied chairs filled the space on his right. The two sections converged on the same hallway, a brightly lit, but dim corridor with alternating curtains. Each pale-blue fabric, open or scrunched, faced a wall.

James slowly passed several vacant rooms, and a few with curtains pulled. When he reached an occupied room with the drape scrunched to one side, he stopped at its threshold. He saw a young man sitting next to an older woman's bed.

"Excuse me," James whispered. Still finding nowhere to put his hands, he raised one halfway into the air. "Um, excuse me."

The young man turned around.

"I was hoping…" James paused. He'd rehearsed nothing. The resolve he had coming out of the bathroom diminished. He had to find it again. "I'm sorry to bother you. I was just hoping that when… If…something was to happen… If you could donate…"

The young man raised a brow into the black and shaggy hair that'd crawled across his forehead.

"If you could donate your IP…their IP." James nodded at the older woman. "My son…"

The young man took a minute to process James' words. "Are you kidding me?"

"No. I didn't mean to say…It's just that, my son. He needs—"

"Get out!"

James bit his lower lip and stepped backwards out of the room. He stood in the hallway for a few seconds before he walked in again. "Please, I don't want you to misunderstand."

The man shot James a sharp look. He almost stood, shifting in the chair and planting his feet.

"My son is dying. He needs an IP. I'm just asking…please think of him."

"I said get out! Asshole!" The man stood.

James raised his hands and stepped out of the room. He half walked, half ran down the hallway. Nobody followed him. He passed two occupied rooms before he found the resolve to enter another. Every minute without an address felt wasted, and he couldn't afford to lose more time.

"Excuse me," James said to two women sitting on either side of a man almost his age. Tight-lipped, he fought back the tears that sought to speak instead. They spoke volumes to the women in front of him. "I just… I don't mean to bother you. My son is… I was just hoping that maybe…" How could he ask? James staggered back out of the room. "I'm sorry. I'm sorry."

A woman startled him. "Excuse me, sir. What are you doing?" She wore a gray uniform and a sizable belt with a baton, pepper spray, and handheld scanner. A badge sat on her left breast pocket and a radio hung a few inches above it.

"I… I walked into the wrong room."

"Uh huh. I'm going to need you to come with me."

James shuffled his feet. "I'm sorry. I went into the wrong room. My wife—we had a son and I'm trying to find her. Emilia Alexander."

"Let me see your wrist." She unclipped the scanner from the belt and held it over James' unmarked skin. After it beeped, she spoke into the radio on her shoulder. She enunciated each number: 192.168.22.8. Moments later, an operator verified James' story.

The female officer holstered the scanner. "We received a report about a man asking for IP addresses from the sick. I'm just reminding folks that solicitation of IP addresses is illegal and carries a fine of five hundred thousand dollars or ten years in prison." She peered down at James, as if she expected him to admit to a crime through an apology.

"I'm looking for my wife," he said.

The officer nodded at the now alert receptionist. "You can get that information up front."

She escorted James to the counter. The young man he'd visited earlier pulled the curtain across the opening. The fabric hadn't settled yet, still flapping from the force applied when James walked past.

At the counter, the receptionist scanned James' wrist. "Your wife is on the first floor in recovery. Room 144." She paused and stared hard at the screen. "Mr. Alexander, are you aware that your son is in intensive care?"

James looked away and nodded. "The doctors spoke to me. I went to tell my wife and got turned around."

"Your son doesn't have—"

"I know! I know." James lowered his voice the second time.

The officer stood next to him, behind his right shoulder. If he hadn't already known she was there, he'd have felt her overbearing presence. He took two steps away and half-turned toward the officer as he spoke to the receptionist. "I need to go to IPAC. The hospital…they can't see his IP."

The officer glanced at the receptionist. "Trish, I'll make another round." She knocked on the counter twice and walked away.

"Thanks, Michelle!" Trish waved with enthusiasm and then addressed James. "There's an IPAC hub a couple of blocks down the road. We send patients that way for IP conflicts. Would you like me to check on your son's IP?"

"No! No, thank you. There's some ongoing legal issues. I need to go there. But thank you…"

Chapter 3

James couldn't fathom the chaos outside the hospital doors. He'd spent last night and the better half of the morning inside. People crowded the entrance like the first day of a major event. They walked among the bumper-to-bumper traffic of vehicles attempting to drop passengers off at the front doors.

Red and blue lights attempted to set up a late barricade. The police instructed pedestrians inside the newly established zone to proceed onto the sidewalk and threatened to arrest anyone who blocked an ambulance.

The hum of various engines contributed to the noise floor. Horns honked. Slurs followed. James focused on a chant rising above the cacophony. Protesters added to, if not caused, the mayhem that hadn't existed last night when he'd dropped Emilia off. They blocked a major intersection, which forced traffic down another street and caused it to bottleneck.

Multiple people bumped into James. He forced his way through, against the flow, and into the grass to the left of the curved pavement. A policeman shouted at him and then waved him off on account of attempting to escape the entrance.

James moved from one bustling spot to another. He stood at the back of the protester line, rising on his toes to peer over the professional and homemade signs in search of the IPAC logo, which comprised several colored dots surrounding one large circle like knights at a round table. James couldn't see past the disgruntled group in front of him. He turned around to find another way, but the rear had already filled with more people.

"The fight is that way!" A young woman pointed behind James. She had "IP" painted in black on her rosy right cheek and "V6" in the same Sans Serif font above her left dimple.

"I'm trying to get to IPAC."

"We all are!" She raised the sign in her hand: WHY WAIT? MOVE TO IPV6 TODAY.

"My son…I'm trying to…"

"What? I can't hear you!"

James moved closer, careful not to step on her slip-on shoes. "My son! He's—he needs an IP!"

The woman shrugged. "I don't know!"

James felt his face flush red-hot with frustration. The crowd shifted, and he lost the young woman in the torrent. Signs similar to what she carried passed him. His eyes couldn't keep up with their constant bobbing and rotating. The various bright colors and rounded typeface didn't help.

The wave carried conversation. "They should've put us on IPv6, too. Whose idea was it to use IPv4? Why aren't we natting? Because the government wants to keep better track of you."

James didn't fully understand the technical jargon, but he understood the protesters were lobbying against the implementation of policies governing the system that prevented his son from getting a heart. Among the crowd, there were more questions than answers. Most people seemed confused and irritated. A few ecstatic protesters seemed happy, claiming that the institution they despised was on its knees.

Sensing no clear path forward to the IPAC hub, James swam several feet against the current. He stopped when a televised voice stilled the flow of the masses and silenced their conversation. James turned around to a tall building across the street. Ten floors of high-definition advertisement transitioned to an interview already in progress.

The host, a man with short, light-brown hair, sat on the edge of a beige leather seat. He wore a navy suit with a wheat-colored shirt underneath. As he spoke, he waved a stack of cards above his crossed leg. "Why shouldn't we go to IPv6 if it's already established and can handle our numbers?"

The words "Mr. Jordan Stone" scrolled across the bottom of the screen. The interviewee also sat on the seat's edge. He leaned forward in a steel-gray shirt colored with purple buttons and nodded. "Great question, Mike. IPv4 was well-managed for over half a century. Transitioning devices to IPv6 took decades to fully implement because the cost of upgrading network infrastructure around the world was enormous. We learned from that. When the country transitioned from social security numbers to IPv4, we made use of this well-developed design to help connect artificial organs."

Mike uncrossed his legs and planted both feet square on the ground. "But that doesn't answer the question. Why haven't we moved to IPv6?"

Mr. Stone brought his hands together, like a prayer, but pointed at Mike and with both thumbs up. "Similar to the transition of electronic devices, it will take time to develop the infrastructure. The low-power chips implanted in people aren't powerful enough to handle IPv6 traffic." He adjusted his seated posture, placing both elbows on his knees. "And since IPv6 is not directly backward compatible with IPv4, we reduced the risk of hackers accessing the human network because computer devices no longer share the same protocols. For now." He rubbed his hands together and grinned, eliciting boos from the crowd outside.

After a brief pause, Mr. Stone coughed into his fist and adjusted his casual tone to be more serious. "Mike, here's exclusive news just for you. We're planning to roll out Artificial Intelligent Identification (AI2) in the next five years, giving digital lenses, such as cameras, glasses, and artificial eyes, the power to identify objects within their field of view and overlay metadata. At a glance, you'll know everything about a product—details, costs, reviews, availability—and compare vendors around the globe." Mr. Stone moved closer. Passion accompanied his lowered tone of voice. "The program will tell you the history of that specific item using its unique protocol address."

Mike looked at his watch, a shiny black band with a bronze ring around the face. "You mean you'll know the history of this specific watch? Who wore it and when?"

"More than that, we'll know the history of an artificial organ—its performance, maintenance, degradation, and operational hours. When we can move an organ from one individual to another, we'll have extended the life of product, too." Mr. Stone leaned back and placed both arms on the armrests. "We need IPv6 address architecture and space for that future and we need time to ensure the proper security measures are in place so we don't expose humanity to nefarious people."

"Mr. Stone, I hear what you're saying and it sounds wonderful. There's a bright future ahead for resource management. But what about now? What about this shortage of human IP space? Newborns require addresses so they can get the medical care needed. The longer we wait—"

"I understand. *We* understand. The increased birth rate and reduced death rate are phenomenal numbers that we didn't predict. We're going to adjust."

The advertisement returned, replacing the interview on-screen with a dark-skinned woman applying pastel-rose lipstick.

Murmurs erupted throughout the crowd about the broadcast's sudden end. People shouted obscenities, and some threw full cups of liquid into the air with no hope of reaching the display. The reactions prompted some pushing and shoving among the protesters.

James didn't wait around for crowd control to begin. Tear gas, water hoses, and sonic vibrations were a few of the non-violent measures the police had used to disperse past gatherings.

Forcing his way through the crowd seemed impossible, especially after it turned violent. Multiple people crashed into James. Most moved on, but one stayed. A young man with hazel eyes looked up at James.

He shouted, "Come with me if you're looking for an IP."

James hesitated for a moment and then followed the green hoodie through the crowd. He reached an edge of the formation between two buildings on the sidewalk. The young man's brisk walk led James down an alley between the buildings. Their brick walls turned darker the further into the shadows he went. Sounds of the streets faded and the young man's footsteps echoed louder.

They reached a rusty metal door. The young man swung it open and stood to the side. James stopped a few feet short of the entrance.

"Why here? Who are you?"

The young man shook his head disappointedly, stepped out from behind the door, and walked inside. The door threatened to close behind him. James grabbed its edge before it shut, almost smashing his fingers between it and the metal frame. He looked down both ends of the alley before he entered the building.

The slamming of the door echoed inside the thirty-foot high ceilings of a warehouse. Light came in through several skylights above. Fifteen to twenty people stood underneath the sun's filtered rays. They looked James' way before returning to the tables they hunched over—the tables full of guns.

Immediately, James turned to leave, but two men in the shadows behind him stood in his way. They nodded in the opposite direction. Their stout figures pressured him further inside the room. James trekked backwards, before he turned, stumbled over his own feet, and hurriedly walked toward a bald man sitting on a makeshift throne between two rows of tables.

"This him?" the bald man asked.

"I'm not. I don't know—" James saw the young woman from earlier, the one with IP and V6 painted on her face. Then he noticed that the bald man had a similar design above his left brow. Many of the others wore the marking in visible, but unique, places. Combined with the slacks, coats, and loafers most of them wore, they reminded him of the gangs he'd seen in movies.

The young woman nodded. "Yep. Trying to save his kid."

James couldn't stop glancing at the surroundings. He was certain he'd walked into an illegal operation focused on selling news media equipment. Dated microphones, and cameras with compartments for removable media, shared table space with guns and ammunition. Big cameras. Big guns.

James took one step forward. "I'm sorry. I didn't mean to come here. I'm just a salesman. My son is dying. He needs an IP address. I'm just trying to get him one so he can get a heart transplant." James touched his chest.

"I know." The bald man rubbed his right temple where the tattoo sat. "The question is, what are you willing to do to save him?"

"Anything!"

A few watched the transaction while others returned to work. The bald man never glanced elsewhere. He stared straight into James' eyes as if the message they conveyed rang truer than his words. "We're going to raid IPAC. There are a couple of nerds here who can reallocate IPs. We need strength in numbers, distractions, and shit. If you make it to the mainframe with us, you'll get an IP. You in?"

Chapter 4

The bald man had a cigar in his mouth, one he'd repeatedly pulled out and turned sideways to read the label. Then he blew the smoke into the air. "Call me Santiago," he said. "You're going undercover as the news crew scheduled to interview some jokers in IPAC. We got everything you need. The owners'll get it back when we're done. We're on at three o'clock, so sign in at two-thirty. The media entrance is around back. Timing is everything, so don't be late."

James recalled Santiago's words from the back of the second news van his men had stolen. He leaned forward to prevent his head from hitting the wall-mounted racks above the benches. They housed monitors and computers. Multiple cables of various colors ran along the tracks, connecting one system to another. He could see out the front window. Police had barricaded an alley leading to the back of the building, where the delivery entrance poked its head out from behind a fence line.

Three people sat around James. They were distractions, too. A woman named Candice sat on his left. She'd mentioned her daughter losing her IP address when it conflicted with a celebrity, a battle she lost before it ever started. George, the older man who sat across from James, said the hospital prematurely pronounced his father dead and released the associated IP address, despite him being next of kin. Matt's wife had the same conflict as Candice's daughter, which occurred more as the available numbers dwindled and concurrent allocations took place.

"They'll scan your IPs when you get to the gate. We spoofed them to look like the news crew. They won't need 'em for a minute. A Faraday cage will prevent their IPs from broadcasting, so you won't show up in two different locations."

The van slowed and climbed over a speed hump as if the driver cared about the equipment in the back. A wide hump gave the security system time to scan visitor IP addresses. The government didn't mandate public key infrastructure because humans weren't simple networks that would toggle on and off. They'd always be pinging a server like cell phones. But the lack of additional authentication meant that hackers could spoof IP addresses; however, pinging from multiple locations resulted in immediate disconnect and investigation of the source device—the implanted chips—and carried a federal sentence exceeding a decade. With the Faraday cage in place to block the original IPs from broadcasting, IPAC didn't flag James and the crew, just as Santiago had calculated.

"Just play it cool. Don't look nervous. You're professionals, remember? Act like a fucking professional. They'll want to run your equipment through a machine. Don't let 'em. If they ask, say it'll ruin the film. Blame their scrutiny of electronic recording devices."

Security directed the van around the building, and another team showed them where to offload equipment. James carried one of the large cameras. Its strap dug into his right shoulder. He leaned to his left to offset the weight.

Inside, he saw multiple conveyor belts, each with a horizontal cylindrical chamber at its center. Two people from Santiago's crew took the lead. A man with short black hair and a woman with a dirty-brown ponytail each flashed their badges and then walked through the scanners without issue. They warned the security team about the sensitivity of the film and then watched them carry two units around the scanners and set them onto a different table.

"After a couple of you get through security, be prepared. Xavier will trigger the fire alarm. When that happens…"

The alarm sounded. Right on time. The man and the woman on the other side of security grabbed one of the cameras set aside for manual inspection. They flipped the device's side compartment open and pulled two guns out. The man aimed his pistol at the security team poised to inspect the other system. "Get your hands up! Move away from the desk!"

The woman stood between the two scanners and called out to the team operating the other conveyor belt. "You, too! Get out of there!"

Candice and Matt acted like bystanders, while two people from Santiago's crew brought up the rear. They shoved the last guard inside and smacked him across the back of the head.

"The place will be a mess 'cause everyone wants to evacuate, but the protesters are blocking the main exit. So they'll use the sky bridge crossing the road, the one connected to the big screen building, which means most of the rear hallways will be clear. The engineers will hang back to secure the servers. Get them to open the doors."

One of Santiago's men directed James and the other distractions to keep carrying the equipment. James hoisted the camera on his hip, rushed up a flight of stairs, ran down a long empty corridor, and filed through a door that led into the main building. Yellow-plastered walls turned to steel gray across the threshold. Chill air welcomed them, and another person from Santiago's crew directed them onward. The armed man and woman brought up the rear and then led the way, followed by the two nerds Santiago had mentioned.

"Don't worry about security cameras. IPAC doesn't use them. They rely on IP scans throughout the building cause 'you can't hide your face from them.' People would've lost faith in their product if they used tech other than their own. They dug their own ditch."

James panted. His legs wobbled. He couldn't recall the last time he exercised. He was a salesman over the phone and in the office when required, not door to door.

George, who carried a bag equal in size, straightened James twice. "Think about your kid," he said. He was panting, too. "A few minutes of exercise for a lifetime of laughs." He tried to laugh, but coughed and ran into a wall. He slung the bag over the other shoulder and almost hit James. An exasperated apology escaped him.

"The vault is in the middle of the building. There are four doors, two bidirectional and two exit-only. The engineers are supposed to use the exit-only doors when leaving, but the evacuation routes direct them out of the entrances. Get there before they lock up."

Two engineers exiting the vault froze when they saw Santiago's crew. They raised their hands as the doors slammed shut. The gunwoman lunged for the handle but missed it by a few inches.

The engineers wore white polos with the IPAC logo above a single breast pocket holding a couple of pens. Lanyards around their necks carried a flat transparent case with multiple cards inside. Glare on the IPAC ID cards made their names difficult to read, but the gunwoman didn't care.

"Get in and get out. The longer you take, the more time you give someone to cut our connection. This IPAC is just a hub. Nobody'll miss it."

"Open the door! Now!" the gunwoman exclaimed.

"I...I can't... I'm not authorized—"

BANG!

The man fell to the floor. James felt sick, a knotting of his stomach that caused him to slouch against a nearby wall. Blood quickly spread into a pool around the engineer, and James saw his own reflection in it.

The woman turned the gun on the other engineer. "Open the fucking door!"

He complied. Panic caused him to fumble the transparent case in his hands before he turned it upside down and dumped the cards onto the floor. Their slick surfaces caused them to scatter.

"Pick them up! Come on, man! I'll blow your fucking brains out, too!"

"Please, I'm trying. I...I'm scared."

"You'll be dead if you don't open that door."

"If you get caught after completing the mission, who cares? You'll be an accessory at most. Your loved ones will have more than a few years to see you when you get out. Life in prison is still life."

George nudged James. "Hold it in, man. You don't wanna leave evidence behind when we get out."

"Get out? No way," James huffed. "There's no way."

"Who gives a shit? Get your kid that IP so they can get out. You feel me?"

The engineer, on his hands and knees, slammed a card against the reader above his head. Lights flickered across the top of the pad. Then he crawled to his feet, punched in a code, and opened the door. Cool air rushed out of the room as the gunwoman shoved the engineer inside.

"Freeze! Stop right there!" Multiple security guards ran up the corridor. Surprised by the gunman, they immediately exchanged fire and struck him in the leg. "Drop it! Drop it now!" they shouted until the gunman tossed his weapon aside.

George adjusted the strap on his shoulder. "We're not gonna make it inside—"

"Put your guns down or I'll blow his brains out!" The gunwoman grabbed James and pressed her pistol against the side of his head. "Do it! Drop it! I already killed one!" She dragged James backwards and posted against the open door.

"What…Wait…What is this?" James no longer leaned over and countered the camera's weight. Slowly, it slid off his shoulder and crashed against the floor. Multiple canisters and grenades rolled out. One of them stopped in the slain man's blood.

"No…No, those aren't mine!"

The men and women at the other end of the corridor inched their way backwards.

"Shut up!" The woman tapped James' temple with the gun. She jostled him left and right as she scanned the floor around their feet for rolling grenades. One almost touched her foot. She scooted more toward the open door, as if contact with the grenade would trigger an explosion.

The two techs from Santiago's crew tip-toed across the battlefield and entered the room. Then Matt followed one more of Santiago's men inside. Candice and George locked up, pressed against a nearby wall. IPAC security seemed helpless until one pulled out a radio.

"They're going to cut our connection!" the gunwoman shouted before she shoved James aside and opened fire.

James fell to the floor as bullets flew overhead. His shoes smeared the nearby blood, and his hands caused pinned grenades to roll in circles. He heard Candice cry out and George soon after. The gunwoman dropped to one knee. She picked up a grenade, pulled its pin, and threw it at the security guards before two shots ripped through her neck.

Chapter 5

The gunwoman had thrown a flashbang grenade. The sound startled James. He'd turned around and faced the corridor behind him in search of a way out when the light filled his peripheral vision. Temporary blindness caused the hallway ahead to look distorted, and as if a few steps would get him around its far corner.

That's when he recalled Santiago's words. Anyone who made it to the mainframe would get IP addresses allocated to whomever they wanted. James paused for a second longer. The consequences weighed heavily on his conscience, but a few months or years in prison paled compared to a lifetime for his son. George was right.

James turned around and crawled toward the open door. He slipped into the room amid the chaos. After scurrying to his feet, he stopped when a gun pressed against his forehead. Santiago's man took a second to recognize James and then helped him up. He shoved James toward the techs before he grabbed the door's handle and pulled the massive metal plate shut.

Evan and Sara, their nametags belonging to the actual news crew, sat in front of two square pillars filled with computers. Activity lights flickered at each system's top left corner. Cables from the towers ran up to the ceiling and routed to several more cabinets at the center of the room.

The engineer that opened the door stood between the first and second row of servers. One of Santiago's men held him by the shoulder. He also blocked a walkway leading to another exit. One of the large camera cases sat on the floor next to him.

Evan and Sara had plugged keyboards into two systems and furiously typed with elegance. The text on the screen attached to the racks scrolled faster than James could read. He'd made it to the vault, but didn't know what to do or what to say. How was he going to get his son an IP address? Then he saw a list of names in Evan's lap. The man didn't object when James grabbed the piece of paper; he adjusted himself on the stool and typed faster.

James read the list, which included the full names and deposit locations for IP addresses. Forrest wasn't one of the fifteen names. James patted himself down for a pen. He usually carried one for his job, and a backup in case a new client forgot to return it, but he wasn't dressed for work.

So he turned to the engineer Santiago's man dragged into the room with them. He had a pen in his breast pocket. James ran across the room and grabbed it. He scribbled Forrest's name on the paper and listed the hospital as the deposit location.

"I'm in!" Evan snatched the paper from James and began copying the information. "I'm assigning new IPs. Take down the outbound firewall."

"You got it!" Sara plugged another cable into her computer.

The engineer struggled. The man behind him said nothing, but Matt, with a gun in hand, warned him. "I ain't gonna hurt you, but if you try anything—help me god—I'll shoot you in the face. I ain't got nothing against you, brother. I'm just trying to help my family." He adjusted his hold on the gun. "Let's both go home to our families."

Leaning his left shoulder against the wall, Matt stood ready to shoot anything that opened a door, the one a couple of steps away and the one down the walkway Santiago's man partially defended.

"Yo, I'm ready to send," Evan said.

Sara shook her head. "I knew something wasn't right. Man, look at this shit."

Both looked at the same white text flowing up a black screen. James stood behind them. He wanted to ask if his son had the IP address, but didn't know when or how to interject. The information on the screen meant nothing to him, but he scanned the wall of evenly spaced letters and numbers for

Forrest's name.

Sara looked at Evan. "Three billion people and four billion IPs. How the fuck are we running out? They're selling that shit to other countries. My brother is dying so this fucker can get into the country once a year without a passport." Sara turned back to the panel. She licked her lips and nodded several times. "Yeah, fuck this guy." She fervently typed and then smacked a single key hard. "IP released," she said.

"What are you doing?" Evan grabbed her shoulder.

"I'm freeing IPs. We're out here trying to survive, giving up our IPs for our loved ones. They should be out here, too." She scrolled through the text. "Mostly middle-aged white men and women with techplants getting updates on a beach somewhere. Millionaires, billionaires, and government officials from other countries and their families. None of them live in this country. They don't pay taxes here!" Sara continued typing, not with the same speed and grace from earlier, but with careful precision as she navigated the on-screen information. "Hm, I can only change the accounts of people serviced by this hub." She looked up at the engineer.

"I don't have the credentials—seriously!" He raised both hands as if he'd suffer the same fate as his coworker. "I can't even cheat them. Separation of duties. Please don't hurt me."

Sara hit several keys a few times. "Fuck, they cut the connection to the main server. Did those addresses get out?" She looked at Evan, brows furrowed.

"What about my son's IP?"

Evan looked up at James. "They're out. I think." Then to Sara, "pretty sure. Question is, how are *we* going to get out of here?"

The white text reflected in Sara's eyes. "Y'all go. I'll stay here and finish this. I can't let them get away with murder."

"What are you going to do without a connection to the main server?" Evan asked as he unplugged his keyboard.

Sara raised her voice, a slight shrill at the end. "I don't

know." She adjusted the stool underneath her. "I really don't know. Copy the data?"

Evan shook his head. He looked up at the stacks as if he counted them. "There's gotta be hundreds of terabytes worth of data in here. We don't have time. Even if you get it copied, we're not gettin' out with it. We might not make it out at all."

"We won't, but he will." Sara nodded at James. "But yeah, that doesn't solve the copying issue."

The man holding the engineer hostage stepped on the camera next to his foot. "Why don't we stream it?"

"You're right!" Evan leaped from the stool and picked the camera off the floor. He held it up to his face and inspected it for a moment before he lowered it. "But they cut our connection, and this thing doesn't have wireless. So our video ain't going anywhere."

"We didn't bring our cellphones either," Sara frowned and then crossed her arms. "Not that I wanted mine pinging from inside this place, anyway."

"Maybe…" James stepped forward and stopped when everyone looked at him. "Maybe the people can be our signal."

Silent glances made several hops before they all returned to him. "We can do it like the interview. Play it on the screen outside. Let the people out there record and share it with their phones."

"My man!" Evan smacked James on the back. "That network's all internal, so we should have access to it, right Mr. Engineer?"

Chapter 6

James hadn't volunteered to deliver the message, but everyone else had jobs. Evan set up and operated the camera. Sara forced the engineer to route the video to the outside screen before she took control and pushed the traffic to all channels connected to the hub. Matt and Santiago's man guarded the entrances with multiple guns and clips shoved into their waistbands and pockets.

"You're a salesman, right?" Evan said from behind the camera. He stood next to one rack. Several cables ran over his shoulder and into a computer. "Sell your soul to those people."

James stared at the black lens, his back to the servers. He crossed his arms in front of him, then behind his back, and then lowered them to their respective sides. He rubbed his hands against his pants until Evan tossed him a folded piece of paper. James picked it up and unfolded it. The list of names from earlier stared back at him. A check mark next to Forrest's name made him smile and gave him confidence.

Evan signaled for him to start.

"My name is… I'm a father. I'm somebody's son. A husband. I'm somebody…" he raised his head, "…like you. My son was born today. Forrest. His name is Forrest. He's perfect. So perfect. He looks like me. A tiny miniature version of me." James brought his hands together and shaped Forrest's body. "But right now, he's at a hospital right up the road." James pointed, ignorant of direction. "Right over there. He's in intensive care because his heart is too small. And they—the hospital—won't give him a heart because he doesn't have an IP address." James paused. He commanded the tears back, placed a hand on his hip, and then rubbed his forehead. "He doesn't have a number, so he's not allowed to live." His voice broke. "He's dying…"

A banging at the door behind Evan startled James. The men at each entrance, captivated by James' words, snapped free of the emotional journey. Hastily, they knotted network cables around the door handles and tied them off to nearby posts.

James wiped tears from his face. Time was limited. He needed to be a salesman. The one that sold products from local businesses to the surrounding community. That's what he knew. He had data, charts, and numbers.

Sara gave James a thumbs up after she patched the list of names and IP addresses to the video feed and displayed it alongside his face.

"Three billion people in the country. Four billion addresses. How are there not enough numbers? These guys figured it out. They figured it out. It's clear in the data that they put their lives on the line for—that people have died for…" He paused again.

The banging at the door grew louder. Someone shook the handle after entering a valid code, but one of Santiago's men pushed back on the door to relieve the strain from the cords and forced it to latch. The locking mechanism reset.

James raised his voice. "We're fighting for the IP addresses IPAC sold to people in other countries. To IPAC, those lives are more important than my son's. More important than you and your family." He shook his head. "I get it. My taxes don't amount to much, but I paid them! I get up every day, put the same clothes on, and work from six in the morning until six in the evening to put food on my family's table. My wife does the same. The government takes money from both of us." James lowered his voice. "I'm a salesman, but I'm not trying to sell you anything—not like them. The data's there. You can read it for yourself. I'm just asking you to look at the truth…Help me share the truth."

An explosion shot the main door handle off. Matt fell to the floor. Cords tied to the silver lever lashed out in a flurry of blue and yellow whips. Six men rushed into the room with their guns drawn.

"Freeze! Let me see your hands! On your knees!"

Santiago's man lowered his weapon. Evan dropped the camera and Sara raised her hands. Everyone followed the commands except for James.

He looked at the space where the camera used to be, believing that the world could still hear him, and said, "Thank you for listening."

***

Each officer grabbed the elbow of a cuffed man or woman and escorted them out of the building. Outside, James expected the noise he'd heard hours ago when he first tried to walk up the very steps the police accompanied him down, but their exit was met with silence. The crowd was just as large and the signs flashy still, but the shouting, screaming, and chanting had ended.

James felt the nervousness of the policeman handling him as they plunged into the eerie sea of people. The grip around his elbow tightened and loosened. He stumbled and kicked the back of James' heel several times. Their bodies collided, too. When they reached the bottom of the steps, the crowd didn't let them through.

"Alright, break it up. Coming through." The policeman stepped into the crowd, but nobody moved. As he weaved his way through, people's gaze gravitated towards James. They surrounded him after one to two steps, obstructed the policeman despite his objections and warnings, and cleared a path for James alone.

"Hey! Stop! You're under arrest!" the policeman shouted after him.

He flowed through the crowd for several more steps before the people paved the way to the hospital. Hands still bound, he picked up the pace and jogged. Many faces greeted him. Tears, smiles, nods, and silent approvals. Two stood out among the crowd. The woman with the IP and V6 tattoo and Santiago's bald head. She waved with enthusiasm, and Santiago nodded once with a smile and a second time toward the hospital.

James ran past the police blockade, through the yard, across the circular entrance, and into the building. He never tired. A nurse met him at the glass doors, and with haste, navigated him to a room where Emilia lay. James ran up to her bedside.

The nurse warned them to take it easy, but Emilia met him halfway out of bed with a solid embrace. He lost balance and fell onto her. She cried into the side of his neck, touched his head and hair, and inspected him with red eyes. She shouted love, muffled against his skin and smothered between the kisses.

"Is he…Is our son okay?"

Emilia nodded against his head. Her voice cracked and then escaped with joy. "Yes. Yes! They took him." She pulled away and looked at James. "You did it. *You* saved our son. He's gonna be fine…thanks to you."

Science Fiction

Chapter 1

The FBI banged on my front door at five in the morning. I watched them through a surveillance camera mounted in the corner. Three black sports utility vehicles idled in the background. Sunrise colors saturated the front windshield of the middle vehicle, obscuring the reflections of the navy-blue sky, a nearby rocky stream, and a line of trees in the west whose leaves and branches swayed in the other vehicles' windows like animated images. There were no flashing red and blue lights illuminating the countryside, and the headlights dimmed, as if they'd disturb the nearest neighbor half an hour away.

I hesitated to open the door. From the end of my driveway to the five wooden steps leading up to my porch, six agents stood like a condensed forest of sequoias. The morning sunlight filtered between them and darkened the black jackets they wore. They looked like space invaders under the light of a UFO.

Had they come to abduct me? I wondered if my computer search history put me on their radar. More than half the words I typed into the query were fictional. Another large percentage resulted in the definitions of basic words. Perhaps only one or two key words were enough to raise suspicion. I don't know. I'm not a morning person.

When I opened the door, two of them stepped forward in anticlimactic fashion—without guns, handcuffs, or warrants at the ready. Instead, with little variance in his voice, one presented me with a summons from the President of the United States.

The procession of dark tinted windows escorted me to the airport, where I took a chartered flight to Washington, D.C., and then sat in a lounge ten feet away from the Oval Office.

The wait reminded me of the doctor's office. People came and went in no particular order. I stared at the lounge decor but didn't commit any of the pieces to memory. The space lacked the sleek lines and simplicity of the modern era. Its colors were bland and uninspiring, bathed in a reality I thought I'd escaped by moving to the country. The lounge screamed the past, and I dreamed of the future.

At last, a young woman in a long gray skirt suit guided me into the Oval Office. In the presence of the young woman, and at the sight of others in the room, I breathed a sigh of relief that I'd worn khaki slacks and a white dress shirt. Despite the long itinerary that brought me here, I had kept my shirt tucked.

She directed me to a couch seat next to a middle-aged woman wearing a black pants suit. She had shoulder-length brown hair. A pair of rose gold glasses sat above her nose and matched the hair clip holding the shorter strands back. She sat with her left leg over her right and rested her folded hands in her lap.

I sat across from a seasoned man. He reminded me of a university professor. Gray evenly peppered his head but scattered about his stubble. He adjusted a navy-blue blazer around his shoulders and ignored the wrinkles in his dark brown khakis. He held a folder close to his chest, almost inside the blazer's left breast.

Another man walked into the room. His square face rounded at the jaw. His hair seemed unnaturally dark. He unbuttoned his black suit jacket, sat next to the seasoned man, and straightened his rich cherry tie.

Nobody spoke, as if silence was proper etiquette. I wondered if the black suits at the ends of the couches knew each other. Both sat like regulars at a bar. The woman flashed a smile that suggested she had an upper hand in whatever competition they competed.

Everyone stood when President Sable Jackson and Vice President Sanya Richardson walked into the room. They sat in two chairs facing the couches.

President Jackson crossed his legs, revealing his famous

mismatched socks beneath the black pant legs. The light-blue clouds of one sock bobbed above the dark-blue city pattern of the other sock. Gray hairs struggled to maintain presence across his balding head. His upper body withstood the test of time courtesy of his military days, and his broad shoulders seemed wider than the chair his back rested against.

Vice President Richardson's makeup hid the aging lines of a woman who'd sat in that seat for six years. She seemed relaxed, at home, and very much the woman who'd served as CEO for multiple corporations. I'd seen her on the news, simultaneously giving hope to people while threatening wrongdoers with a single smile.

President Jackson said, "Good Morning, Mr. Emmanuel. Thank you for agreeing to meet on such short notice. Normally, I'd apologize for the early wake-up call, but like many, I assume you welcomed an escape from the nightmares plaguing the country—the world, really."

He spoke with his hands, their movements as casual as his demeanor and tone of voice. I thought he'd be more intimidating in person. He made solid yet gentle eye contact that put me at ease.

"Thank you for having me, Mr. President."

President Jackson brought his hands together. A small clap preceded his words. "I'll go around the room. To my left is Dr. Naomi Sanders, a retired psychologist who uses artificial intelligence to recognize patterns in human behavior. Next to her is the renowned science fiction author, Mr. Kenny Emmanuel. Across from him is Dr. Miguel Rodriguez. He's a psychologist from Blake Grove University. To his left is my technical advisor, Mr. Ryan Albright.

"I called all of you here to discuss the dreams. Dr. Sanders wrote an excellent paper on the recurring nightmares after she'd discovered something intriguing about their existence. I think it's worth exploring. Doctor, the floor is yours."

Dr. Sanders sat up straight. She pushed the thin glasses

further up the bridge of her curved nose. Its inward arch prevented the frames from sliding off and onto the floor after she quickly glanced down at the pages in her hands and then raised her head to President Jackson.

"Good morning, Mr. President. Thank you for having me. I've been studying the recurring dreams over the past couple of months, using complex statistical analysis algorithms and artificial intelligence to find patterns among various reports, including official, news, and social media. We designed the application to accept prompts like an internet search engine, analyze comments and visualizations from those various media sources, and generate results that represent the correlation between reported dream sequences.

"For example, I typed: What is the origin of the widespread recurring dreams? And it responded with several of Mr. Emmanuel's books. I asked again, shifting the question around each time, and found that ninety-six percent of the responses included your books, Mr. Emmanuel."

I understood the relationship between my books and my dreams. My stories played out like a movie in my head, and I sought to transcribe those motion pictures into words. I designed the stories to lure people into a science fantasy-like world until reality beckoned their return or the last page turned. Reviews spoke of my success, so I kept dreaming. That my stories shared a likeness with whatever nightmares were running rampant was absurd and fascinating.

Mr. Albright rolled his head away from the President and toward the rest of us. "Can we really trust an AI application? It can only provide results based on existing data, right? These dreams are unprecedented." His gaze leaped from Dr. Rodriguez to me before he turned back to the President. "We're wasting the President's time on inconclusive data and hunches."

Dr. Sanders cleared her throat and spoke over Mr. Albright's objections. "After the results were *calculated*," she dragged the syllables and then paused, "I reached out to Dr.

Rodriguez for concurrence. We'd met at an artificial intelligence summit in Sweden. He agreed that many concepts from Mr. Emmanuel's books were evident in the dreams he's been having, and most importantly, predate the dreams."

Dr. Rodriguez cleared his throat. He spoke in short bursts. The rise and fall of enthusiasm matched his breath, and he almost left the couch with each inhalation. "After I received Dr. Sanders's email, I began researching Mr. Emmanuel's novels. The dreams are almost a reimagining of his stories and have maintained the tone, pacing, genre, style, and world-building his readers are familiar with. While reading his stories, I sometimes couldn't tell if I was still reading or dreaming with my eyes open." He chuckled and then shook his hands, desperate to prevent others from interrupting his train of thought while he caught his breath. "It's not uncommon for dreams to be influenced by events in our daily lives, from tragic experiences to something as simple as a story we read; however, the idea that an entire species is dreaming about the same world from their individual perspectives, and that *that* world can be traced back to a common source, is a significant step towards understanding this phenomenon."

Mr. Albright huffed. "With all due respect, Mr. President, this is absurd. They're suggesting that the dreams are somehow related to Mr. Emmanuel's science-fiction books. There'd have to be some kind of hypnosis or subliminal message in the pages, and the entire world would've had to have read them at relatively the same time. Next, you'll tell me that reading his stories was another social media challenge." He leaned to his right and planted his cheek against his fist, his elbow rested on his crossed knee.

President Jackson interlocked his fingers under his chin. "I read one of Mr. Emmanuel's books and agree with Dr. Sanders and Dr. Rodriguez. The resemblance of his stories to the dreams is undeniable, which is why I called this meeting today. Let's be clear, I'm not suggesting that you're at all responsible for the dreams, Mr. Emmanuel, but I'd like you to work with Dr. Sanders to investigate them and maybe shed some light on its source. You'll have resources for travel, lodging, and food. I assigned an FBI agent to your team to help expedite your needs."

Dr. Sanders held back her jubilation, but the grin on her face sold her out. "Thank you, Mr. President." She turned to me. "Mr. Emmanuel, I'm honored to work with you and hope we can make artificial intelligence breakthroughs in both investigations and magical realism?" she questioned at the end.

I shook my head. "Dr. Sanders, I assure you, there are no pendulums in the pages of my books."

She shrugged. "One can always hope."

Vice President Richardson smiled. "Let us know if you need anything else."

After President Jackson stood, I asked, "Mr. President, can you tell me about your dream?"

"You don't get to ask him that," Mr. Albright said.

He glared at me, but I didn't take offense. He was a man of the past, and I dreamed of the future, which included his demise in my next book.

"It's alright, Ryan. This is exactly what I asked him to do."

President Jackson thrust his hands into his pants pockets. He looked up at the fifty bulbs comprising a circular, multi-tiered chandelier.

"It's the same dream every night. A blue sky in the middle of summer. A few clouds overhead. I'm standing at the edge of somewhere—a city, a fort, or a sanctuary. The location changes, as do the bystanders on a nearby sidewalk who are curious about what's happening where I am.

"A chain-link fence stands between me and the archangel Michael. I don't know how I knew his name other than I did. Behind us both—way back—are our respective military forces. Both sides seem restless and eager to do something.

What, exactly, I don't know, but they're waiting on whatever resolution comes out of a discussion between Michael and me.

"How do you negotiate with someone four feet taller than you, arms larger than your head, and six wings spanning, oh I don't know, fifteen feet? Making eye contact was like finding two drones flying in front of the sun. I've had this dream a hundred times, and that sun was always above and behind him as if it'd chosen his side.

"*Him.* I don't really know their gender. Some nights, a man stood in front of me. Other nights, a woman? Neither? They were beautiful all the time—what little I could see of their face. White feathers resembling armor covered most of the shimmering scales that comprised their body up to the underside of their chin, where a gradual transition resulted in a perfect racial mix of human-like skin.

"I spent most of the dream trying to look at them, half turned away and shielding my eyes from their radiance. Their presence weighed on me like atmospheric pressure, crushing and suffocating me in a satisfying way, like sleeping under a heavy blanket." President Jackson shook his head and then looked at us. "The Bible calls the day Armageddon. The end of all things. This felt like the end of mankind alone."

Mr. Albright raised a hand toward the President. "It was just a dream, sir."

"I thought the same thing, Ryan. I really did. But the words that wake me every morning beg to differ. In a deep, harmonious tone, Michael always says, 'Oh, humanity. To believe in us, yet label us fictional, is fallacy.'"

Chapter 2

I wasn't sure what President Jackson expected from me. I was an author, not an investigator. He teamed me up with a psychologist and a very green Agent Jones. I understood not sending your best man for the job, but I would've preferred someone with experience using the promised powers a veteran agent might be more familiar with exercising.

Dr. Sanders nudged me with her elbow, as if we were childhood friends. She towered over me. Black heels contributed an inch.

"It's not every day you get tasked with a super-secret mission by POTUS himself," she said, with the grin of a tenacious reporter on the cusp of a big scoop.

We stood beside the desk of Heather Robertson, the woman who'd escorted me into the Oval Office earlier. The bright computer screen flickered in her eyes as she downloaded the contract someone had already drafted for this mission, as if the President knew I'd take the job.

"Hm, I'm not sure how I feel about that—about any of this." I folded my arms and sighed. "I want to say that being woken up at five in the morning, flown up the east coast, and told that your books are tied to recurring nightmares plaguing the world isn't exactly exciting, but those sequence of events sounds like something I'd write, which means it has to be a thrilling adventure, or I'd have been selling a lie to my readers all these years."

Dr. Sanders slowly shrugged her shoulders and raised her hands with palms up. "Surely your readers don't expect you to be whisked away to another world after being summoned by the government."

"How can I expect my readers to be on the edge of their seats and engrossed in my stories if I don't feel that way after experiencing similar events in real life?"

I paused and glanced at Dr. Sanders, a delayed response to her statement about being summoned by the government, and then whisked away. Being transported to another world was a common trope in the animated shows I watched, and I found the comment attractive.

She grinned. "I read *The Witch's Trial*—and the second *Vanguard*—and thought: What if some artificial intelligence program calculated your future and is warning the world about your crime through dream sequences broadcast using wireless networks?" Her eyes widened. The fluorescent lighting brightly reflecting in her glasses darkened after she lowered her chin to make better eye contact. "And what if these events led to your capture, and subsequently, your banishment to another world?"

After a moment of silence from me, she laughed wholeheartedly. I couldn't be angry at the genuine glee she expressed. It suggested true happiness and inner peace. If Dr. Sanders was at all bothered by the dreams, it'd be from the recurrence and not the grim content I'd heard about.

"That's not funny at all," I said flatly. "Especially since I don't know that much about these dreams."

She chuckled anyway. "Where have you been these past few months?"

"As far away from people as possible, yet still not far enough. I don't watch the news much, and while I'm always interacting with my fans on social networks, I don't follow anyone's account. A few people left comments about having dreams similar to my stories, but I didn't know their frequency or their dark nature, apparently."

Dr. Sanders raised her head and pushed several strands of hair back behind her shoulder. "To be fair, your stories are frighteningly grounded. And you can mix and match the worlds, themes, and plots to make other coherent stories, which is probably what contributes to the variance of the dreams." She paused for a second before her eyes lit up again. "If you publish mix-and-match stories after this conversation, I want to be acknowledged!"

Heather raised her brows. "Now that you've mentioned

it, Dr. Sanders, my dreams resemble one of Mr. Emmanuel's stories. It was also called *Vanguard.* You mentioned a second one, so I wasn't sure if we were talking about the same story. I read the one where that winged lady fought people falling from the sky. That happened in my dream."

She leaned back in the chair. There was a distant gaze in her hazel eyes as she nodded her head. "Every night, I dream about the Monday morning commute to work. That and the traffic jam never change, but the car I'm driving, the vehicles around me, and other minor, often cosmetic things, vary; things that are easily different that you just don't think about, unless you've seen it over and over again one hundred-plus nights in a row. Occasionally, there'll be odd dream things, like a streetlight in the middle of the interstate or something."

As she spoke, she pulled several pages off the printer next to her desk. She tapped their bottoms several times to line them up and then fastened them together with an electric stapler.

"So there I am in traffic with an iced macchiato—sometimes caramel and other times vanilla—while listening to the same radio station playing some combination of my favorite songs, when I see people getting out of their cars and running for the hills, if you know what I mean. I watched an old lady vault over the freeway median."

She widened her eyes, suggesting disbelief at what she'd seen, while she absent-mindedly collected more documents from the printer.

"I didn't know what was happening. People ran in every direction, looking back behind them and sometimes up at the sky. I couldn't see anything from inside the car, so I went to get out and couldn't open the door. The vehicle next to me was too close. I reached for the passenger side door handle, and it was the same thing over there. Some white sedan stopped right beside my car. I was trapped."

Heather took a deep breath, as if rising anxiety impacted

her breathing. She continued in a calm voice. "So I started rolling down the window. I didn't know how I was going to get my big ole behind out, but I wasn't gonna sit there and let whatever happens happen, you know? Man, I rolled the window halfway down and then immediately rolled it back up after I saw these semitransparent things with wings falling from the sky. At first, I wasn't sure what they were. I couldn't see them very well, but I saw what they were doing to people. They landed on men, women, and even children, and then disappeared inside of them like they'd possessed them. Then those people began assaulting other people—including other possessed. I swear it was like some battle royale to see who can control the strongest person. They were just beatin' each other up. It was crazy.

"I panicked because the chaos started moving toward me. Like, the fights were getting closer and so were the people getting possessed. I decided I'd crawl out of the passenger side window, so I climbed over the gearbox and into the passenger seat. As I touched the window controls, I looked up and saw five teenagers standing on a sidewalk alongside the interstate. Of course, I've seen them before. Their faces never change, but their clothes and the things they carried did. One boy always had something under his arm, such as a skateboard, a notebook, or crutches. Another boy held onto the shoulder straps of various types of backpacks, some designed for school and others created for hiking. A girl with long pale-blue hair stood behind and between the boys. She's always staring right at me over the guys' shoulders. Two other girls stood at the left end of the group, in front of a deer crossing sign. My gut instinct told me they were twins. I couldn't tell with my eyes because one always had a hoodie pulled over her head. The other always had an arm raised, which partially obscured her face while pointing toward the sky, as if she were telling her sister to look. I should've already known to look up. Same dream every night. I know what's going to happen, but to the me in the dream, it's always the first time.

"I leaned back in the chair and looked up. The beige ceiling of my car had turned into glass, and I could see through the roof. Let me tell you, there was this faceless human-like creature, like a mannequin, descending toward me. It didn't wear clothes like you or me or the ones on display at the mall, but it wasn't naked, either. The textures across its body varied, but I was too scared to focus on any one thing.

"I did notice the two wings on its back and the four arms, two of which replaced its feet. When it landed on my car, it crushed the frame, almost sandwiching me inside. I didn't cry or scream. I just froze and stared in horror.

"Just imagine four muscular hands clamped to the sides of your car, and this blank, white face slowly getting closer until a vertical crease giving its head dimension touches the glass and cracks it."

Chapter 3

I met Dr. Sanders in the hotel lobby at eight the next morning. She sat at a high-top near a line of windows facing D.C. traffic and stared at the steam from a cup of coffee she held with both hands. I envied her morning posture, the straightened lower back that supported a head held high. Her right leg crossed over her left and pointed at the windows, as if she were a mannequin on display advertising a sleek woman's navy-blue business suit and matching high heels. The white glow that fluorescent lights bathed her in reminded me of the angels President Jackson had mentioned when he'd recounted his dream. Maybe they too had breakfast before attacking the town.

I lurched toward her table like a zombie. Despite the extra sleep I got, I still hadn't recovered from yesterday's early morning wake-up call. I was a night owl, awake long enough to see the oncoming dawn and destined to sleep in its warmth until the lunch crowd returned to their cubicles, where I then dragged myself out of bed only because city offices closed a few hours later, and I required their services to adult.

Mere steps away from Dr. Sanders, I noticed the discomfort of the surrounding people—a here-we-go-again reminiscent of Mondays when I'd worked nine-to-five. People in the lobby were mostly quiet, as if they'd already conversed about their dream many times before, and where they would normally talk about their flight, the city, or last night's outing, the recurring dreams had sapped them of their energy to socialize.

"Good morning, Dr. Sanders," I said, awkwardly climbing into the high-back chair across from her. The blue jeans I'd found at the hotel shop didn't fit comfortably. Maybe stretching them would loosen the fabric. The last light-gray long-sleeve tee on the rack hugged my chest. I liked the simple coffee mug graphic, even if I didn't care for the beverage.

Dr. Sanders greeted me with a smile above the white

porcelain rim of her mug. "Please, call me Naomi." She lowered the cup and then curled her fingers further around it, obscuring the dull, printed hotel logo of two birds in a nest.

"Good morning…Naomi."

She wasn't wearing her glasses. The morning light enriched her hazel eyes when she turned her head back toward the windows. Her contact lenses briefly shimmered. She seemed lonely. Maybe she too was processing last night's dream.

"What have *you* been dreaming about?" I asked, unsure how else to drive the conversation. I didn't dream like everyone else. What they experienced as recurring nightmares, I sought to repeat each night for the sake of a novel.

Naomi shrugged. "Not to be rude, but I dream about the same thing every night and sift through similar data every day. The last thing I wanna do is relive mine a third time, you know?"

I nodded. "Fair. So what's the plan?"

Naomi raised a brow. "Your guess is as good as mine. I've never done this before. I've mulled over some data, but I can't make heads or tails of it. Dream analysis really is its own field. And because I'm unfamiliar with the data, I'm not sure what to ask Danni."

"Who is Danni?"

Naomi sipped her coffee. At last, she loosened her hold on the mug and used her free hand to push several strands of hair away from the right side of her face. A leaf-shaped hair clip added color to the left side of her head.

"DANNI stands for Data Analysis Neural Network Informant. It's the system grad students at the university helped me develop to analyze the dreams." She sets the mug down on the table. "I feel as if giving DANNI a bad prompt will send me down the wrong rabbit hole."

The clever acronym made me smile. Naomi didn't see it. She still stared out the window. Considering she'd only recently discovered my work, she probably didn't know that I enjoyed creating acronyms for my stories.

Naomi rolled her eyes and tilted her head at me. "A fourth time, actually, since I've been reading your stories. My dreams aren't much different from what you've heard about so far. I feel like we need to explore the variations and find more correlation between other people's dreams and your stories. Are there meanings behind the themes portrayed? Is there a pattern? Or a sequence? Can we predict what's coming next?"

I cupped my chin in my hands and rested my elbows on the table. Then I looked out the window, too, at all those people sitting in traffic waiting for the day to start and end. How similar were their dreams? Of the two versions I'd heard about so far, both featured winged creatures.

Next to elves and vampires, angels—assuming they were the creatures in Heather's story too—were one of my favorite fantasy beings. I loved the light that surrounded them and the hope or despair they brought to the fight—physical and psychological—good and evil. Yes, I enjoyed a compelling villain, too.

A sidewalk was also something both dreams shared. It meant nothing to me, though. I grew up in a middle-class home and rode my bike around the neighborhood streets more than the sidewalks, but none of that made it into my stories. I grounded my characters in reality, just not *my* reality.

Turning my attention to Naomi, I focused on the topic of angels. "So far, both dreams featured winged creatures, bystanders, and sidewalks. Heather's version had more detail than the President's. Maybe the President didn't have time to elaborate. But he mentioned not being able to see Michael's face, and he talked about the people in the rear, but didn't describe them, whereas Heather detailed both the angels and the people on the sidewalk."

Naomi looked through me with a distant gaze that suggested she was piecing the puzzle together in her head. I imagined the narratives we'd heard, the dreams she'd had, the data she'd collected, and the books I'd written were all sections of a puzzle, each with multiple missing pieces. The puzzle didn't come in a box. If I could help find and place the pieces related to my stories, that might give us a hint at the larger picture.

"Naomi, what if you asked DANNI about the most popular or controversial report about winged creatures? Maybe we can find someone with even more detail."

Naomi pulled out her phone. "Sure thing. I should be able to start a remote session with our lab network and send the inquiry. Might take a minute to return a result."

I nodded. From the corners of my eyes, I saw Agent Jones headed our way with a cup of coffee in hand. There was nothing remarkable or distinguishable about him. He had short brown hair and wore a black suit. That was it. No accessories, battle scars, or personality in his facial expression. He could easily be a robot replica of himself.

We nodded at each other before he said, "Mr. Emmanuel. Dr. Sanders. How can I assist you today?"

Before I could respond, Naomi said, "There's a social media account that recently received some major attention and then controversy. A video by user LadyAmethystMoon received more than a few million views in a couple of hours."

"Can we watch it?" I asked, sitting up higher and ready to lean over to view the phone's screen.

Naomi shook her head. "The platform took it down for violating terms and conditions." She glanced at me before adding, "In other words, it pissed somebody off." She swiped her finger several times across the glass display in her hands. "Looks like she insulted an entire community when she called them wannabe practitioners of magic. Then she made the church mad when she said witches defeated angels. After hundreds of thousands of people corroborated her dream, the Pope addressed her comments as misguided."

"The Pope? That popular, huh?" I sat back in the chair. "Neither of the other two dreams mentioned witches. The President alluded to an oncoming war, but it hadn't started yet. In Heather's dream, the angels were attacking. Amethyst's dream could be the next chapter in the story. Can we send her a message?"

"I don't know where to send a message. The video was taken down and the account deactivated."

"Then where are you getting all this information from?"

"I'm skimming social media comments from various forums. People don't stop talking just because they've been silenced."

"You trust the comment section?"

She laughed. "The comments section is the best place for verifying information. The people using them are everywhere, and their sheer numbers ensure a singular, biased political or social agenda is a drop of water in an ocean."

Naomi found value in the comments section. I'd always seen it as a wasteland filled with chittering birds; a vast landscape where nothing of value grew from the social interactions. And every now and again, their presence would annoy a lower god, and they'd be forced to migrate. So they flocked to the next apocalypse like a plague.

Naomi grinned at the screen. "And the comment section says…drum roll please…the owner of the video is Lady Amethyst of Morrigan's Lunar Circle, a coven of witches in Virginia."

Chapter 4

Lady Amethyst had brown frizzy hair, styled as long twists with slivers of gray strands or cobwebs. Ghostly skin suggested she'd risen from a corpse buried in the backyard cemetery. Black lipstick and dark-blue eye shadow gave her face dimension. She sat with legs crossed underneath a long, black dress with its sleeves rolled up to her elbows. Bronze runes colored the outfit and matched the polish on her fingernails. She held a pipe-shaped electronic cigarette in her hand that she puffed every few statements.

"We didn't *defeat* the angels," she said. "We held them back with a barrier."

She sat across from Naomi and me, at a round table on the back porch of an aged boarding school. Old wooden planks stepped down to a graveyard and then a thick forest. Black birds perched on the heads of tombstones. One bird looked at us often, repeatedly turning its head to the side as if it were paranoid about our presence. I thought it might be a familiar spying on us. They—the other witches—were protective of Lady Amethyst.

The few residents we'd encountered at the front door greeted us with a warning glance at the chalk pentagram we'd stood on. I didn't blame them for being cautious, considering the newly gained attention they'd received online that resulted in offensive letters and the occasional unruly visitor. The barrier Lady Amethyst mentioned didn't protect them from the real world. The coven relied on an old iron gate five hundred feet away from the front porch. Threats against the property prompted Agent Jones to secure the perimeter.

Naomi looked at me. "I thought you wrote science fiction. Is there magic in your stories?"

I met her gaze and nodded. "In some fantasy worlds I haven't published yet…" I said, my mind preoccupied with a different question. Tapping my fingers against the wooden surface of the table, I asked, "Being grounded made some dreams scarier, right? If people could just use magic, then why aren't more of them overcoming their situations? Sounds like it'd be easy."

"Do all of your characters overcome their situations?" Naomi asked. She dusted a couple of her long brown hairs from her navy-blue pants. "Some of them even died."

I frowned and shook my head. Excitement would've been my usual response because I loved talking about how I'd created the worlds in my stories, and how they'd go on to develop on their own, sometimes for the better of the characters and sometimes for the worst. That world-building autonomy engrossed my readers and made each character's journey less predictable. But I realized that lack of control echoed in the widespread dreams.

Lady Amethyst blew a cherry-scented mist into the air. "People aren't overcoming their situations with magic because they're unpracticed. Imposters. To feel like they're part of the conversation, people on the internet will say anything, and they'll act like experts on something they know nothing about. They'll talk out of their ass for a like or two."

She took a deep breath and then raised her eyes toward the sky. Her face resembled a painting—an oval sheet of canvas nestled among rolls of thick brown yarn, and facial features defined by sharp black lines sketched with chalk, and the brush strokes of a light-blue sky smeared in the eyes. The mist she blew from her pipe drifted across the portrait like cirrus clouds.

"What we're experiencing aren't simple dreams, Dr. Sanders. Or fictional stories, Mr. Emmanuel. They're prophecies. Each is different because our individual strengths and weaknesses vary, as will our role in the upcoming battle. Through these dreams, Morrigan showed us—and the world—just how powerful her coven can be." She lowered her head and then her tone, down from the casual high pitch to a desolate monotone voice. "There's a war coming. You can't turn to magic without a source, but you can turn to God at the darkest hour, apparently."

Lady Amethyst's words rattled me. A chill ran down my spine as an ominous feeling stoked the fear that the surrounding gloom had sparked. Had we been in a movie, a howling wind would've blown the leaves littering the backyard across the porch. I was ready to hear Lady Amethyst's dream and leave.

I leaned back in the folding chair, my long sleeve tee protecting me from the cold metal. The wooden floor squeaked, and I worried it'd collapse. I waited for its silence before I asked, "Can you tell us about your dream in as much detail as possible?"

Lady Amethyst blew another scented mist into the air, this time from the corner of her lips and away from us. "Dreams can be difficult to remember after you wake up, even if they are recurring. At most, we recall fragments, and our ambition fills the gaps. So don't believe everything you hear."

She uncrossed her legs and slouched in the seat, resting the base of her neck against the high back of her chair. She blew another mist cloud into the air and then said, "Fortunately for you, my girls and I tapped into Morrigan's power so that I could remember every detail of my dream. I was going to tell the full story in a book, or even a podcast, but the Pope ruined that venture with his passive-aggressive slander. Platforms took my videos down and threatened my livelihood." With her head still tilted, she lowered her eyes to me. "Since you agreed to protect my home until this shit passes, I'll give you the first-hand tale of the century that began one gorgeous morning.

"The day was nothing like the dark and cloudy ones of the foretold apocalypse. Angels descended from a clear, sunny sky. We can all agree on that. They attacked schools, homes, and government buildings, but ignored the churches. Not a denomination or two, but all of them, as if they were equal regardless of their belief.

"Attacks centered on key locations in the world. Washington, D.C., being one of them. Every channel on the television streamed some news station rambling about the end times—unprecedented this and extraordinary that.

"Flocks of angels swarmed the cities. The winged ones near us resembled crimson locusts as the dark red rooftops of houses reflected off the undersides of their semitransparent bodies. And in their wake, deranged and bloodthirsty neighbors chased each other. People fought for control of their own bodies; their limbs jerked in unexpected ways from contradictory commands.

"The possession of human bodies meant spiritual energies were at play. With Morrigan's guidance, I gathered the girls into the sunroom. There, five of us formed a pentagram that created a barrier over northern Virginia. Centered on us, it spread to the greater D.C. area and pushed the angels back and out. We even managed to exorcise those who'd been possessed, which is something the church failed to do, but tried to take credit for.

"I saw the clergyman on TV," she sneered. "A bishop. Or a priest. I dunno. There was a man in a robe claiming to be God's messenger. He stood in the Oval Office, advising the President of the United States of God's will, and the President believed every word spoken. This country's leaders and its people thanked and praised the man for doing absolutely nothing.

"I wanted to bring down the barrier. I wanted to watch their religion crumble on national television, but I wouldn't risk my girls' lives over trivial pride. And I didn't have to. People quickly realized that no other man of faith in all the world could raise the same barrier. Not even the Pope.

"And the scientists were already hard at work trying to prove or disprove the invisible force keeping the angels out. After they calculated the barrier's diameter and found its center, law enforcement and military surrounded our home.

I stood on the front porch, between them and my girls, because I wasn't sure if they'd come to protect us or control us."

Lady Amethyst paused and looked at me. A cloud of vape sat in her mouth, swirling, and then slowly escaped when she exhaled. "Mr. Emmanuel, have you ever felt someone's emotions, such as hate or lust? Some of us are more sensitive to those energies than others. They often radiate from people like musk.

"Standing on the porch in front of those soldiers, the stench of fear drifted over me. I saw trembling hands attempting to steady automatic weapons. Sweat ran out from under helmets and dripped off the chins of adolescent adults. I gazed into conflicted eyes and surmised that they too were confused by this new reality because the church protected everyone within its walls—good and evil alike, and a commander ordered them to protect witches from angels. And from ourselves, apparently.

"That's when the real test began. A test of time and mental fortitude. A test of our patience and our faith. Fourteen of us called the coven home and five were required to maintain the barrier. Channeling Morrigan's power through the human form exhausted us. I developed a schedule, but the girls' recovery times varied and were often longer than a shift. We struggled, but we endured. That wasn't enough for the military. They required certainty and contingencies. So they called for any and all who practiced witchcraft to come into *our* home and support."

Lady Amethyst snickered. "The military gathered a crowd of fools; wannabes who couldn't maintain the current barrier, never mind put up their own at an alternate site. Those who answered the call believed they'd receive the rewards of magic without actual practice, knowledge, or consequence. Worse," she dropped her right elbow on the table, leaned toward me, and furrowed her brows, "how could they draw power from a source they didn't devote themselves to?"

She leaned back in the chair and sighed. Another misty cloud scented the air. "Anyway, my girls maintained the barrier for five days before the angels bypassed it. Like something out of a science-fiction movie, three warships exited light-speed travel in the sky above D.C. I saw one in detail, briefly, after the displaced air flattened the capital, but before the dust from debris obscured the horizon. It was massive. Several large halos rotated around sections of a long three-dimensional trapezoid, and the angels poured out of it like a disturbed beehive. And that's when I wake up."

Lady Amethyst stared at us in silence for a moment, perhaps waiting to see if we'd criticize her tale. I absorbed everything she'd said, once again holding back my inner child at the excitement of spacecraft warping into battle above the enemy's capital. Yet something seemed off. Missing.

I looked to my left, away from Naomi. The porch we sat on extended the length of the building and sharply turned right. I imagined myself walking down its wooden baseboards with an oil lamp from the Middle Ages in hand, extended out in front and raised above my shoulders to illuminate *something*. It felt like a haunted house hiding its tragic history, but instead, it hid in the shadows of Lady Amethyst's words.

She raised a brow. "You seem disappointed."

"Not at all," I said, closing my eyes to the corridor and reopening them to her. "I was just wondering if there was more to your dream. Feels like you skipped to the end there."

Naomi shot me a hard glance. She started to apologize on my behalf, but Lady Amethyst interrupted her.

"It's okay. He's right. I omitted the actual nightmare," she said.

The excluded parts of her story reflected in her distant gaze. She resembled an artistic statue the birds could've perched on. The vape pipe was motionless, too, clasped between her fingers as her wrist balanced on the chair's arm-rest. She parted and closed her lips several times until she came to terms with whatever lingered on her mind. After a deep breath, she spoke aloud.

"There was this girl among the volunteers. An eerie and stoic girl with long pale-blue hair. She stood alone. There were others who came by themselves, but they…*belonged.* She occupied space but didn't seem to exist to anyone else but me. Some of my girls had noticed her in their dreams, but not to the extent I had. We thought maybe Morrigan had taken a new form—that she was testing us from behind those unusual light-blue eyes. But I've felt Morrigan's presence before, and that girl was not her. I couldn't feel anything from that girl, and at the same time, I felt everything. Her presence saturated my sixth sense. It shook my faith.

"I felt this growing urge to walk toward her—to-ward…oblivion. My feet moved on their own. They took slow and steady steps and then stopped thirty feet away. I followed her pointed finger toward the sky seconds before the warships appeared."

Lady Amethyst lowered her gaze. She stared at the table. The color of reality slowly returned to her eyes. She raised the electronic cigarette to her lips but didn't put it into her mouth. Her right arm trembled, so she steadied it with her left hand. Then she closed her eyes and took a few deep breaths.

I wasn't sure if the girl she'd mentioned or the flicker in her belief or both was the actual nightmare. I wasn't going to ask. She panted while holding her chest. I'd done enough.

Naomi looked at me, as if she'd find the answer to a question or the result of an ongoing mental search in my eyes. "Is there a girl with pale-blue hair in any of your stories?" she asked.

I shook my head. "Not even in the slush pile."

Naomi reached for the glasses she wasn't wearing, as if to adjust them out of habit. She rubbed her temples instead and then pushed her hair back behind her ears. "So…Heather, the admin at the White House, also mentioned a girl with pale-blue hair. That same girl was also in my dream pointing at the sky." Naomi nodded several times to herself and then added, "I know our next stop."

Chapter 5

"Dr. Sanders, I need an official reason to escort civilians into this facility," Agent Jones said from the driver's seat of a black SUV. He'd parked in front of a cement building with two rows of covered windows separated by a floor. He glanced at the rearview mirror. "Dr. Sanders…"

Naomi stared at the phone in her hands. Her thumb glided across the glass. "Is this the extent of your superpowers, Agent Jones?"

"Ma'am?"

Naomi smirked. "I don't need to go inside." At last, she looked up from the screen. "Sorry, I was double-checking my notes. I've never been to this base before. In my dream, there was a Captain Davis stationed here. Can we talk to him? In the car? In the lobby, maybe or outside?"

Agent Jones nodded. "Stand by," he said and exited the vehicle.

I watched Naomi from the corner of my eyes, as hers followed Agent Jones' brisk pace up the sidewalk leading to the building's side entrance. She'd untucked her brown hair out from behind her ear, so I couldn't quite see her face, mostly just its dim reflection in the window.

"What?" she asked without turning her head.

"I didn't say anything."

Naomi looked at me through the reflection and raised a brow. "It's called body language for a reason."

I averted my gaze and pulled on the seat belt strap across my chest to loosen its tightness around my waist. "Are you referring to the 'musk' Lady Amethyst talked about?"

Naomi laughed. "Don't mock her. She might curse you."

My joke seemed to ease whatever discomfort I'd felt from her. She hadn't told me anything about her dream, just bits and pieces here and there. I could tell from the growing social distance between us that she'd recollected something painful. A persistent memory, once she recalled it. Something she'd have to work hard at burying again.

I unbuckled the seat belt, pulled on it for additional slack, and then re-fastened it. I asked, "Weren't you hoping for magical realism? Isn't that about as real as it gets?"

She rolled her eyes and smirked.

I shifted in the seat, turning my body a few degrees to face Naomi. "So you've never been here before, except in your dream?"

Naomi seemed to understand the rhetorical nature of the question. Or she ignored me.

I sat straight again and stared at the back of the passenger seat headrest. "It's not unusual to dream of a place you've never been to before. However, accurately leading us to this specific building was unexpected." I turned to Naomi again. "What if Lady Amethyst was right, and these dreams are prophecies? What if the events in your dream start now, and this investigation led you to the place where those events will take place?"

I glanced up. The dreams we'd heard about so far had mentioned the same beautiful sky Naomi and I currently sat under. The sun would set soon instead of rise.

Naomi planted the left side of her face into her palm. "You don't know how scary accurate your words are right now." She paused for a long, suspenseful moment. Then, in a flat tone, she added, "We're following my dream. It started with the drive here. Sort of."

"Wait…what?"

I hoped she'd turn around and explain her words with the same zest she'd shown back at the Oval Office, but she didn't. Perhaps because the conversation was about her.

"I was in your dream?" I asked.

My overexcitement could've made her uncomfortable, too. I felt like a kid asking a girl to go steady, and the answer wasn't exactly no. Instead of romantic interest, Naomi gave me an idea for a story, where a woman dreams about the love of her life and follows that dream's events step-by-step in the real world, hoping to meet him. Through physical pain, emotional heartbreak, and paranormal obstacles, she knows he'll be in her arms at the end of the road, if she can survive the trek.

Naomi's voice split my attention. "I trusted DANNI when it returned you as the result to my query. I'd never shared my dream with anyone, so it couldn't have used data on me to draw that conclusion. And it couldn't be a coincidence that the two distinct paths had crossed—DANNI's result and your presence in my dream.

"We had this conversation. The words we exchanged varied, but I had the gist of it: use my connections through the university to publish a white paper about DANNI's findings. That got me an audience with the President, which then led to you."

It was my turn to speak. Developing the new story in my head caught me flat-footed, so that the silence carried on for too long. I blurted out the first thing that came to mind.

"How did you know the President would read it?"

"I didn't know that *he* would read it, but I knew that *somebody* would and that I'd somehow end up here with you." Naomi sighed. "Otherwise, no harm and no foul. The paper would've just been another publication."

Another publication. It pained me to hear those words. I'd been told that my stories were just another book. They weren't. To somebody, they were a valuable escape. I opened my mouth to tell her that, but Agent Jones startled me when he tapped on Naomi's window.

He waited for Naomi to sit up straight before opening the door. "Captain Davis will meet us at the gazebo over there." He nodded toward a wooden structure in the middle of the parking lot.

The gazebo sat on a sidewalk that served as a walkway between the split lot. A couple of trees shaded the areas the cone top exposed to the sun. Cigarette butts filled a tin can sitting on the interior floor. Ashes stained the surrounding wood. A few spiders called the upper interior corners home, having woven sparse webs like the events that might've brought us all together.

Naomi and I sat on the same side of the bench. She sat next to the opening, which faced the building. We watched Agent Jones cross the parking lot with a young man wearing a coyote-brown operational camouflage uniform. He and Agent Jones had the same purposeful stride. If the young man had longer legs, they would've walked in sync.

After both stepped onto the sidewalk in front of the gazebo, I saw the name "Davis" on the right breast of the young man's uniform. Two coyote-brown vertical bars at the center of his chest represented the rank of captain.

His jaw dropped when he saw Naomi. He glanced at me and then at Agent Jones. An unlikely trio.

"So you recognize me," Naomi said.

Davis re-focused his attention on her. "Um…yes ma'am." His fingers fidgeted at his sides, and he adjusted his posture after his right shoulder slumped. He patted down his pants' right-side cargo pocket, as if to hide his nervousness behind a deliberate action.

"At ease, Captain," Agent Jones said, placing a hand on the young man's right shoulder. "You're not in trouble. Dr. Sanders and Mr. Emmanuel would like to ask you a few questions about your dream."

Davis exhaled. His brown boots made solid impact with the wood floor as he stepped into the gazebo and sat on the opposite bench, equally spaced between Naomi and me. His eyes shifted from Naomi to the floor and back, as if he doubted the scene in front of him, or didn't want to stare but needed to look at her long enough to clear his doubt.

"I'm here, too," I said, having only seen the right side of his low top fade since he'd sat down.

"Uh, yes sir," Davis said. He lowered his chin. "Sorry, it's been a little crazy here lately. You know, with everything going on." Davis dried his fingers across his fatigues and then extended his hand toward us. "I'm Captain Davis, United States Air Force," he said.

I went to shake his hand. "Kenny Emmanuel," I said, but he shook Naomi's instead, flashing her a wide, embarrassed grin. I looked at my hand and slowly lowered it into my lap.

Naomi folded her arms. "Of all the people in your dream, you remembered me."

"Yes, ma'am. I didn't think you'd be real, though."

"Hm, you didn't look for me, either." Naomi teased.

Davis blushed. It didn't show through his dark complexion, but his smile and dilated pupils lit up the gazebo like a bonfire inside the wood rails. He clasped his hands together in front of him.

"I got used to seeing a lot of different people. Mostly from my time in the sandbox. But even here, I learned to remember faces."

"Good," Naomi said. She crossed her legs and kicked her foot back and forth. "Do you remember a girl with pale-blue hair in your dream?"

"Yes, ma'am."

"Can you tell us about your encounter with her?"

Davis lowered his chin. He seemed to gather his thoughts before he said, "An evacuation order came after the warships entered our airspace. Command directed us to escort the civilians away from the battle. Sergeant Cooper joined me. We followed the emergency action plan, but when we got outside, chaos swallowed us.

"Angels were everywhere. At least, I called them angels. They flew down and into—inside of—people and turned them into…zombies, I guess. They ran real fast, drooled a lot, and attacked anything that moved, except other zombies and the dead." Davis raised his eyes to us. "The dead didn't get back up though, so I guess they weren't zombies."

"They were possessed," Naomi added. She smoothed the wrinkles out of her suit pants and then cupped her knee with both hands.

"Yeah. Well, we got the order to kill the possessed…"

Davis paused. He stared at the gazebo floor, curled his lips, and slowly rubbed his hands together, tightening and then loosening his grip often. An uneasy smile parted his lips. He said, "This lady thought one of the dead had turned into an angel—that God had called them home just then. I wanted to believe, so I turned around to look. I saw this spectral figure stand up and out of someone laying on the ground. It kinda looked like the person, like it'd transformed into them and slowly reverted to itself." Davis stared off into space with dreamy eyes. "It was beautiful, though. No face. Long and ghostly-white curly hair down to the knees. A similarly colored and flowing robe covered its body. Bare feet and shins were visible below the robe's uneven ends." Davis frowned and then bit his lips. "I could see through it—robe, hair, and everything. I could see people dying through its body.

"Then it saw us, and I just froze. It's like that dream where danger's in front of you, but you can't move, even though you're screaming at yourself to go. Anyway, the angel took two steps forward and then leaped toward us. It went inside Mr. Park, one civilian, and then Mr. Park tried to choke Ms. Kathy.

"Sergeant Cooper shot Mr. Park five—ten times until he stopped moving. The angel slowly rose from Mr. Park's body. It had his short, straight hair, which gradually grew longer. Sergeant Cooper fired his gun at it, but the bullets went through its body. It stepped out of Mr. Park and walked toward Sergeant Cooper with reserved purpose.

"Cooper looked at me and shrugged. He smiled and flicked his head to the right; told me to get outta there. I watched that thing step into his body and start taking over.

"I grabbed Ms. Kathy's hand and told everyone to run. We dodged as many of the possessed as we could, ran out of the parking lot, and onto the main road. That's when I saw you, Dr. Sanders," Davis nodded at her. "You told us to evacuate to the chapel because the angels wouldn't attack it."

"I wonder how I knew that," Naomi said.

I wondered if Davis saw me alongside Naomi. He seemed smitten with her, which added bias to his re-telling. He remembered the girl with pale-blue hair, so maybe he just ignored me.

Davis shrugged. "I don't know, but it worked. The angels chased people up to the chapel's doorstep and just gave up. They didn't even really fight anyone on the lawn. But they—the possessed—charged at us in the street. I shot them. I had to shoot them—innocent people." Davis choked. Teardrops hit the deck. He wiped them with the back of his hand. "Sorry. I shouldn't be crying over a dream. But man, it felt so real."

Naomi grabbed the edge of the bench to either side of her. "You'll be stronger after talking about it," she said.

Davis sat up and rested his back against the gazebo frame. He shook his head. "I felt everything. I watched the same people die every night, and there was nothing I could do about it. The angels took control of people, made them kill each other, and then just left their bodies to rot."

Naomi looked to her right, at the building Davis worked at. She said, "Isn't it crazy how we always cross paths even though we tried different things to change course? It's almost like we're being guided. I remember. No matter how many times I told you to get inside, you refused. There was always one more person to help."

Davis blinked several times and then said, "The woman with blue hair."

Naomi bobbed her foot back and forth again. I hadn't noticed when she'd stopped. She seemed distant again, in a faraway land. Davis held a similar look in his eyes. For a moment, I thought they were dreaming together.

"The woman with blue hair," Naomi repeated in a soft

voice and then continued in her regular tone, "She stood in the middle of the street, her back to the chapel, staring and pointing up at the sky. Not even at one of the ships. Just at the sky. That's where my dream always ended. With you running toward her and the chapel doors slamming shut."

Davis snapped out of his daydream. "I'm about as stubborn as you are, ma'am. The chapel's always nearing max capacity before I convince you to go inside. And yeah, I couldn't leave the girl. I knew I'd have to take her somewhere else, but every time I stepped within inches of her, an angel gets me, and I wake up."

I tilted my head and asked, "Were they protecting her?"

At last, Davis saw me. "I don't know, sir. They always get me from behind. I tried to run backwards once, thinking maybe I could see it coming, but I couldn't turn around. My body just kept running forward."

Naomi faced Davis again. "Where would you have taken her?"

Davis's forehead scrunched. "What do you mean?"

"If you ever caught up to the woman with blue hair, where would you have taken her?" After a brief silence, Naomi turned to me, perhaps assuming I too was confused. "I came looking for a man I'd never met at a place I'd never been. Both exist. I'm willing to bet she exists, too. Somewhere."

Chapter 6

The woman with pale-blue hair, whom we've started calling "Blue", appeared in an absurd number of dreams, according to DANNI. The artificial-intelligence application drilled down into data during our drive to the Air Force base's medical center, where Captain Davis said he would've taken Blue had he been able to reach her in his dream. From the accounts DANNI had mined, most people overlooked the woman, describing her only in passing along with others. We focused on Blue's hair color, but it wasn't exactly an unusual shade among young folks.

As a researcher, Naomi saw something more in the data, hidden information that proved Blue's uncanny existence. Unlike everyone else, Blue simultaneously existed in multiple dreams occurring at different physical locations. Position data for other people matched across several dream instances, like how Naomi and Captain Davis appeared in each other's dream despite having never met.

Unknown to Naomi, my presence in her dream deviated from her analysis of DANNI's findings. While I dreamed of related events, species, and structures present in many of the nightmares, I didn't share the same end-of-the-world vision, and I didn't dream about her or this Air Force base.

Agent Jones tapped on the SUV's window again, startling me…again. We exited the vehicle and followed him into the medical center's lobby, where two servicemen greeted us.

"Dr. Sanders and Mr. Emmanuel, this is Captain Sullivan and Sergeant Ross. They can answer any questions you have about patients in this facility."

We shook their hands and shared the usual nod and professional smile that accompanied a greeting. Captain Sullivan towered over all of us. He had short, brown hair. A horizontal scar originated from the left side of his nose and faded halfway across his cheekbone. Sergeant Ross had large hands and looked sturdier than his commanding officer. The coyote-brown uniform complemented his bronze complexion, and both shimmered gold when they crossed the ray of sunlight filtering through the front doors.

Captain Sullivan lightly grabbed his hips. "I don't know how far you all traveled, and I'd hate to say you've wasted your time, but there are a ton of privacy laws that prevent me from sharing information about patients."

Naomi didn't bat an eye in the face of regulation. "We're looking for a woman with blue hair."

Captain Sullivan addressed all of us professionally. "If you're a family member of a patient, we'll need to verify your identity before we can answer questions."

I had a feeling the captain wouldn't budge. I stepped back and let Agent Jones negotiate. Naomi did, too. She meandered to the left side of the entrance and looked at various model aircraft on display inside a wooden cabinet behind glass French doors. Framed photos of prior Air Force units decorated the surrounding wall space. She glanced over her shoulders every ten seconds to check Agent Jones' progress with Captain Sullivan.

I sat down in one of five chairs positioned against the wall to the right of the entrance. When I looked up, Naomi crossed my line of sight. The sunlight briefly made her hair glow a copper-red hue. She stared at the interior doors to either side of the receptionist counter, a semi-circular block of concrete in front of four workstations, before sitting down next to me. She placed her chin in her palms and her elbows on her knees.

"This is taking forever," she muttered, the gap her chin settled within impeding speech clarity.

It's only been a minute, I thought to myself. Then I asked aloud, "Are you anxious about being incorrect or correct?"

Naomi didn't respond. She shifted her gaze from side to side, from one door behind the counter to the other and then from Agent Jones to Captain Sullivan. Her bland fingernails drummed against her left temple, and she tapped the floor with her opposite foot.

"Who knew the government took our privacy so seriously?" I asked.

"They don't. The captain's taking his job seriously."

"Doesn't your profession have similar laws?"

Naomi raised her chin out of her hands. "I don't have patients. I have data. So long as I don't publish the two together, nobody cares." She frowned. "Honestly, I didn't care to know their names until now." She leaned forward and looked back at me. "I wonder what Blue dreams about. If you're in everyone else's dream, what are your dreams like?"

"Did you ask DANNI?"

Naomi sighed. "Needle in a massive haystack. There's just too many answers—"

"Captain Sullivan," Agent Jones said in a stern voice. "The President of the United States has directed us to investigate the recurring nightmares. I've shown you the directive." Agent Jones held up his phone at the two men. "The woman we're looking for is a person of interest. If you have any information, I'd *prefer* your cooperation."

Naomi stood and walked over after the servicemen exchanged uneasy glances.

Captain Sullivan nodded at Sergeant Ross, who turned to Agent Jones and said, "Sir, a young woman named Euphoria Gallatin checked in a few months ago. She has long pale-blue hair."

Agent Jones' eyes widened, the first I'd seen his face stray from composure. "Surely not in relation to the two-star general?" he asked.

Sergeant Ross nodded. "She's his adopted daughter. He brought her in himself. Said she wouldn't wake up."

From behind Naomi and Agent Jones, I asked, "Why is an army general's daughter at an Air Force base's medical facility?"

Sergeant Ross said, "This is a joint base. General Gallatin lived here."

"Lived?" Agent Jones asked.

Captain Sullivan looked around, as if to make sure no one else was nearby. "We haven't been able to contact General Gallatin over the past couple of months. I informed the MPs of the situation, and haven't heard from them, either. We've been taking care of her ever since, but to be honest, we don't know what to do."

Naomi adjusted her suit jacket. "Can we talk to her?"

Captain Sullivan briefly closed his eyes and shook his head. "She's in a coma."

***

Euphoria. An exotic name suited for the characters in my stories and for the young woman lying in the hospital bed. Pale-blue hair brought the room to life as if it were the only color in a gray scale setting. Its owner slept peacefully, like a wild child after terrorizing the house. No. The more I looked at her, the more she emanated an atmosphere reminiscent of a nap underneath bed sheets hung out to dry in a green field somewhere in the countryside. I felt the warmth of the day and the occasional breeze. It nearly lulled me to sleep.

"What's wrong with her?" Naomi asked. She stood next to me, several feet away from Euphoria's bed, at the corner of the room where Captain Sullivan had first pulled back a dark blue curtain separating the space from the hallway.

Sergeant Ross walked further into the room. He grabbed a clipboard hanging at the foot of the bed. "Other than being asleep, she's perfectly healthy. I'm unaware of any underlying conditions. The medical history we have for her is clean, and we haven't seen—she hasn't shown—any signs of trouble."

Naomi folded her arms. "This girl's our best lead." She

raised crinkled eyes to me. "So now we wait on Jones?"

After hearing about the General's disappearance, Agent Jones verified Euphoria's identity and then left to get answers from the military police. He also wanted her moved, again citing her as a person of interest in a major investigation. I wasn't sure what moving her to a larger hospital would accomplish but agreed that a woman appearing in multiple strangers' disparate dreams where spatial positioning across the variations had otherwise been realistic was fascinating indeed. It gave me an idea.

If Naomi believed the dreams echoed my stories, a theory I struggled to fully embrace, then I could, theoretically, apply logic from my fictional worlds to help us take the next step.

I cleared my throat. "In *The Witch's Trial*, a character believed that being asleep made the brain sensitive to external signals of thought that were otherwise lost in the noise of being awake." My words engrossed the others. I felt three pairs of eyes on me while I stared at Euphoria. "In other words, our dreams are composed of other people's realities, and the inability to fully interpret those signals fabricates the fantastical scenes during REM sleep. If Euphoria's constantly dreaming, does that mean those external thoughts are her reality, which are then received by others when they sleep?"

Restlessness sat on Captain Sullivan's broad shoulders, as if I wasted his time spewing nonsensical theories. A long and flat 'uh' escaped Sergeant Ross. Wide eyes betrayed the grin he held back for the sake of being professional. Naomi seemed deep in thought. She looked at Euphoria with intense eyes, possibly frustrated by the answers that were so close yet so far away.

I continued talking, with one foot in reality and the other in Somnia. "She could simultaneously appear in multiple dreams if her external thoughts reached many people. Or maybe she's dream-walking at the intersection of this complex highway of other people's nightmares. Something must explain her presence in all those dreams."

"Or she's at the origin of that highway," Naomi said. Her eyes brightened. "Or *is* the origin. But how would she transmit those thoughts across the globe and control people's locations?"

I shrugged. Nothing came to mind that could answer Naomi's question because a valid reason had to obey the laws of physics. Even if I could prove Euphoria's dream had engulfed everyone, I couldn't explain how one person's actions carried across multiple people's dreams. Like Ethan in *The Witch's Trial*, I couldn't do the math.

Naomi and I faced each other, and then we looked at Euphoria. Her face kept innocence and serenity. The steady beeping of the heart-rate monitor made the only sound. The sheet over her body rose and fell, maintaining the suspenseful mood Naomi and I had created.

"One foot in reality and the other in Somnia," I said. Naomi didn't understand, and she wouldn't understand. I hadn't published that book yet. The dreams had mostly incorporated ideas from my science-fiction stories, but there'd been a couple of minor similarities to my unpublished fantasy pieces. *Somnia* came to mind.

Ideas for the story flooded my thoughts and coaxed me to talk about them, perhaps the same way Lady Amethyst felt compelled to walk toward Euphoria in her dream. Instead of my legs, my lips moved on their own and said, "*Somnia* is an unpublished, urban fantasy story I've been writing. It's about a dream world that exists in an individual's mind. The story follows a dream watcher who divined the future based on the dreams they watched, and the dreams they watched were based on real-world events outside of the imaginary world called Somnia." I zoned out. Scenes from the untold story played in my head. An answer to *some* question sat on the tip of my tongue, and I kept talking to prevent it from escaping. "Everything took place in a dream world, and the main character was determined to save Somnia from the external threat of reality…"

I shook my head, once again fighting the urge to sleep. At least, in that moment. I pushed back an adjacent curtain and slipped into the next room.

Naomi called after me. "Where are you going?"

Captain Sullivan used my name. He sounded distant. I unwillingly ignored him and sat on an empty bed. The same type of machines and tubes attached to Euphoria silently stood next to me. The cold scent of sterile equipment filled the room.

Sergeant Ross pulled the curtain all the way back as I lay across the bed and faced the ceiling. I turned my head toward him. He must've seen me looking past him because he stepped aside. Euphoria's gentle visage caused my eyelids to grow heavier. I thought her hair glowed, too, a soft neon-blue glow-in-the-dark tint. At last, it was my turn to sleep…to visit…Somnia…

Chapter 7

"I didn't know that *he* would read it, but I knew that *somebody* would and that I'd somehow end up here with you." Naomi exhaled. "Otherwise, no harm and no foul. The paper would've just been another publication."

Déjà vu, I thought.

I sat in the middle row of an SUV. Black leather creaked as I moved. Naomi occupied the seat to my left. She leaned against the window with her chin in her palm and her elbow against the door's armrest. She stared off into the distance, her reflection mirroring her visage. I reached for her shoulder and then lowered my hand to the back of her elbow to avoid touching her brown hair, which had fanned across her shoulder blades.

Naomi jerked around, rolling her shoulder back and into the leather seat. An apology sat on my lips; except I hadn't touched her yet. Naomi's eyes widened. She glared at the SUV's front windshield and then at the driver side door as it swung open.

A man entered the vehicle, sat in the driver's seat, and slammed the door shut. He wore a black suit like Agent Jones. Quick movements, like camera cuts of a stunt double, made seeing his face difficult. In a deep and raspy voice, he said, "They're headed this way!"

Who's headed this way? I thought, but couldn't ask.

The man threw the car in reverse. He used the side-view mirrors to look behind. Still moving too fast for me to scratch the familiarity itch, the I've-seen-him-somewhere feeling. He reversed and slammed on the brakes multiple times to avoid hitting people running across the parking lot.

"Get down!" he suddenly shouted.

The SUV shook violently. Multiple flying objects, obscured by the dusty wind, crashed against the driver side windows and doors, and a follow-on gust of wind lifted the SUV off its driver side tires. After the gale, the vehicle slammed back down, throwing Naomi against the window. I would've landed in her lap if I hadn't grabbed the door handle.

The man tried to throw the car into gear, but nothing worked. He leaned over to the passenger seat and pulled a pistol and several clips out of the glove box. He checked the gun's chamber and then loaded the weapon. "We're evacuating." He spoke over his shoulder. "Stay close to me."

We stepped out of the SUV. Dust made seeing anything difficult. Car alarms inundated my senses. I'd heard them from inside the SUV, all sounding off before and after the sound of a distant boom, but I didn't realize they'd be this loud together. People shouting and screaming added to the cacophony.

"Kenny!" Naomi yelled. She stood several feet away from the SUV swatting at the dust and chasing the man in black while half-turned and waving at me.

I ran after her. We dashed through the back half of the parking lot and cut across a green field between the building and the main road. Abandoned and crashed vehicles littered the once-scenic landscape, some of their doors left ajar. A couple of trunks remained opened, too.

The man slowed down. He scanned the area ahead and then turned around to survey the damage we'd left. I saw his face then—Agent Jones' twin brother's face, if he had one. I called twin Jones TJ.

"Get down!" TJ's chiseled jaw lined up with the pistol he aimed at Naomi and me.

Naomi squatted in place and then yanked me down. TJ opened fire. I covered my head with both arms and then peeked around one forearm in time to see two people fall to the ground. TJ circled around us and slowly walked toward the bodies. When one person twitched, he fired two more shots into their back.

Alas, I shared the common dream.

My surroundings were nothing short of what others had

described. People chased and murdered each other. The killings were as swift and merciless as they could be. Nobody played with their food. Both assailants and victims abandoned worldly possessions. Angels rose from the dead and sought their next host to carry on their rampage.

TJ discharged the gun again. He'd fired the pistol at two angels, their semitransparent bodies doing little to throw off his aim and the bullets doing much less to their celestial forms—curving and reflecting light as they moved. One angel strode toward him and the other reverted its transformation from an older gentleman to an equally tall and dashing figure dressed in long, flowing robes.

The angels' presence weighed on me. I felt helpless and wondered if an ant shared the same overwhelming sense of defeat when a human stood over their dirt mound. Instinct compelled ants to move. I froze, just as Captain Davis had. The magic I thought others could wield to overcome their nightmares didn't answer my call. I, whose imagination captured the worlds of so many, couldn't even teleport away.

"Come on!" Naomi shouted. She grabbed my hand and pulled me along.

We ran down the street. I heard gunshots, one fired after another. I glanced over my shoulder and saw TJ hunting people down with a smile on his face. That expression didn't belong to him, though. An angel must've forced its will through his weeping eyes.

Naomi and I ran into Captain Davis with a few others in tow on the next block. Echoing the captain's dream, Naomi suggested we go to the chapel. So we did. Others had the same idea. I saw the windows Naomi would eventually take shelter behind. She'll watch Captain Davis try to save one more person. The woman with blue hair. Euphoria.

Thinking her name caused the scene to skip ahead several minutes, displacing everything except me. Then my surroundings slowed. Motion came to a crawl. Naomi pounded on a window from inside the chapel. I heard her silent plea as Captain Davis sprinted across the lawn. We saw the angel that would possess him. After he left the chapel yard, it majestically glided down to him and then took two graceful steps into his body. He never stood a chance against the bodily invasion.

I wanted to help him but remembered him and Naomi saying they couldn't change the outcome despite their best efforts.

The surrounding chaos continued, slowing only with the growing body count. Euphoria stood in the street, just as Captain Davis had described. She pointed at the sky. The massive warships others had mentioned, simply put, took my breath away. On a beautiful, sunny day, they floated in the sky like rain clouds. They occupied space like they'd always been there, as if their presence was natural.

And as quickly as their existence swept me into their exhilarating calmness, everything except me stopped moving.

"Eu…phoria?"

I lowered my gaze to the long pale-blue hair that reached and curled around the back of her ankles. She wore the same flowing robe as the angels. Both pure white and without blemish. Both short of covering shins and feet. Only the color of her hair distinguished her from the invaders.

"I've been waiting for you," she said. Her voice caressed my ears, a harmony that beckoned me to my knees and simultaneously empowered me to stand.

I wanted to walk up to her, but the angels, though suspended in animation, were nearby. Their presence remained strong. They wore inhumane facial expressions of the people they controlled, including elongated jaws and over-exaggerated grins. Their victims had frozen mid dash, flight, and scramble.

"Don't be afraid." Euphoria tilted her head toward me. Steel-blue eyes caused my heart to rush, as if I'd kayaked rich-blue rapids. "I command this realm."

Tilting my head slightly, I sought her radiant visage as it

had shone so brightly in the hospital bed. And I found it matched to perfection. Pale, as if she lacked a lifetime of exposure to ultraviolet rays. Pale, as if her cheeks never once flushed.

I took a deep breath after she looked away. The anxiety I'd felt dissipated. After a few minutes in her presence, I found her being there comforting, like a long-time friend.

"Why do I feel like I know you?" I asked.

"I'm represented in every character you've ever dreamed of. To know them is to know me."

I laughed in disbelief—at something that'd been gnawing at me for years. "They were never my own creations, were they?"

Euphoria tilted her head again, this time looking down first and then up at me. "No."

I watched her from the corner of my eyes, unable to look straight into the depths of hers. "And the worlds they call home? You showed me them, too?"

Euphoria blankly stared ahead and didn't respond.

"Where did you come from?"

She pointed at the sky. Not at the spacecraft occupying most of it or the flock of angels surrounding it. Perhaps just beyond it.

"Are you one of them?" I nodded at the closest angel. "What's happening? Why are you showing the world this dream?"

She turned her palm upward and studied it as she brought it closer to her face. "I am…refracted light. We are luminescent. And I…am astray."

I lowered my gaze and fought her overwhelming aura with a deep, suppressed breath.

"When conditions permit and enough of my light refracts in the presence of intelligent life, I evaluate the incident rays that caused my refraction."

"Incident rays as in…humanity?"

She nodded once.

"When conditions permit…are you saying you wait for a species to evolve and then judge them? So you've been evaluating humanity for, what, millions of years?"

"Twenty."

"Twenty years?" My voice cracked. "We've been evolved a longer time than that." Humanity's long history came to mind. "Perhaps it was best that you waited."

Her tone remained the same, mimicking the harmonic vibrations of a fifteen-year-old choir girl. "Is that amount of time insufficient for a fleeting existence that understands tomorrow's never promised?"

She caught me unaware. Speechless. I didn't know if God evaluated me as an individual or humanity as a whole. Did a longer life mean more opportunities for repentance or more chances to go…astray?

"You said you were astray. What did you mean by that?" I asked.

No response. She didn't even blink. Those blue irises likely cooled any strain suffered from unblinking eyes. Lost in her endless awe, my thoughts had drifted again. Socializing wasn't my strong suit. My characters carried on better conversations than I did. Other than spacing out or rambling on, I didn't know how to continue the dialogue after someone ignored my question or statement.

"Okay. Um, how's humanity doing?" I asked.

She pointed at the sky, this time at the spacecraft. She used the same thin arm extending out from under the swirling sleeves of light.

"Not well, huh? If that's indeed envoy to the end of the world." I grabbed my hips. "Angels? Did God send you?"

She shook her head. Her long hair remained in place, possibly weighed down by its length. "Every intelligent species believes in something. We take on the form of those beliefs to dissuade resistance."

I'd never written a character determined to end or take over the world. Perhaps because my characters represented everyday people struggling to do what's right, as opposed to some global nemesis or pandemic that seemed too far-fetched. But I could tell that the unique challenges my characters faced, and the clever tactics required to overcome those challenges, originated from Euphoria. Mostly. She revealed a flawless plan, something only her species could execute. Probably.

I folded my arms. "So, by taking on the form of angels, you hope to reduce opposition. Some believers may even join your crusade. And when the atheists are no more, you'll turn on the rest of humanity. And you ignored the churches, to what, further sell the lie?"

Euphoria frowned. "You understand."

"I may have written something similar."

"I reached out to humanity through your stories. It wasn't sufficient."

"I mean, I write science fiction. Emphasis on fiction. I'm also one man. My individual ideas about the future are insignificant."

"Agreed." She looked up at me. I half-expected a charming smile from the sly diss she made about my insignificance, but her expression remained neutral. She added, "Thus, the dreams."

Lady Amethyst's intuition had been spot-on. The dreams were prophecies, indicative of our perilous path. I wondered if the barrier she raised in her dreams would work in reality when the time came.

"How do we stop them—your kind?"

"You can't. You can only prevent them. The world—your species—must change."

"The morals of my stories and the struggles of those characters aren't impacting people the way you imagined. Again, fiction. The dreams aren't exactly working, either. Nothing's changing. At least the dreams got our attention."

"Agreed."

Alas, she blinked. I felt humanity's last chance close

with her eyelids, and then hope after she opened them. Astray. Perhaps she strayed from her mission by warning us.

"I refracted too much of my light showing humanity its future. My luminescence is fading. Use it, your stories, and the dreams…wisely…"

***

I opened my eyes. Naomi, Captain Sullivan, and Sergeant Ross surrounded Euphoria's bed. Wide eyes and hands clasped to heads came into focus. Panicked movement finally gave me a clear view of Euphoria's empty bed. Somehow, I had to share her message with the world. If I failed, we, too, would disappear.

About the Author

KENNY EMMANUEL creates original science fiction and fantasy worlds that immerse readers in unique characters and settings, via short stories, novels, and video games. Visit www.kennyemmanuel.com to dive into more worlds.

www.ingramcontent.com/pod-product-compliance
Lightning Source LLC
Chambersburg PA
CBHW070201310726
48976CB00001B/174